Horace Smith

The Tin Trumpet

Horace Smith

The Tin Trumpet

ISBN/EAN: 9783337314255

Printed in Europe, USA, Canada, Australia, Japan

Cover: Foto ©Andreas Hilbeck / pixelio.de

More available books at **www.hansebooks.com**

THE
TIN TRUMPET.

BY

HORACE SMITH.

THE
TIN TRUMPET.

BY

HORACE SMITH,

AUTHOR OF "REJECTED ADDRESSES," "BRAMBLETYE HOUSE,"
ETC , ETC.

AUTHORISED EDITION.

LONDON
GEORGE ROUTLEDGE AND SONS, Limited
BROADWAY, LUDGATE HILL
GLASGOW, MANCHESTER, AND NEW YORK
1890

NOTICE.

THE TIN TRUMPET is the whimsical name of a work which, when published thirty-three years ago, had but a small success, through the vagueness of its title, through the concealment of its authorship, and through the boldness of some of its opinions. It is, however, a very remarkable work, full of wit and wisdom, and is greatly prized by collectors, both for its worth and for its scarceness. Its authorship has been confidently ascribed to various writers, and particularly to Thackeray. The real author's name is now for the first time acknowledged, and that by permission of his family.

(*Original Title.*)

THE TIN TRUMPET;

OR

HEADS AND TALES

FOR THE WISE AND WAGGISH.

EDITED BY

JEFFERSON SAUNDERS, Esq.

" Misce stultitiam consiliis brevem."—HORACE.

LONDON:

PRINTED FOR WHITTAKER & Co.

AVE MARIA LANE.

—

1836.

INTRODUCTION.

BY THE EDITOR.

TO say that my deceased friend had always been an eccentric creature, a humorist, an oddity, will scarcely be received as a sufficient explanation of the quaint title which he has thought proper to affix to his work, and for which, therefore, I feel it my first duty as an Editor, to account. After the death of his wife, and, subsequently, of his only child, to both of whom he had been most tenderly attached, Dr. Chatfield sought relief from sorrow by frequent changes of scene, and found such alleviation of mind in wandering over the wilder and least frequented districts of the north of England, as well as such an expanded field for the exercise of his philanthropy, the ruling passion of his soul, that he formed the Quixotic resolution of abandoning his regular professional pursuits, then highly profitable, and of exercising them gratuitously for the benefit of such remote and forlorn objects, as he might encounter in that erratic life which he had now determined on adopting. Born in Yorkshire, and well acquainted with its loneliest recesses, experience had convinced him that there were many remote hamlets, as well as solitary hovels of wood and turf-cutters, charcoal burners, and other peasants, where much sickness and suffering were endured, either from local difficulties, or from pecuniary inability to employ even a village practitioner. To this class of indigent and obscure sufferers, whom he visited in regular periodical excursions, he devoted, for several years, his eminent professional skill, his time, his cheerful powers of consolation, and no small portion of his fortune, (which, since his retirement from productive practice, was restricted to rather less than five hundred a-year,) with a zeal, perseverance, and success, utterly unparalleled, as I verily believe, except in the wonders of charity, accomplished with a similar income, by the celebrated Man of Ross.

For the sake of his own health, which was now occasionally impaired, as well as for the purpose of meeting a circle of cherished friends, who usually betook themselves to Harrowgate during the season, the Doctor made that place his head-quarters for a portion of every summer. Upon one of these visits he established a little society, which met weekly at his lodgings, under the name of " The Tea Party," to participate in his favourite beverage, and to pass a few hours in rational conversation. From every thing in the nature of a club, as the reader will perceive, on a reference to that word in the present work, my friend recoiled with an insurmountable aversion, only consenting to be named President of the Tea Party, on condition that it should consist of both sexes, and be governed by the rules that he had drawn up for its regulation. These exhibited, in several instances, their author's characteristic whimsicality. To avoid the use of a hammer, which was associated, in his mind, with the chairman of a club, it was his good pleasure to suspend from his neck a small Tin Trumpet, by sounding an alarum upon which he procured order, when there was the smallest irregularity or deviation from a punctilious courtesy on the part of any member. The same Tin Trumpet, with a transferable steel-pen affixed to its narrow end, served to register the proceedings of the society in a book kept for that purpose; as well as to write on a slip of paper, for the information of the associates, the subjects upon which they were to converse at their next meeting. Not in any degree, however, could this friendly party be assimilated to a debating society, though its founder was anxious to avoid the common trivialities of chit-chat, by devoting an hour and a half of their meeting ot the consideration of some specific objects, of which several were sometimes proposed for a single night. The remaining hour and a half, for they met at seven, and parted at ten, was given to tea, and such passing topics as might be spontaneously suggested, and which generally assumed a greater latitude, and more playful character, from the previous limitation and partial restraint upon the general volubility. In the presence of the Doctor, indeed, it was almost impossible not to sympathise with his remarkably cheerful temperament.

It was the founder's custom to note down in a commonplace book, such brief heads, or extracts, or allusions as might bear upon the subject next to be considered; for it will readily be conjectured that he himself was the principal speaker. Loving truth better even than my late friend, I am bound to confess that apophthegms, epigrammatical turns, terse sayings, antithetical phrases, and even puerile conceits, were his hobby-horse, and one which he occasionally rode even to a tiresome excess. Whatever of this sort was elicited at the meetings, or subsequently presented itself in his superficial reading, for he did not affect profound literature, was transferred to his common-place book, under different alphabetical *heads*, a process in which he invariably employed the writing instrument to which we have already alluded. This will explain the title of "The Tin Trumpet"—given to his book, as well as the first part of its second appellation—"HEADS and TALES."

In elucidation of this latter word we must state that the most important personage of the party, after its president, was one Timothy Harrison, an independent Yorkshire yeoman, and a not less singular character, though in a different way, than his bosom friend, and latterly his almost inseparable companion—the Doctor. Honest Tim, who was the installed punster and wag, or, as the reader may rather think, the Merry Andrew of the party, made it his business to *cap* every grave remark or serious discussion with some foolery, either in the shape of quibble, joke, anecdote, or appropriate *tale*, most of which found their way to the common-place book, and were generally assigned to their author, under his initials of T. H. Many of these *caudal vertebræ*, or *tale-joints*, as he himself banteringly termed them, I have ventured to expunge, as they would have swelled the work to a disproportionate size; several of his *bon-mots* have suffered a similar fate; though I am still apprehensive that I may be thought to have used the pruning knife much too sparingly. By his droll and flexible features, his power of mimicry, and his broad rustic humour, TIM was expressly qualified to be the wag of a provincial *coterie;* but where you cannot print the countenance and manner, it is sometimes dangerous to publish the joke. Not a few of his jests, for he was as bold a plagiarist as his friend, were stolen from newspapers, or other equally accessible sources; while others may even be traced back to Joe Miller, an authority which is occasionally acknowledged under the Latin alias of *Josephus Molitor*.

It will be seen, therefore, that the following little work cannot set up much claim to originality, either in its serious or jocose departments; while even its form was suggested, as I have heard its author admit, by some humorous alphabetical definitions which appeared several years ago in one of our magazines. From the writer of those papers, as well as from all others who might serve his purpose, not excepting the Edinburgh Review, of which he was a constant reader, he borrowed without compunction. Wherever he made verbal quotations of any extent, it will be seen that he refers to the original; and he often regretted that the omission of noting down his authorities, prevented him from acknowledging them upon other and all occasions. With the materials thus accumulated, he interspersed, as he proceeded, his own sentiments upon every topic that called for their avowal. Knowing that they express the conscientious convictions of an eminently pious and virtuous man, I have published them without hesitation, but I think it right to put upon record my total dissent from many of his views and doctrines. Intimate, indeed, as was our friendship for a long course of years, we differed, *toto cœlo*, upon most of the leading subjects that divide the opinions of mankind. In his Liberal, not to say Radical notions, I was decidedly opposed to him; while my reverence for the Established Church, of which I am proud to

call myself a member, made the discussion of its discipline
and tenets, in both of which he maintained the necessity of
a Reform, a forbidden subject between us.

Deeming it impious to suppose that the investigation of
truth, conscientiously pursued, could possibly lead to any
other results than an additional confirmation of the greatness, goodness, and glory of God, Dr. Chatfield was a
fearless and zealous explorer of many questions which would
have been avoided by the timid and the indifferent. Creeds,
articles, and all the ceremonials of religion, he held in slight
estimation, compared to heart-felt, practical, vital Christianity; yet a more devout man I never knew. His religion
was a sentiment in which his whole heart was steeped, and
which exhibited itself in an ever present sense of profound
gratitude to the Creator, and an all embracing love of his
creatures. His strange, and sometimes startling notions
exposed him to occasional attacks of considerable sharpness, which he invariably bore with such a Christian meek-
ness, and defended himself with a sweetness so conciliatory
and unassuming, that even those who impugned his opinions, could not help admiring their placid and philosophic
maintainer.

With such gentleness of disposition, it may seem that
the satirical character, occasionally perceptible in his book,
is not altogether in accordance; but it may literally be
affirmed of him, to use a homely saying, that his bark was
worse than his bite. Personalities there are none throughout
the whole work. Taking for his motto—" parcere personis,
dicere de vitiis,"—he visited the offence not the offender,
regardless of the hacknied objection that, to exercise such
a misplaced lenity, is to lash the dice and to spare the dicer.

That predilection for point and antithesis to which we have already alluded, and which forms the besetting sin of his stile, often betrayed him into a severity of expression quite foreign to his real nature. He might be caustic with his pen, especially if an epigrammatic turn were at stake; but his lips could not utter anything intentionally bitter, nor could his heart harbour a single angry feeling. This is not the place, however, to expatiate upon his character, as it is my intention to make his life, for which I had been collecting materials long before his decease, the subject of a second volume; and I avail myself of the present opportunity, to request that his Yorkshire and other correspondents will add to my large stock of his amusing letters, by forwarding any that they may possess, to the Publisher of this work, under whose inspection they will be copied, and punctually, as well as thankfully returned, to their respective owners.

Most of the peasants and cotters in the northern and western wapentakes of Yorkshire, were familiar with the Doctor's old white-tailed dun horse, as well as with his antique broad-winged whiskey. In the boot of this rickety vehicle were usually stowed a medicine-chest, a box of linen, and other travelling indispensables, the respective packages being steadied by a few well-worn books wedged in between them. Latterly he had seldom made an excursion without "honest Tim," whose pranks, jokes, and buffooneries, lent some support to the idea entertained by many strangers, on their first appearance, that the companions were an itinerant Quacksalver and his Zany. Nor was it easy to remove this impression, so far as the Merry Andrew was concerned; but it was impossible to gaze upon

the benevolent countenance of his friend, whose Quaker's
attire, bald forehead, and silver side locks descending to
his shoulders, gave him altogether a most venerable appearance, without a quick conviction that his errand was one
of pure philanthropy,—and that his purposes, like his aspect,
were high and holy.

By his will, Dr. Chatfield bequeathed to the Editor, the
whole of his manuscripts, consisting of tales, ancient and
modern—fugitive poems—a few essays on medical subjects,
and the volumes now submitted to the public. From his
poems I have made such a selection as will afford a fair
sample of his general powers in this department of literature. They exhibit much smoothness and facility in the
versification, and no small diversity of stile, since they are
perfectly free from the forced conceits and artificial glitter
of his prose compositions. Respecting the Tales, he left
no instructions — and future circumstances must decide
whether any of them shall ever see the light; but it was
one of his last requests that "The Tin Trumpet" should
be prepared for immediate publication. The quantity and
the confusion of the materials, rendered their selection and
arrangement a matter of no small difficulty and of some
unexpected delay; but I have executed my task to the best
of my ability and judgment, and I now commit the work to
the indulgence of the reader, again requesting him to bear
in mind that I broadly dissent from many of the crude
notions and fanciful theories broached by my late excellent
but eccentric friend.

J. S.

HARROWGATE,
 February, 1836.

THE AUTHOR'S PREFACE.

Ad Candidum Lectorem.

Cum legis hunc nostrum, Lector studiose, libellum,
　Decedat vultu tetrica ruga tuo.
Non sunt hæc tristi conscripta Catonibus ore,
　Non Heraclitis, non gravibus Curiis :
Sed si Heracliti, Curii, si fortè Catones,
　Adjicere huc oculos et legere ista velint,
Multa hic invenient quæ possint pellere curas,
　Plurima quæ mæstos exhilarare queant.

THE TIN TRUMPET;

OR,

HEADS AND TALES.

.B.C.DARIAN—seems to have been an ancient term for a pedagogue. Wood, in his Athenæ Oxonienses, speaking of Thomas Farnabie, says—" When he landed in Cornwall, his distresses made him stoop so low, as to be an A.b.c.darian, and several were taught their horn books by him." By assuming this title, its wearer certainly proves himself to be a man of letters ; but my friend T. H. suggests, that the schoolmaster who wishes to establish his aptitude for his office, instead of taking the three first, had better designate himself by the two last letters of the alphabet.

ABLATIVE CASE—one that now is, or very soon will be, applicable to usurped power, to unjust privileges, and to abuses of all sorts. Though the schoolmaster is abroad, the times are more ungrammatical than ever. A borough-monger has ceased to be in the nominative case ; there is no longer a dative case to the Pension List ; and when the public is in the accusative case, it governs the party or thing implicated, and makes it fall into the ablative case absolute. Though corruptions are nouns substantive, they cannot

stand by themselves ; and abuses, which used to be plural,
will soon become singular. The verb " to love" is declined,
not conjugated. Standard words, to which the utmost importance was attached by the wisdom of our ancestors, such,
for instance, as " rotten boroughs," are arbitrarily cut off by
elision. When John Bull is in the imperative mood, he is
now, at the same time, in the potential ; while the present
tense has no longer the smallest reference to the past, provided it can improve the future. But we have still more
startling changes ;—Lady A. is a masculine, and Lord B. is
a feminine person. What can be expected but irregularity
and disturbance, when our grammar is in such a state of
anarchy? This comes of Reform ! ! Ah ! it is to be feared
that we shall none of us have the consolation of Danjeau,
the French grammarian, who, when told that a revolution
was approaching, exclaimed, rubbing his hands, " Well, come
what may, I have two hundred verbs well conjugated in my
desk !"

ABLUTION—a duty somewhat too strictly inculcated in
the Mahometan ritual, and sometimes too laxly observed
in Christian practice. As a man may have a dirty body,
and an undefiled mind, so may he have clean hands in a
literal, and not in a metaphorical sense. All washes and
cosmetics without, he may yet labour under a moral hydro-
phobia within. Pleasant to see an im-puritan of this stamp
holding his nose, lest the wind should come between an
honest scavenger and his gentility, while his own character
stinks in the public nostrils. Oh, if the money and the
pains that we bestow upon perfumes and adornments for
the body, were applied to the purification and embellish-
ment of the mind ! Oh ! if we were as careful to polish our
manners as our teeth, to make our temper as sweet as our
breath, to cut off our peccadilloes as to pare our nails,

to be as upright in character as in person, to save our souls as to shave our chins, what an immaculate race should we become ! Exteriorly, we are not a filthy people. We throw so much dirt at our neighbours, that we have none left for ourselves. We are only unclean in our hearts and lives. As occasional squalor is the worst evil of poverty and labour, so should constant cleanliness be the greatest luxury of wealth and ease ; yet even our aristocracy are not altogether without reproach in this respect. It is well known, that the celebrated Lord Nelson had not washed his hands for the last eight years of his life. Alas ! upon what trifles may our reputation for cleanliness depend ! Even a foreign accent may ruin us. In a trial, where a German and his wife were giving evidence, the former was asked by the counsel, " How old are you ?"—" I am *dirty.*" —" And what is your wife ?"—" Mine wife is *dirty-two.*"— " Then, Sir, you are a very nasty couple, and I wish to have nothing further to say to either of you."

ABRIDGMENT—anything contracted into a small compass; such, for instance, as the abridgment of the statutes in twenty volumes, folio. To make a good abridgment, requires as much time and talent as to write an original work ; a fact of which the reader will find abundant proof as he proceeds ! When Queen Anne told Dr. South that his sermon had only one fault—that of being too short,—he replied, that he should have made it shorter if he had had more time. How comes it that no enterprising bookseller has ever thought of publishing " an Abridgment of the Lives of the Fathers ?" I know not whether the religious public would give it encouragement, but I am confident, that in this land of primogeniture and entailed estates, there is not an heir in the three kingdoms who would not exert himself to ensure its success.

ABSCESS—a morbid tumour, frequently growing above the shoulders, and swelling to a considerable size, when it comes to a head, with nothing in it. It is not always a natural disease, for nature abhors a vacuum; yet fools, fops, and fanatics are very subject to it, and it sometimes attacks old women of both sexes. "I wish to consult you upon a little project I have formed," said a noodle to his friend. "I have an idea in my head—" "Have you?" interposed the friend, with a look of great surprise; "then you shall have my opinion at once: *keep it there!*—it may be some time before you get another."

ABSOLUTE GOVERNMENT.—There is a simplicity and unity in despotism, which is not without its advantages, if every despot were to be a Titus or a Vespasian—to unite great talents with a clement and benevolent heart. But the chances against such a fortunate conjunction are almost incalculable; and even where it occurs, its effects may be suddenly defeated, and the best sovereign be converted into the worst, by an attack of gout, or a fit of indigestion. Besides, there are few who can drink of unrestrained power, without being intoxicated, or, perhaps, maddened. Nero, before he succeeded to the crown, was remarkable for his moderation and humanity. So true is the dictum of Tacitus, that the throne of a despot is generally ascended by a wild beast. Free institutions are the best, indeed the only security, both for the governed and the governor; for there is no remedy against a tyrant but assassination, of which *ultima ratio populi*, even our own times have furnished instances at St. Petersburg and Constantinople. An hereditary monarchy with institutions adapted to the state of knowledge, and the diffusion of moral power, or, in other words, leaning towards republicanism, seems to be the form of government most appropriate for a civilized and enlightened nation in the nineteenth century. The greatest strength should be at the base, not at the top; for it is as difficult to overturn a pyramid, as to preserve the equilibrium of an inverted cone. What an illustration of the spirit of the times, and what an instructive lesson to monarchs, is the startling fact, that the present rulers of Sweden, France, and Belgium, are not the regular inheritors of the crowns they wear, but sovereigns elected by the most powerful of all sovereigns—the people; while the pseudo-legitimate kings of Portugal and Spain have been formally repudiated, and are wanderers on the face of the earth! Few modern despots can calculate on being so fortunate as the Turk Mustapha, who, having rebelled against his brother, was taken prisoner, and ordered for execution on the following morning. The Sultan, however, being suddenly seized with the colic, accompanied, perhaps, with some fraternal, as well as internal qualms, ordered the decapitation to be deferred for two days, during which he died, and his imprisoned brother quietly succeeded to the throne. "O happy Mustapha!" exclaimed the Sultaness, "you were born to be lucky, for you have not only derived life from your mother's stomach, but from your brother's!"

ABSOLUTION, Self — generously pronouncing our own pardon. Such is the power in the human mind of adapting itself to circumstances, that we can reconcile ourselves, at least, partially, to our own crimes and infamy. The stings of conscience would be intolerable, could we not lay some flattering unction to our souls, and steal relief from self-delusion. It may be doubted, whether the greatest villain in the world ever thought himself much worse than some of his neighbours, or was ever without his share of those extenuating pleas, subterfuges, and shufflings, in which the mind is so subtle a casuist. A man is sure of his own good word, and if it be the only one he has to expect, he draws upon it the more liberally. Another is worse than himself, or he fancies him to be so, and he forthwith imagines that he is a moral character, because he is not the basest profligate in existence. We claim praise for not having pushed our vices farther, but we feel no shame for having carried them so far; as if there were a positive merit in sinning, provided we stop short of the *ne plus ultra* of turpitude.

ABSURDITY—anything advanced by our opponents, contrary to our own practice, or above our comprehension,—and, therefore, a term very liberally used, because it is applied in exact proportion to our own ignorance. Nothing to which we are so quick-sighted in another, so blind in ourselves, not only individually, but nationally. "*Comment!*" exclaims the French sailor in Josephus Molitor, when he saw Ironmonger Lane written on the corner of a street in London, which he read, "*Irons manger l'ane.*"—"*Comment! Es çe qu'on mange des anes dans çe pays ci? Mais, quelle absurdité!*" How many of us, in travelling, exhibit our own, in imputing an imaginary absurdity to others! "How ridiculous!" exclaims the travelled servant in one of Dr. Moore's novels, "to dress the French regiments of the line in blue, —a colour which, as all the world knows, is only proper for the Oxford Blues and the Artillery." Some of our highest classes are unconscious imitators of the knight of the shoulder-knot.

Of the *Reductio ad absurdum*, a very useful weapon of logic in arguing with ultras of any class, I know not a happier illustration than the Duke of Buckingham's reply to Dryden's famous line—

"My wound is great, because it is so small."
"Then 'twould be greater were it none at all."

ABUSE, Intemperate—excites our sympathies, not for the abuser, but the *abusee*, a fact which some of our virulent critics and political writers are very apt to forget. Like other poisons, when administered in too strong a dose, it is thrown off by the intended victim, and often relieves, where it was meant to destroy. If the wielder of the weapon be such an unskilful sportsman as to overcharge his piece, he must not be surprised if it explode, and wound no one but himself. Dirt wantonly cast, only acts like fullers' earth, defiling for the moment, but purifying in the end ; so that those who are the most bespattered, come out the most immaculate. Pleasant was the well-known revenge of the vilipended author, who having in vain endeavoured to propitiate his critic by returning eulogy for abuse, sent him at last the following epigram :—

> " With industry I spread your praise,
> With equal you my censure blaze ;
> But faith ! 'tis all in vain we do,
> The world believes nor me, nor you."

ABUSES—see Tory Administration, *passim*. Thank Heaven, the times are changed, and those who refuse to give up abuses, will inevitably be called upon to surrender uses. Will they take a hint, and make a compromise in time, or like the boroughmongers, dig a pit for themselves to fall into ? For their own sakes I hope they will yield in time ; for the sake of the country I might wish them to be obstinate.

ACCIDENT.—Fanatics, whose inordinate conceit prompts them to believe that the Deity must be more engrossed with the affairs of an obscure Muggletonian in Ebenezer Alley, Shoreditch, than with the general and immutable laws of the universe, presumptuously wrest every unexpected occurrence, in which themselves are concerned, into a particular Providence, more especially if it be an escape from any sort of danger. As the risk, however, must come from the same source as the deliverance,—as a providential escape, may with equal propriety be termed a providential exposure to imminent peril,—this hazardous doctrine, like a two-edged sword, must cut both ways ; and according to the sanguine or desponding temperament of the expounder, will tend to generate either an overwhelming arrogance, or a dark despair. A plot is formed, to way-lay and murder a man, on his way home at night. He gets drunk, takes the wrong road and escapes. Even a Muggletonian would hesitate at calling this a providential intoxication, and yet he often uses the term when it is quite as inapplicable and indecorous. Occurrences of this description may be improved into moral warnings without supposing any special deviation from the laws of nature. There is a Providence ever watching over the destinies of mankind, but we should not the less on that account observe the maxim of Horace—*Nec Deus intersit nisi dignus vindice nodus.* The uncharitable forgetfulness of this rule was once well reproved by Voltaire, who happened to be in company with a fanatical old lady during a violent thunder storm, when she screamed out, that the house would be dashed to pieces upon their heads on account of his impiety. " Know, madam," said the Patriarch —" that I have said more good of the Deity in a single verse, than you will ever think of him in the whole course of your life."

Father Mabillon, who had been of a very narrow capacity in his youth, fell, at the age of twenty-six, against a stone staircase, fractured his skull, was trepanned, and after that operation, possessed a luminous understanding, and an astonishing zeal for study. We submit this accident to the joint and serious consideration of the Muggletonians and Phrenologists, but without recommending either party to

anticipate the same results, should they be disposed to make
a similar experiment upon their own skulls.

ACCOMPLISHMENTS—in women all that can be supplied by the dancing-master, music-master, mantua-maker
and milliner: in men, tying a cravat, talking nonsense,
playing at billiards, dressing like a real, and driving like an
amateur coachman. The latter is an excusable ambition,
even in our noblemen, for it shows that they know themselves, and have found a properer place, and more congenial
elevation than the peerage. Some there are, who, deeming
dissolute manners an accomplishment, endeavour to show
by their profligacy that they know the world, an example
which might be dangerous, but that the world knows them.
Accomplishments are sociable—but nothing so sociable as a
cultivated mind.

ACTOR.—How often do we quote Shakspeare's dictum,
that—

> —— "All the world's a stage,
> And all the men and women merely players,"

without reflecting upon its close applicability, not only to the
classes he has specified, but to almost every individual in
existence. The laws of society, and the restraints upon
opinion, compel us all to be actors and hypocrites, simulators
and dissimulators; and the more servile the observance of
this slavish disingenuousness, the greater the assumed civilization! Oh, for a week's social intercourse in the Palace of
Truth of M. de Genlis, that we might see what capital actors
we have all been when out of it; especially those who had
been playing the parts of Maw-worm and Cantwell!

Diderot has endeavoured to prove that in the delineation
of the passions—" He best shall paint them who shall feel
them least," and that an actor, injured rather than benefited

by an intense feeling of the emotions he represents, is never so sure to agitate the souls of his hearers, as when his own is perfectly at ease. We believe that he may excite without being excited, for the same reason that the most sensitive young lady will remain unmoved at the hundredth re-perusal of the tragedy, which at first drew a flood of tears from her eyes; but the mimic, in order to carry our sympathies with him, must at least have a certain degree of susceptibility in himself. How can he successfully study or understand a character if totally incapable of feeling it? Speaking, as it were, an unknown language, he must deliver it, without adaptation or expression, and consequently without effect.— His emotion may be as transient as you please, but it must be *once* felt, once impressed upon the actor, if it is to impress the audience. To suppose that studied and artificial, can be more appropriate to the stage than real passion, is a contra-diction in terms, for it is a remarkable fact, that deep and genuine emotion, even in the humblest persons, is never un-dignified, never ungraceful.

An adherence to nature, however, is by no means incom-patible with a due regard to the Thespian art, which requires elaborate study, and to a heightening of the effect by profes-sional, or even mechanical aids. Vivid conception, and keen sensibility, will not of themselves make a good actor; but it may be questioned, whether a good actor can be made without them. Rare indeed is the physical and moral com-bination that produces a superior performer, as will at once appear if we compare the best amateur, with a second or even a third rate professional actor. What miserable mum-mery are private theatricals! At those given last year at Hatfield House, old General G—— was pressed by a lady to say whom he liked best of all the actors. Notwithstanding his usual bluntness, he evaded the question for some time, but being importuned for an answer, he at length growled,—

" Well, madam, if you will have a reply, I liked the prompter
the best, because I heard the most of him, and saw the least
of him !"

ADDRESS—generally a string of fulsome compliments
and professions, indiscriminately lavished upon every king
or individual in authority, in order to assure him of the particular, personal, and exclusive veneration in which he is
held by those who, being the very obedient humble servants
of circumstances, would pay equal homage to Jack Ketch, if
he possessed equal power. In the latter case, they would
perhaps attempt to dignify his person, and his office by some
courteous periphrase, or concealing both beneath the appropriate veil of a *dead* language, would speak of him as—*Vir
excellentissimus, strangulandi peritus.*
In a Shrewsbury Address to James I., his loyal subjects
expressed a wish that he might reign over them as long as
sun, moon, and stars should endure.—"I suppose, then,"
observed the monarch, "they mean my successor to reign
by candle-light."

ADMIRATION.—We always love those who admire us,
says Rochefoucauld,—but we do not always love those whom
we admire. From the latter clause an exception might have
been made in favour of *self,* for self-love is the source of self-
admiration ; and this is the safest of all loves, for most
people may indulge it without the fear of a rival.

ADMITTING yourself out of court—a legal phrase, signifying a liberality of concession to your opponent by which
you destroy your own cause. This excess of candour was
well illustrated by the Irishman, who boasted that he had
often skated sixty miles a day. " Sixty miles !" exclaimed
an auditor—"that is a great distance : it must have been

accomplished when the days were longest."—" To be sure it was ; I admit that," cried the ingenious Hibernian.

ADULTERER—one who has been guilty of perjury, commonly accompanied with ingratitude and hypocrisy, an offence softened down by the courtesy of a sympathising world, into " a man of gallantry, a gay person somewhat too fond of intrigue ;" or a woman "who has had a little slip, committed a *faux pas*," &c.—" Pleasant but wrong," was the apology of the country squire, who being detected in an intrigue with the frail rib of his groom, maintained that he had not offended against the law, since we are only commanded not to sin with another man's wife, whereas, this was his own man's wife.

ADVERSITY—is very often a blessing in disguise, which by detaching us from earth and drawing us towards heaven, gives us, in the assurance of lasting joys, an abundant recompence for the loss of transient ones. " Whom the Lord loveth he chasteneth." Many a man in losing his fortune has found himself, and been ruined into salvation ; for though God demands the whole heart, which we could not give him when we shared it with the world, he will never reject the broken one, which we offer him in our hour of sadness and reverse. Misfortunes are moral bitters, which frequently restore the healthy tone of the mind, after it has been cloyed and sickened by the sweets of prosperity. The spoilt children of the world, like their juvenile namesakes, are generally a source of unhappiness to others, without being happy in themselves.

ADVICE—almost the only commodity which the world is lavish in bestowing, and scrupulous in receiving, although it may be had *gratis*, with an allowance to those who take a quantity. We seldom ask it until it is too late, and still more rarely take it while there is yet time to profit by it. Great tact and delicacy are required, either in conferring or seeking this perilous boon, for where people do not take your counsel they generally take offence; and even where they do, you can never be sure that you have not given pain in giving advice. We have our revenge for this injustice. If an acquaintance pursue some unfortunate course, in spite of our dissuasions, we feel more gratified by the confirmation of our evil auguries, than hurt by the misfortunes of our friend; for that man must be a sturdy moralist who does not love his own judgment better than the interest of his neighbours. This may help to explain Rochefoucauld's dictum, that there is something, even in the misfortunes of our best friends, which is not altogether displeasing to us.

To decline all advice, unless the example of the giver confirms his precepts, would be about as sapient as if a traveller were to refuse to follow the directions of a finger-post, unless it drew its one leg out of the ground, and walked, or rather hopped after its own finger.

ADVOWSON — the purchaseable right (purchaseable even by a Jew, Pagan, or Mahometan,) of controlling the souls of a whole parish by appointing the clergyman, from whom its inhabitants must receive their spiritual instruction, and to whom they are compelled to pay tithes, even although they should disapprove his doctrine, despise his abilities, and dislike his character. Advowsons are temporal inheritances, which may be granted by deed or will, and are assets in the hands of executors; so carefully is the worship of Mammon preserved by those who solemnly protest that they are not given to filthy lucre! A clergyman may purchase a next presentation, provided the living be not actually vacant at the time; and even where it is, he may accomplish that object, through the instrumentality of friends, without incurring the penalties of Simony. We should deem it a monstrous oppression, were an apothecary or a lawyer to be imposed upon a populous and enlightened parish at the arbitrary fiat of a patron, who would not hear of objection, or even of inquiry into his character and capacity; and yet the wrong in the imposition of a spiritual guide is still more flagrant, by the whole difference between the soul and the body, between time and eternity.

Can the clerical purchaser of a next presentation be always sure that he will not sigh for the *death* of the incumbent, because he sighs for his living? If not, religion, reason, and justice, seem equally to require that the temptation of saleable advowsons should be removed from his path, and that these spiritual rotten boroughs should be consigned to the tomb of their parliamentary brethren in schedule A.

AFFECTION, Filial—an implanted instinct, exalted by a feeling of gratitude and a sense of duty.—The Roman daughter, who nourished her imprisoned father, when condemned to be starved to death, from her own breast, has generally been adduced as the noblest recorded instance of filial affection; but the palm may almost be contested by an Irish son, if we may receive without suspicion the evidence of a fond and doting father—"Ah now, my darlint!" exclaimed the latter, when his boy threatened to enlist in the army—"would you be laving your poor ould father that doats upon ye? You, the best and the most dutiful of all my children, and the only one that never struck me when I was down!"

AFFLICTION.—A French writer, arguing, perhaps, from the analogy of the English language, wherein two negatives constitute an affirmative, observes that *deux afflictions mises*

ensemble peuvent devenir une consolation, an experiment
which few, we apprehend, will be anxious to try.   Man has
been termed the child of affliction, an affiliation of which the
writer does not recognise the truth ; but for the benefit of
those who hold a contrary opinion, he ventures to plagiarise
a few stanzas versified from a prose apologue of Dr.
Sheridan—

> Affliction one day, as she hark'd to the roar
>   Of the stormy and struggling billow,
> Drew a beautiful form on the sands of the shore,
>   With the branch of a weeping willow.
>
> Jupiter, struck with the noble plan,
>   As he roamed on the verge of the ocean,
> Breathed on the figure, and calling it man,
>   Endued it with life and motion.
>
> A creature so glorious in mind and in frame,
>   So stamp'd with each parent's impression,
> Among them a point of contention became,
>   Each claiming the right of possession.
>
> "He is mine," said Affliction ; " I gave him his birth,
>   I alone am his cause of creation."—
> "The materials were furnished by me," answered Earth—
>   "I gave him," said Jove, "animation."
>
> The gods all assembled in solemn divan,
>   After hearing each claimant's petition,
> Pronounced a definitive verdict on man,
>   And thus settled his fate's disposition.
>
> "Let Affliction possess her own child, till the woes
>   Of life cease to harass and goad it ;
> After death give his body to earth, whence it rose,
>   And his spirit to Jove, who bestowed it."

AGE, Old—an infirmity which nobody knows.   Nothing
can exceed our early impatience to escape from youth to
manhood, and appear older than we are, except our subse-

quent anxiety to obtain the reputation of being younger than we are. The first longing is natural, for Hope is before us, and it seems possible to anticipate that which we must soon reach ; but the second is a weakness, not less strange than general, for we cannot expect to recover that from which we are perpetually flying, or avoid that to which we are incessantly approaching. If by putting back our own date, we could arrest the great clock of time, there would be an intelligible motive for our conduct. Alas ! the time-piece of old Chronos never stops.

Women, who imagine their influence to depend upon their personal attractions, naturally wish to preserve their youth. It is in their power to do so; for she who captivates the heart and the understanding, never grows old: and as men are generally estimated by their moral and intellectual, rather than their baptismal recommendations ; as a philosopher of fifty is preferred, by all those whose preference is worth having, to a fool of twenty, there is something very contemptible in a male horror of senility. So prevalent, however, is the feeling, that, with the exception of one individual, who has obtained an enviable immortality as "*middle age* HALLAM," we have no chronology for men and women at, or beyond the meridian of life. They are all " persons of a certain age," which is the most *un*certain one upon record. Complimentary in everything, the French say of a woman thus circumstanced, that she is *femme d'un age raisonnable*, as if she had gained, in her reasoning faculties, what she had lost in personal charms; and this, doubtless, ought to be the process with us all. To our mind, as to a preserving green-house, should we transfer, in the winter of life, the attractions of our spring and summer.

As variety is universally allowed to be pleasing, the diversity occasioned by the progress of age should, in itself, be a source of delight. Perpetual sunshine would soon be found more annoying than an alternation of the seasons ; so would a continuous youth be more irksome than the gradual approach of old age. Existence may be compared to a drum, which has only one single tone ; but change of time gives it variety and cheerfulness enough.

The infirmity of falsifying our age is at least as old as Cicero, who, hearing one of his contemporaries attempting to make himself ten years younger than he really was, drily observed—" Then at the time you and I were at school together, you were not born."

ALCHYMIST.—The true possessor of the philosopher's stone is the miner, whose iron, copper, and tin are always convertible into the more precious metals. Agriculture is the noblest of all alchymy, for it turns earth, and even manure, into gold, conferring upon its cultivator the additional reward of health. Most appropriate was the rebuke of Pope Leo X., who, when a visionary pretended to have discovered the philosopher's stone, and demanded a recompence, gave him an empty purse.

ALCORAN.—In the life of Mahomet, prefixed to Reland's work, " De Religione Mohammedica," is the following passage, allusive to the peculiar tenets of the Moammarites, a famous sect among the Mahometans :—" Suppose," say they, " we should resolve all our faith into the sole text of the Alcoran, the difficulty and uncertainty will still remain, if we consider how many metaphors, allegories, and other figures of speech,—how many obscure, ambiguous, intricate, and mysterious passages are to be met with in this infallible book,—and how different are the opinions, expositions, and interpretations, of the most subtle doctors and learned commentators on every one of them. The only sure way, then," add they, " to come to the certain knowledge of the truth, is to consult God himself, wait His inspirations, live just and honest lives, be kind and beneficent to all our fellow-creatures, and pity such as differ from us in their opinions about the authority, integrity, and meaning of the Alcoran."—What a contrast does the charitable and Christian-like feeling of these Moammarites afford to some of our own unchristian fanatics, who, setting themselves up for stewards of the mysteries, affix their own meaning—often a very revolting one—to "the letter that killeth;" and if we hesitate to receive their interpretations, immediately begin to "deal damnation round the land!"

ALDERMAN—a ventri-potential citizen, into whose mediterranean mouth good things are perpetually flowing, although none come out. His shoulders, like some of the civic streets, are "widened at the expense of the corporation." He resembles Wolsey; not in ranking himself with princes, but in being a man "of an unbounded stomach." A tooth is the only wise thing in his head, and he has nothing particularly good about him, except his digestion, which is an indispensable quality, since he is destined to become great by gormandising, to masticate his way to the Mansion-house, and thus, like a mouse in a cheese, to provide for himself a large dwelling, by continually eating. His talent is in his jaws; and like a miller, the more he grinds the more he gets. From the quantity he devours, it might be supposed that he had two stomachs, like a cow, were it not manifest that he is no ruminating animal.

ALMS.—To this word there is no singular, in order to teach us that a solitary act of charity scarcely deserves the name. Nothing is won by one gift. To render our bounties available, they must be in the plural number. It is always wise to be charitable, but it is almost peculiar to my friend

L—— that he is often witty in his bounties. He was about to assist with a sum of money a scribbler in distress, when he was reminded that he had on more than one occasion been libelled and maligned by the intended object of his bounty. "Pooh," said L——, "I have so long known all his slanders by heart, that they have quite gone out of my head."

ALPHABET—twenty-six symbols which represent singly or in combination, all the sounds of all the languages upon earth. By forming letters into words, which are the signs of ideas, we are enabled to embody thought, to render it visible, audible, perpetual, and ubiquitous. Embalmed in writing, the intellect may thus enjoy a species of immortality upon earth, and every man may paint an imperishable portrait of his own mind, immeasurably more instructive and interesting to posterity than those fleeting likenesses of the face and form entrusted to canvas, or even to bronze and marble. What myriads have passed away, body and mind, leaving not a wreck behind them, while the mental features of some contemporary writer survive in all the freshness and integrity with which they were first traced. Were I a literary painter how often should I be tempted in the pride of my heart, to exclaim with the celebrated artist, "*Ed io anche sono Pittore.*"

Although the word be derived from the two first letters of the Greek, every ALPHABET now in use may be traced with historical certainty to one original—the Phenician or Syriac. "Phenicia and Palestine," says Gibbon, "will for ever live in the memory of mankind; since America, as well as Europe, has received letters from the one and religion from the other."

One of the earlier French princes being too indolent or too stupid to acquire his alphabet by the ordinary process, twenty-four servants were placed in attendance upon him, each with a huge letter painted upon his stomach ; as he knew not their names, he was obliged to call them by their letter when he wanted their services, which in due time gave him the requisite degree of literature for the exercise of the royal functions.

AMBIGUITY—a quality deemed essentially necessary to the clear understanding of diplomatic writings, acts of parliament, and law proceedings.

AMBITION—a mental dropsy, which keeps continually swelling and increasing, until it kills its victim. Ambition is often overtaken by calamity, because it is not aware of its pursuer and never looks behind. " Deeming naught done while aught remains to do," it is necessarily restless ; unable to bear anything above it, discontent must be its inevitable portion, for even if the pinnacle of worldly power be gained, its occupant will sigh, like Alexander, for another globe to conquer. Every day that brings us some new advancement or success, brings us also a day nearer to death, embittering the reflection, that the more we have gained, the more we have to relinquish. Aspiring to nothing but humility, the wise man will make it the height of his ambition to be un-ambitious. As he cannot effect all that he wishes, he will only wish for that which he can effect.

AMBLE.—Of this indefinite and intermediate pace, which, (to adopt the Johnsonian style) " without the concussiveness of the trot, or the celerity of the canter, neither contributes to the conservation of health, nor to the economy of time, nothing can be pronounced in eulogy, and little therefore need be said in description." To those elderly gentlemen, nevertheless, who are willing to sacrifice the perilous reputation of a good seat for the comfort of a safe one; an ambling nag has always been an equestrian beatitude. Such was the feeling of the Sexagenarian, who took his horse to the *ménage*, that it might be taught the "old gentleman's pace." As the riding-master, after several trials, could not immediately succeed in his object, the owner of the animal petulantly cried out—"Zooks, Sir, do you call this an amble?"—"No, Sir," was the reply, "I call it a pre-amble."

ANCESTRY.—

> " They who on length of ancestry enlarge,
> Produce their debt instead of a discharge."

They search in the root of the tree for those fruits which the branches ought to produce, and too often resemble potatoes, of which the best part is under ground. Pedigree is the boast of those who have nothing else to vaunt. In what respect, after all, are they superior to the humblest of their neighbours? Every man's ancestors double at each remove in geometrical proportion, so that after only twenty generations, he has above a million of progenitors. A duke has no more; a dustman has no less.

A river generally becomes narrower and more insignificant, as we ascend to its source. The stream of ancestry, on the contrary, often vigorous, pure, and powerful at its fountain head, usually becomes more feeble, shallow, and corrupt as it flows downwards. Some of our ancient families, whose origin is lost in the darkness of antiquity, and into whose hungry maws the tide of patronage is for ever flowing, may be compared to the Nile, which has many mouths, and no discoverable head. *Nobles* sometimes illustrate that name about as much as an Italian Cicerone recalls the idea of Cicero.

It is a double shame to a man to have derived distinction

from his predecessors, if he bequeath disgrace to his posterity.

ANCIENTS—dead bones used for the purpose of knocking down live flesh. Every puny Samson thinks he may wield his ass's jaw-bone in assaulting his contemporaries, by comparing them with their predecessors. If architects attempt any thing original, they are ridiculed for their pains, and desired to stick to the five orders. This is the sixth order of the public. If artists follow the bent of their own genius, they are tauntingly referred by their new masters to the old masters, and desired not to indulge their own crude *capriccios.* Authors are schooled and catechized in the same way; but when either of the three conform to the instructions of their critics, they are instantly and unmercifully assailed as servile imitators, without a single grain of originality. Whether, therefore, they allow the ancients to be imitable or inimitable it is manifest that they only exalt them in order to lower their contemporaries, and that their suffrages would be reversed, if the ancients and moderns were to change places. With a similar jealousy we give a preference to old wine, old books, and an old friend, unless the latter should appear in the form of an old joke, when he is treated with the utmost scorn and contumely. As this is equally reprehensible and inconsistent, I shall endeavour to cure my readers of any such propensity, by habituating them to encounters with some of their old Joe Miller acquaintance.

ANGER—punishing ourselves for the faults of another; or committing an additional error, if we are incensed at our own mistakes. In either case, wrath may aggravate, but was never known to diminish our annoyance. "I wish," says Seneca, "that anger could always be exhausted, when its first weapon was broken, and that like the bees, who leave their stings in the wound they make, we could only inflict a single injury." To a certain extent this wish is often fulfilled, for the same writer observes, that anger is like a ruin, which, in falling upon its victim, breaks itself to pieces.

Without any other armour than an offended frown, an indignant eye, and a rebuking voice, decrepit age, timid womanhood, the weakest of our species, may daunt the most daring, for there is something formidable in the mere sight of wrath; even where it is incapable of inflicting any chastisement upon its provoker. It has thus a preventive operation, by making us cautious of calling it forth, and restrains more effectually by the fear of its ebullitions, than it could by their actual outbreakings; while it still retains a positive influence when aroused. Anger, in short, is a moral power, which tends to repair the inequalities of physical power, and to approximate the strong and the weak towards the same level.

So carefully, however, are our constitutional instincts guarded against abuse, that the moral and physical vigour imparted to us by anger as a salutary means of defence, is immediately lessened, when by its intemperate and reckless exercise, we would pervert it into a dangerous instrument of aggression. Blind and ungovernable rage, approaching to the nature of madness, not only obscures the reason, but often paralyses, for the moment, the bodily energies; a paroxysm which fortunately serves as a protection both to ourselves and others. This seasonable arrest of our functions gives us time to sanify, and we are allowed to recover them, when their exercise is no longer dangerous. Protective nature makes us sometimes blind and weak, when highly excited, for the same reason that the fleet greyhound has no sense of smell, and the quick-scented bloodhound no swiftness of foot.

Queen Elizabeth discovered qualities in anger which may not be obvious to common observers. "What does a man think of when he thinks of nothing?" her Majesty demanded of a choleric courtier, to whom she had not realised her promise of promotion. "He thinks, madam, of a woman's promise," was the tart reply. "Well, I must not confute him," said the Queen, walking away, "anger makes men witty, but it keeps them poor."

ANGLER—a fish-butcher—a piscatory assassin—a Jack Ketch—catcher of jack, an impaler of live worms, frogs, and flies, a torturer of trout, a killer of carp, and a great gudgeon who sacrifices the best part of his life in taking away the life of a little gudgeon. Every thing appertaining to the angler's art, is cowardly, cruel, treacherous, and cat-like. He is a professional dealer in "treasons, stratagems, and plots;" more subtle and sneaking than a poacher, and more exclusively devoted to snares, traps, and subterfuges; he is at the same time infinitely more remorseless, finding amusement and delight in prolonging, to the last gasp, the agonies of the impaled bait, and of the wretched fish writhing with a barb in its entrails.

The high priest of the anglers is that demure destroyer, old Izaak Walton, who may be literally termed the HOOKER of their piscatory polity. Because he could write a line as well as throw one, they would persuade themselves that he has shed a sort of classical dignity on their art, and even associated it with piety and poetry,—what profanation! The poet is not only a lover of his species, but of all sentient beings, because he "looks through nature up to Nature's God." But how can an angler be pious? How can a tormentor of the creature be a lover of the Creator? Away with such cant! Old Izaak must either have been a demure hypocrite, or a blockhead, unaware of the gross inconsistency between his profession and his practice. If he saw a fine trout, and wished to trouble him with a line, just to say he should be very happy to see him to dinner, he must first torture his postman, the bait, and make him carry the letters of Bellerophon. Hark how tenderly the gentle ruffian gives directions for baiting with a frog : " Put your hook through the mouth, and out at his gills, and then with a fine needle and silk, sew the upper part of his leg, with only one stitch, to the arming wire of the hook, and in so doing, *use him as though you loved him.*"

Tender hearted Izaak !—What would be his treatment of animals whom he did *not* love?

An angler may be meditative, or rather musing, but let him not ever think that he thinks, for if he had the healthy power of reflection, he could not be an angler. If sensible and amiable men are still to be seen squatted for hours in a punt, " like patience on a monument, smiling at grief," they are as much out of their element as the fish in their basket, and could only be reconciled to their employment by a resolute blinking of the question. In one of the admirable papers of the " Indicator," Leigh Hunt says—" We really cannot see what equanimity there is in jerking a lacerated carp out of the water by the jaws, merely because it has not the power of making a noise ; for we presume, that the most philosophic of anglers would hardly delight in catching shrieking fish." This is not so clear. Old Izaak, their patriarch, would have probably maintained that the shriek was a cry of pleasure. We willingly leave the anglers to their rod, for they deserve it, and we allow them to defend one another, not only because they have no other advocates, but because we are sure that the rest of the community would be glad to see them *hang together*, especially if they should make use of their own lines.

Averse as we are from extending the sphere of the angler's cruelty, we will mention one fish which old Izaak himself had never caught. A wealthy tradesman having ordered a fish-pond at his country-house to be cleared out, the foreman discovered, at the bottom, a spring of ferruginous coloured water ; and, on returning to the house, told his employer that they had found a chalybeate. " I am glad of it," exclaimed the worthy citizen, "for I never saw one. Put it in the basket with the other fish, and I'll come and look at it presently."

ANNUALS, Illustrated—the second childhood of Literature, the patrons of which carefully look over the plates, and studiously overlook the letter-press. Its object is to substitute the visible for the imaginative, a sensual for an intellectual pleasure, and to teach us to read engravings instead of writings.

ANSWERS—*to* the point are more satisfactory to the interrogator, but answers *from* the point may be sometimes more entertaining to the auditor. " Were you born in wedlock ?" asked a counsel of a witness. " No, Sir, in Devonshire," was the reply.—" Young woman," said a magistrate to a girl who was about to be sworn, " why do you hold the book upside down ?"—" I am obliged, Sir, because I am left-handed." — See Josephus Molitor. A written *non sequitur*, not less amusing, was involved in the postscript of the man who hoped his correspondent would excuse faults of spelling, if any, as he had no knife to mend his pens.

ANTINOMIANS—an antithesis to the Society for the Suppression of Vice. If we did not know that the best

things perverted become the worst, we might wonder that
the Christian religion should have ever generated a sect,
whose doctrines are professedly anti-moral. Many, however, are still to be found, who, maintaining that the moral
law is nothing to man, and that he is not bound to obey
it, avow an open contempt for good works, and affirm, that
as God sees no sin in believers, they are neither obliged
to confess it, nor to pray for its forgiveness. In this most
perilous spirit many tracts have been published,

> " Which, in the semblance of devotion,
>   Allure their victim to offence,
> And then administer a potion,
>   To soothe and lull his conscience ;
> Teaching him that to break all ties,
> May be a wholesome sacrifice ;—
> That saints, like bowls, may go astray,
> Better to win the proper way ;
> Indulge in every sin at times,
>   To prove that grace is never lacking ;
> And purify themselves by crimes,
>   As dirty shoes are clean'd by blacking."

ANTIPATHY.—As most men imagine themselves to have
an abundance of good reasons for dislike of their fellow-
creatures, they should be careful not to indulge imaginary
ones. And yet some people, forgetting the precept of " *Fas
est et ab hoste doceri*," have such a blind antipathy against
a political opponent, that they will disclaim any opinion
which he adopts, and adopt those that he disclaims, which,
as Bacon pithily observes, " is to make another man's folly
the master of your wisdom." Bentham, in his Book of
Fallacies, has ably pointed out the absurdity of this indiscriminate oppugnancy.—" Allow this argument the effect of
a conclusive one, you put it into the power of any man to
draw you at pleasure from the support of every measure

which, in your own eyes, is good; to force you to give your support to any and every measure which, in your own eyes, is bad. Is it good?—the bad man embraces it, and, by the supposition, you reject it. Is it bad?—he vituperates it, and that suffices for driving you into its embrace. You split upon the rocks, because he has avoided them; you miss the harbour, because he has steered into it! Give yourself up to any such blind antipathy, you are no less in the power of your adversaries than if, by a correspondently irrational sympathy and obsequiousness, you put yourself into the power of your friends."—pp. 132, 133.

ANTIQUARY—too often a collector of valuables that are worth nothing, and a recollector of all that Time has been glad to forget. His choice specimens have become rarities, simply because they were never worth preserving; and he attaches present importance to them in exact proportion to their former insignificance. A worthy of this unworthy class was once edifying the French Academy with a most unmerciful detail of the comparative prices of commodities at various remote periods, when La Fontaine observed, "Our friend knows the value of everything,—except time." We recommend this anecdote to the special consideration of *ci-devant* members of the Roxburgh Club, as well as to the resuscitators of the dead lumber of antiquity.

ANTIQUITY—the stalking horse on which knaves and bigots invariably mount, when they want to ride over the timid and the credulous. Never do we hear so much solemn palaver about the time-hallowed institutions, and approved wisdom of our ancestors, as when attempts are made to remove some staring monument of their folly. Thus is the youth, nonage, ignorance, and inexperience of the world invested by a strange blunder, which Bacon was the first to indicate, with the reverence due to the present times, which are its true old age.

Antiquity is the young miscreant, the type of commingled ignorance and tyranny, who massacred prisoners taken in war, sacrificed human beings to idols, burnt them in Smithfield as heretics or witches, believed in astrology, demonology, sorcery, the philosopher's stone, and every exploded folly and enormity; although his example is still gravely urged as a rule of conduct, and a standing argument against innovation,—that is to say, improvement ! If the seal of time were to be the signet of truth, there is no absurdity, oppression, or falsehood, that might not be received as gospel; while the Gospel itself would want the more ancient warrant of Paganism. Never was the world so old, and consequently so wise, as it is to-day; but it will be older, and therefore, still wiser, to-morrow.

In one generation, the most ancient individual has generally the most experience; but in a succession of generations, the youngest, or last of them, is the real Methuselah and Mentor. To this obvious distinction, nothing can blind us but gross stupidity, or the most miserable cant. To plead the authority of the ancients, is to appeal from civilized and enlightened Christians, to fierce, unlettered Pagans ; for no one has decided where this boasted wisdom begins or ends, though all agree that it is of great age. Every elderly man is an ancestor to his former self. Let him compare his boyish notions and feelings with his matured judgment, and he will form a pretty correct notion of the wisdom of our ancestors ; for what the child is to the man, are the past generations to the present.

Let us learn to distinguish the uses from the abuses of antiquity. Not to know what happened before we were born, is always to remain a child: to know, and blindly to adopt that knowledge, as an implicit rule of life, is never to be a man.

APOLOGY—as great a peacemaker as the word " if." In all cases, it is an excuse rather than an exculpation, and if adroitly managed, may be made to confirm what it seems to recall, and to aggravate the offence which it pretends to extenuate. A man who had accused his neighbour of false-hood, was called on for an apology, which he gave in the following amphibological terms :—" I called you a liar,—it is true. You spoke truth : I have told a lie."

APPEARANCES, Keeping up—a moral, or, rather, immoral uttering of counterfeit coin. It is astonishing how much human bad money is current in society, bearing the fair impress of ladies and gentlemen. The former, if carefully weighed, will always be found light, or you may presently detect if you *ring* them, though this is a somewhat perilous experiment. Both may be known by their assuming a more gaudy and showy appearance than their neighbours, as if their characters were brighter, their impressions more per-fect, and their composition more pure, than all others.

APPETITE—a relish bestowed upon the poorer classes, that they may like what they eat, while it is seldom enjoyed by the rich, because they may eat what they like.

ARCHITECTURE. — Nothing more completely esta-blishes the absence of any standard of intrinsic or inherent beauty in architecture, than the fact that we may equally admire two styles so totally dissimilar, both in their outlines, proportions, and details, as the Grecian and the Gothic,—an apparent inconsistency which has been accounted for by the plastic power of association. Independently of our impressions of the convenience, stability, skill, magnificence, and antiquity connected with the classical structures, they appeal more especially to our imagination, as the handiworks and records of those great nations, for which, even from our boyish days, we have ever felt the deepest reverence. And association can find the identical elements of beauty, dissimilar as they may seem, in the Gothic architecture, where a sense of religious veneration, and all the romantic recollections of chivalry, produce the same hallowing and ennobling effect as our classical impressions in the former instance. Alison has further observed, too, that a taste in architecture, when once established, is generally permanent, because the costliness of public edifices, as well as their great durability, prevent their renewal, until they have acquired, in the eyes of succeeding generations, all the sanction of antiquity, and have rooted themselves in the public mind. This accounts for the long-continued uniformity of style among the ancient Egyptians, and other people of the East, as well as for our own habitual imitation of ancient standards.

Why we should continue to enslave ourselves to the five orders of Vitruvius, I cannot well see. To the art of the statuary there is a conceivable limit, but that of the architect seems to admit a much wider range, and greater variety, than can be circumscribed within five orders. All structures should be adapted to the climate, and there is, therefore, *primâ facie* evidence that the fitting style for Greece and Asia Minor can scarcely be the proper one for England. A Grecian temple, many of whose ornaments are heathen symbols, is not the best model for a Christian church, which is but a solecism in stone when thus paganized ; nor can I admit the wisdom of our imitating an Italian villa, with its open balconies, and shady colonnades, unless we could, at the same time, import the Italian climate. The five orders are, to architecture, what the thirty-nine articles are to the church,—they do not ensure uniformity;—and if they did, it would not be desirable, because they are not adapted to the present state of knowledge, and the wants and feelings of the community. In either instance, this slavery of opinion must eventually yield to the growing freedom of thought.

Is there any valid reason why the Doric capital should be peculiar to a pillar whose height is precisely eight diameters, the Ionic volute to one of nine, and the Corinthian foliage to one of ten? Custom has assigned these ornaments and proportions, but one can imagine others which would be equally, or, perhaps, more agreeable to an unprejudiced eye. The first columns were undoubtedly trees, which diminished as they ascended. The stems of the branches, where they were cut off, suggested the capital; the iron or other bandages at top and bottom, to prevent the splitting of the wood, were the origin of the fillets; the square tile which protected the lower end from the wet, gave rise to the plinth. But why should a stone pillar be made to imitate a tree, by lessening as it rises? Custom alone has reconciled us to an unmeaning deviation, which throws all the inter-columnar spaces out of the perpendicular, and presents us with a series of long inverted cones, the most ungraceful of all forms. As if sensible of this defect, the Egyptians made the outline of some of their temples conform to the diminution of the columns, rendering the whole structure slightly pyramidical, and thus preserving the consistency of its lines.

Observing some singular pilasters at Harrogate, surmounted with the Cornua Ammonis, I ventured to ask the builder to what order they belonged. "Why, Sir," he replied, putting his hand to his head, "the horns are a little order of my own." Knowing him to be a married man, I concluded he had good reason for appropriating that peculiar ornament to himself, and made no further objections to his architecture.

The bow windows and balconies that scallop the narrow side streets at our watering-places, in order that their occupants may have a better opportunity of seeing nothing, are excrescences which ought to be cut away. I admit, however, the disinterestedness of the architect; he *can* have no view in them.

ARGUMENT — with fools, passion, vociferation, or violence: with ministers, a majority: with kings, the sword: with fanatics, denunciation: with men of sense, a sound reason.

ARISTOCRACY.—In ancient Greece this word signified the government of the best; but in modern England, if we are to judge by the present majority of the House of Lords, the term seems to have fairly "turned its back upon itself," and to have become the antithesis to its original import; even as beldam (or *belle dame*), formerly expressive of female beauty, is now defined by Dr. Johnson as, "a term of contempt, marking the last degree of old age with all its faults and miseries."

If we have noblemen whose titles are their honour, we have others who are an honour to their titles. Happy he, who deriving his patent from nature, as well as from his sovereign, may be dubbed, "*inter doctos nobilissimus,—inter nobiles doctissimus,—inter utrosque optimus.*"

ARITHMETIC.—The science of figures cuts but a poor figure in its origin, the term calculation being derived from the *calculus* or pebble used as a counter by the Romans, whose numerals, stolen from the ancient Etruscans, and still to be traced on the monuments of that people, seem to have been suggested in the first instance by the five fingers. Indeed, the term *digit* or finger, applied to any single number, sufficiently indicates the primitive mode of counting. The Roman V is a rude outline of the five fingers, or of the outspread hand, narrowing to the wrist; while the X is a symbol of the two fives or two hands crossed. In all probability the earliest numerals did not exceed five, which was repeated, with additions, for the higher numbers; and it is a remarkable coincidence that to express six, seven, eight, the North American Indians repeat the five, with the addition of one, two, three, on the same plan as the Roman VI, VII, VIII. Our term eleven is derived from the word *ein* or one, and the old verb *liben*, to leave; so that it signifies one, leave ten. Twelve means two, after reckoning or laying aside ten; and our termination of *ty*, in the words twenty, thirty, &c., comes from the Anglo-Saxon *teg*, to draw; so that twenty, or twainty, signifies two drawings, or that the fingers have been twice counted over, and the hands twice closed.

From the hands also, or other parts of the human body, were derived the original rude measurements. The *uncia*, or inch, was the first joint of the thumb, which being repeated three times, gave the breadth of the hand; and this product, quadrupled, furnished the measure of the foot. The *passus*, or pace, was the interval between two steps, reckoned at six feet; and a mile, as the word imports, consisted of a thousand paces. Other portions of the human body furnished secondary measures; the width of the hand gave the palm, reckoned at three inches :—the distances of the elbow from the tips of the fingers, the cubit; the entire length of the arm, the yard;—and the extreme breadth of the extended arms, across the shoulders, the fathom or six feet.

The Arabic numerals, derived, in all probability, from the Persians, and brought into Europe by the Moors, were a great improvement upon the clumsy system of the Romans; but it is to be regretted that we have not adopted the duodecimal in preference to the decimal scale, as it mounts faster, and being more often divisible in the descending series, would express fractions with a greater simplicity.

ART—Man's nature. Of all cants defend me from that cant of Art which substitutes a blind and indiscriminate reverence of the painter, provided he be dead, for a judicious admiration of his paintings. Our connoisseurs reverse the old adage, and prefer a dead dog to a living lion. They are Antinomian in their critical creed; they substitute faith for *good works*, and will fall prostrate before any daub provided it be sanctified by a popular name.

It may be objected that no artist would have acquired a great name unless he had been a great painter; a position to which there are exceptions, although we will grant it for the sake of argument. But an artist who might command universal admiration in the clden times, is no necessary model for the present. Surely our portrait painters need not study Holbein. Many of the old masters, avowedly deficient in drawing and composition, were celebrated for their colouring, a merit which the mere effects of time, in the course of three or four centuries, must inevitably destroy: and yet Titian, the great colourist of his day, but whose pictures have mostly faded into a cold dimness, is still held up to admiration, because his bright and blended hues delighted the good folks of the fifteenth century. The pictures of Rubens preserve the richness of their broad tints, which we can admire without being blind to the vulgarity of his taste and his bad drawing, for his females are little better than so many Dutch Vrowes—coarse, flabby and clownish. To a genuine connoisseur, however, every one of them is, doubtless, a Venus de Medici; not because she is handsome or well-proportioned, for she is neither, but because she is painted by Rubens.

This idolatry of the artist and indifference to art, has had

a very mischievous effect in England ; first, by withdrawing
encouragement from our countrymen and contemporaries
and, secondly, by injuring their taste in holding up as model
for imitation, not the paintings of nature, but old Continenta
pictures, which, even supposing them to be genuine, hav
often lost the sole distinction that once conferred a valu
upon them. But in many instances they are spurious, fo
the high prices which we so absurdly lavish upon them, hav
called into existence, in the chief Italian towns, manufactorie
of copies and counterfeits for the sole supply of England, i
which happy and discerning country may be found ten time
more pictures of each of the old masters, than could hav
been painted in a long life. Neither the most experience
artist, nor knowing virtuoso, can guard against this specie
of imposition. It is well known that Sir Joshua Reynolds
even in that branch of the art with which he was most con
versant, was perpetually deceived, his collection swarmin
with false Correggios, Titians, and Michael Angelos. Wha
wonder, then, that an old picture, as often happens, shall se
to-day for a thousand pounds, and that to-morrow, strippe
of its supposed authenticity, *stat nominis umbra*, and sha
not fetch ten? And yet it is as good and as bad one day a
it was the other, viewed as a work of art. So besotting is th
magic of a name.

To these pseudo-connoisseurs, who bring their own narro
professional feelings to the appreciation of a work of art, w
recommend the following authentic anecdote :—A thrivin
tailor, anxious to transmit his features to posterity, inquire
of a young artist what were his terms for a half length. "
charge twenty-five guineas for a head," was the reply. Th
portrait was painted and approved, when the knight of th
thimble, taking out his purse, demanded how much he was t
pay. "I told you before that my charge for a head wa
twenty-five guineas."—"I am aware of that," said Snip

"but how much more for the coat?—it is the best part of the picture."

ART, Origin of.—We are struck with an admiration almost amounting to awe, when we contemplate a noble building, a fine statue, or a grand painting, and feel a pride in our species when we term them the noblest productions of human art; but such objects have a still more sanctifying effect if we suffer them to raise our thoughts to Him who made the artist, and benevolently endowed him with faculties of which the exercise can bestow such pure delight, not only on his contemporaries, but on a long succession of generations. The races of spectators who have been gratified by the beautiful products of Grecian art, form, perhaps, but a tithe of those who are to succeed to the same pleasure, for celebrated statues are almost immortal—they can only perish at least with the civilization that has enshrined them. The humblest work of nature, as well as the most perfect one of art, are alike exalted by tracing them to their divine original.

ARTICLES, The Thirty-nine—spiritual canons, drawn up with the most subtle complication for the purpose of establishing a general simplicity and unity in matters of faith. Of these Polyglot persuaders to the use of one religious language, there were originally forty-two, composed in the year 1552, "by the bishops and other learned and good men in Convocation, to root out the discord of opinions, and establish the agreement of true religion." But it appears that these infallible bishops and other learned and good men, who had undertaken to fix and determine the only right road to heaven, were themselves but blind guides, for, in the year 1562, their Confession of Faith was altered and reduced to thirty-nine articles. Alas! this Convocation was no more infallible than its predecessor, for in 1571 these Articles were again revised and altered, since which time they have continued to be the criterion of the faith of the Church of England. They profess for their object—"the avoiding of diversities of opinions, and the establishing of consent touching true religion," and their eminent success is attested by the fact that, if we include Ireland, Scotland, and the various dissenters, both from Episcopalianism and Presbyterianism, little more than one-third of the inhabitants of Great Britain are calculated to belong to the Established religion; while, even of that third, owing to different interpretations of these articles, framed for producing universal consent, there are various sects opposed to one another within the walls of the Church, not less zealously than to the common enemy without!

Mark the opinion upon this subject entertained by a distinguished prelate. "I reduced the study of divinity," says Bishop Watson, "into as narrow a compass as possible, for I determined to study nothing but my Bible, being much unconcerned about the opinions of councils, fathers, churches, bishops, and other men, as little inspired as myself. I had no prejudice against, no predilection for the Church of England; but a sincere regard for the Church of Christ, and an insuperable objection to every degree of dogmatical intolerance. I never troubled myself with answering any arguments which the opponents in the divinity-schools brought against the Articles of the Church, nor ever admitted their authority as decisive of a difficulty; but I used, on such occasions, to say to them, holding the New Testament in my hand, '*En sacrum codicem!*' Here is the fountain of truth; why do you follow the streams derived from it by the sophistry, or polluted by the passions of man? If you can bring any proofs against any thing delivered in this book, I shall think it my duty to reply to you. Articles of churches are not of divine authority; have done with them, for they may be true, they may be false, and appeal to the book itself."

No Christian Church ought to exact from its ministers a Confession of Faith upon numerous and intricate articles of human construction, though it may fairly claim a declaration of belief that the Scriptures contain a revelation of the divine will. Such, at least, was the opinion of Bishop Watson, as it had been previously professed by the celebrated Bishop Hoadly, and other distinguished members of the Church of England.

Xerxes, we are told, ordered the non-conforming waves of the ocean to be scourged with rods and confined within certain boundaries; in imitation of which sapient example, our Church has provided a cat-o'-thirty-nine-tails, to lash back the tide of human thought and circumscribe the illimitable range of opinion. In both instances the success has been worthy of the attempt.

ASCETIC.—Dr. Johnson has observed that the shortness of life has afforded as many arguments to the voluptuary as to the moralist, and there can be no doubt that the ascetic, in his cell, is seeking his own happiness with as much selfishness as the professed epicurean: one betakes himself to immediate, the other to remote gratifications; one devotes himself to sensuality, the other to mortification; one to bodily, the other, perhaps, to intellectual pleasures; one to this world, the other to the next; but the principle of action is the same in both parties, and the ascetic is, perhaps, the most selfish calculator of the two, inasmuch as the reward he claims is infinitely greater and of longer endurance. He is usurious in his dealings with heaven, and does not put out the smallest mortification except upon the most enormous interest. His very self-denial is selfish, for

the odds are incalculably in favour of the man who bets
body against soul.

They who impiously imagine that the happiness of the
Creator consists in the unhappiness of the creature, are
thus offending Him in their very fear of giving offence,
since they find sweetness even in their sourness, and a joy
in the very want of it. Well for them, too, if they go not
astray, in their over anxiety to walk straight. " As for those
that will not take lawful pleasures," says old Fuller, "I am
afraid they will take unlawful pleasure, and, by lacing themselves too hard, grow awry on one side."

To the same purport we may quote the observation of
the French writer, Balzac : " *Si ceux qui sont ennemis des
divertissemens honnêtes avoient la direction du monde, ils
voudroient ôter le printemps et la jeunesse,—l'un de l'année,
et l'autre de la vie.*"

ATHANASIAN CREED, Character of, by a bishop.—
"A motley monster of bigotry and superstition, a scarecrow
of shreds and patches, dressed up of old by philosophers
and popes, to amuse the speculative and to affright the
ignorant; *now* a butt of scorn, against which every un-
fledged witling of the age essays his wanton efforts, and
before he has learned his catechism, is fixed an infidel
for life."*

In Bishop Watson's proposed bill for revising the Liturgy
and Articles, the omission of the Athanasian Creed was one
of the principal improvements ; and, long before his time,
Bishop Burnet had not scrupled to pronounce it a forgery
of the eighth century. We know, from the authority of Dr.
Heberden, that the pious George III. refused, in the most
pointed manner, to make the responses when this creed was

* Misc. Tracts, by Watson, Bishop of Llandaff, v. ii., p. 49.

read in Windsor Chapel. Dr. Mant, quoting from Dean Vincent, says, "this creed *is supposed* to have been framed from the writings of Athanasius. It was not, however, admitted into the offices of the Roman church, at the earliest, till the year 930, in which it has continued ever since, and was received into our liturgy at the time of the Reformation."—(Mant's Common Prayer, p. 57.)

In spite of the damnatory clauses at the conclusion of this theological puzzle, this *Ignotum per ignotius*, it appears that Christendom did very well without it for 900 years; and, probably, very few of the rationally devout would complain if it were placed in the same situation for 900 years to come. It was a saying of the Dutch General, Wurtz, "that when men shall have once taken out of Christianity all that they have foisted into it, there will be but one religion in the world, and *that* equally plain in doctrine, and pure in morals." The Scriptures warn us against "teaching the doctrines of men as the commandments of God;" or, as Paley has said, "imposing, under the name of revealed religion, doctrines which men cannot believe, or will not examine." When objections are made to the Mosaic account of the creation, as being inconsistent with the modern state of science, it is indignantly urged that Moses did not undertake to expound astronomy or geology to ignorant shepherds, but that he spoke popularly, and adapted himself to the comprehensions of his auditors. And yet, when any attempt is made to popularize our liturgy, by the omission of any such objectionable portions as the Athanasian Creed, we hear a Pharisaical cry of impiety and profanation, and are solemnly warned that to remove a single stone, however cankered or superfluous, is to endanger the whole edifice of the church. Strange! that we may suppress truth and yet not expunge a forgery. Strange! that we may adapt the liturgy and formularies of religion to the ignorance of the age, and yet not adjust them to its knowledge !

This incredible creed, which it is above all things necessary to hold, may be defined, like Aristotle's Materia Prima, as, "*nec quid, nec quale, nec quantum, nec aliquid eorum de quibus Ens denominatur.*" Nevertheless, there are golden reasons, which may induce a profession of belief in it. Mr. Patten, a curate of Whitstable, was so much averse to it that he always omitted it from the service. Archbishop Secker, being informed of his recusancy, sent the archdeacon to ask him his reason. "I do not believe it," said the priest.—"But your metropolitan *does*," replied the archdeacon.—"It may be so," rejoined Mr. Patten; "and he can well afford it. He believes at the rate of *seven thousand* a-year, and I, only at that of *fifty*."

ATHEIST.—Supposing such an anomaly to exist, an atheist must be the most miserable of beings. The idea of a fatherless world, swinging by some blind law of chance, which may every moment expose it to destruction, through an infinite space, filled, perhaps, with nothing but suffering and wretchedness, unalleviated by the prospect of a future and a happier state, must be almost intolerable to a man who has a single spark of benevolence in his bosom. "All the splendour of the highest prosperity," says Adam Smith, " can never enlighten the gloom with which so dreadful an idea must necessarily overshadow the imagination ; nor in a wise and virtuous man, can all the sorrow of the most afflicting adversity ever dry up the joy which necessarily springs from the habitual and thorough conviction of the truth of the contrary system."

The word atheist has done yeoman's service as a nickname wherewith to pelt all those who disapprove of the thirty-nine articles, or who venture to surmise that there are

.buses in the church which need reform; but this sort of
lirt has been thrown until it will no longer stick, except to
he fingers of those who handle it. The real atheist is the
Mammonite, who, making "godliness a great gain," wor-
hips a golden calf, and calls it a God: or the miserable
anatic, who, endowing the phantom of his own folly and
ear, with the worst passions of the worst men, dethrones the
eity to set up a dæmon, and curses all those who will not
urse themselves by joining in his idolatry.

AUDIENCE—a crowd of people in a large theatre, so
alled because they cannot hear. The actors speak to them
vith their hands and feet, and the spectators listen with
heir eyes.

AUTHOR, Original—one who copying only from the
vorks of the great Author of the world, never plagiarises,
xcept from the book of nature; whereas the imitator de-
ives his inspiration from the writings of his fellow-men, and
as no thought except as to the best mode of purloining the
houghts of others. Authors are lamps, exhausting them-
elves to give light to others; or rather may they be com-
ared to industrious bees, not because they are armed with
sting, but because they gather honey from every flower,
nly that their hive may be plundered when their toil is
ompleted. By the iniquitous law of copyright, an author's
roperty in the offspring of his own intellect, is wrested from
im at the end of a few years; previously to which period,
ne bookseller is generally obliging enough to ease him of
ne greater portion of the profit.
Against the former injustice, however, most writers secure
nemselves by the evanescent nature of their works; and as
) the latter, we must confess after all, that the bookseller is
ne best Mæcenas.

For the flattery lavished upon a first successful work, an author often pays dearly by the abuse poured upon its successors; for we all measure ourselves by our best production, and others by their worst.—Writers are too often treated by the public, as crimps serve recruits,—made drunk at first, only that they may be safely *rattaned* all the rest of their lives.

An author is more annoyed by abuse than gratified by praise ; because, he looks upon the latter as a right and the former as a wrong. And this opens a wider question as to the constitution of our nature, both moral and physical, which is susceptible of pain in a much greater and more intense degree than of pleasure. We have no bodily enjoyment to counterbalance the agony of an acute toothache ; nor any mental one that can form a set-off against despair. Nowhere is this more glaringly illustrated than in the descriptions of our future rewards and punishments, the miseries and the anguish of hell being abundantly definite and intelligible, while the heavenly beatitudes are dimly shadowed forth, as being beyond the imagination of man to conceive.

An author's living purgatory, is his liability to be consulted as to the productions of literary amateurs, both male and female. The annoyance of reading them can only be equalled by that of pronouncing upon their merits. Oh, that every scribbler would recollect the dictum of Dr. Johnson upon this subject. "You must consider beforehand, that such effusions may be bad as well as good; and nobody has a right to put another under such a difficulty, that he must either hurt the person by telling the truth, or hurt himself by telling what is not true."

Between authors and artists there should be no jealousy, for their pursuits are congenial ; one paints with a pen, the other writes with a brush; and yet it is difficult for either to be quite impartial, in weighing the merits of their different avocations. The author of the Pleasures of Hope, being at a dinner-party with Mr. Turner, R.A., whose enthusiasm for his art led him to speak of it and of its professors as superior to all others, the bard rose, and after alluding with a mock gravity, to his friend's skill in varnishing painters as well as paintings, proposed the health of Mr. Turner, and the worshipful company of Painters and Glaziers. This, (to use the newspaper phrase) called up Mr. Turner, who with a similar solemnity, expressed his sense of the honour he had received, made some good humoured allusions to blotters of foolscap, whose works are appropriately bound in calf; and concluded by proposing in return, the health of Mr. Campbell, and the worshipful company of Paper-stainers—a rejoinder that excited a general laugh, in which none joined more heartily than the poet himself.

AUTHORITY, Submission to, in matters of opinion—making names the measure of facts,—deciding upon truth by extrinsic testimony, not intrinsic evidence—surrendering our reason, which is the revelation of God, to the reasons of men, not necessarily more competent to judge than ourselves. Better to be a slave with an unfettered mind, than a pseudo freeman whose opinions, his most precious birthright, are bondslaves to a name. Had authority always been our guide, we should still have been savages. "The woods," says Locke, " are fitter to give rules than cities, where those that call themselves civil and rational, go out of their way by the authority of example." Are we to follow every Will-o'-the-wisp because it is literally a precedent?

Although it condemns the same assumption in the Pope, our Church in its twentieth article, claims " power to decree rites or ceremonies, and authority in controversies of faith." It has been affirmed that this article has neither the sanction of parliament nor convocation; but if it possessed both, it would still want the authority of reason and justice, and the possibility of enforcing that which is quite beyond the reach of mortal jurisdiction. Christianity, its own best and surest authority, is only weakened by arbitrary enactments. To a calm inquirer, it must seem marvellous that any fallible man, or council of men, should set themselves up as directors of the consciences of others.

Surely the time will come when even the stoutest sticklers for compulsory act of parliament faith, becoming convinced of their error, will join in the following prayer of the learned and pious Dr. Chandler—"'Tis my hearty prayer to the Father of Lights, and the God of Truth, that all human authority in matters of faith, may come to a full end; and that every one, who hath reason to direct him, and a soul to save, may be his own judge in every thing that concerns his eternal welfare, without any prevailing regard to the dictates of fallible men, or fear of their peevish and impotent censures."

At present it is to be feared, there are many churchmen, reformed as well as Roman, who hold with Cardinal Perron, when he says, "We must not pretend to convince an Arian of his errors by scripture evidence—we must have recourse to the authority of the Church." That this was not the opinion of our English Bishop Hoadly, will appear from the following extract :—

"Authority is the greatest and most irreconcilable enemy to truth and argument that this world ever furnished out. All the sophistry, all the colour of plausibility, all the argument and cunning of the subtlest disputer in the world, may be laid open and turned to the advantage of that very truth, which they designed to hide or to depress: but against authority there is no defence. It was authority which would have prevented all reformation where it is;

and which has put a barrier against it wherever it is not."

AUTO-BIOGRAPHY—drawing a portrait of yourself with a pen and ink, carefully omitting all the bad features that you have, and putting in all the good ones that you have not, so as to ensure an accurate and faithful likeness ! Publishing your own authentic life is telling flattering lies of yourself, in order, if possible, to prevent others from telling disparaging truths. No man's life is complete till he is dead, an auto-biography is therefore a *mis-nomer*. As such works, however, generally fall still-born from the press, an author may fairly be said to have lost his life, as soon as he is delivered of it, so that this objection is, in fact, removed.

AUTO DA FE, or act of faith—roasting our fellow creatures alive, for the honour and glory of a God of mercy. The horrors of this diabolical spectacle, which was invariably beheld by both sexes and all ages with transports of triumph and delight, should eternally be borne in mind, that we may see to what brutal extremities intolerance will push us, if it be not checked in the very outset. Thanks to the progress of opinion, the inquisition and its tortures are abolished; but fanatics, whether Romish or Reformed, still reserve the right of punishing Heretics, (that is, all those who differ from themselves on religious points,) with fire, pillory, imprisonment, and odium in this world ; while they carefully retain the parting curse of the inquisition, " *Jam animam tuam tradimus Diabolo*," and consign them to eternal fire in the next. This moral inquisition remains yet to be suppressed. It is only a postponed *auto da fé*. And all this hateful irreligion for the sake of religion ! How truly may Christianity exclaim—" I fear not mine enemies, but save, oh ! save me from my pretended friends."

AVARICE—the mistake of the old, who begin multi-plying their attachments to the earth, just as they are going to run away from it, thereby increasing the bitterness without protracting the date of their separation. What the world terms avarice, however, is sometimes no more than a compulsory economy; and even a wilful penuriousness is better than a wasteful extravagance. Simonides being reproached with parsimony, said he had rather enrich his enemies after his death, than borrow of his friends in his lifetime.

There are more excuses for this "old gentlemanly vice," than the world is willing to admit. Its professors have the honour of agreeing with Vespasian, that—"*Auri bonus est odor ex re quâlibet*," and with Dr. Johnson, who maintained, that a man is seldom more beneficially employed, either for himself or others, than when he is making money. Wealth, too, is power, of which the secret sense in ourselves, and the open homage it draws from others, are doubly sweet, when we feel that all our other powers, and the estimation they procured us, are gradually failing. Nor is it any trifling advantage, in extreme old age, still to have a pursuit that gives an interest to existence ; still to propose to ourselves an object, of which every passing day advances the accomplishment, and which holds out to us the pleasure of success, with hardly a possibility of failure, for it is much more easy to make the last *plum* than the first thousand. So far from supposing an old miser to be inevitably miserable, in the Latin sense of the word, it is not improbable that he may be more happy than his less penurious brethren. No one but an old man who has withstood the temptation of avarice, should be allowed to pronounce its unqualified condemnation.

ACHELOR—one who is so fearful of marrying, lest his wife should become his mistress, that he not unfrequently finishes his career by converting his mistress into a wife. "A married man," said Dr. Johnson, "has many cares; but a bachelor has no pleasures." Cutting himself off from a great blessing, for fear of some trifling annoyance, he has rivalled the wiseacre who secured himself against corns, by amputating his leg. In his selfish anxiety to live unencumbered, he has only subjected himself to a heavier burthen : for the passions, who apportion to every individual the load that he is to bear through life, generally say to the calculating bachelor —"As you are a single man, you shall carry double."

We may admire the wit, without acknowledging the truth of the repartee uttered by a bachelor, who, when his friend reproached him for his celibacy, adding that bachelorship ought to be taxed by the Government, replied, "There I agree with you, for it is quite a luxury !"

BAIT—one animal impaled upon a hook, in order to torture a second, for the amusement of a third. Were the latter to change places, for a single day, with either of the two former, which might generally be done with very little loss to society, it would enable him to form a better notion of the pastime he is in the habit of pursuing.—N.B. To make some approximation towards strict retributive justice, he should gorge the bait, and his tormentor should have all the humanity of an experienced angler !

BALLADS—vocal portraits of the national mind. The people that are without them, may literally be said not to be worth an old song. The old Government of France was well

defined as an absolute monarchy, moderated by songs ; and
the acute Fletcher of Saltoun was so sensible of their importance, as to express a deliberate opinion, that if a man
were permitted to make all the ballads, he need not care who
made the laws of a nation. They who deem this an ex-
aggerated notion, will do well to recollect the silly ballad
of Lilliburlero, the noble author of which publicly boasted,
and without much extravagance in the vaunt, that he had
rhymed King James out of his dominions.

BALLOT—an equal security against aristocratical corruption, and democratical intimidation : the only security
for the free and impartial exercise of the elective franchise,
to extend which to the poor and dependent, without the
protection of secrecy, is only to throw the representation
more completely into the hands of the rich and powerful.
Sad rogues must be the lower classes, as we are told, thus
to be bought or browbeaten. No doubt : and their superiors,
who bribe and intimidate them, are all marvellous proper
gentlemen ! Against a proposition for the ballot, the established arguments are, a shrug of the shoulders, a look of
disgust, and an exclamation of horror ;—conclusive modes
of reasoning, adopted rather from necessity than choice, for
we are not aware of any more convincing objections. Some,
indeed, are so consistent as to tell us, that the practice is
mean, degrading, contemptible, un-English, at the very time
that it is openly practised in the Committee business of the
House of Commons, in the elections at the East India
House, and in those of almost every club throughout the
kingdom. Though such noodles have short memories, they
cannot be called great wits.

BANDIT—an unlegalised soldier, who is hanged for
doing that which would get him a commission and a medal,

had he taken the king's money, instead of that of travellers. "*Ille crucem sceleris pretium tulit, hic diadema.*"

BAR, Independence of the.—Like a ghost, a thing much talked of, and seldom seem. If a barrister possess any professional or moral independence, it cannot be worth much, for a few guineas will generally purchase it. It must be confessed, that he is singularly independent of all those scruples which operate upon the consciences of other men. Right and wrong, truth or falsehood, morality or profligacy, are all equally indifferent to him. Dealing in law, not justice, his brief is his bible, the ten guineas of his retaining fee are his decalogue : his glory, like that of a cookmaid, consists in wearing a silk gown, and his heaven is in a judge's wig. Head, heart, conscience, body and soul, all are for sale : the forensic bravo stands to be hired by the highest bidder, ready to attack those whom he has just defended, or defend those whom he has just attacked, according to the orders he may receive from his temporary master. Looking to the favour of the judge for favour with their clients, and to the government for professional promotion, barristers have too often been the abject lickspittles of the one, and the supple tools of the other.

M. de la B——, a French gentleman, seems to have formed a very correct notion of the independence of the bar. Having invited several friends to dine on a *maigre* day, his servant brought him word, that there was only a single salmon left in the market, which he had not dared to bring away, because it had been bespoken by a barrister.—" Here," said his master, putting two or three pieces of gold into his hand, " Go back directly, and buy me the barrister and the salmon too."

BARRISTER—a legal servant of all work : one who

sometimes makes his gown a cloak for browbeating and putting down a witness, who, but for this protection, might occasionally knock down the barrister. Show me the conscientious counsellor, who, refusing to hire out his talents that he may screen the guilty, overreach the innocent, defraud the orphan, or impoverish the widow, will scrupulously decline a brief, unless the cause of his client wear at least a semblance of honesty and justice;—who will leave knaves and robbers to the merited inflictions of the law, while he will cheerfully exert his eloquence and skill in redressing the wrongs of the injured. Show me such a Phœnix of a barrister, and I will admit that he richly deserves—not to have been at the bar !

"Does not a barrister's affected warmth, and habitual dissimulation, impair his honesty?" asked Boswell of Dr. Johnson.—"Is there not some danger that he may put on the same mask in common life, in the intercourse with his friends?"—"Why no, Sir," replied the Doctor. "A man will no more carry the artifice of the bar into the common intercourse of society, than a man who is paid for tumbling upon his hands will continue to do so when he should walk on his feet." Perhaps not ; but how are we to respect the forensic tumbler, who will walk upon his hands, and perform the most ignoble antics for a paltry fee ?

All briefless barristers will please to consider themselves excepted from the previous censure, for I should be really sorry to speak ill of any man *without a cause.*

BATHOS—sinking when you mean to rise. The waxen wings of Icarus, which, instead of making him master of the air, plunged him into the water, were a practical Bathos. So was the miserable imitation of the Thunderer by Salmoneus, which, instead of giving him a place among the Gods, consigned him to the regions below.

Of the written Bathos, an amusing instance is afforded in the published tour of a lady, who has attained some celebrity in literature. Describing a storm to which she was exposed, when crossing in the steam-boat from Dover to Calais, her ladyship says,—" In spite of the most earnest solicitations to the contrary, in which the captain eagerly joined, I firmly persisted in remaining upon deck, although the tempest had now increased to such a frightful hurricane, that it was not without great difficulty I could—hold up my parasol !"

As a worthy companion to this little *morçeau,* we copy the following affecting advertisement from a London newspaper : —" If this should meet the eye of Emma D——, who absented herself last Wednesday from her father's house, she is implored to return, when she will be received with undiminished affection by her almost heart-broken parents. If nothing can persuade her to listen to their joint appeal—should she be determined to bring their grey hairs with sorrow to the grave—should she never mean to revisit a home where she has passed so many happy years—it is at least expected, if she be not totally lost to all sense of propriety, that she will, without a moment's further delay,—send back the key of the tea-caddy."

BEAUTY—has been not unaptly, though somewhat vulgarly, defined by T. H. as " all my eye," since it addresses itself solely to that organ, and is intrinsically of little value. From this ephemeral flower are distilled many of the ingredients in matrimonial unhappiness. It must be a dangerous gift, both for its possessor and its admirer, if there be any truth in the assertion of M. Gombaud, that beauty "*représente les Dieux, et les fait oublier.*" If its possession, as is too often the case, turns the head, while its loss sours the temper; if the long regret of its decay outweighs the fleeting pleasure of its bloom, the plain should rather pity than envy the handsome. Beauty of countenance, which, being the light of the soul shining through the face, is independent of features or complexion, is the most attractive, as well as the most enduring charm. Nothing but talent and amiability can bestow it, no statue or picture can rival, time itself cannot destroy it.

Wants are seldom blessings, and yet the want of a common standard of beauty has incalculably widened the sphere of our enjoyment, since all tastes may thus be gratified by the infinite variety of minds, and the endless diversities in the human form. Father Buffier maintains, that the beauty of every object consists in that form and colour most usual among things of that particular sort to which it belongs. He seems to have thought that there was no inherent beauty in anything except the *juste milieu*, the happy mean. "The beauty of a nose," says Adam Smith, following out the same idea in his Theory of Moral Sentiments, is the form at which Nature seems to have aimed in all noses, which she seldom hits exactly, but to which all her deviations still bear a strong resemblance. Many copies of an original may all miss it in some respects, yet they will all resemble it more than they resemble one another. So it is with animated forms; and thus beauty, though, in one sense, exceedingly rare, because few attain the happy mean, is, at the same time, a common quality, because all the deviations have a greater resemblance to this standard than to one another.

Even this, however, is not a certain criterion, for our estimate of beauty, depending mainly upon association, will be influenced by the predominant feeling in the mind of the spectator, whether he be contemplating a woman or a landscape. Brindley, the civil engineer, considered a straight canal a much more picturesque and pleasing object than a meandering river. "For what purpose," he was asked, "do you apprehend rivers to have been intended?"—"To feed navigable canals," was the reply. Dr. Johnson maintained, that there was no beauty without utility, but he was not provided with a rejoinder, when the peacock's tail was objected to him. What so beautiful as flowers, and yet we cannot always perceive their utility in the economy of nature. There are belles, to whom the same remark may be applied.

As the want of exterior generally increases the interior beauty, we should do well to judge of women as of the impressions on medals, and pronounce those the most valuable which are the plainest.

BEER, Small—an undrinkable drink, which if it were set upon a cullender to let the water run out, would leave a residuum of —— nothing. Of whatever else it may be guilty, it is generally innocent of malt and hops. Upon the principle of *lucus a non lucendo*, it may be termed liquid bread, and the strength of corn. Small-beer comes into the third category of the honest brewer, who divided his infusions into three classes—strong table, common table, and *lamen-table*. An illiterate vendor of this commodity wrote over his door at Harrogate, " Bear sold here !" " He spells the word quite correctly," said T. H., " if he means to apprise us that the article is his own *Bruin !*"

BELIEF—an involuntary operation of the mind, which we can no more control, however earnestly we may wish or pray for it, than we can add a cubit to our stature by desiring to be taller. " Belief or disbelief," says Dr. Whitby, " can neither be a virtue nor a crime in any one who uses the best means in his power of being informed. If a proposition is evident, we cannot avoid believing it, and where is the merit or piety of a necessary assent? If it is not evident, we cannot help rejecting it, or doubting of it ; and where is the crime of not performing impossibilities, or not believing what does not appear to us to be true?" Throughout the world belief depends chiefly upon localities, and the accidents of birth. The doctrines instilled into our infant mind are, in almost every instance, retained as they were received—without inquiry; and if such a passive acquiescence deserve the name of an intelligent belief, which may well be questioned, it is manifest that we ourselves have no merit in the process. And yet, gracious Heaven! what wars, massacres, miseries and martyrdoms, to enforce that which it does not depend upon the human will, either to adopt or to repudiate!

Perhaps the world never made a more mischievous mistake, than by elevating the meritoriousness and the rewards of belief, which is not in our power, above the claims of good works, which depend entirely upon ourselves; a perversion operating as a premium upon hypocrisy, and a positive discouragement to virtue. Whatever desert there may be in mere belief, we share it with the devils, who are said, in the Epistle of James, "to believe and tremble;" a tolerably conclusive answer to those who maintain that good works are the inevitable result of faith.

We will put a case to the sincere bigot. If fifty, or five hundred, or five thousand, of the most learned and clearsighted men in the kingdom, were solemnly to warn him that his salvation or perdition depended on his believing the sky to be of a bright orange colour, what would be his reply, if he was an honest man? "Gentlemen, most implicitly do I believe that, to your eyes, the sky is of a bright orange colour; but, owing to some singularity or defect in the construction of my visual organs, a misfortune for which I ought to be pitied rather than hated and anathematized, it has always appeared to me of a mild blue colour; nor can I ever believe, such being the case, that a God of truth and justice, will reward me with eternal happiness for uttering a falsehood; or condemn me to endless torments for avowing that which I most conscientiously believe to be true." Let the bigot, upon questions as to the colour of faith, infinitely more difficult of proof than the hues of visible objects, grant the indulgence he is thus described as claiming; let him do as he would be done by, and he will soon lose the reproach of his name, while enlightened and philanthropic Christianity will gain a convert. But, alas! it is so much easier to observe certain forms involving no self-denial, or to profess a belief, which may be simply an uninquiring assent, than to practise virtue, that the fanatics will always have numerous followers, who will hate the moralists even as the ancient Pharisees detested the Christians.

Shaftesbury, in his "Characteristics," has thus defined the different forms of belief :—

"To believe that everything is governed, or regulated for the best, by a designing Principle or Mind, necessarily good and permanent, is to be a perfect Theist."

"To believe no *one* supreme designing Principle or Mind, but rather *two, three,* or more, (though in their nature good) is to be a Polytheist."

"To believe the governing mind or minds not absolutely and necessarily good, nor confined to what is best, but capable of acting according to mere will or fancy, is to be a Dæmonist !"

God forbid ! that anything here set down, should be construed into an encouragement of unbelief, when its sole object is the discouragement of unchristian intolerance, by showing the real nature and value of faith. They who persecute, or even hate their fellow creatures for opinion's-sake, want the power rather than the inclination to restore the inquisition, with all its diabolical cruelties. We are told, in the 7th Psalm, that "the Lord ordaineth his arrows against the persecutors." They who practise, therefore, not those who deprecate persecution, are the real unbelievers. Hacknied

as is the quotation, we cannot, perhaps, better close this
article than with Pope's couplet :—

> " For modes of faith let zealous bigots fight;
> His can't be wrong whose life is in the right."

BENEFICENCE — may exist without benevolence.
Arising from a sense of duty, not from sympathy or compassion, it may be a charity of the hand rather than of the
heart. And this, though less amiable, is, perhaps, more
certain than the charity of impulse, inasmuch as a principle
is better to be depended upon than a feeling. There is an
apparent beneficence which has no connection, either with
right principle or right feeling, as, when we throw alms to a
beggar, not to relieve him of his distress, but ourselves of his
importunity or of the pain of beholding him : and there is a
charity which is mere selfishness, as when we bestow it for
the sole purpose of ostentation. We need not be surprised
that certain names should be so pertinaciously blazoned
before the public eye in lists of contributors, if we bear in
mind that " charity covereth a multitude of sins."

BENTLEY, Doctor.—In the lately published life of this
literary Thraso, the editor has omitted to insert an anecdote
which is worth preserving, if it were only for the pun that it
embalms. Robert Boyle, afterwards Earl of Cork, having,
as it was generally thought, defeated Bentley in a controversy
concerning the authenticity of the letters of Phalaris, the
Doctor's pupils drew a caricature of their master, whom the
guards of Phalaris were thrusting into his brazen bull, for
the purpose of burning him alive, while a label issued from
his mouth with the following inscription, " Well, well ! I had
rather be roasted than *Boyled.*"

BIGOT.—Camden relates that when Rollo, Duke of Normandy, received Gisla, the daughter of Charles the Foolish, in marriage, he would not submit to kiss Charles's foot; and when his friends urged him by all means to comply with that ceremony, he made answer in the English tongue—NE SE BY GOD—*i. e.*—*Not so by God.* Upon which the king and his courtiers deriding him, and corruptly repeating his answer, called him *bigot,* which was the origin of the term. Though modern bigots resemble their founder in being wedded to the offspring of a foolish parent, viz. their own opinion, they are unlike him in every other particular; for they not only insist upon kissing the foot of some superior authority, the Pope of their own election, but they quarrel with all the world for not following their example. Generally obstinate in proportion as he is wrong, the bigot thinks he best shows his love of God by hatred of his fellow creatures, and his humility by lauding himself and his sect. Vain is the endeavour to argue with men of this stamp—

> For, steel'd by pride from all assaults,
> They cling the closer to their faults ;
> And make self-praise supply an ointment
> For every wound and disappointment,
> As dogs by their own licking cure
> Whatever soreness they endure.
> Minds thus debased by mystic lore,
>   Are like the pupils of the eye,
> Which still contract themselves the more,
>   The greater light that you supply.
> Others by them are prais'd or slander'd,
> Exactly as they fit their standard,
> And as an oar, though straight in air,
>   Appears in water to be bent,
> So men and measures, foul or fair,
>   View'd through the bigot's element,
> (Such are the optics of their mind,)
> They crooked or straightforward find.

But, ought we not to treat even the most intolerant with

forbearance? On this subject, hear what Goethe says, when writing of Voss the German Poet.—" If others *will* rob the poet of this feeling of universal, holy complacency; if they *will* set up a peculiar doctrine, an exclusive interpretation, a contracted and contracting principle,—then is his mind moved, even to passion; then does the peaceful man rise up, grasp his weapon, and go forth against errors which he thinks so fearfully pernicious; against credulity and super-stition; against phantoms arising out of the obscure depths of nature and of the human mind; against reason-obscuring, intellect-contracting dogmas; against decrees and anathemas; against proclaimers of heresy, priests of Baal, hierarchies, clerical hosts, and against their great common progenitor, the devil himself."

" Ought we to accede to the apparently fair, but radically false and unfair maxim, which, impudently enough, declares that true toleration must be tolerant, even towards in-tolerance? By no means; intolerance is ever active and stirring, and can only be maintained by intolerant deeds and practices."

BIRTH, Low — an incitement to high deeds, and the attainment of lofty station. Many of our greatest men have sprung from the humblest origin, as the lark, whose nest is on the ground, soars the nearest to heaven. Narrow circum-stances are the most powerful stimulant to mental expansion, and the early frowns of fortune the best security for her final smiles. A nobleman who painted remarkably well for an amateur, showing one of his pictures to Poussin, the latter exclaimed—" Your lordship only requires a little poverty to make you a complete artist." The conversation turning upon the antiquity of different Italian houses, in the presence of Sextus V. when Pope, he maintained that his was the most illustrious of any, for being half unroofed, the light entered on all sides, a circumstance to which he attributed his having been enabled to exchange it for the Vatican.

BISHOP—a Protestant Cardinal. Everything appertaining to a bishop tends, unfortunately, to place him in a false position. Disclaiming all intention of irreverence towards those who are Right Reverend by title, we cannot help saying, that when we compare their ostensible objects and professions with their practice, they may be more pertinently defined as solecisms in lawn sleeves, mitred anomalies, and cassocked catachreses. Claiming authority and succession from those apostles who were desired by their heavenly Master to provide neither gold, nor silver, nor brass, nor scrip for their journey, the Episcopal Apostle forswears pomps, vanities, and filthy lucre, at the very moment when he is about to revel in their enjoyment. His revenues, exceeding those of learned and laborious judges and prime ministers, may appear enormous ; but they will not be deemed disproportionate, if we reflect that his office, being nearly a sinecure, is remunerated in the inverse ratio of its claims. Scandal, indeed, is thus brought upon the whole priesthood, by the indecent opulence and luxury of one extremity, and the degrading poverty of the other : but it must be confessed that the bishop is not answerable, either for the excess or the deficiency. Before the Reformation, being compelled to celibacy, he shook that superflux to the poor, which he now accumulates for the enrichment of his children. It seems to have been thought, even at the Reformation, by not giving his lordship a title *for* his wife, that he had no title *to* one.

Forgetting Wesley's assertion, that the road to heaven is too narrow for wheels, and that to ride in a coach here, and go to Paradise hereafter, is too great a happiness for one man, the Bishop, whom St. Peter enjoins to be an "ensample of the flock," lives in a palace with little less than regal pomp; is paraded about in a stately carriage; and by a singular want of tact which has the air of a mockery, decks his very servants in the purple and fine linen which are condemned in scripture, as the types of a vainglorious and worldly grandeur. More punctual in his attendance at the House of Lords, than in the Lord's House, and oftener seen at the court of the king than in that of the temple, he faileth not to do homage to the monarch, whenever there is prospect of a translation, of which he covets every good one, save that of Enoch. His struggles for divine grace may be very earnest; but they are less apparent than his anxiety to be made an Archbishop, that so he may receive the worship of " Your Grace," from the mouths of men. In title he is Right Reverend, but there are many who doubt whether the Episcopal office with all its unseemly state and splendour, be either right or reverend. The Bishop adheres, however, to the Greek origin of his name—he is literally an *overlooker* of his flock.

Lycurgus being asked why he had commanded offerings of such little value to be made to the Gods, replied—" In order that we may not cease to honour them. We have pursued a contrary course with our Episcopal Gods, and the honour they receive is too little, precisely because their revenues are too large. Their greatness has made them small, their wealth poor, their power weak, and we hold them cheap in exact proportion as they are *dear* to us. As if to complete the gross inconsistency between his life and its ostensible objects, the lordly successor of the lowly apostles, abandoning his diocess during a great portion of the year, sits as a peer of parliament, and mixes in all the unholy strife of the political arena. He takes his seat, we are well aware, not in his episcopal capacity, but as a feudal baron: if, however, he sustains two characters, which incapacitate him from properly discharging the duties of either, he must share the odium that may attach to failure in both. If the baron, moreover, should chance to be consigned to a place which is never mentioned to "ears polite," what is to become of the unfortunate Bishop? How must he envy his mitred brother of Sodor and Man! Having little antiquarian lore, the writer is quite ignorant by what right the Bishops of Gloucester, Peterborough, Oxford, Bristol, and Chester, sit in the House of Lords. They cannot plead usage from time immemorial, for their sees were created by patent of Henry VIII., in which there is no mention of sitting in parliament; they cannot plead their temporal baronies, for they do not hold by barony, but in *franc almoigne;* they cannot plead their spiritualities, for the Bishop of Sodor and Man is quite as spiritual as they are, and he has no seat. They may plead their writ of summons, but a curious consequence would follow the allowance of this right; for a writ of summons and sitting, is allowed on all hands to confer a barony in fee tail, the holder and the heirs of his body become noble in blood, and thus a descendant, male or female, of every clergyman who has ever held any one of these sees, and has sat in parliament, becomes entitled to a peerage.

"They have reigned, but not by me; they have become princes, but I know them not." For this, however, we repeat, the present Bishops are not answerable; they have found, not formed the existing system, and we cannot expect that they should willingly forego its advantages. It is one of those monuments of the "wisdom and Christian humility of our ancestors," which successfully imitate the Athenian altar, erected to the unknown God. Pity it is, nevertheless, that the original and most exorbitant endowment of the episcopal office should have provoked Milton to exclaim, in his *Letters on Reformation,*—"They are not Bishops; God and all good men know that they are not, but a tyrannical crew and corporation of impostors, that have blinded and abused the

world so long, under that name. When he steps up into a
a chair of pontifical pride, and changes a moderate and exemplary house for a misgoverned and haughty palace,
spiritual dignity for carnal precedence, and secular office and
employment for the high negociations of his heavenly em-
bassage, then he degrades, then he unbishops himself."

Far be it from us to insinuate that the present episcopal
bench are liable to all the thunderbolts so fiercely fulminated
against their predecessors; but their whole system is in
grievous need of amendment, and adaptation to the spirit of
the age. The signs of the times are not to be mistaken, the
handwriting on the wall is flagrant and patent, and if they
will not take the warning and set their house in order by
making some slight approximation towards a more equitable
division between the dignified drones and the toiling bees;—
if they are determined to illustrate the " *Quos Deus vult
perdere prius dementat*," and obstinately refuse to reform the
church from within, they may rest assured that it will soon
be reformed with a vengeance from without.

Let it be stated, in justice both to the present bench and
the people of England, that if the former are unpopular, it is
from a dislike of their anomalous office, with its corruptions
and abuses, rather than from any disaffection to themselves
and still less to religion. The general learning and piety of
their lordships, as well as their private characters, are perfectly unimpeachable, in spite of the candour of one of their
body, who being asked why he had not been more careful to
promote merit, in some of his recent appointments, is re-
ported to have jocosely replied—" Because merit did not
promote me."

BLIND, The—see—nothing.

BLOOD—the oil of our life's lamp :—the death signature

of the destroying angel.   Of blood, eight parts in ten consist
of pure water, and yet into what an infinite variety of substances is it converted by the inscrutable chemistry of
nature !   All the secretions, all the solids of our bodies, life
itself, are formed from this mysterious fluid.

T. H., who, whenever he gets beyond his depth in argument, seeks to make his escape by a miserable pun, was once
maintaining that the blood was not originally red, but acquired that colour in its progress.—" Pray, Sir," demanded
his opponent—" what stage *does* the blood turn red in ? "—
" Why, Sir," replied T. H., — " in the *Reading Stage*, I
presume."

BLUSHING—a suffusion least seen in those who have
the most occasion for it.

BODY —that portion of our system which receives the
chief attention of Messrs. Somebody, Anybody, and Everybody, while Nobody cares for the soul.—Body and mind are
harnessed together to perform in concert the journey of life,
a duty which they will accomplish pleasantly and safely if
the coachman, Judgment, do not drive one faster than the
other.   If he attempt this, confusion, exhaustion, and disease
are sure to ensue.   Sensualists are like savages, who cut
down the tree to pluck all the fruit at once.   Writers and
close thinkers, on the contrary, who do not allow themselves
sufficient relaxation, and permit the mind to " o'er-inform its
tenement of clay," soon entail upon themselves physical or
mental disorders, generally both.   We are like lamps ; if we
wind up the intellectual burner too high, the glass becomes
thickened or discoloured with smoke, or it breaks, and the
unregulated flame, blown about by every puff of wind, if not
extinguished altogether, throws a fitful glare and distorting
shadows over the objects that it was intended to illuminate.

The bow that is the oftenest unbent, will the longest retain its strength and elasticity.

> ———— " Quondam cithará tacentem
> Suscitat musam, neque semper arcum
> Tendit Apollo."

BON-MOT—see the present work—*passim*. "Collectors of *ana* and *facetiæ*," says Champfort, "are like children with a large cake before them; they begin by picking out the plums and tit-bits, and finish by devouring the whole." He might also have compared their works to a snowball, which, in our endeavours to make it larger and larger, takes up the snow first, and then the dirt.

Sheridan, when shown a single volume, entitled "The Beauties of Shakspeare," read it for some time with apparent satisfaction, and then exclaimed, "This is all very well, but where are the other seven volumes?"

BOOK—a thing formerly put aside to be read, and now read to be put aside. The world is, at present, divided into two classes—those who forget to read, and those who read to forget. Bookmaking, which used to be a science, is now a manufacture, with which, as in everything else, the market is so completely overstocked, that our literary operatives if they wish to avoid starving, must eat up one another. They have, for some time, been employed in cutting up each other, as if to prepare for the meal. Alas! they may, have reason for their feast, without finding it a feast of reason.

BOOKS, Prohibited.—Attempting to put the sun of reason into a dark lantern, that its mighty blaze may be hidden or revealed, according to the will of some purblind despot. When W. S. R. published his admirable " Letters from the

North of Italy," they were found so little palatable to the Austrian emperor, that they were prohibited throughout his dominions. This honour the author appreciated as he ought, only regretting that the interdict would prevent his sending copies to some of his Italian friends; a difficulty, however, which was soon overcome. Cancelling the original title page, he procured a new one to be printed, which ran as follows :—
" A Treatise upon Sour Krout, with full directions for its preparation, and remarks upon its medicinal properties." On their arrival at the frontiers, the inspector compared the books with the Index Expurgatorius, but as he did not find any imperial anathema against sour krout, they were forwarded without further scrutiny, and safely reached their respective destinations.

Rabelais said, that all the bad books ought to be bought, because they would not be reprinted ; a hint which has not been thrown away upon our Bibliomanians, who seem to forget that, since the invention of printing, no good book has ever become scarce.

BOOKSELLER.—There is this difference between the heroes of Paternoster Row, and the Scandinavian warriors in the Hall of Valhalla,—that the former drink their wine out of the skulls of their friends, the authors, whereas the latter quaffed their's out of the skulls of their enemies. In ancient times, the *Vates* was considered a prophet as well as bard, but now he is barred from his profit, most of which goes to the bookseller, who, in return, generously allows the scribbler to come in for the whole of the critical abuse. It has been invidiously said, that as a bibliopolist lives upon the brains of others, he need not possess any himself. This is a mistake. He has the wit to coin the wit that is supplied to him, and thus proves his intellectual by his golden talents. Many a bookvender rides in his own carriage ; but I do not

know a single professional bookwriter who does not trudge
a-foot. "*Sic vos non vobis*" — the proverb's somewhat
musty.—If they take our honey, they cannot quarrel with us
if we now and then give them a sting.

BORE—a brainless, babbling button-holder. A wretch
so deficient in tact that he cannot adapt himself to any
society, nor perceive that all agree in thinking him disagreeable. Nevertheless, we forgive the man who bores us much
more easily than the man who lets us see that we are boring
him. Towards the former, we exercise a magnanimous compassion ; but our wounded self-love cannot tolerate the latter.
A newly-elected M.P. lately consulted his friend as to the
occasion that he should select for his maiden speech. A
very important subject was suggested, when the modest
member expressed a fear, that his mind was hardly of sufficient calibre to embrace it. "Poh! poh!" said the friend,—
"don't be under any apprehensions about your calibre : depend upon it, they will find you *bore* enough."

BOROUGHMONGERS—an extinct race of beasts of
prey. If, as historians assert, we owe gratitude to King
Edgar for having extirpated the wolves from England, and
to Henry VIII. for having suppressed the monks, what do
we not owe to the Whigs for having delivered us from the
borough-mongers, who were, at the same time, both wolves
and monks?

BREATH—air received into the lungs by many young
men of fashion, for the important purposes of smoking a
cigar, and whistling a tune.

BREVITY—the soul of wit, which accounts for the tenuity
of the present work! Into how narrow a compass has Seneca

compressed his account of the total destruction of Lyons by fire.—"*Inter magnam urbem et nullam nox una interfuit*,"—between a great city and none, only a single night intervened!

BRIEF—the excuse of counsel for an impertinence that is often inexcusable.

BUFFOON—a professional fool, whereas a wag is an amateur fool.

BULL.—A copious and amusing book might be made, by collecting the bulls and blunders of all nations, except the Irish, whom we would exclude, upon the principle that determined Martial not to describe the nose of Tongilianus, because "*nil præter nasum Tongilianus habet*." Of the French bulls, there are few better than the following. A Gascon nobleman had been reproaching his son with ingratitude. "I owe you nothing," said the unfilial young man; "so far from having served me, you have always stood in my way; for if you had never been born, I should at this moment be the next heir of my rich grandfather."

Worthy of a place by the side of this Gallic Hibernicism is the *niaiserie* of Captain Baudin, the Commander of a French expedition of discovery. On opening a box of magnetic needles, they were found to be much rusted, which sensibly impaired their utility. "What else can you expect?" exclaimed the irritated captain;—"all the articles provided by Government are shabby beyond description. Had they acted as I could have wished, they would have given us silver instead of steel needles."

An Irishman may be described as a sort of Minotaur, half man and half bull. "*Semibovemque virum, semivirumque bovem*," as Ovid has it. He might run me into a longer essay than Miss Edgeworth's, without exhausting the subject,

I shall therefore content myself with a single instance of his felicity in this figure of speech. In the examination of a Connaught lad, he was asked his age.—" I am just twenty, your honour; but I would have been twenty-one, only my mother miscarried the year before I was born."

One American bull, and we have done. " Do you snore, Abel Adams?" inquired a Yankee of his friend.—" No, Seth Jefferson, I do never snore."—" How do you know, Abel?"—" Because t'other day I laid awake the whole night on purpose to see!"

BURGLARY.—If the burglar who craftily examines a house or a shop, to see how he may best break into it and steal its contents, be a knave, what name should we bestow upon the Old Bailey barrister, who, in the defence of a confessed thief, sifts and examines the laws to ascertain where he may best evade or break through them, for the purpose of defrauding justice and of letting loose a felon to renew his depredations upon society? Bentham compares the confidence between a criminal and his advocate, to a compact of guilt between two confederated malefactors.

 AGE—an article to the manufacture of which our spinsters would do well to direct their attention, since, according to Voltaire, the reason of so many unhappy marriages is, that young ladies employ their time in making nets instead of cages. Putting the same thought in another form, we might say, that our damsels, in fishing for husbands, rely too much upon their personal and too little on their mental attractions, forgetting that an enticing bait is of little use unless you have a hook, line, and landing-net, that may secure the prey.

CANDIDATES for Holy Orders—are sometimes persons claiming authority to show their fellow-creatures the way to heaven, because they have been unable to make their own way upon earth.

Some of the clamourers against the abuses of the church, object that the greatest dunce in our families of distinction, is often selected for the ministry. How unreasonable! is it not better that the ground should be ploughed by asses, than remain untilled? I cannot, by any means approve the fastidiousness, any more than the bad pun of the Canadian Bishop, who, finding, after examining one of the candidates for holy orders, that he was grossly ignorant, refused to ordain him. "My lord!" said the disappointed aspirant, "there is no imputation upon my moral character—I have a due sense of religion, and I am a member of the *Propaganda* Society."—"*That* I can easily believe," replied the Bishop, "for you are a *proper goose.*"

CANDIDATES for Parliament—self-trumpeters. In reading their addresses to electors, it is amusing to observe how invariably, and how very impartially, each candidate, when describing the sort of representative whom the worthy and enlightened constituents ought to return, *draws a portrait of himself,* blazoning the little nothings that he has achieved, and, sometimes, like the Pharisee, introducing a fling at his opponent, by thanking heaven that he is not like yonder Publican. For the benefit of such portrait painters, I will record an apposite anecdote of Mirabeau, premising that his face was deeply indented with the small-pox. Anxious to be put in nomination for the National Assembly, he made a long speech to the voters, minutely pointing out the precise requisites that a proper and efficient member ought to possess, and, of course, drawing as accurate a likeness as possible of himself. He was answered by Talleyrand, who contented himself with the following short speech : "It appears to me, gentlemen, that M. de Mirabeau has omitted to state the most important of all the legislative qualifications, and I will supply his deficiency by impressing upon your attention, that a perfectly unobjectionable member of the Assembly ought, above all things, to be very much marked with the small-pox." Talleyrand got the laugh, which in France always carries the election.

CANDOUR—in some people may be compared to barley-sugar drops, in which the acid preponderates over the sweetness.

CANT—originally the name of a Cameronian preacher in Scotland, who had attained the faculty of preaching in such a tone and dialect, as to be understood by none but his own congregation.   This worthy, however, has been outcanted by his countryman, Irving, whose Babel tongues possessed the superior merit of being unintelligible not only to his flock, but even to himself.

In the present acceptation of the word, as a synonyme of hypocrisy—as a pharisaical pretension to superior religion and virtue, substituted by those great professors of both, who are generally the least performers of either, *cant* may be designated the characteristic of modern England.   Simulation and dissimulation are its constituent elements—the substitution of the form for the spirit, of appearances for realities, of words for things.

CARE—the tax paid by the higher classes for their privileges and possessions.   Often amounting to the full value of the property upon which it is levied, care may be termed the poor-rate of the rich.   Like death, care is a sturdy summoner, who will take no denial, and who is no respecter of persons. Nor is the importunate dun a with improved in his manners since the time of Horace, for he beards the great and the powerful in their very palaces, and scares them even in their throne-like beds, while the peasant sleeps undisturbed upon his straw pallet. Under the perpetual influence of these drawbacks and compensations, the inequalities of fortune, if measured by the criterion of enjoyment, are rather apparent than real; for it is difficult to be rich without care, and easy to be happy without wealth.

CASTLE.—In England every man's cottage is held to be his castle, which he is authorised to defend, even against the assaults of the king; but it may be doubted whether the same privilege extends to Ireland.—"My client," said an Irish advocate, pleading before Lord Norbury, in an action of trespass, "is a poor man—he lives in a hovel, and his miserable dwelling is in a forlorn and dilapidated state; but, still, thank God! the labourer's cottage, however ruinous its plight, is his sanctuary and his castle. Yes—the winds may enter it, and the rains may enter it, but the king cannot enter it."—"What! not the *reigning* king?" asked the joke-loving judge.

. CASUISTS, A question for.—Lord Clarendon, speaking of Fletcher of Saltoun, says, "he would willingly have sacrificed his life to serve his country, though he would not have committed a base action to save it." *Quære?*—Can any action be termed base which has for its object the salvation of our native country? Was Brutus a murderer or a patriot, when he delivered Rome from the usurper of its liberties by assassinating Cæsar? Is tyrannicide justifiable homicide? —"*Non nobis est tantas componere lites.*"

CAT—a domestic quadruped, commonly, but, we believe, erroneously supposed to have nine lives; whence, we presume, a whip, with the same number of lashes, is called a cat-o'-nine tails. Few creatures have more strikingly exhibited the caprice and folly of mankind, for the cat, according to times and localities, has been either blindly reverenced or cruelly persecuted. Among the Egyptians it was a capital punishment to kill this animal, which was worshipped in a celebrated temple dedicated to the goddess Bubastis, who is said to have assumed the feline form to avoid Typhon ; a fable, reversed in the fairy tale of the cat metamorphosed into a young lady. The sympathies of the Egyptians seem to have descended to the Arabians, for it is recorded of Mahomet, that when a favourite cat had fallen asleep, on the sleeve of his rich robe, and the call to prayers sounded, he drew his scymetar and cut off the sleeve, rather choosing to spoil his garment, than disturb the slumbers of his four-footed friend.

In England, on the contrary, owing partly to the superstitious connection of this animal with witches, and partly to that barbarism which never wants an excuse for cruelty, the unfortunate cat appears to have been always considered a proscribed creature, against one or other of whose nine lives, if it ventured beyond the threshold of its owner's house, every hand might be lifted.

CATACHRESIS—the abuse of a trope, or an apparent contradiction in terms, as when the law pronounces the accidental killing of a woman to be manslaughter. The name of the Serpentine River, which is a straight canal, involves a catachresis, and we often, unconsciously, perpetrate others, in our daily discourse ; as when we talk of wooden tomb-stones, iron mile-stones, glass ink-horns, brass shoeing-horns, &c.

Every one recollects the fervent hope expressed by the late Lord Castlereagh, that the people of this happy country would never turn their backs upon themselves. This was only a misplaced trope ; but there is, sometimes, among his fellow-countrymen, a confusion of ideas that involves an impossibility. An Irishman's horse fell with him, throwing his rider to some distance, when the animal, in struggling to get up, entangled its hind leg in the stirrup. " Oh, very well, sir," said the dismounted cavalier ; "if you're after getting up on your own back, I see there will be no room for me."

The following string of Catachreses is versified, with some additions and embellishments, from a sermon of an ignorant field-preacher :—

Staying his hand, which, like a hammer,
  Had thump'd and bump'd his anvil-book,
And waving it to still the clamour,
  The tub-man took a loftier look,
And thus, condensing all his powers,
Scatter'd his oratoric flowers.—
''What ! will ye still, ye heathen flee,
  From sanctity and grace,
Until your blind idolatry
  Shall stare ye in the face ?
Will ye throw off the mask, and show
Thereby the cloven foot below ?—
Do—but remember, ye must pay
What's due to ye on settling day !
Justice's eye, it stands to sense,
  Can never stomach such transgressions,
Nor can the hand of Providence
  Wink at your impious expressions.
The infidel thinks vengeance dead,
  And in his fancied safety chuckles,
But atheism's Hydra head
  Shall have a rap upon the knuckles !"

CELIBACY—a vow by which the priesthood, in some countries, swear to content themselves with the wives of other people.

CEREMONY—all that is considered necessary by many in religion and friendship.

CENSORIOUSNESS—judging of others by ourselves. It will invariably be found, that the most censurable are the most censorious; while those who have the least need of indulgence, are the most indulgent. We should pardon the mistakes of others as freely as if we ourselves were constantly committing the same faults, and yet avoid their errors as carefully as if we never forgave them. There is no precept, however, that cannot be evaded. "We are ordered to forgive our enemies but not our friends," cries a quibbler. "We may forgive our own enemies, but not the heretics, who are the enemies of God," said Father Segnerand to Louis XIII. Many people imagine that they are not only concealing their own misconduct in this world, but making atonement for it in the next, by visiting the misdeeds of others with a puritanical severity. They may well be implacable! "I should never have preserved my reputation," said Lady B—, "if I had not carefully abstained from visiting demireps. I must be strait-laced in the persons of others, because I have been so loose in my own."—"My dear Lady B—!" exclaimed her sympathising friend, "upon this principle you ought to retire into a convent!"

CHALLENGE—calling upon a man who has hurt your feelings to give you satisfaction by—shooting you through the body.

CHANCELLOR, The present Lord.*—One who throws his own lustre upon that high office, from which all his predecessors have borrowed their's. It has been objected to

* For *present*, we must now read *late*.

Lord Brougham that he is ambitious, and long had his eye upon the Great Seal before he obtained it. So much the better. If nature had not stamped him with *her* great seal, he would never have obtained that of England. What is it to us that the Chancellor's wig was in his head, long before his head was in the wig? We know that they fit one another admirably, and that is enough. Lord Brougham has experienced the usual fate of reformers—gross ingratitude; but what can he expect, when he provokes all by his superiority to all, in virtue as well as talent? His disinterestedness is a reproach to the sordid, his prudence to the destructives, his determined spirit of reform to the conservatives; and because he is too independent and lofty to belong to any party, he is outrageously abused by all. This cry confused—"Of owls and monkeys, asses, apes, and dogs,"—"full of sound and fury, signifying nothing," obscures his lustre about as much as the baying of wolves, or the cackling of goslings, darkens the moon. If he does not immortalize them by his notice, as Pope did his contemptible detractors, what will posterity know of the serpents and geese who combine to hiss at him? There are savages who, in an eclipse of the sun, endeavour to drive away the interceptor of their light, by the most hideous clamour they can raise. The enemies whom the Chancellor has thrown into the shade, have tried a similar experiment; but, strange to say, they still remain eclipsed!

In my high opinion of Lord Brougham, I have sometimes been too prone to fatigue my friends with his praises; a tendency which, upon one occasion, elicited a pun bad enough to be recorded. My assertion, that he was the greatest man in England, being warmly contested, I loudly exclaimed, "Where is there a greater?"—"Here!" said the punch-making T. H., with a look of exquisite simplicity, at the same time holding up a nutmeg *grater*.

CHANGE—the only thing that is constant ; mutability being an immutable law of the universe.

> " Men change with fortune, manners change with climes,
>   Tenets with books, and principles with times."

CHARACTER, Individual—a compound from the characters of others. If it be true that one fool makes many, it is not less clear that many fools, or many wise men, make one. The *noscitur à socio* is universally applicable. Like the chameleon, our mind takes the colour of what surrounds it. However small may be the world of our own familiar coterie, it conceals from us the world without, as the minutest object, held close to the eye, will shut out the sun. Our mental hue depends as completely on the social atmosphere in which we move, as our complexion upon the climate in which we live.

Nevertheless, it must be admitted that it is sometimes profitable to associate with graceless characters. A reprobate fellow once laid his worthy associate a bet of five guineas that he could not repeat the creed. It was accepted, and his friend repeated the Lord's prayer. " Confound you ! " cried the former, who imagined that he had been listening to the creed,—" I had no idea you had such a memory. There are your five guineas ! "

CHARITY—the only thing that we can give away without losing it.

> " True charity is truest thrift,
>   More than repaid for every gift,
>   By grateful prayers enroll'd on high.
>   And its own heart's sweet eulogy,
>   Which, like the perfume-giving rose,
>   Possesses still what it bestows."

Charity covereth a multitude of sins, and the English are

the most bountiful people upon earth ! The best almsgiving, perhaps, is a liberal expenditure; for that encourages the industrious, while indiscriminate charity only fosters idlers and impostors. The latter is little better than mere selfishness, prompting us to get rid of an uneasy sensation. Sometimes, however, we refuse our bounty to a suppliant, because he has hurt our feelings ; while the beggar who has pleased us by making us laugh at his buffoonery, seldom goes unrewarded. Delpini, the clown, applied to the late king, when Prince of Wales, for pecuniary assistance, drawing a lamentable picture of his destitute state. As he was in the habit of thus importuning his Royal Highness, his suit was rejected. At last, as he met the Prince coming out of Carlton House, he exclaimed—"Ah, votre altesse ! Ah, mon Prince! if you no assist de pauvre Delpini, I must go to your papa's bench !" Tickled by the oddity of the phrase, the Prince laughed heartily, and immediately complied with his request.

CHEERFULNESS—"The best Hymn to the Divinity," according to Addison, and all rational religionists. When we have passed a day of innocent enjoyment ; when "our bosom's lord sits lightly on his throne ;" when our gratified and grateful feelings, sympathising with universal nature, make us sensible, as John of Salisbury says, that " *Gratior it dies, et soles melius nitent,*"—we may be assured that we have been performing, however unconsciously, an acceptable act of devotion. Pure religion may generally be measured by the cheerfulness of its professors, and superstition by the gloom of its victims. *Ille placet Deo, cui placet Deus.*—He to whom God is pleasant, is pleasant to God.

CHESS—a wooden or ivory allegory. Sir William Jones, who claims the invention of this game for the Hindoos, traces the successive corruptions of the original Sanscrit term, through the Persians and Arabs, into *scacchi*, echess —chess ; which, by a whimsical concurrence of circumstances, has given birth to the English word *check*, and even a name to the Exchequer of Great Britain. In passing through Europe, the Oriental forms and names have suffered material change. The ruch, or dromedary, we have corrupted into rook. The bishop was with us formerly an archer, while the French denominated it *alfin*, and *fol*, which were perversions of the original Eastern term for the elephant.

The ancient Persian game consisted of the following pieces :—

1.	*Schach* . . .	The King.
2.	*Pherz* . . .	The Vizier, or General.
3.	*Phil*	The Elephant.
4.	*Aspen Suar* .	The Horseman.
5.	*Ruch*	The Dromedary.
6.	*Beydal* . . .	The Foot-soldiers.

In process of time, the Persian names were gradually translated into French, or modified by French terminations. Schach was translated into *Roy*—the King ; Pherz, the Vizier, became *Fercié—Fierce—Fierge—Vierge;* and this last was easily converted into a lady—*Dame*. The Elephant *Phil* was altered into *Fol* or *Fou;* the Horseman became a Cavalier or Knight, while the Dromedary, *Ruch*, was converted into a *Tour*, or Tower, probably from being confounded with the Elephant, which is usually represented as carrying a castle. The foot-soldiers were retained by the name of *Pietons*, or *Pions*, whence our Pawns.

In its westward progress, the game of chess adapted itself to the habits and institutions of the countries that fostered it. The prerogative of the King gradually extended itself, until it became unlimited : the agency of the Princes, in lieu of the Queen, who does not exist in the original chess-board, bespeaks forcibly the nature of the oriental customs, which exclude females from all influence and power. In Persia, these Princes were changed into a single Vizier, and for this Vizier the Europeans, with the same gallantry that had prompted the French to add a Queen to the pack of cards, substituted a Queen on the chess-board.

We record the following anecdote, as a warning to such of our male and married readers as may be in the perilous habit of playing chess with a wife. Ferrand, Count of Flanders, having constantly defeated the Countess at chess, she conceived a hatred against him, which came to such a height, that when the Count was taken prisoner at the battle of Bovines, she suffered him to remain a long time in prison, though she could easily have procured his release.

CHILD, Spoilt—an unfortunate victim, who proves the weakness of his parents' judgment, much more forcibly than the strength of their affection. Doomed to feel by daily experience, that a blind love is as bad as a clear-sighted hatred, the spoilt child, when he embitters the life of those who have poisoned his, is not so much committing an act of ingratitude, as of retributive justice. Is it not natural that he should love those too little, who by loving him too much have proved themselves his worst enemies ?—How can we expect him to be a blessing to us, when we have been a curse to him? It is the awarded and just punishment of a weak over-indulgence, that the more we fondle a spoilt child, the more completely shall we alienate him, as an arrow flies the farther from us the closer we draw it to our bosom.

As a gentle hint to others similarly annoyed, we record

the rebuke of a visitor, to whom a mother expressed her apprehension that he was disturbed by the crying of her spoilt brat.—"Not at all, Madam," was the reply; "I am always delighted to hear such children cry."—"Indeed! why so?"—"Because in all well-regulated families, they are immediately sent out of the room."

CHRISTIANITY, Primitive.—"There hath not been discovered in any age," says Lord Bacon, "any philosophy, opinion, religion, law, or discipline, which so greatly exalts the common, and lessens individual, interest as the Christian religion doth." The perpetual denunciations of the rich and the great, the repeated averment that the Lord is no respecter of persons, the lowly origin of Jesus Christ in His earthly capacity, the selection of his Apostles and chief missionaries from among the labouring poor, or from women, a class which had previously exercised no influence in society, all tend to confirm the assertion of Bacon, and to impart to primitive Christianity a character which, in modern times, would almost be termed radical; while it forms a most significant contrast to the wealth, splendour, and haughty pride of all those spiritual corporations, which are called Established Churches.

He that would form a correct notion of primitive Christianity, should study the following character of its Founder, as drawn by an eloquent divine:—"Christ in his sympathetic character, was fairer than the sons of men, therefore full of grace were his lips. His humanity was not, like ours, degenerate, but refined and exalted. God breathed direct into him. Sin had not impaired the delicate and sensitive perceptions of his nature; had not chilled the fountain of his feelings, nor the warm current of his affections. Prompt to feel the woes of others, the sympathetic strings of his heart, constantly attuned and tremulously sensitive, vibrated at every sigh of the sorrowful spirit, and responded full and deep to every sound of human woe. He identified himself with disgrace and sorrow, and even with sin. He sympathised with the sufferers in his humanity, before he exerted the power of his divinity for their relief."

CHRISTIANITY, Fashionable—keeping a pew at some genteel church or chapel, to which ladies pay a civil visit when the weather is fine, when they have got a new bonnet or pelisse to display, and a smart livery servant to follow them with a prayer-book. They curtsey very low at the mention of the Lord's name, making the homage of the knees a substitute for that of the heart ; and duly receive the sacrament, which, by a strange perversion of ideas, they look upon as a proof of the sincerity of their belief, and an absolution for the laxity of their practice.

Fashionable male Christianity is demonstrated by an occasional nap in a cushioned and carpeted pew ; in cheerfully paying Easter offerings and Church dues ; in maintaining a certain decency of appearance ; and more especially in hating those who presume to differ in matters of religion.

That they possess the outward and visible signs of Christianity, both sexes exhibit incontestable proofs ; but as to the inward and spiritual grace, they leave it to the vulgar and the fanatical. They are too polite to travel Zionward in such company, and would rather sacrifice heaven altogether, than reach it by any ungenteel mode. Provided they may be among the exclusives here, they will cheerfully run the risk of being among the excluded hereafter.

Christianity will never have received its full development, and have accomplished its final triumph, until its spirit shall have surmounted its ceremonials, and the reformed religion shall have undergone a new and more searching reformation.

CHURCH and STATE, Alliance of—an interchange of contamination; a league between the civil magistrate and the priesthood, ostensibly for the maintenance of loyalty, and the suppression of heresy;—in reality for the enforcement of political and religious subjection. If an establishment be right, religious liberty is not: and if religious liberty be right, an establishment is not. The compact between Pontius Pilate and the chiefs of the Synagogue, which ended in the crucifixion of Christ, was but a foreshadowing of that unscriptural union of Church and State, which may almost be said to have crucified Christianity. Dr. Warburton, and others, regard the religion of the *majority*, as the religion of the State: so that if the Church be united with the State, through the king at its head, it has in England an Episcopalian, in Scotland a Presbyterian, and in Ireland a Catholic head. History and experience attest that this coalition is equally degrading and mischievous to *both* parties. Equality of civil and religious rights being the grand basis of all safe and healthy government, the State ought not to identify itself with one sect, even where it tolerates all others; it is its duty to protect all alike, without favour or discountenance. For the information of the worthy inhabitants of Noodledom, and of those old women in petticoats or pantaloons, who imagine that the dissolution of this unsanctioned union would extinguish religion and dissolve the whole frame of civil society, we will state the principal changes that it would effect. The king, no longer the head of the Church, would cease to appoint the Bishops; the Lords spiritual would have no seats as such in parliament; the doctrines and worship of the Church would not any longer be regulated and enforced by act of parliament; civil penalties for religious offences would cease to exist, and all Toleration Acts would die a natural death. Unless it can be shown that the Dissenters, who have no lordly Hierarchy, and no Church and State union, are less religious and less patriotic than the Episcopalians, which no one will be hardy enough to assert, what injury could piety or patriotism sustain by placing both parties upon the same broad level of independence ? Manifest, however, and manifold would be the blessings springing from such a change. Jealousies and heartburnings would be healed ; it is not too much to assert that whatever the Church might lose, would be so much clear gain to Christianity ; while the State would be benefited by the removal of all grounds of discontent or disaffection from the numerous and hourly increasing class of conscientious Dissenters.

That great advantage would accrue to *both* parties from a severance of the Church and State, is no new-fangled notion of radicals or visionaries, but an opinion which has been deliberately formed and frankly expressed by many wise and pious men, even among the dignitaries of the Church itself. Such were the sentiments of the good and the illustrious Locke. "The single end," says Dr. Paley, "which we ought to propose by religious establishments, is the preservation and communication of religious knowledge. Every other idea, and every other end that have been mixed with this,— as the making of the Church an engine, or even *an ally* of the State, converting it into the means of strengthening or *of diffusing* influence,—or regarding it as a support of regal *in opposition to popular* forms of government,—have served only to debase the institution, and to introduce into it numerous corruptions and abuses."* And again in his " Evidences of Christianity," p. ii. ch. 2, the same writer says, "We find in Christ's religion, no scheme of *building up a hierarchy*, or of *ministering to the views of human govern-ments*." " Our religion, as it came out of the hand of its

* Moral and Political Philosophy, vol. ii. p. 305.

founder and his apostles, exhibited a *complete abstraction from all views, either of ecclesiastical or civil policy.*" In fact it is little better than profanation to imagine that the religion of God and of truth stands in need of the support of the State. "An alliance between Church and State in a Christian Commonwealth," says Burke, "is in my opinion, an idle and a fanciful speculation."

Many of the most temperate and enlightened members of the establishment are ashamed of their connection with the State, and would willingly see it quietly dissolved. On their account, and not in apprehension of the clamorous and sordid brethren, who deal in fulminations and menaces, rather than arguments, may the sincere Christian desire to see the Church divorced from an union which many have pronounced adulterous. Herein he will agree with Bishop Warburton, who says in his letters, "The Church, like the Ark of Noah, is worth saving ; not for the sake of *the unclean beasts and vermin that almost filled it, and probably made most noise and clamour in it;* but for, the little corner of rationality, that was as much distressed by the stink within, as by the tempest without."

To a rotten ship, say the Italians, every wind is contrary. No wonder, therefore, that the Church finds so many opponents of its course :—but for those who have occasioned the clamour to complain of it, and fulminate anathemas and nick-names, will but aggravate the evil, and make its inevitable remedy more quick and unsparing. What renders the folly and inconsistency of such conduct more glaring, is the fact that some of the most distinguished prelates of the Church have been the most strenuous advocates of Reform. "A Reformer," says Bishop Watson, "of Luther's temper and talents, would, in five years, persuade the people to compel the parliament to abolish tithes, to extinguish pluralities, to enforce residence, to confine episcopacy to the overseeing of dioceses, to expunge the Athanasian Creed from our Liturgy, to free Dissenters from Test Acts, and the ministers of the establishment from subscription to human articles of faith. These, and other matters respecting the Church, ought to be done."—*Letter to the Duke of Grafton.*

CHURCH and KING, Toast of—usually means, according to Dr. Parr, a Church without the gospel, and a King above the law.

CIGAR-SMOKING—vomiting an offensive exhalation in the face of every passenger. As it was said of Virgil that, in his Georgics, he threw his dung about him with an air of dignity, so may we allow Vesuvius and Mount Etna to smoke, without conceding that privilege to every puny whiffler who may think fit to poison the air with the contents of his mouth. Every such culprit ought to be made to swallow his own smoke, like the improved steam-engines. It is a solecism in good manners, that a quasi gentleman should adopt this ploughman's habit, even in the open air; but to attempt it in any sort of mixed society, whether in a public room or on the top of a stage-coach, should subject the perpetrator to an unceremonious expulsion. It has, nevertheless, one advantage, it entices fools to be silent, or only to talk smoke, which is at least an inaudible annoyance.

After all, perhaps, there is much to be said on both sides,—not of the cigar, for there both sides are alike,—but of the question—*audi alteram partem :* condemn not a cigar before you have smoked one. Of this last enormity I was never guilty, but, methinks I might point the wit of some fumigator to give a reason for the smoke that is in him ; even as the grindstone may sharpen, though it was never known to cut :

"Ego fungar vice cotis, acutum
Reddere quæ ferrum valet, exsors ipsa secandi."

Voyons ! there is an inspiration that may vindicate tobacco without its aid ; suppose we, therefore, some puffer of Havannah, to evaporate the following :—

EFFUSION—(By a Cigar-Smoker).

Warriors ! who from the cannon's mouth blow fire,
  Your fame to raise,
  Upon its blaze,
Alas ! ye do but light your funeral pyre !—
  Tempting fate's stroke,
Ye fall, and all your glory ends in smoke.
Safe in my chair from wounds and woe,
My fire and smoke from mine own mouth I blow.

Ye booksellers ! who deal, like me, in puffs,
  The public smokes,
  You and your hoax,
And turns your empty vapour to rebuffs.
  Ye through the nose
Pay for each puff; when mine the same way flows,
It does not run me into debt ;
And thus, the more I fume, the less I fret.

Authors ! created to be puff'd to death,
  And fill the mouth
  Of some uncouth
Bookselling wight, who sucks your brains and breath,
  Your leaves thus far
(Without its fire) resemble my cigar ;
But vapid, uninspired, and flat :
When, when, O Bards, will ye *compose* like *that ?*

Since life and the anxieties that share
  Our hope and trust,
  Are smoke and dust,
Give me the smoke and dust that banish care.—
  The roll'd leaf bring,
Which from its ashes, Phœnix-like, can spring ;
The fragrant leaf whose magic balm
Can, like Nepenthe, all our sufferings charm.

Oh, what supreme beatitude is this !
    What soft and sweet
    Sensations greet,
My soul, and wrap it in Elysian bliss !
    I soar above,
Dull earth in these ambrosial clouds, like Jove,
And from mine Empyrean height,
Look down upon the world with calm delight.

CIRCLE, The social—a dull merry-go-round which makes us first giddy, and then sick. What is called the round of pleasure, may be compared to a knife-grinder's wheel. When its rotations are duly regulated and adapted to the end proposed, it gives point to the wit, while it brightens, sharpens, and polishes the general surface of the mind and manners. But if we whirl it round with an unintermitting rapidity, it takes off the edge of enjoyment, and soon wears out that which it was intended to refresh and renovate. We have Christian epicureans, who advocate a short life and a merry one, as staunchly as their pagan predecessors, and cry out, with Sir Henry Wotton, that they had rather live five Mays than fifty Novembers. But unfortunately, a short life is not always a merry one, nor is a merry one necessarily short. We must live our appointed term, whether for good or evil, for we cannot suck out the sweets of life, and then lay it down like a squeezed orange. Throwing it away is not getting rid of it. A merry youth may turn to a mournful old age ; we may make a boast of leaving our sins when they have deserted us, and of having mastered our passions when we have only worn them out ; but their ghosts may haunt us in the shape of gout, dropsy, dyspepsia and other torments, when we are only living to do penance for the excesses of our youth.

An old rake who has survived himself, is the most pitiable object in creation. If we discount our allotted portion of pleasure, and live upon the capital instead of the interest, at the outset of life, we must expect to be bankrupts at its close. If we cut down the tree for the sake of its spring blossoms, we cannot apply to it for fruits in autumn, or shelter in the winter. The hours may seem short that are passed in revelry and dissipation ; but to suppose that as a matter of course we can thus abbreviate our prescribed term, and make death become due, just as we are tired of life, is to fall into the ludicrous error of the Irishman, who applied to his friend to discount a bill of exchange, stating that it had only thirty days to run. When he brought it, however, it was found that forty days would elapse before it became due, in consequence of which his friend objected to cash it. "Ah, now !" said the Hibernian, " you've forgotten that it is Christmas time. Look how short the days are ! Sure, if it was summer, the whole forty wouldn't make more than thirty."

CIRCUMSTANCES.—If a letter were to be addressed to this most influential word, concluding thus—" I am, Sir, your very obedient humble servant ;"—the greater part of the world might subscribe it, without deviating from the strictest veracity.

CIVILIZATION, Advancement of—a consolatory progression, which ought to make us proud of the present, and to inspire us with confidence in the future. If one of our savage ancestors, slaughtered, we will suppose, by the incursions of some hostile horde, or burnt as a sacrifice in the wicker cages of the Druids, were to revive in the present era, he would find it difficult to pronounce whether the greatest change had occurred in the physical or moral state of his native land. When he expired, our island, covered with dense unhealthy forests, or noxious swamps and wildernesses, was thinly inhabited by half-naked tribes, for ever contending with cold and famine, with the beasts of the field, or with fellow barbarians still more ferocious. At his resuscitation he beholds, with utter amazement, how all the past centuries have been the diligent slaves of the present, clearing the forests, draining morasses, digging canals and wells, levelling hills, filling up valleys, making innumerable roads and railways, converting the whole surface of the country into a beautiful and productive garden, or studding it with churches and noble or elegant buildings for every imaginable purpose of use and ornament.

As yet, however, he will have seen nothing. To give him some faint conception of what civilization has effected since the time of his death, I would read to him a striking passage from a modern writer,* showing how the comforts and luxuries which no king could command a few centuries ago, are now, under the influence of peace and commerce, brought within the reach of the meanest peasant;—how ships are crossing the seas in all directions to minister to his enjoyments;—how in China they are gathering tea; in the West Indies sugar and cotton; in Italy feeding worms, in Saxony shearing sheep;—how steam engines are spinning and weaving, and pumping out mines;—how coaches are travelling night and day to expedite letters;—how vessels and vehicles are conveying fuel to every door;—how fleets are sailing, and armies are sustained to secure for every subject of the realm protection from foreign or domestic violence. I would endeavour to make my barbarian auditor understand that our progress in the intellectual world has been still greater and more marvellous; I would tell him that almost every man in modern England can read and write; that penny magazines and halfpenny newspapers are composed by authors of talent for the instruction and amusement of

* See Dr. Arnott's "Elements of Physics."

the poor; that in intellectual pleasures, the purest and most exalted of all, the mechanic is upon a par with the monarch; and that under the salutary influences of Reform, our legislature, instead of upholding, as heretofore, the privileges of the few, and increasing the oppression of the many, will study to secure the greatest happiness to the greatest number. I would point out to him that as improvement must now advance in an incalculably accelerated ratio, the melioration of the last thousand years will probably be surpassed in the course of the next one or two centuries; and then, desiring him to throw his mind forward, if he could, to the termination of that period, I would lead him to form a notion of what has been, and will be accomplished by the march of intellect and the progress of civilization.

CLUB.—Dr. Johnson, himself a member of one of these societies, designates a club as "an assembly of good fellows, meeting under certain conditions;" a definition which would be hardly applicable now-a-days, unless the words "for nothing" were inserted after the adjective "good." Far from originating in sociableness, professional sympathies, or a love of intellectual improvement, our modern clubs, enrolling without associating a mob of strangers, are simply and solely founded upon selfishness and sensuality. What are their leading objects, is thus stated by a writer in one of our magazines:—"Epicurism, in the least elevated acceptation of that misunderstood word—to place the greatest possible luxury, but more especially the pleasures of the palate, within reach of the lowest possible sum—to combine exclusiveness with voluptuousness—to foster, at the same moment, the love of self, and the alienation from others—to remove men from their proper and natural mode of living —to enable five hundred a-year to command the state, style, and splendour of five thousand—to destroy the taste for simple and domestic pleasures—and to substitute a longing for all the expensive and sensual enjoyments that might have gratified an ancient Sybarite."

A professional or exclusive club is the most shy, sullen, reserved, and unamiable of all institutions.—"Its union of one class is a separation from all others; the junction of its members is a dismemberment from the general body of citizens; it is dissocial in its very association. It is a cabal, a caste, a *clique*, a coterie, a junto, a conspiracy, a knot, a pack, a gang; anything, in short, that is close, selfish, disjunctive, and inhospitable: but if there be in such narrow fellowship any single element of sociability, why then the monks who planted their convents in the desert of the Thebaid, were sociable beings, and useful members of society. Goldsmith very properly condemns the man of talent,

> " ' who narrowed his mind,
> And to party gave up what was meant for mankind.'

"If the division of the male community into grades and classes be a confessed evil, what shall we say to the wide separation of the sexes which this club-mania is daily and rapidly effecting. It will be admitted, that man and woman were meant for one another, collectively as well as separately. Socially speaking, they are as naturally married to each other, in the aggregate, as are the individual husband and wife; and 'whom God hath joined together let no man put asunder.' The beneficial, the civilizing influences, which the sexes mutually impart and receive in society, are best to be appreciated by the deep and instant degradation which Nature, who never suffers her laws to be violated with impunity, has invariably entailed upon their disjunction. For evidence of this fact, it will be only necessary to refer to the monasteries and convents. In the society of man, the softer sex, discarding some portion of its frivolity and inherent weakness, acquires mental corroboration, and is imperceptibly imbued with the best and finest emanations of masculine character. In female society, the lord of the creation, losing the ruggedness, arrogance, and licentious coarseness of his nature, becomes softened, courteous, and refined, chastening himself with feminine graces, while he loses not a fraction of his proper manliness and dignity. Polish is the result of collision, both morally and physically; and man's iron nature is not injured, or unduly mollified, but made more useful and attractive, by coming in contact with the magnet of beauty. Acting at once as a stimulant and a restraint, the social intercourse of the two sexes draws forth and invigorates all the purifying, exalting, and delightful qualities of our common nature; while it tends to suppress, and, not seldom, to eradicate those of an opposite character. From this unrestricted communion flow the graces, the affections, the charms, the sanctities, the charities, of life; and as benignant Nature ever blesses the individual who contributes to the advancement of his species, from the same source is derived our purest, most exquisite, and most enduring happiness.

" I lay it down as a broad, incontrovertible axiom, that no married man has a right to belong to a club, and to become an habitual absentee from his home, indulging in hoggish epicurism, while his wife and family are perhaps keeping Lent, that he may afford to feast. What hath he sworn to in his marriage-oath? Merely to maintain his wife, and to make her the mother of his children? No such thing; he hath sworn to forsake all others, and to cleave only unto her, until death shall part them. Is it consistent, either with the letter or the spirit of this vow, that he should deprive her of his society, and make a sort of concubine of his club? Is a virtuous, honourable, and accomplished wife to be treated like an impure Delilah, into whose house her paramour sneaks in the dark, and skulks away again in the early morning? The little occasional bickerings, from which few married couples are totally exempt, not unfrequently prove, under the soothing influences of children, and the pleasures of the domestic meal, a renewal and confirmation of love; but *now*, the sullen husband escapes to his still more sullen club; he becomes embittered by feeding upon his own angry heart; a reconciliation is rendered every day more difficult; he begins to hate his home; and his occasional absence is soon made habitual. Meanwhile, the children lose the benefit of the father's presence and example; the father, whose loss is of still more mischievous import, is deprived of all the heart-hallowing influences of his offspring: and the neglected wife, thinking herself justified in seeking from others that society which is denied to her by her husband, is exposed to temptations and dangers, from which she cannot always escape without contamination. To over-rate the conjugal and domestic misery now in actual progress, and all springing from this prolific source, would, I believe, be utterly impossible. How many married couples are there in the middling classes of society, the course of whose alienation and unhappiness might be traced out in the following order?—

"HUSBAND. The club—a taste for French cooks, expensive wines, and sensual luxuries—fastidious epicurism— a dislike of the plain meals which he finds at home, although the only ones adapted to his fortune and his station—confirmed absenteeism and clubbism—hatred of the wife, who reproaches him for his selfish desertion—late hours—estrangement—profligacy—misery!

"WIFE. Natural resentment of neglect—reproaches— altercations—diminution of conjugal affection—dissipation, as a resource against the dulness of home—expensive habits

—embarrassment—total alienation of heart—dangerous con-
nections—infidelity—misery !

"Of this account-current, the items may vary, either in
quality or sequence, but the alpha and omega will ever be
the same.   It will begin with the club, and end with misery."

COLLEGE—an institution where young men are apt to
learn everything but that which professes to be taught,
although that which professes to be taught falls very short
of what a modern gentleman ought to learn. As a type of
the olden times, with all their unredeemed bigotry and prejudice, our colleges are sadly out of keeping with the nineteenth century. Their whole system is a specimen of the
moral, as some of their structures are of the architectural
gothic. Mark the opinion of no incompetent witness, since
he was himself an Oxford collegian.

" Were there no public institutions for education, no system, no science would be taught, for which there was not
some demand, or which the circumstances of the time did not
render it either necessary or convenient, or at least fashionable to learn. A private teacher could never find his account
in teaching either an exploded and antiquated system of a
science acknowledged to be useful, or a science universally
believed to be a mere useless and pedantic heap of sophistry
and nonsense. Such sciences, such systems, can subsist
nowhere but in those incorporated societies for education,
whose prosperity and revenue are, in a great measure, independent of their reputation, and altogether independent of
their industry. Were there no public institutions for education, a gentleman, after going through, with application and
abilities, the most complete course of education which the
circumstances of the time were supposed to afford, could not
come into the world completely ignorant of everything which
is the common subject of conversation among gentlemen

and men of the world."—*Smith's Wealth of Nations*, bk. v. ch. 1, part 3, art. 2.

If our colleges be still the seats of learning, it can only be for the reason assigned in the old epigram—

> " No wonder that Oxford and Cambridge profound,
> In learning and science so greatly abound,
> Since some carry thither a little each day,
> And we meet with so few who bring any away."

COMFORT.—"Ah!" said a John Bull to a Frenchman, " you have no such word as 'comfort' in your language."— " I am glad of it," replied the Gaul ;—" you Englishmen are slaves to your comforts, in order that you may master them." There is some truth in this reproach. Perpetually toiling for money, with the professed object of being enabled to live comfortably, we sacrifice every comfort in the acquisition of a fortune, in order that when we have obtained it, we may have an additional discomfort from our anxiety to preserve or increase it. Thus do we " lose by seeking what we seek to find." On the other hand, we may find a comfort where we never looked for it ; as, for instance, in a great affliction, the very magnitude of which renders us insensible to all smaller ones. Comfort, in our national acceptation of the word, has been stated to consist in those little luxuries and conveniences, the want of which makes an Englishman miserable, while their possession does not make him happy.

COMMISERATION, Felonious.—There is a large class of idle people in this country, whose palled and jaded feelings can only be roused by some powerful excitement, whence they derive so much pleasure, that they immediately yearn towards the exciter, however undeserving of their pity. They like a murderer, because he relieves them for a moment from listlessness and *ennui*, and assists in committing another murder, by helping them to kill their greatest enemy—time. The spurious, morbid, perverted sympathy which can only be elicited by criminals and malefactors, generally increasing with the enormity of their offences, and which I have stigmatised as the " felonious commiseration," may be compared to the diseased taste of certain epicures, who attach no value to a cheese while it is sound, but doat upon it when it becomes corrupt, rotten, and rank with all sorts of offensive abominations.

COMMON-PLACE PEOPLE—are content to walk for life in the rut made by their predecessors, long after it has become so deep that they cannot see to the right or left. This keeps them in ignorance and darkness, but it saves them the trouble of thinking or acting for themselves.

COMPETENCY—a financial horizon, which recedes as we advance. This word is by no means of indefinite meaning. It always signifies a little more than we possess. We are none of us wealthy enough in our own opinion, although we may be too much so in the judgment of others. Content is the best opulence, because it is the pleasantest, and the surest. The richest man is he who does not want that which is wanting to him ; the poorest is the miser, who wants that which he has.

COMPLIMENT—a thing often paid by people who pay nothing else :—the counterfeit coin of those who substitute the form, fashion, and language of politeness, for its substance and its feeling. Throwing compliments, like dice, is a game of hazard, at which the incautious player may get nothing but a sharp rap on the knuckles. He who sports compliments, unless he knows how to take a good aim, may miss his mark, and be wounded by the recoil of his own gun.　Above all things, it is incumbent upon him to reflect, that even a blue-stocking will look black at him, if he attempt to flatter her mental, at the expense of her personal attractions. At a dinner-party in Paris, an ugly and dull German baron, finding himself seated between the celebrated Madame de Stael, and Madame Recamier, the *belle* of the day, whispered to the former—" Am I not fortunate, to be thus placed between beauty and talent?"—" Not so very fortunate," replied the offended authoress, " since you possess neither one nor the other ! "

" *Hélas, le pauvre duc d'Aumont !*" exclaimed one of his female friends,—" who would have thought that he would have been carried off so suddenly ?—On the very morning of his death, he had played as usual with his parroquet and his monkey ;—he had said, give me my snuff-box, brush this arm chair, let me see my new court dress ;—in fact, he possessed all his ideas and faculties with as much strength and vigour as ever he had done at the age of thirty." What an unintended satire in these tender compliments. Not more so, however, than in the *naïf* remark of a lady, when a censorious and conceited neighbour, vaunting of her good figure, boasted that herself and her sister had always been remarkable for the beauty of their backs. " That is the reason, I suppose, that your friends are always so glad to see them." A sarcasm may often wear the garb of a compliment, and be taken for one by the simple-witted. The Abbé Voisenon once made a complaint that he was unduly charged with the absurd sayings of others. " *Monsieur l'Abbé,*" replied D'Alembert, " *on ne prête qu'aux riches.*"

Not altogether unworthy of being recorded is the compliment attributed to a butcher at Whitby.—" This fillet of veal seems not quite so white as usual," said a fair lady, laying her hand upon it.—" Put on your glove, Ma'am, and you will think otherwise," was the complaisant reply.

CONCEIT—taking ourselves at our own valuation, generally about fifty per cent. above the fair worth. Minerva threw away the flute, when she found that it puffed up her own cheeks ; but if we cast away the flute now-a-days, it is only that we may take a larger instrument of puffing, by becoming our own trumpeters. Empty minds are the most prone to soar above their proper sphere, like paper kites, which are kept aloft by their own lightness ; while those that are better stored are prone to humility, like heavily laden vessels, of which we see the less the more richly and deeply they are freighted. The corn bends itself downward when its ears are filled, but when the heads of the conceited are filled with self-adulation, they only lift them up the higher.

Perhaps it is a benevolent provision of Providence, that we should possess in fancy those good qualities which are withheld from us in reality ; for if we did not occasionally think well of ourselves, we should be more apt to think ill of others. It must be confessed, that the conceited and the vain have a light and pleasant duty to perform, since they have but one to please, and in that object they seldom fail. Self-love, moreover, is the only love not liable to the pangs of jealousy. Pity ! that a quick perception of our own deserts generally blinds us to the merits of others ; that we should see more than all the world in the former instance, and less in the latter ! In one respect, conceited people show a degree of discernment, for which they deserve credit,—they soon become tired of their own company. Especially fortunate are they in another respect ; for while the really wise, witty, and beautiful, are subject to casualties of defect, age, and sickness, the imaginary possessor of those qualities wears a charmed life, and fears not the assaults of fate or time, since a nonentity is invulnerable. Even the really gifted, however, may sometimes become conceited. Northcote, the artist, whose intellectual powers were equal to his professional talent, and who thought it much easier for a man to be his superior than his equal, being once asked by Sir William Knighton what he thought of the Prince Regent, replied, "I am not acquainted with him."—"Why, his Royal Highness says he knows you."—"Know me !—Pooh ! that's all his brag."

CONGREGATION—a public assemblage in a spiritual theatre, where all the performers are professors, but where very few of the professors are performers.

"Taking them one with another," said the Rev. S— S—, "I believe my congregation to be most exemplary observers of the religious ordinances ; for the poor keep all the fasts, and the rich all the feasts." This fortunate flock might be matched with the crew of the A—— frigate, whose commander, Capt. R—, told a friend that he had just left them the happiest set of fellows in the world. Knowing the captain's extreme severity, his friend expressed some surprise at this statement, and demanded an explanation. "Why," said the disciplinarian, "I have just had nineteen of the rascals flogged, and they are happy that it is over, while all the rest are happy that they have escaped."

CONSCIENCE—something to swear by. Conscience being regulated by the opinion of the world, has no very determinate standard of morality. Among the ancient Greeks and Romans, suicide was a magnanimous virtue, with us it is a cowardly crime. The Spartans taught their children to steal ; we whip and imprison ours for the same act. No man's conscience stings him for killing a single adversary in a duel, or scores in war, because these deeds are in accordance with the usages of society ; but he may, nevertheless, be arraigned, perchance, for murder, at the bar of the Almighty. Terror of conscience, therefore, would seem to be the fear of infamy, detection, or punishment in this world, rather than in the next. Criminals, who voluntarily surrender themselves to justice, and confess their misdeeds, are, doubtless, driven to that act of desperation by their conscience; but it is from a dread of Jack Ketch, and the intolerableness of suspense. They would rather be hanged once in reality than every day in imagination. Pass a law that shall legalize their offences, or let them be tried and acquitted, from some flaw in the indictment, and their minds will be wonderfully tranquillized. How much safer a guide and monitor would our conscience become, if we adapted it to the immutable laws of God, instead of the fluctuating opinions of man, and were penetrated with the great truth that, whatever may be our present feelings, there is an inevitable ultimate connection between happiness and virtue, misery and vice.

CONSERVATIVE—one who has evinced a good sense, that entitles him to our respect, by becoming ashamed of the word Tory. With the exception of the mere boroughmonger, whose sordid motives deserve no indulgence, every generous reformer will give credit to his conservative opponent for the same sincerity of feeling, and purity of purpose, that he himself professes and claims. Invective and personality prove nothing on either side, but a lamentable want of good taste and good argument. There is one party to which all aspire to belong, and whose characteristics none can mistake—that of the GENTLEMAN; not limiting this all-embracing appellation to the vulgar distinctions of rank and external appearance, but to the innate gentleness and liberality, which a peasant or an artisan may possess in as eminent a degree as a peer or a prince. Let the reformer, whose victory is won, grace it by forbearance—let the conservative, whose further opposition is useless, disdain the guerilla warfare of faction. The former should now employ himself in realising the advantages he so confidently anticipated from his great measure ; the latter, in guarding against the dangers he not less positively prognosticated. Gladly holding out the right hand of fellowship to each other, both should unite in endeavouring to accomplish their mutual object—the advancement, the glory, and the happiness of their common country. So shall old England, with improved institutions, renovated energies, and an united people, re-assert her proud prerogative of teaching the nations how to live.

CONSOLATION for unsuccessful authors.—" Many works," says Chamfort, " succeed, because the mediocrity of the author's ideas exactly corresponds with the mediocrity of ideas on the part of the public." Writers who fail in hitting the present taste, are apt to appeal to posterity, which, even if it should ratify their fond anticipations, (a rare occurrence,) will only show that they have still failed, because they have gained an object which they did not seek, and missed that which they sought. Let him profess what he will, every man writes to be read by his contemporaries ; otherwise why does he publish ? It would be a poor compliment to a sportsman to say—" You have missed all the birds, at which you took aim, but you fire so well that your shot will be sure to hit something before they fall to the ground." He who professes to do without the living, and yet wants the suffrages of the unborn, stands little chance of obtaining his election, and is sure that he cannot enjoy it, even if he succeed. Few will possess such claims to celebrity as Kepler, the German astronomer ; and yet there was a sense of mortification, as well as an almost profane arrogance, when, on the failure of one of his works to excite attention, he exclaimed, " My book may well wait a hundred years for a reader, since God himself has been content to wait six thousand years for an observer like myself."

CONTENT—a mental Will-o'-the-wisp, which all are seeking, but which few attain. And yet every one might succeed, if he would think more of what he has, and less of what he wants. Daily experience may convince us that those who possess what we covet, are not a jot more happy than ourselves : why then should we labour and toil in chasing disappointment? How few feel gratitude for what they have, compared to those who pine for what they have not ! *Aut Cæsar aut nullus* is the prevalent motto : not to have everything, is to have nothing. Like the famous Duke of Buckingham, some are more impatient of successes, than others are of reverses ; by basking in the sunshine of fortune, they become sour, and turn to vinegar.

> "Let this plain truth those ingrates strike,
>   Who still, though bless'd, new blessings crave,
> That we may all have what we like,
>   Simply by liking what we have."

Or, if this fail, let us call arithmetic to our aid, and learn content from comparing ourselves and our lot with the many who want what we possess, rather than with the few who possess what we want.

CONTROVERSY.—What a blessing to the world if it had exemplified the dictum of Sir William Temple, that all such controversies as can never end, had much better never begin ! At the present moment, when the necessity of a Church reformation is so generally discussed, it may not be uninteresting to reprint the lines on the famous controversy between John Rainolds and one of his brothers, wherein *each converted the other.*

> " In points of faith, some undetermin'd jars,
>   Betwixt two brothers, kindled civil wars ;
>   One for the Church's reformation stood,
>   The other held no reformation good.
>   The points propos'd, they traversed the field
>   With equal strength ; so equally they yield.
>   As each desir'd, his brother each subdues ;
>   Yet such their faith, that each his faith does lose.
>   Both joyed in being conquered, strange to say,
>   And yet both mourn'd, because both won the day."

As to religious controversy, we will set an example worthy of all imitation, by saying nothing about it, further than to refer the curious in such matters, to the tomb of Sir Henry Wotton, in the chapel at Eton, whereon is the following inscription—"Hic jacet hujus sententiæ primus auctor :—*Disputandi pruritus Ecclesiæ scabies.*" "Here lies the first author of this sentence :—*The itch of disputation is the scab of the Church.*"

CONVERSATION, Rational—see Library, Solitude, anything but company. Despotic but civilized countries, such as France under the old monarchy, where the men having little or no share in the government, and being unembittered by party politics, threw their whole minds into social intercourse, are the best adapted for conversational excellence. In England we have too much business, and too much political acrimony to allow us either time or aptitude for the enjoyment of society in all its nonchalance, sprightliness and vivacity ; while even the narrow bounds left to us, are still further restricted by our pride, reserve, and exclusiveness. On these accounts English women are in general much better conversationalists than the men. In many families, the daughters have more cultivated minds than the sons, and will discourse of literature and the arts, while their brothers can talk of little but dogs and guns, a horse-race, or a boxing-match.

Even upon politics, when they will discuss them, women are more philosophical than men, because their passions and interests are not so deeply embarked. Not being educated for the business of life, they are more dispassionate, and are only the more agreeable for being ornamental instead of useful.

How incalculably would the tone of conversation be improved, if it offered no exceptions to the example of Bishop Beveridge: "I resolve never to speak of a man's virtues to his face, nor of his faults behind his back." A golden rule! the observation of which would at once banish flattery and defamation from the earth. Conversation stock being a joint and common property, every one should take a share in it; and yet there may be societies in which silence will be our best contribution. When Isocrates, dining with the King of Cyprus, was asked why he did not mix in the discourse of the company, he replied, "What is seasonable I do not know, and what I know is not seasonable."

A brilliant talker is not always liked by those whom he has most amused, for we are seldom pleased with those who have in any way made us feel our inferiority. "The happiest conversation," says Dr. Johnson, "is that of which nothing is distinctly remembered, but a general effect of pleasing impression."—"No one," says Dean Locker, "will ever shine in conversation, who thinks of saying fine things: to please, one must say many things indifferent, and many very bad." This last rule is rarely violated in society!

COQUETTE—a female general who builds her fame on her advances. A coquette may be compared to tinder, which lays itself out to catch sparks, but does not always succeed in lighting up a match. Men are perverse creatures; they fly that which pursues them, and pursue that which flies them. Forwardness, therefore, on the part of a female makes them draw back, and backwardness draws them forward. There will always be this difference between a coquette and a woman of sense and modesty, that while one courts every man, every man will court the other. When the coquette settles into an old maid, it is not unusual to see her as staid and formal as she was previously versatile :—

> " Thus weathercocks which for a while,
>   Have turned about with every blast,
> Grown old, and destitute of oil,
>   Rust to a point, and fix at last."

CORPORATION and TEST ACTS.—The obstinacy, the blindness, the fanatical fury with which the repeal of these obnoxious acts was opposed, from the days of James II. to our own ; the total oblivion into which their recent abrogation has already fallen ; and the consequent proofs of their absolute nullity, as affecting the security of the Church, forms the bitterest satire upon the ignorance and intolerance of those who so long and so fiercely opposed their repeal.

COUNTERACTION—a balancing provision of nature, for the prevention of excess, whether in morals or mechanics. But for this salutary restraint, even our virtues would be pushed to a vicious extreme. How many men do we encounter in society whose praises of their friends, when speaking to their faces, would appear fulsome flattery, were it not qualified by their disparagement of the same friends behind their backs ! Others there are whose warm offers of assistance, to such as do not need their aid, would appear generous even to a fault, did we not invariably find that they are equally cold, shy, and cautious where there is any probability of their professions being accepted. People may run into excess with their vices, but their virtues, thanks to this wholesome principle of counteraction, are seldom urged beyond the boundaries of prudence.

COURAGE—the fear of being thought a coward. The reverence that withholds us from violating the laws of God or man, is not infrequently branded with the name of cowardice. The Spartans had a saying, that he who stood most in fear of the law, generally showed the least fear of an enemy. We may infer the truth of this dictum from the reverse of the proposition, for daily experience shows us that they who are the most daring in a bad cause, are often the most pusillanimous in a good one. Bravery is a cheap and vulgar quality, of which the highest instances are frequently found in the lowest savages, and which is often still more conspicuous in the brute creation, than in the most intrepid of the human race. Equally signal were the courage and the candour of the man of Amiens, who being driven to the gates of his own city, cried out, " Come on, if you dare, cuckolds of Abbeville ; we are *here* four to one of you."

COURT.—"*La Cour*," says La Bruyere, "*ne rend pas content; mais elle empêche qu'on ne le soit ailleurs.*" If there be truth in this position, a luckless courtier must somewhat resemble the showman's amphibious animal—" who cannot live on the land, and dies in the water."

COUSIN—a periodical bore from the country, who, because you happen to have some of his blood, thinks he may inflict the whole of his body upon you during his stay in town. We do not mention his mind, because it is generally a nonentity.

CREATION, Lord of the—an ephemeral insect, the slave, too often, of his own passions. If this magisterial worm contemplates a map of the world, he will find that nearly three-fifths of it are covered by the sea and polar ice, and appear consequently to have been made for the occupation and accommodation of fishes, rather than of human beings ; while no small portion of the earth is in the possession of wild beasts and savages. If he considers his body, he will find it inferior, in some of its most important functions, to many of the animals ; but if he look into his mind, he will instantly discover sufficient vindication for the proud title he has assumed. By the study of Geology, he can throw back his existence into the remote æras, long before the creation of man. History makes him contemporary with all the celebrated nations of antiquity; speculation carries his life forward into an illimitable futurity ; Astronomy enables him to develope the laws by which the universe is governed, and to penetrate, as it were, into the secrets of the Deity. Thus doth he conquer both time and space. The beautiful and majestic earth is his footstool, he walks between two eternities, God is everywhere round about him, a beatific immortality is before him. Truly this august creature may justly term himself the Lord of the Creation.

CREDULITY—an instinct of youth. "The simple believeth every word, but the prudent man looketh well to his going." Prov. xiv. 15. Credulity diminishes as we gather wisdom by experience, and yet, even among the old and suspicious, it is probable that many falsehoods are believed, for a single truth that is disbelieved. The young having a constant tendency to welcome pleasant and repel disagreeable impressions, reject as long as they can the painful feeling of suspicion. Belief, like a young puppy, is born blind ; and must swallow whatever food is given to it ; when it can see, it caters for itself. Or it may be better compared to the block of marble, and Truth to the statue within it, at which we can only arrive by perpetually cutting away the fragments that enclose and conceal it. As a good workman is known by the quantity of his chips, so may a penetrative mind by the rubbish and heaps of discarded credulity with which it is surrounded. Taking the whole world at the present moment, can it be said to believe a thousandth part of what it believed a thousand years ago?

CREED, Compulsory—an attempt to cast the minds of others in the same mould as our own, which is about as likely to be successful as if a similar experiment were applied to the body. Hear the opinion of St. Hilary upon this subject—"It is a thing equally deplorable and dangerous, that there are at present as many creeds as there are opinions among men. We make creeds arbitrarily, and explain them as arbitrarily. We can't be ignorant that, since the council of Nice, we have done nothing but make creeds. We make creeds every year, nay every morn: we repent of what we have done; we defend those that repent; we anathematize those we have defended; we condemn the doctrine of others in ourselves, or our own in that of others; and reciprocally tearing one another to pieces, we have been the cause of one another's ruin."—(*Ad Constant.*)

Creeds are doubly injurious in their operation; they occasion a positive as well as a negative evil to the Church, by excluding the conscientious and upright, while they admit the subservient and unscrupulous. "Though some purposes of order and tranquillity," says Paley, "may be answered by the establishment of creeds and confessions, yet they are at all times attended with serious inconvenience: they check inquiry; they violate liberty; they ensnare the consciences of the clergy, by holding out temptations to prevarication."—*Moral and Political Philosophy*, bk. vi. ch. 10.

The same writer notices another, and still more crying

evil to which they inevitably tend—" Creeds and confessions, however they may express the persuasion, or be accommodated to the controversies or to the fears of the age in which they are composed, in process of time, and by reason of the changes which are wont to take place in the judgment of mankind upon religious subjects, they come at length to *contradict the actual opinions* of the Church, whose doctrines they profess to contain."—*Ibid.* bk. vi. ch. 10.   So that these tyrannical and useless shackles of the mind actually promote perjury or equivocation in the pastor, while they obstruct the progress of knowledge and of Christianity among the flock !—What more can be added to show the necessity for their abolition ?

CRITICISM—very often consists in measuring the learning and the wisdom of others, either by our own ignorance, or by our little technical and pedantic partialities and prejudices.   Every one has heard of the mathematician who objected to Shakspeare, that his works *proved* nothing. Equally luminous was the remark of the lawyer, who happening to catch the words—" a deed without a name,"—uttered by the witches in Macbeth, repeated—" A deed without a name !—why, 'tis *void.*"   In the same enlarged spirit is much of our criticism written ; but even this is better than the feeling of rancour and bitterness by which it is too often perverted from its legitimate ends, and rendered subservient, by the most disingenuous acts, to the gratification of personal pique, or party malevolence.   As the devil can quote scripture for his purpose, so can the practised critic, by severing passages from their context, and placing them in a ridiculous or distorting light, make the most praiseworthy work appear to condemn itself.   A book thus unfairly treated, may be compared to the laurel, of which there is honour in the leaves, but poison in the extract.

Of much of our contemporary criticism, which consists rather in reviewing writers than writings, we may find a fair type in the following passage from a letter of the celebrated Waller: " The old blind schoolmaster, John Milton, hath published a tedious poem on the fall of man ; if its length be not considered as merit, it hath no other."

Pepys, in his Memoirs, thus speaks of Hudibras—" When I came to read it, it is so silly an abuse of the Presbyter knight going to the wars, that I am ashamed of it ; and by and by, meeting at Mr. Townsend's at dinner, I sold it to Mr. Battersby for 18*d.* !"   There are living critics who seem to have caught the mantle of these sapient judges.

CRY, Conservative—an imitation of the cunning rogue who calls out " Pickpocket ! "—in order that, by diverting our attention to others, he may effect his own escape with the plunder he has made.   This is a favourite device with corruptionists of all sorts.   Whenever there is a cry that the State is in danger, we may be confident that it is about to be rendered more secure by some popular concession ; and when our ears are stunned by vociferations of the Church being in danger, we may safely suspect that it is about to be fortified by the removal of some act of intolerance, or the reform of some gross abuse.   It is one of the most encouraging signs of the times, that this interested clamour, once so influential, is now little better than a *brutum fulmen*.

CUNNING—the simplicity by which knaves generally outwit themselves.   As the ignorant and unsuspicious are often protected by their singleness of purpose, so are the crafty and designing not unfrequently foiled by their duplicity.   It is not every rogue that, like a bowl, can gain his object the better by deviating from the straight line ; although there is one straight line to which the rogue's deviations are very apt to conduct him.

CURIOSITY—looking over other people's affairs, and overlooking our own. If a spy may be executed by the laws of war, surely a Paul Pry may be kicked or horsewhipped by the laws of society. There is no peace with such a man, unless you declare war against him. Xenocrates, reprehending curiosity, said, "It was as rude to intrude into another man's house with your eyes, as with your feet."

CUSTOM—a reason for irrational things, and an excuse for inexcusable ones. While we exercise our own judgment in all matters of importance, we should do well, in trifles, to conform, without inquiry, to existing modes. "A froward retention of custom," says Lord Bacon, "is as turbulent a thing as an innovation;" a *dictum* which we recommend to the special consideration of our Conservatives. Most shrewd and discreet was the advice of the old lady, who, on her first settlement at Constantinople, advised her children to conform strictly to the manners and customs of the inhabitants, adding—"When people are in Turkey, they should live as turkeys live." Perhaps the power of custom was never more strongly exemplified than in the case of Ariosto's hero, who was so habituated to fighting, that he went on combating, even after he was dead.

> " Il pover uomo che non se n'era accorto,
> Andava combattendo—ed era morto."

AY AND MARTIN—falsifiers of prophecy. Thirty years ago, our wiseacres predicted, that when all could read and write, we should find none to black our shoes. The day of evil has arrived: everybody *can* read and write; our shoes are not only better blacked than ever, but they are polished by comparatively polished people; our blacking-makers acquire fortunes, and build palaces, thus giving encouragement to other arts than the black one; and it is even reported, that a London firm keeps a regular bard upon the establishment, to write poetical puffs.

Nevertheless, we *have* heard of a saucy knight of the shoulder-knot, who, on applying to the irascible Colonel B——, while he was at his desk, for the vacant situation of valet, asked permission to state beforehand that he never touched a boot, and inquired who was to do the black work? —"*That* I do myself," cried the Colonel, throwing the ink-stand in his face;—"and as you never touch a boot, I must make my boot touch you,"—with which words he kicked him down stairs.

DEATH—the sleeping partner of life—a change of existence. This great and insolvable mystery, which we are ever flying from and running towards, is by no means the φοβερὸν φοβερώτατον that our fancy somtimes represents it. To live is, in fact, to die, and to die is to live; for the body is the grave of the soul, and death the gate of life. If to expire be an evil, it is only a negative one, which might well be endured, since it terminates those that are positive. If it be a rod, it is like that of Aaron, which blossoms and bears the fruit of peace. Why should a long, be less pleasant than a short sleep? Post-natal, cannot differ from ante-

natal unconsciousness : we were dead before we lived ;
ceasing to exist is only returning to our former state, speaking always with reference to this world.

It is what we are flying *from*, rather than *to*, that often
makes us unwilling to sustain so " violent a wrench from all
we love ;" an argument which one of the fathers adduces as
an excuse for the bitterness of the world. "*Amarus est mun-
dus, et diligitur. Puta, si dulcis esset, qualiter amaretur.*"
A French monarch being told, in his last moments, that he
would soon be a saint in heaven, exclaimed, sorrowfully, " I
should have been quite content to remain King of France
and Navarre."

" Ah, David, David !" said Johnson to Garrick, who had
been showing him his house and grounds at Hampton,—
"these are the things that make a death-bed terrible !" Had
he been reading in the Alceste—

> " Ce sont les douceurs de la vie,
> Qui font les horreurs du trepas ;"—

or Horace's

> " Linquenda tellus, et domus, et placens
> Uxor, neque harum quas colis arborum,
> Te, præter invisos cupressos,
> Ulla brevem dominum sequetur ! "

Montaigne makes Nature address man in the following
words :—"*Sortez de ce monde comme vous y êtes entré ; le
même passage que vous avez faie de la mort à la vie, sans
passion et sans frayeur, refaites-la de la vie à la mort. Votre
mort est une des pièces de l'ordre de l'univers ; une pièce
de la vie du monde.——Si vous n'aviez la mort, vous me
mauderiez sans cesse de vous en avoir privé.*"

" O Death, I bless thee !" exclaims Le Mercier, in a tone
of bitter eloquence—" Thou shakest tyrants ; thou reducest
to dust those whom the world had flattered, and who made

mankind their footstool. They fall, and we breathe more freely. Hope of the unfortunate! terror of the wicked! stretch out thine arm, and strike the persecutors of the earth. And ye voracious worms! my friends and my avengers! hasten in crowds to the feast of their crime-fattened carcasses!"

He that would die sooner or later than he ought, is equally a coward. Cæsar, when he heard of any sudden death, used to wish—"*sibi et suis euthanasiam similem*," and he was right; for the aspect, the threats, and the bark, of death, are worse than his bite.

The author of the following stanzas seems to have been of Cæsar's opinion :—

> " Oh ! come not, thou skeleton king, in the garb
>   Of a lingering sickness to summon thy prize,
> To hover above me with menacing barb,
>   And dangle its ominous glare in mine eyes—
> For see ! I have open'd my breast, that thy dart
> May be steadily aim'd at a resolute heart.

> " Be the grass of the meadow my pillow of death,
>   And the friends that surround it—the sea and the sky;
> May the angel-wing'd breezes receive my last breath,
>   To be borne to its heavenly giver on high !—
> Be the spot where I fall unprofaned by a tear,
> Save the dews of the night that descend on my bier."

Death is the only subject upon which everybody speaks and writes, without a possibility of having experienced what he undertakes to discuss. Contempt of it is seldom real; it is but the love of glory: many, besides Mirabeau, have dramatized their own exits. Most consolatory is the reflection, that if this great consummation puts an end to the enjoyments of some, it terminates the sufferings of all. Death is a silent, peaceful genius, who rocks our second childhood to sleep in the cradle of the coffin.

It is the proud prerogative of noble natures, that they
retain their influence after death. The lamps which guided
us on earth, become stars to light us from above, and the
beneficent may still claim our aspirations as the blessed ;—a
species of apotheosis equally honourable to the living and the
dead.

DEBT, National — mortgaging the property of our
posterity, that we may be better enabled to destroy our contemporaries. It may be questionable, whether any community has a moral right to discount the future, for the purpose
of tormenting or corrupting the present ; to exhaust the
resources of many ages, that it may render the pugnacity
and ambition of its own more extensively mischievous. Is
there no limit to this right, or, rather, wrong ; no check, but
the frightful one of a national bankruptcy? If parliament,
for instance, for the purpose of raising a large loan, were to
sell all our unborn children into slavery, would our offspring
be legally bound to submit to bondage? and, if not, are there
not limits to financial bondage? To a certain extent, the
latter includes the former ; for the person is often fettered
where the purse is crippled and straitened.

Well is it that these questions should be discussed, for the
universal discontinuance of the funding system would be an
incalculable blessing to the world, by cutting the sinews of
war. While it lasts, however, let its engagements be sacredly
observed.

The injurious persons who maintain that the weight of our
debt gives solidity to our political institutions, and that its
increase only adds to our security, remind one of the sapient
Justice, who, finding the ice begin to crack, as he was crossing the frozen Thames, cried out to his servant—" John,
there seems to be some danger here ; so, for our mutual
safety, do prythee help me over on your back."

Speaking of the difference between laying out money in land, or investing it in the funds, it was said by Soame Jenyns, that one was principal without interest, and the other interest without principal.

DECEPTION—a principal ingredient in happiness. Did we possess the spear of Ithuriel, or could we realise the suggestion of Momus, we should gain a fearful loss. An enemy to education, when told that the schoolmaster was abroad, replied, "I am very glad to hear it ; I hope he will remain there !" A friend to his species will utter a similar aspiration respecting Truth, if he believe the popular saying, that she lies at the bottom of a well. Instead of regretting that we are sometimes deceived, we should rather lament that we are ever undeceived. But, alas ! as Seneca says— "*Nemo omnes, neminem omnes fefellerunt.*"—None deceives all, and none have all deceived.

DEDICATION—inscribing to an individual that, which, if it be worth encouragement, will find its best patron in the public. Kopp, the German, prefixed the following short, but pithy dedication to his Palæographia Critica :—"*Posteris hoc opus, ab æqualium meorum studiis fortè alienum, do, dico, atque dedico.*" Upon these occasions, one cannot help sharing the apprehension expressed by Voltaire, that the work may never reach the party to whom it is addressed !

DESCRIPTION.—A living critic has laid it down as a rule, that no author can succeed in describing what he has not seen, forgetting that Dante was never in hell, nor Milton in Paradise ; and that it is the highest praise of Shakspeare to have "exhausted worlds, and then imagined new." Inventive writers evince their talent by portraying the invisible and non-existent, snatching a grace, not only beyond the reach of art, but beyond the reach of nature. Little right had the critic in question to expect imagination in others, for it is manifest that he possessed none himself.

DESPONDENCY—ingratitude to heaven, as cheerfulness is the best and most acceptable piety. H—, who is bilious and hypochondriacal, may be termed a constitutional grumbler. "If my future life," he one day exclaimed, "be only an executed copy, an unheard echo, an invisible reflection of the past, I wish it not to be prolonged. Running after happiness, is only chasing the horizon, or seeking the philosopher's stone, and I am already

> " ' Tired of toiling for the chymic gold,
>   That fools us young, and beggars us when old.' "

D— does not possess the talents of H—, but his bile is never deranged ; he has a fortunate organisation ; he is a happier, and, so far, a wiser man. Like the bee, which extracts honey even from bitter flowers, he can derive cheerfulness from the most unpromising elements. Are his companions gloomy, disagreeable, silent,—he calls forth his own stores of pleasantness, and if he do not succeed in enlivening others, which is but rarely the case,—for good humour and good spirits are often catching,—he finds cause for gratitude that he himself possesses a constant aptitude for the enjoyment of existence, while so many are enacting the part of Terence's Heautontimorumenos. Is the scenery picturesque, it exalts his admiration into rapture : is it flat and commonplace, it still possesses an interest for one who feels that every spot of ground, however unattractive, conduces to some benevolent purpose of utility or enjoyment. Does the sun shine, its jocund beams heighten his natural exhilaration, by lifting up his thoughts to the great Source of all light, solar, as well as intellectual. Is it a rainy day, he sees the outstretched hand of the same beneficent Deity, guiding the clouds over the earth, that they may dispense fertility and gladness to the creatures whom He has called into existence, and around whom He is for ever scattering blessings. I know not how H— may feel upon the occasion, but, for my own part, I would gladly give up whatever I may possess of talent and learning—(deem me not overweening, gentle reader! for, perchance, I may reckon them as Indians do rupees—by the *lack*)—I would give them all up, I repeat, to possess the happy disposition of D—.

DESPOTISM—allowing a whole people no other means of escape from oppression, than by the assassination of their oppressor. If tyranny be an unjustifiable liberticide, may not tyrannicide be termed justifiable homicide? We moot the point, without presuming to decide it. Despotism, nevertheless, has its advantages in a barbarous and ignorant country, where its evils are little felt. Peter the Great, of Russia, could hardly have accomplished so much in civilizing his subjects, if he had not been an absolute monarch. Even among a comparatively enlightened people, such is the force of habit, that a long-established despotism may continue unabated, without being resented by its victims. For two centuries, at least, the French presented the anomaly of a polished, intellectual, enslaved people. Nay, they could record their degradation, and seem to glory in it. The terror of Europe, named *par excellence*, the *Grand Monarque*, was the puppet of an old woman, the widow of Scarron, the buffoon, whom he had clandestinely married. "The State is myself," said Louis XIV.; an ebullition of despotism imitated in our own times by Napoleon; so besotting is the cup of unlimited power. In its self-punishing operation, it generally weakens the mind, until the enslaver becomes a slave, either to a mistress or a favourite, if not to both.

There is a natural connection between despotic government and depraved manners,—free governments and comparative purity. Free institutions not only open to the rich higher and more worthy objects of ambition than the gratification of the senses, but operate as a wholesome restraint upon the upper ranks, by making them dependent, in some degree, on the good opinion of the lower classes. Where character is power, we have the best security for general morality.

Perhaps the worst thing ever uttered by Madame de Stael, was her speech to the Emperor of Russia :—" Sir, your character is a constitution for your country, and your conscience its guarantee;" nor is there a better kingly speech upon record than his reply,—" Even if it were so, I should never be anything more than a lucky accident."

DESTINY—the scapegoat which we make responsible for all our crimes and follies; a necessity which we set down for invincible, when we have no wish to strive against it.

DIET—the edibles and potables that we turn into blood and bone—the matter that we metamorphose into mind. —"Sir," said Bentley to one of his pupils, who had a predilection for malt liquor—" if you drink ale you will think ale;" and there was more truth in the averment than might at first sight be imagined, for body and mind must assimilate, to a certain extent, with that which sustains them. Look at the difference of disposition between the carnivorous and graminivorous animals : the latter, who seem to be nature's unweaned favourites, are peaceful as the bosom upon which they browse; the former, doomed to be constantly tearing one another, and to live by blood and slaughter, are constitutionally savage and ferocious. Varieties of temperament in animals will often be found to have reference to the different food in which each race delights, and it is by no means improbable that the national character of human societies may be modified by their favourite diet. The taste of each, taking that word in its most extended acceptation, may be traceable to the palate. The suppleness and levity of the Italian may be derived from maccaroni and vermicelli; Dutch phlegm and obstinacy, from flat-fish, water-zootje and schiedam; German acerbity, mysticism and melancholy, from sour-krout, sausages, and vin de grave; the insubordination of the Irish peelers and repealers, from potatoes; French levity and vivacity, from ragouts and champagne; and the solid but somewhat crude and uncivilized character of John Bull, from his feeding upon huge joints of underdone beef.

Potables have a more immediate effect upon the formation of character than Edibles, because we like them better, and therefore sympathise with them more intimately. *In vino veritas*, saith the proverb: intoxication is thought to draw forth the real character; but this is a mistake; it creates instead of developing. Ebriety varies not with the man, but with the liquor. That of ardent spirits is fierce, maddening, and pugnacious; of strong beer, stupifying and somniferous; of port and heady wines, fond, maudlin, hic-coughing, and heavy; of champagne, gay, noisy, vivacious, shrieking, and saltatory. I have heard an old naval captain declare that, during the late war, a complete change was produced in the manners of the petty officers, by Sir George Rose's regulation, which substituted duty-free wines for their previous allowance of new rum and grog. When they had indulged a little too freely in the latter, (no very unusual occurrence,) strife, blackguardism, and outrage too often ensued; a similar excess in wine evaporated in laughter and hugging. "Besides, Sir," added my informant, "when we were drinking our wine, like gentlemen, we felt it incumbent

upon us to behave accordingly." Could anything more
effectually confirm the doctrine of Bentley? Perhaps the
notion was first suggested by his classical studies, and a
perusal of the speech wherein Silenus tells the Cyclop that
if he eats the tongue of Ulysses, he will acquire all his
eloquence.

DILEMMA for the doctors.—Complaint having lately
been made in a Yorkshire hospital, that an old Hibernian
would not submit to the prescribed remedies, one of the
committee proceeded to expostulate with him, when he
defended himself by exclaiming—" Sure, your honour, wasn't
it a blister they wanted to put upon my back? and I only
tould 'em it was althegither impossible, for I've such a mighty
dislike to them blisters, that put 'em where you will, they are
sure to go agin my stomach."

DILEMMA, Logical—a verbal check-mate. Aristotle
wishing to refute the opinion of Protagoras, who maintained
that there was nothing true in the world, argued thus:—
" Your proposition is either true or false; if it is false we
are not, of course, bound to believe it: if it is true, there *is*
such a thing as truth in the world, and consequently your
proposition is false." These clinches were once in great
favour with the sophists and logicians, but they were never
worth the pains bestowed upon them, and have deservedly
fallen into oblivion. The puzzling instance given in Johnson's Dictionary under the word Dilemma, is recorded by
Apuleius, as well as by Aulus Gallius in his Attic Nights.
Our special pleading is the last remnant of these verbal
quibbles, and the sooner it is exploded the better. The age
of words is passing away, as well as the impostures and
delusions to which they gave a species of sanction. Injustice, delay, and robbery will no longer be called law;

tithes and bishoprics, Christianity; rotten boroughs, representation; negro slavery, a mild and happy servitude; or public wrongs, private rights. In exploding these verbal frauds it should be well understood that they may be still practised, if we can reduce the great enemy of mankind to a *non plus*, in imitation of the wily friar, who sold his soul to him upon condition that all his debts should be paid. Money was supplied in abundance, until he was extricated from his difficulties; but when Satan came to claim the soul that was due to him, the friar answered, "Begone, thou swindler! If I owe thee anything, I am not yet out of debt, and if I do not owe thee anything, why dost thou trouble me?"

Shrewd and quickwitted was the reply of the miser, who on being requested by a dervish to grant him a favour, said, "On one condition I will do whatever you require."—"What is that?"—"Never to ask me for any thing."

DINNER—a meal taken at supper time; formerly considered a means of enjoying society, and therefore moderate in expense, and frequent in occurrence; now given to display yourself, not to gratify your friends; and inhospitably rare, because it is foolishly extravagant.

John Bulwer, a quaint writer of the seventeenth century, especially recommends the following three dinner rules:— *Stridor dentium—Altum silentium—Rumor gentium;* which has been humorously translated, "Work for the jaws—A silent pause—Frequent Ha—has!"

DISCIPLINE, Military—that subordination which is maintained upon the continent by the hope of distinction, in England by the fear of the cat-o'-nine-tails. Nothing is so reluctantly abandoned by despots, whether kings, pedagogues, officers, or magistrates, as any oppressive cruelty, which they imagine to be connected with the maintenance of their authority. A tyrant not only gratifies his malignity, but saves all trouble of argument or proper management, by the use of the whip, which may account for the disgraceful floggings still so prevalent in our schools, army and navy. This remnant of a barbarous age must soon pass away, and if our flogging disciplinarians would pass away at the same time, we should all be gainers by their loss. The cat-o'-nine-tails must have as many lives as tails, or it never could have lasted so long.

DISCONTENT—being unhappy at the non-possession of that, of which the possession would not make us happy. Whence comes it that most men are satisfied with their country, to whatever sufferings its climate may expose them, while few or none are satisfied with their lot? In the former instance, a man is on a par with his neighbours; in the latter, the mass being necessarily inferior to the few, pride makes them imagine that they are all too low, because they are not all at the top.

To those who repine at the humbleness of their lot, without knowing to what eventual distinctions they may be destined, we recommend a perusal of the apologue with which Addison concludes one of his moral essays. A drop of water falling from the clouds into the ocean, became discontented with its insignificance, and complained that in the loss of its identity, it was in fact annihilated. In the midst of these murmurs, it was swallowed by an oyster, became converted, in process of time, into a gem, and finally constituted that celebrated pearl which adorns the top of the Persian diadem.

DISCOVERY—differs from invention. The former may

be accidental, and only makes known that which had previously existed; the latter implies creation, or, at least, a new
combination of old materials.

To surrender the fair honour of any discovery, by naming
it after the reigning monarch, is an absurd act of sycophancy,
which the world has too much good sense to confirm. No
family ever deserved better of literature and science than the
Medici; and yet the name of the Medician stars, assigned
by Galileo to the satellites of Jupiter, never travelled beyond
the confines of Tuscany, and was quickly dropped even in
that country. At a later date, when the planet Ceres was
discovered by Piazzi, it received the royal cognomen of
Ferdinandea, an addition never recognised by Europe, and
now forgotten everywhere. Botanists have very properly
bestowed their own names, or those of their friends, upon
the new or exotic plants which they have discovered or imported; nor is it easy to conceive a more pleasing immortality than to descend to posterity, enshrined in the petals of
a flower, like Hyacinthus, or the supposed child-deity of
India. Sir Anthony Ashley, who first planted them in this
country, has a cabbage sculptured at his feet upon his
monument; a much more honourable trophy than all the
herald's mummery, or the emblems of military prowess. A
potatoe plant would have afforded the noblest crest for Sir
Walter Raleigh, were it not deemed more honourable to
destroy our fellow-creatures in war, than to minister to their
gratification and support in peace.

DISEASE, A new and fatal.—During the prevalence
of the cholera in Ireland, a soldier hurrying into the mess-
room, told his commanding officer that his brother had been
carried off two days ago by a fatal malady, expressing his
apprehensions that the whole regiment would be exposed to a
similar danger in the course of the following week. "Good

heavens !" ejaculated the officer, "what then did he die of?"
"Why, your honour, he died of a Tuesday."

DISSENT.—When upon honest conviction, a man rejects
the faith in which he has been educated, he at least affords a
proof that he has inquired into its truth, which is by no
means the case with nine-tenths of the religious world, who
take up their father's creed, like his name, as a mere matter of
course. "He who has inquired, and come to a wrong conclusion," says the pious Locke, "is in a more gracious state,
in the sight of heaven, than he who is in the right faith, not
having inquired at all !"

DISSENTER—one who refuses the communion of the
English Church, under the fantastical notion that Christianity
may exist without a state religion, an enormously endowed
priestly nobility, wealthy spiritual sinecures, pluralities and
non-residence, overpaid drones, hunger-pinched workers,
and all the other advantages that so happily characterise our
established Church. Really these non-conformists are the
most unreasonable people upon earth ! Who but a captious
puritan would, for such trifling objections as these, undertake
the burthen of supporting *two* churches, shut himself out
from all the tempting flesh-pots of Egypt, from benefices,
dignities, rich revenues, college education, professorships,
and the innumerable fat things that may be scrambled for
within the golden pale of episcopacy? For such a perverse
self-denial there is but one way of accounting ; the man
who practises it must be neither more nor less than——
conscientious !
Causes quite independent of discipline or doctrine must
furnish a continual increase to the Dissenters. "In an intellectual pursuit of the highest order, there is a rivalry
between two classes, one feeling itself dependent for success

upon talents, zeal, piety, perseverance, and good conduct; the other being independent of all these stimulants, if they choose to disregard them, and supported in their office by the force of law, by nomination of patrons, by succession, by simonaiacal or allowed purchase, by any power or preference, in short, *except that of their flocks.* In such a contest for opinion and favour, putting differences of doctrine out of view, there can be little doubt which must ultimately prevail. The law will uphold the Church, and the people will uphold the chapels, until they become tired of supporting both, when they will determine on paying that clergyman alone, by whose services they benefit." To this consummation have the Irish dissenters already been driven by spiritual oppression; and as their English brethren are in a precisely similar predicament, it is not difficult to foresee that they will, ere long, do themselves the same justice. A plethora of dignities and wealth, combined with an atrophy of merits and followers, can never be symptoms of longevity in any Church, however firmly it may seem to be established.

DISTINCTION—*with* a difference.—" I have no objection," said a leveller, " that the ranks below me should be preserved just as they are now, but I wish to have none above me ; and that is my notion of a fair and perfect equality."

An instance of the distinction *without* a difference was offered by the Irishman who, having legs of different sizes, ordered his boots to be made accordingly. His directions were obeyed ; but, as he tried the smallest boot on his largest leg, he exclaimed, petulantly, " Confound the fellow ! I ordered him to make one larger than the other ; and, instead of that, he has made one smaller than the other."

DISTINCTIONS.—It is idle to talk of the abolition of distinctions, for Nature herself has created them. A great and happy change, however, is taking place in our estimate of these honours. Every day adds to our reverence of *in-*trinsic, and diminishes our respect for *ex*trinsic superiority. Patents of nobility, signed by the hand of God, are rising in general esteem, while those merely signed by the hand of a king are declining. Hereditary distinctions, whether of an exalting or degrading aspect, generally deteriorate their objects. It was once questioned, whether a villein, or serf, could enter heaven, and the very doubt rendered him unfit for it, just as the certainty of succeeding to honours often disqualifies their inheritor from wearing them becomingly.

DISTRESS—even when positive or superlative, is still only comparative. "Such is the pressure of the times in our town," said a Birmingham manufacturer to his agent in London, "that we have good workmen who will get up the inside of a watch for eighteen shillings."—"Pooh! that is nothing, compared to London," replied his friend;—"we have boys here who will get up the inside of a chimney for sixpence!"

DIVINITY.—If the real divinity within our souls were not more pure and consoling than the false one which fanatics create, how deplorable would be the lot of human nature! Happily, we cannot altogether get rid of the internal God, even by worshipping an external dæmon. The mercy of the Heavenly Father is indefeasible; we may desert Him, but He will not utterly desert us.

DRAM—a small quantity taken in large quantities by those who have few grains of sobriety, and no scruples of conscience. Horace Walpole records, that when one of his contemporaries died, in consequence, as it was currently said, of an over-addiction to brandy, the escutcheon affixed to the house of the deceased exhibited the common motto of "*Mors janua vitæ;*" upon which a wag observed—" Surely there has been a mistake in this inscription : it should have been ' *Mors aqua vitæ.*'"

DRAMA, Modern—every sort of drama, except tragedy and comedy;—such as melo-drama, hippo-drama, &c.

DRAWING.—This most moral of all accomplishments, as Goethe terms it, is, at the same time, the most delightful ; almost endowing its possessor with an additional sense. A landscape is the silent voice of nature, speaking in forms and colours ; and the artist who can reduce these vocal visions to painted writing, has a companionship with the outward world, an enjoyment of its beauties, and a consequent sweetness in his communion with its great Creator, of the most hallowing and enviable description. He who can thus read the face of nature, or listen to her inaudible effusions, may indeed be said to find

> " Tongues in the trees, books in the running brooks,
> Sermons in stones, and good in everything."

DREAMS—the invisible visions to which we are awake in our sleep ; the life of death ; the sights seen by the blind ; the sounds heard by the deaf ; the language of the dumb ; the sensations of the insensible ; a mystery which may afford us some vague notion of the undeveloped powers of the human mind, waiting, perhaps, the longer sleep of death, before they receive a full expansion. Objects thus presented to us can only be a wild combination, we are told, of those with which we have been previously conversant ; but in these revelations, there seems to be an occasional apocalypse of another world, or, at least, a different state of being from our present existence. What are the prevalent dreams of persons born blind? This subject has not excited inquiry, but it seems of a nature to deserve it, as it might lead to some very curious results. Are forms and figures presented to them, either animate or inanimate, and if so, do they bear any resemblance to their originals? Everything thus flitting before the mind's eye must be a creation, not a recollection, to him who can only have gathered vague notions of form from the touch, and can have no idea of colour. The dreams of maniacs, could they be detailed, would supply matter for not less interesting speculation. We may imagine them to embody forth all that is gorgeous, magnificent, rapturous, and paradisaical; or to evoke the most hideous and terrific phantasmagoria, according to the different moods of their madness. Somnambulism, which may be termed an intermediate affection between dreaming and insanity, would also present many mental diagnostics, of the most curious character, could we " observingly distil them out."

It has been asserted by medical writers, who have attentively considered the subject, that our senses and organs sink to sleep in the following succession :—1st, the sense of sight; 2nd, the taste; 3rd, the smell; 4th, the hearing; 5th, the touch. The powers of the mind may, in the meantime, be inert, active, or deranged, according to circumstances; but they are never altogether coherent. The two principal theories of dreams suppose them to originate wholly in direct impressions on the senses during sleep; or to be ascribable to the supremacy of the mind, which, being unfettered by objects of sense, takes a wider range. According to this latter supposition, how inconceivably eccentric and illimitable may be its flight, when it is released from its earthly tegument, and revels in the boundless wilds of imagination, as a liberated balloon soars into the invisible empyreum!

To illustrate the total absence of judgment in all these phantasms, Dr. Johnson used to relate the following dream.

He imagined himself to be engaged in a contest of wit, before a large literary party, with an adversary whose superior talents compelled him to retreat, filled with shame and mortification. "Had my judgment," argued the Doctor, "been as clear and active as my other mental powers, I should have recollected that my own head had furnished all the repartees of my supposed antagonist, and that I could not fail to be the victor, however the battle might terminate."

An exceedingly corpulent man, who had suffered much from the intense heat of summer, dreamt, one sultry night, that, for the sake of cooling himself, he got out of his flesh, and sate in his skeleton, suffering the air to blow through his ribs ; a mode of refrigeration which he found so delicious, that on awaking he could almost have cried, like Caliban, to fall asleep again.

DRESS—external gentility, frequently used to disguise internal vulgarity. Wise men will neither be the first to adopt a new fashion, nor the last to abandon an old one; for an affectation of singularity is only the desire to set, instead of following, the mode. Eccentricity of appearance is the contemptible ambition of being personally known to those who do not know you by name. We may hold it slavish to dress according to the judgment of fools, and the caprice of coxcombs ; but are not we ourselves *both*, when we are singular in our attire ? Mean indeed, though, doubtless, very just, must be the self-opinion of that man, who can only hope to achieve distinction by the cut of his garments. The proverb tells us, to cut our coat according to our cloth ; but we are nowhere enjoined to cut out a character by a coat.

Malvezzi says—"*i vestimenti negli animali sono molto sicuri segni della loro natura ; negli uomini del lor cervello.*"

This may be illustrated by rags as well as finery. Socrates told Antisthenes, who affected shabbiness, that he saw his pride through the holes in his coat ; and the gay attire of the coxcomb only serves to prove the more clearly, that he is "a leaden rapier in a golden sheath"—a cork leg in a silken stocking.

DRUNKENNESS—a beastly, detestable, and often punished vice, in the ignorant lower orders, whose ebriety is thrust upon the public eye as they reel along the streets,—but softened into "a glass too much," or being "a little elevated," when a well-educated gentleman is driven home in his own carriage, in a state of insensibility, and put to bed by his own servants. The half-starved wretch, who finds in casual intoxication meat, drink, clothing, fuel, and oblivion, may be fined, or put in the stocks, because he cannot afford to conceal his offence ; but the *bon vivant*, whose habitual intemperance has none of these excuses, shall escape with impunity, because he sins in a dining, instead of a tap-room. "A drunkard," says Sir Edward Coke, "who is a voluntary madman, hath no privilege thereby ;"—but he should have added, except he be a gentleman in station. To the credit of modern manners, it must be admitted that the two characters are now hardly ever found united.

Droll, though not very logical or conclusive was the reply of the tipsy Irishman, who, as he supported himself by the iron railings of Merrion Square, was advised by a passenger to betake himself home. "Ah now, be aisy ; I live in the square ; isn't it going round and round, and when I see my own door come up, won't I pop into it in a jiffey ?"

DUELLING, How to avoid.—This desirable immunity may be accomplished by a pleasanter method than by plagiarising Mr. O'Connell's oath,—videlicet, by falling in

love, when you may decline a challenge after the following
fashion of one of our old amatory poets—

> " 'Tis not the fear of death or smart,
>   Makes men averse to fight,
>   But to preserve a tender heart,
>   Not mine but Celia's right.

> " Then let your fury be supprest,
>   Not me, but Celia, spare,
>   Your sword is welcome to my breast,
>   When Celia is not there.",

DUELLIST—a moral coward, seeking to hide the pusil-
lanimity of his mind, by affecting a corporeal courage. Instead of discharging a pistol, the resort of bullies and
bravoes, the really brave soul will dare to discharge its duty
to God and man, by refusing to break the laws of both. He
is the true hero who can exclaim in the sublime language of
Voltaire, " *Je crains Dieu, cher Abner, et je n'ai d'autre
crainte.*"

DULNESS—Do *not* see the present work.—" I cannot
exactly perceive the scope of your argument, and therefore I
cannot adopt your opinion," said a gentleman with whom
Dr. Parr had been arguing. " Then, Sir," said the doctor,
" I can only say that you have the dulness of lead without
its malleability." Serjeant K—— having made two or three
mistakes, while conducting a cause, petulantly exclaimed,
" I seem to be inoculated with dulness to-day." " Inoculated, brother ? " said Erskine, " I thought you had it in the
natural way."

DUMBFOUNDER—a verbal checkmate which incapa-
citates your adversary from making another move of his
jaws. " I do not write for fools," said a boastful and asinine

pretender to literature : "I only wish to please those who have the same taste as myself, and to do this, every leaf that I produce must be full of point. Such being my feelings, what would you have me give to the world?" "Thistles!" replied a wag.

Dr. Parr was celebrated for the unsparing severity with which he could deal out his dumbfounders, when the occasion justified their infliction. A flippant chatterer, after having spoken slightingly of the miracles, exclaimed, "Well but, Doctor, what think you of the mark of the cross upon the ass's back, which they say indicates the precise spot where the animal was smitten by Balaam?"—"Why, Sir," replied the doctor, "I say that if you had a little more of the cross, and a good deal less of the ass, it would be much better for you." Upon another occasion, a shallow smatterer tauntingly asked him why he did not write a book :—"Sir, I know a method by which I might soon write a very large one." "Ay, Doctor! how so?" "Why, Sir, by putting in all that I know, and all that you do not know."

DUTY—financially, a tax which we pay to the public excise and customs ; morally, that which we are very apt to excise in our private customs. "*Les hommes*," says Voltaire, "*se piquent toujours de remplir un devoir qui les distingue.*" If singularity be a distinction, they might easily attain it by a conscientious discharge of religious and moral duty.

DUTY, Parental—sometimes consists in making our children a stalking-horse for our own failings and vices. Of all the virtuous disguises which self-love is made to assume, the most accommodating, the most sanctimonious, the most demure-looking, is the mask which gives to us the appearance of loving others.

The avaricious man, the gambling speculator, the fraudulent dealer have all the same plausible excuse; they are making fortunes for their children, which, however, they never give to them, when acquired, until the hand of death wrenches the booty from their grasp. It is remarkable too, that many of the loving fathers who boast what great things they are thus doing for their offspring, are the last to do small things for them, refusing them the most trivial indulgence, ruling them with a rod of iron, and making them at one time the stalking-horse, and at another the scape-goat of their own humours and propensities. Oh! how pleasant is it when the affectionate parent can in this manner throw a garb of goodness over his evil passions, and sin with a safe conscience!

AR, Pleasures of the—the most spiritual of all enjoyments, the least sensual of the senses. Where can its sensibilities be so well cultivated, and impart such a hallowing character to delight, as amid the various and exquisite harmonies of nature, the vocal fields, the rustling woods, the deep-mouthed and sonorous sea? Let each of these pleasant sounds, as it falls upon the drum of the ear, be as a *reveille*, calling upon our thoughts to arise, and be wafted heavenward upon the symphonious air. These are the feelings that make *all* music sacred. No wonder that the deaf are often morose and dejected, while the blind, shut out as they are from the world, almost invariably draw in cheerfulness through the ear.

EATING and DRINKING—supplying the lamp of life with cotton and oil. "The proverb's somewhat musty," but it cannot be too often repeated that we should " eat to live not live to eat," for if we make the stomach a cemetery of food, the body will soon become the sepulchre of the soul.

" Pone gulæ metas, ut sit tibi longior ætas,"

whether in this world or the next : for to make a god of your belly, is to sell yourself to the devil.

One half of mankind pass their lives in thinking how they shall get a dinner, and the other in thinking what dinner they shall get ; and the first are much less injured by occasional fasts, than are the latter by constant feasts.

ECHO—the shadow of a sound—a voice without a mouth, and words without a tongue. Echo, though represented as a female, never speaks till she is spoken to, and at every repetition of what she has heard, continues to make it less, an example recommended to the special imitation of chatterboxes and scandal-mongers.

ECONOMY—a pauper without a parish, whom no one will own or adopt, unless compelled by necessity. It has long since been driven out of every rich house, while the churchwardens and overseers take good care that it shall never be admitted into the poor-house. Government, after having long turned a deaf ear to its remonstrances, must take it up, or the government itself must break down.*

EDUCATION, Modern—a game of cross purposes. "*Aujourdhui,*" says Montesquieu, "*nous recevons trois éducations différentes ou contraires ; celle de nos pères, celle de nos*

---

* Had the author lived, he would doubtless have been gratified to find that this article—thanks to the patriotic exertions of the Whig Government—was no longer applicable, either to our parochial or national expenditure.—ED.

maîtres, celle du monde. Ce qu'on nous dit dans la dernière, renverse toutes les idées des premières. Cela vient en quelque partie, du contraste qu'il y a parmi nous, entre les engagemens de la religion et ceux du monde, chose que les anciens ne connaissaient pas." Every one's experience and observation must have confirmed the truth of this averment. At five years of age, the father begins to rub the mother out of his child ; at ten, the schoolmaster rubs out the father ; at twenty, the college rubs out the schoolmaster ; at twenty-five, the world rubs out all its predecessors, and gives us a new education, till we are old enough to take reason and religion for our pastors, when we employ the rest of our lives in unlearning all that we had previously learnt. The universe is the best university, for it teaches us to forget a great portion of what we have acquired at all the others.

When most of our colleges and public schools were founded, a knowledge of Latin and Greek was the paramount desideratum, not only because the classics were the fashionable study, but because all learning and science, whether ancient or contemporary, was confined to those tongues. The scholars, moreover, were mostly intended for the professions, an object which rendered a knowledge of Latin indispensable, the Bible and the Church service, the law and the law proceedings, as well as the mysteries of medicine, being locked up in that language. All this is now totally changed : the classics are accessible in a variety of excellent translations, —Literati publish in the language of their respective countries,—and the professions, with the solitary exception of medical prescriptions, which may be, and are learnt by heart, without the least knowledge of Latin, are all carried on in English. And yet under circumstances diametrically opposite, our educational system remains precisely the same, and boys, at a costly sacrifice of toil and suffering, waste several of the most precious years of life in laying up stores for oblivion, in composing nonsense verses, which they have the good sense to forget as rapidly as they can, and in acquiring a mere smattering of Latin and Greek, which not one in a hundred retains after he has embarked in the business or pleasures of life. Nothing has so completely survived its original aims and intentions, and nothing therefore so imperatively demands a thorough reform, as our scholastic and collegiate establishments. Aware of this fact, the founders of the London University have given it a system much better adapted to the spirit and the wants of the times. Modern and foreign literature are cultivated under able teachers; lectures are delivered on a variety of useful subjects, totally neglected at our old institutions; and professorships have been established for every branch of science with which an accomplished gentleman ought to be conversant.

It is remarkable, that while our sons continue to be educated at our old colleges and public schools upon the same system that existed several hundred years ago, the tuition of our daughters has undergone a total change. For housewifery, formerly the one thing needful, we have substituted the accomplishments which, however ornamental and attractive, are scarcely more enduring than the nonsense verses of the boy. After a ridiculous waste of money and time upon a French dancing-master, the pupil is told, upon her coming out, that as nothing is so vulgar as to dance, she must forget all her saltatory lessons, and walk through a quadrille as quietly as possible. At a not less costly outlay, she is taught by an Italian to sing a Bravura; but if colds, sickness, or time do not lay siege to her voice, she is sure to lose it when she marries, for few indeed retain their accomplishments after they have answered their purposes of procuring a husband. Thus successfully do they rival their brothers, by forgetting in two or three years, what it has required eight or ten to drill into them.

As a proof how little a college education, even when it has been most successfully prosecuted, qualifies a man for the business and duties of the world, it has been ascertained that very few of those who take their degrees with the greatest eclât, have ever attained any subsequent eminence. In Archdeacon Wrangham's *Sertum Cantabrigiense*—privately printed, Malton, 1824, is a list of those who took honours at Cambridge from 1754 to 1823. Of two thousand nine hundred names thus registered, hardly any in after life obtained the smallest distinction. Even of the seventy senior wranglers, very few became afterwards known. So much for university tests of talent!

Even the partisans of the old system, with all its cherished ineptitudes, are but the blind instruments for advancing that of which they would fain arrest the march. Rough-hew their purposes how they will, individuals, classes, nations, are all receiving an unconscious education, over which they have little control, from the divine Schoolmaster, who, looking upon the whole human race as his scholars, and generations as his successive classes, is preparing us, by the gradual development of our energies and talents, for that loftier position in the scale of existence, to which man is eventually destined.

EFFECTS—do not always result from causes, as many a lawyer, whose bill remains unpaid, knows to his cost. A suitor for the hand of a young lady at Harrogate, had been repeatedly warned that she was of a violent and ungovernable temper, but persisted in attributing the information to envy or mistake.—" At length," said the lover, relating his mishap to a friend, " I got into an argument with my dear Maria about a mere trifle, when she so far forgot herself, in a moment of passion, as to throw a cup of tea in my face." " And what was the effect?" inquired his auditor.—" Oh! *that* completely opened my eyes!"

" I was rather hot at the moment," said a man when asked how he came to commit an assault, "and so I struck the fellow." Here was an instance of an effect before a cause. Percussion generally produces heat, but in this case the heat produced the percussion.

EFFEMINACY—wearing moral petticoats. A masculine woman is much more endurable than an effeminate man; for, though both are abandoning their proper sphere, the former seeks to rise above, the latter to sink beneath, it. There is an ambition about the one, which, though it may be offensive, does not move our scorn; whereas there is a pitiful meanness in the other, which always renders it contemptible.

Even among our senators, we have ringleted effeminates, whom Nature, evidently designing them for barbers, supplied with ready-made blocks, giving them, at the same time, the tonsorial loquacity that enables them to speak to everything —except the point, and to cut everything—except a joke. Let them wield the comb, and leave the making of laws to others ; let them braid their hair, and cease to upbraid reformers ; let them abstain from Parliament, over the doors of which should be inscribed the words of Ovid—

" Sint procul à nobis juvenes ut fæmina compti."

Let them perpend the following passage of Seneca—"*Horum quis est, qui non malit rempublicam turbari, quam comam suam ? qui non sollicitior sit de capitis sui decore, quam de salute generis humani ?* "—"Which of these effeminates would not rather see the State thrown into disorder than his hair ? Which of them is not more anxious about the becoming arrangement of his curls, than the welfare of the whole human race ? "

EGOTISM—suffering the private I to be too much in the public eye. We are offended at the arrogance of Cardinal Wolsey's *ego et rex meus;* but there is a species of egotism so dignified and noble, that in the elevation which it gives to our common nature, we lose all sense of individual presumption.—Such is the character of the following passage from Milton :—

" For the world, I count it not as an inn but a hospital ; and a place not to live but to die in. The world that I regard is myself. It is mine own frame that I cast mine eye on ; for the other, I use it but like my globe, and turn it round sometimes for my recreation. Men that look upon my outside, perusing only my condition and fortunes, do err in my altitude, for I am above Atlas his shoulders. The earth is a point, not only in respect of the heavens above us, but of that heavenly and celestial part within us. That mass of flesh that circumscribes me, limits not my mind. That surface that tells the heavens they have an end, cannot persuade me I have any. I take my circle to be above three hundred and sixty. Though the number of the arc do measure my body, it comprehendeth not my mind : whilst I study to find how I am a microcosm, or little world, I find myself something more than the great. There is surely a piece of divinity to us—something that was before the elements, and owing no homage unto the sun. He that understands not this much, hath not his introductions or first lesson, and is yet to begin the alphabet of man."

ELECTION, General—hiring servants at a statute fair, which, however, will never be a fair statute, until it resumes its original triennial form. A general election, like varnish on a faded picture, draws out all the bright spots and favourable tints of our common nature. How delightful to the philanthropist to contemplate such a galaxy of purity and

glory as is then radiant in a thousand speeches and adver-
tisements. This is not the moment in which the old Member,
who is desirous of remaining as a fixture at St. Stephen's,
should be taken at his own valuation; or when the new
candidate should receive implicit credit for his pledges and
promises. They who can no longer frank letters, now frank
their own praises, which they convey to their constituents
without any fear of their being overweight. The candidates,
instead of wearing white robes, appear in white characters
of their own giving; they are all immaculate, impeccable.
There is a general avalanche of snow-like purity of purpose,
and the cardinal virtues are as common as vices at any other
time. If we had annual parliaments we should soon reach
the Millennium. Pity that men who always represent themselves so amiably in their speeches, should sometimes mis-
represent themselves so lamentably in private, and their
constituents in public life!—If the senatorial dignity could
exempt from reproach, as well as from arrest, and the man
who cannot make laws for himself, could legislate for a
nation, our House of Commons would be no common
house.

ELEVATION—of Station is very often accompanied with
depression of spirits. Success disappoints us; we feel ourselves out of our sphere, and sigh for the lost happiness of
our humbler days. "You see how languid the carp are,"
said Madame de Maintenon to her friend, when looking into
a marble fish-pond at Marly: "they are like me—*they regret
their mud.*"

ELOPEMENT—beginning in disobedience that which
generally terminates in misery.

EMBALMING—making a flesh statue;—eternalising a

corpse ;—perpetuating the perishable with more pains than we take to save that which is immortal.

ENDOWMENTS, Church.—See Poison ; but do *not* see the Bible. An old tradition bears, that when Constantine, the emperor, first endowed the Church, a voice was heard from heaven, crying out, " This day is poison poured into her ! "—Whatever may be thought of the tradition, no one can doubt the fulfilment of the prophecy.

Wherever Religion has been the mother of Wealth, the daughter has invariably devoured the parent.

ENNUI—a French word for an English malady, which generally arises from the want of a want, and constitutes the complaint of those who have nothing to complain of. By the equalising provisions of nature, the rich, idle, and luxurious, are thus brought down to the level of their seeming inferiors, and made to envy those who envy them. When this ugly Goliah haunts the mind, he is only to be subdued by exertion and occupation.—" Throw but a stone, the giant dies." Authors have too much to do with printers' devils, to be annoyed with blue devils. They may inflict, but they seldom suffer, *ennui*. No exorcism for the spleen, and the vapours, like that of the Muse. When Bellerophon went forth to conquer the Chimæra, he mounted Pegasus.

ENTHUSIASM—that effervescence of the heart, or the imagination, which is the most potent stimulus of our nature, where it stops short of mental intoxication. " Conscience," says Madame de Stael, " is, doubtless, sufficient to conduct the coldest character into the road of virtue ; but enthusiasm is to conscience, what honour is to duty : there is in us a superfluity of soul, which it is sweet to consecrate to the beautiful, when the good has been accomplished. Our genius and our imagination require to be gratified in this world; and the law of duty, however sublime it may be, is not sufficient to make us taste all the wonders of the heart and the head."

ENVY—punishing ourselves for being inferior to our neighbours. If, instead of looking at what our superiors possess, we could see what they actually enjoy, there would be much less envy, and more pity, in the world.

" The envious man," says St. Gregory, " is made unhappy, not by his own misfortunes, but by the successes of others; and, on the other hand, he does not enjoy his own good fortune so much as the misfortunes of his neighbours. *"Invidus non suis malis, sed alienis bonis infelix est; et contrà, non suo bono sed malis proximis felix."* Our affected contempt of greatness is only an envious attempt to lift ourselves above the great, and thus achieve an imaginary superiority. "Since we cannot attain grandeur," says Montaigne, "let us take our revenge by abusing it."

The envy that grudges the successes for which it would want the courage to contend, was well rebuked by the French Marshal Lefévre. One of his friends, expressing the most unbounded admiration of his magnificent hotel, and exquisite *cuisine*, exclaimed, at the end of every phrase, " How fortunate you are!" "I see you envy me," said the Marshal; "but come, you shall have all that I possess at a much cheaper rate than I myself paid for it; step down with me into the court-yard, you shall let me fire twenty musket shots at you, at the distance of thirty paces, and if I fail to bring you down, all that I have is yours.—What! you refuse!" said the Marshal, seeing that his friend demurred,—" know, that before I reached my present eminence, I was obliged to stand more than a thousand musket shots, and, *sacre!* those who pulled the triggers were nothing like thirty paces from me."

EPICURE.—An epicure has no sinecure; he is unmade, and eventually dished by made dishes. Champagne falsifies its name, when once it begins to affect his system; his stomach is so deranged in its punctuation, that his colon makes a point of coming to a full stop; keeping it up late, ends in his being laid down early; and the *bon vivant* who has been always hunting pleasure, finds at last, that he has been only whipping and spurring, that he might be the sooner in at his own death !

EPITAPHS—giving a good character to parties on their going into a new place, who sometimes had a very bad character in the place they have just left. For the *de mortuis nil nisi bonum*, it would be an improvement to substitute *nil nisi verum;* since the fear of posthumous disrepute would be an additional incentive to living good conduct. No man could pass through a truth-telling churchyard, without feeling the full value of character.

What can more impressively stamp the evanescency of man and all his works, than an epitaph on a whole nation, which shall afford nearly the sole evidence of its ever having existed? Such are the cinerary urns of the Etruscans, of whose history we have little other record than their tombs, and of whose literature few other remains than their alphabet. A whole empire *stat nominis umbra !* The signs have survived the ideas of which they were the symbols : the chisel has outlasted the statue. Volterra, and other great Etruscan cemeteries, may be termed the skeletons of their cities.

Few more appropriate epitaphs than the common Latin one of " *Sum quod eris, fui quod sis*"—" I am what thou shalt be, I was what thou art."

Beloe, in his anecdotes, gives a good punning epitaph on William Lawes, the musical composer, who was killed by the Roundheads,

> " Concord is conquer'd !   In this urn there lies
> The master of great Music's mysteries ;
> And in it is a riddle, like the cause,
> Will Lawes was slain by men whose *Wills* were *Laws*."

More witty than decorous was the epitaph composed in the reign of Henry III., for a Sir John Calfe, who died young.—

> " O Deus omnipotens, Vituli miserere Joannis,
> Quem mors præveniens noluit esse bovem."

Sir Christopher Wren's inscription in St. Paul's Church—"*Si monumentum quæris, circumspice*"—would be equally applicable to a physician, buried in a churchyard ; both being interred in the midst of their own works.

In the epitaph of Cardinal Onuphrio at Rome, there breathes a solemn, almost a bitter conviction of the vanity of earthly grandeur—"*Hic jacet umbra, cinis—nihil.*"—Here lies a shadow—ashes, nothing. There is great tenderness and beauty in the two lines found upon an ancient Roman tomb, supposed to be addressed by a young wife to her surviving husband :

> " Immatura peri, sed tu, felicior, annos
> Vive tuos, conjux optime, vive meos."

But a still more simple and affecting epitaph is the following, translated verbatim from a tomb at Montmartre, near Paris :—" To the memory of M. Jobart, a most excellent husband and father. His inconsolable widow still continues to carry on the grocery business in the Rue St. Denis, No. 242, near the Café Chinois."

EQUAL—that which a man of talent will seldom find among his superiors. As the winds and waters, abrasion and gravitation, are perpetually tending towards a physical equalisation, by lowering mountains and filling up valleys, so, in the moral world, does the progress of social improvement gradually tend to equalise all ranks, by reducing the higher, and elevating the lower ; a levelling process, equally conducive to the happiness and melioration of both. Civilization is, in fact, a gravitation towards that happy medium which is the centre of attraction to the social circle. Almost every man is a loser by being elevated above the sphere to which he is habituated. When the Duke of Orleans proposed to make Fontenelle perpetual President of the Academy of Sciences, his reply was—"Take not from me, my Lord, the delight of living with my equals."

ERROR of calculation.—The life of nine-tenths of mankind is a gross error of calculation, since they attach themselves to the evanescent, and neglect the permanent, accumulating riches in a world from which they are constantly running away, and laying up no treasures in that eternity to which every day, hour, minute, brings them nearer and nearer.

ESPRIT DE CORPS—is a corporate partiality or prejudice ; a feeling of clanship and confraternity ; a selfishness at second hand, which induces us to prefer the members of our own club, guild, or coterie, not only to others, but to reason and justice. It prefers Plato to truth, even though Plato be personally unknown, provided he belongs to the same *clique*. Nationality is but *esprit de corps* on a large scale, selfishness spread over the surface of a whole country; and the propensity sometimes exhibits itself in still more extensive divisions. In hunting or baiting wild beasts, there is a strong feeling of humanity, or, rather, of inhumanity, against bestiality. We sympathise with the basest of our own species, rather than with the noblest of the animal race.

Among ourselves, there is a sexual *esprit de corps,*—the men siding with the males, the women with the females; the single with the single, and the married with the married. Of this latter propensity advantage was taken by an unfortunate Irishman, who, being arraigned for accidentally killing his wife, contrived, by objecting to the bachelors, to procure a jury of married men, when he stated that the deceased, an habitual drunkard, had used the most insulting language at the moment of the fatal occurrence. This appeal came so completely home to the business and bosoms of his auditors, several of whom had not improbably been placed in similar circumstances, that they were presently agreed in their decision, when the foreman coming forward, and addressing himself to the Judge, exclaimed, with a voice and look of great energy—" Please, my Lord, our vardict is—Sarved her right!"

ESTATE, a landed one for all!—Terra Firma for *my* money. Well may it be called real property; there is none other that deserves the name. What are public securities, as they are impudently termed? Ask the impoverished bond-holders of the South American States, or of Greece. Neither their new nor old governments, neither despotism nor republicanism, can give certain tangibility or visibility to that ghost of defunct money yclept a dividend. What will tithes soon be worth in England?—what they are now worth in Ireland. In ten years, the claim for tenths will be no more observed than are the ten commandments at present. What is the value of houses? It is notorious that they are everywhere falling, especially the very old ones; rents threaten to be all peppercorns; house owners will not get salt to their porridge, even if they distrain upon their tenants, and make quarter day a day without quarter. No—give me land. The man who walks upon his own estate carries himself erect, and plants his foot upon the ground with an air of confidence and consequence.

Perhaps I feel this the more sensibly, because I have not a single acre in possession. Nothing, however, can prevent my succeeding to a small estate which I have lately been inspecting. It certainly possesses many advantages, being tithe-free, and the land-tax redeemed. In this snug retreat, which is perfectly sequestered, you are surrounded with wood, and yet close to a populous neighbourhood, to the parish church, and the high road. Its proprietor enjoys several privileges and advantages: he pays no taxes, is exempt from serving in the militia, or sitting upon juries, his privacy is undisturbed by the impertinent intrusion of neighbours, he has no cares by day, and he is sure of a sound sleep at night. When a new occupant comes to take possession, he usually arrives in a coach and four, with numerous attendants, and he is not only received with bell-ringing, but the clergyman, and a portion of the parishioners, go out to meet him, and escort him home with much ceremony. The house, though it can hardly be called anything better than a mere country box, has so many recommendations, that there is no instance of an occupant quitting it, after he has once given it a fair trial.

Readers! whether gentle or simple, you need not envy me my expectations. A similar landed estate is entailed upon every one of you, and upon your children's children. If you want a description of it, refer to Blair's poem of—"The Grave."

One of the Roman emperors wept that nothing could prevent the master of the wide world from being finally imprisoned in an urn. I would counsel some of our landed proprietors—

> " large-acred men,
> Lords of fat Evesham, and of Lincoln fen "—

who, in the pride of their possessions, "bestride the narrow earth like a Colossus," to cast their eyes downwards, if looking upwards will not teach them humility, and to reflect that their huge estates must inevitably shrink into six feet by two !

ETYMOLOGY—sending vagrant words back to their own parish. It was said of Menage, that in requiring every word to surrender its passport, he not only inquired whence it came, but whither it was going.

An ancient grammarian tells us that the Greek word ἄω, to breathe, consists of alpha and omega, the first and last letters of the alphabet, because to inspire and to expire, form the beginning and ending of man's life. This is a fine instance of ὕστερον πρότερον, or putting the cart before the horse ; the learned philologist having forgotten that men breathe before they speak, and that languages long preceded the time of Cadmus and the invention of letters and alphabets. While upon the subject I may mention that the word *sack* is found in all languages, which a profound antiquary has explained, by suggesting that it was necessary to leave that primitive word, in order that every man, when he took his departure from the tower of Babel, might ask for his own bag. Titles of dignity, derived from age, seem also to have spread from the same root into a great variety of languages ; our sir, signor, senator, and perhaps seneschal, being identical with the scheik, shah, and aga of the orientals, and the schachem of the red Indians. Titles inferring superior age do not, however, always command our respect, as, for instance, in the case of our London elder or aldermen.

Somewhat far-fetched was the conceit of an erudite etymologist, who maintained that the term bag-pipe was originally a Hebrew word, signifying a larger sort of sack-but, sack and bag being synonymous terms, and a butt being half a pipe.

Learned philologists are very apt to imitate the ignorant butcher, who spent a whole morning in searching for the knife which he held in his mouth—a wild-goose chase, which has been eminently illustrated in their endless wanderings for the origin of the word danger, when it was difficult to stir a step without stumbling over its real etymology. We need not go any further back than the siege of Troy to discover it at once. After the capture of that city, by the well-known stratagem of the wooden horse, an event with which every Roman became familiar, only twelve hundred years afterwards, through the writings of Virgil, it was customary to exclaim, whenever any fraud or trick was suspected, "*Danaos gerit?*"—"Are there any Greeks in this pretended horse?" —meaning any cheat or imposture. The phrase was soon proverbial, and with the habitual indolence of the Italians, was eventually contracted into one word, by taking the initial syllable of each; so that whenever they smelt a rat, as we say in English, or anticipated any perils, they exclaimed, interrogatively, "dan-ger?" Is it not almost incredible, that so obvious a derivation should have been overlooked by the most acute of our etymologists? Henceforth let us hear no more of the butcher and his knife.

In searching for the signification of words, we are not, however, always to take them *au pied de la lettre*, or we might define a hypocrite to be a judge of horses—a sycophant, as a fig-seer—a beldam, as a handsome lady— consideration, as a collection of stars—understanding, as a pair of shoes—and sincere as unwaxed. Into these and similar errors, the enlightened etymologist is in no fear of falling, for he will ever bear in mind the fundamental rule of his art, viz., to pay little attention to consonants and none to vowels. Why should letters obstruct him when he is considering things of such importance as words?

EXAGGERATION, Intemperate—diminishing by addition, as the word small is made smaller by appending two more letters to it. When a man asserts too much, whether in the shape of praise or censure, we take our revenge by falling into an opposite error, and believe too little. The same effect is often produced by that confusion of ideas or terms which is designated a bull. A Radical, inveighing against the rapacity of the clergy, gave it as his decided opinion, that if they had their own way, they would raise the tithes from a tenth to a twentieth. On the other hand, an intended diminution, by the same figure of speech, may amount to an exaggeration. "I have just met our old acquaintance Daly," said an Irishman to his friend, "and was sorry to see he has almost shrunk away to nothing. You are thin and *I* am thin, but he is thinner than both of us put together." Did the Hibernian sailor exaggerate or diminish when, in describing the weather, he said, "There was but little wind, but what there was, was uncommonly high."

EXAMPLE.—It is much more easy to imitate bad example than good, because it has our natural inclination on its side. Perverse natures find a positive gratification in doing wrong. A man of this stamp, who was remarkably fond of pork, once expressed his regret that he had not been born a Jew, in order that he might enjoy the double pleasure of eating his favourite viand, and sinning at the same time.

EXCEPTIONS—prove every rule, as we are told, except the rule that "every rule has its exception." Nothing can be rendered more exceptionable than an exception, even when accompanied with an invidious eulogy. According to Saville, poets are the best of all authors—except prose writers. F——, defending a kind-hearted unmarried woman, whose character, however, was far from immaculate, exclaimed "Out of the pale of marriage and celibacy, I protest that I do not know a more respectable person." Cases may occur where parties are not to be conciliated, either by their inclusion or exclusion. "How many fools, including yourself, went to the lecture on phrenology?" demanded a collegian to his comrade, who, instead of answering the inquiry, took the term applied to him in high dudgeon.—"Well, then," resumed his friend; "how many fools were there *without* reckoning yourself?"

Under this head we may insert one of the very few jokes attributed to William Pitt. As Lord Warden of the Cinque Ports, he presided at a public meeting, held in Dover, during the war, for the purpose of raising a volunteer corps, when the secretary, in drawing up the conditions on which they were to be embodied, said to the chairman, "I suppose, sir, that I am to insert the usual clause—not to serve out of the country."—"Certainly, certainly," smiled Pitt, "except in case of invasion!"

Few will be unacquainted with Swift's saving clause, when, in his anxiety to promote the products and manufactures of the Irish, he recommended them to burn everything that came from England, except her coals.

EXCULPATION, A satisfactory.—"My good friend!" exclaimed an enraged author, who had been lampooned and libelled in a review, "I have strong reason to suspect that I have received this stab in the dark from that rascal M——." —"Make your mind perfectly easy," said his friend; "M—— is the last man to give you a stab in the dark; first, because he always held you in light estimation, and, secondly, because I know him to be a fellow who would not stick at anything."

Ingenious enough, though, perhaps, not literally true, was the excuse of the day-boarder, who, being asked one morning why he came to school so late, replied that, owing to the hard frost and the slipperiness of the ground, he had taken two steps backwards for one step forwards. "In that case," inquired the master, "how did you manage to get here at all?"—"Oh, sir! I turned about and came the other way."

EXCUSE—confessing our faults by attempting to excuse them—*Qui s'excuse s'accuse.* Good intentions, with which, according to Wesley, hell is paved, are no defence of evil actions. We have all of us pleas and evasions enough not only for leaving undone what we ought to have done, but for doing what we ought not to have done.

A gentleman, who had just put aside two bottles of capital ale to recreate some friends, discovered, just before dinner, that his servant, a country bumpkin, had emptied them both. "Scoundrel!" said his master, "what do you mean by this?" —"Why, sir, I saw, plain enough, by the clouds, that it were going to thunder, so I drank up the yale at once, lest it should turn sour, for there's nothing I do abominate like waste." Fuseli, when he failed in any of his serious caricatures, used to complain that Nature put him out: and the sluttish house-maid, when scolded for the untidiness of the chambers, exclaimed, "I'm sure, the rooms would be clean enough, if it were not for the nasty sun, which is always showing the dirty corners."

EXPEDIENTS—remedies for half our pains and sorrows, did we but know how to find and to apply them. There must, certainly be a charm in enacting the part of Jaques—

in having "a cue for villanous melancholy," and a "sigh like Tom o' Bedlam." Whether it be that our self-love is gratified by exciting sympathy, or our vanity by being made the subject of conversation, it is unquestionable that we cling to our little ills and ailments as if they conferred a sort of distinction. Never could I entirely agree with the pensive poet when he exclaims—

> "Go ! you may call it madness, folly,
> You shall not chase my griefs away,
> There's such a charm in melancholy,
> I would not if I could be gay."

But I can accord with the French writer, who affirms, that a woman always finds her physician and confessor the most delightful companions in the world, because she is constantly talking to them about herself, her complaints, and her peccadilloes. Men are precisely the same in the auricular confessions of society, and almost any girl may be sure of winning their affections, provided she be a patient and persevering listener to their aches and annoyances, real or imaginary. This must be the secret reason why we often refuse to avail ourselves of expedients which would effectually remove all our grievances, and which are too palpable to have escaped our notice. A lady, of delicate health, who loved to talk of her rheums and rheumatics, complained to S—— that she rarely went out to make purchases without catching cold, because they never kept their shop-doors shut. "My dear madam," said S——, " how easily you might avoid all this ! —You should make it a rule never to go a shopping except on a Sunday." "You sot of a fellow!" exclaimed a poor woman to her husband: "you are always at the public-house, getting drunk with hot purl, while I am at home with nothing to drink but cold water."—" Cold, you silly jade ! " hiccoughed the husband, " why don't you warm it ? "

Strange, that neither of the females should have previously hit upon such obvious and satisfactory expedients ! Infinitely quick and apt in expedients, was the manager of a country theatre, who, when requested, by a lady of rank in the neighbourhood, to get up the play of Henry the VIIIth, regretted that the state of his company would not allow it ; but added that they could very well manage to perform the two parts of Henry the IVth, which would come to exactly the same thing.

EXTEMPORE—a premeditated impromptu.

EYE-GLASS—a toy which enables a coxcomb to see others, and others to see that he is a coxcomb.

ABLES—giving human intellects to brutes, in imitation of Nature, who sometimes gives brute intellects to men.

FACE—the silent echo of the heart.

FAITH.—If all the innumerable false and forgotten faiths, and all the myriads of men who have contentedly died in their belief, after having spent a long life in hating or persecuting those who disbelieved them, could be presented at once to our apprehension and sight, what a lowering impression would it give of human reason, and how forcibly would it inculcate humility as to our own opinions and toleration towards the opinions of others !— And this would be the genuine feeling of Christianity, for the Scriptures assure us, more than once, that the Lord "ordaineth his arrows against the persecutors."

FALSE POINTS.—The author who pays more attention to the manner than the matter of his writings, and excites an expectation by his studied conceits and antitheses, which is not justified by the subject or the sentiment, may be compared to an ill-trained dog, which by stopping to make a false point where there are no birds, only makes game of his master. Punning writers are comical dogs of this sort, who often raise our expectation, but seldom enable us to bring down a thought, or put anything into our memory-bag. There are dull dogs, on the contrary, who weary you by beating about the bush, and who seem to make a point of never making a point, even though they may be surrounded by numerous coveys of intellectual game. The writings of Jeremy Bentham constitute a well-stocked preserve of valuable thoughts, entrenched in such a *chevaux de frise* of crooked, crabbed, and impenetrable language, that nobody can get at them. Some one said of his *style* that it was a five-barred gate with spikes at top, and furze bushes on either side. It is not any known tongue, it is Benthamese, or perhaps a variety of those that sprung up in the hotbed of Mr. Irving's chapel. One cannot defend its obscurity, as Balzac did that of Tertullian, by saying that it resembles the darkness of polished ebony, which throws a certain splendour around. Through such impediments, few men would think of forcing their way, any more than of breaking their teeth with a hickory nut for the sake of the kernel.

There are conversational dogs, who by making a dead point, as if they were about to start a *bon-mot*, will induce you to cock your ear and prepare for an explosion of laughter ; after which they leave you miserably in the lurch. Of this a notable instance was afforded by the late facetious Jack Taylor, who became somewhat forgetful towards the close of his career. "Did I ever tell you," he inquired, " of a famous good thing I once said to Du B——? He was alluding to my former occupation of an oculist, in which he said it was no wonder I had failed, since a man must have been blind indeed before he would apply to *me.*— Well, Sir, that was very good ; but I blew him completely to atoms by a retort I made. I can't recollect just now what it was, but you may depend upon it, my dear friend, it was a most capital thing, and made a great laugh at the time ! "

A man must be reduced to great straits before he can think of living upon the good things he has forgotten.

FAME, Literary—being partially known to-day and universally forgotten to-morrow. To what does this posthumous existence amount? At most it is but a question of one small link in the circular chain of eternity. He who writes in a modern language, is but the suicide of his own fame : scribbling on the sand what the next wave of time will obliterate ; he gets a short respite, not a pardon from oblivion ! Everything is incessantly passing away, the physical and the moral, the corporeal and the intellectual ;—the very elements of nature are subject to decay. Not that this would affect—— as an author, for in his writings there is little or nothing of nature. In one sense they are eternal—" For he who reads them, reads them to no end." Literary fame is more easily caught than kept. If you do nothing you are forgotten, and if you write and fail, your former success is thrown in your teeth. He who has a reputation to maintain has a wild beast in his house, which he must constantly feed, or it will feed upon him. So indifferent was Fontenelle to fame and reputation of all sorts, that he is recorded to have said, " If I had a paper in my bureau, the disclosure of which would make my name infamous and detestable for ever, I would not take the trouble to destroy it, provided I could be quite sure that it would never appear in my lifetime." This is pushing indifference into a heartless misanthropy. What can a man have cared for others, who cared so little for himself?

FANATIC—a religionist, whose irreligious gloom and intolerance are generally ascribable to disease, either bodily or mental. We are told in Scripture, not to be as the hypocrites, who disfigure their faces ; but the sour miserables, who go groaning and scowling about this beautiful and cheerful world, if they do not literally infringe the precept, seem to steep their countenances in vinegar, as if to preserve them from contagion, and, wearing their hearts in their looks, frown both upon God and man. They are the order of men. of whom Lord Bacon says, that they "bring down the Holy Ghost in the shape of a vulture or a raven, instead of in the likeness of a dove ; and hang from the bark of a Christian Church the flag of a bark of pirates and assassins." They appear to think with their spleen, write with their gall, and pray with their bile; no wonder, therefore, that they are perpetually canting about "the beauty of sickness." It is at these seasons that the new light flashes upon their cracked sculls ; so true is the averment of Waller, that—

> " The soul's dark cottage, batter'd and decay'd,
>   Lets in new lights thro' chinks which time has made :"

and the wittier observation of Swift, that—" When our earthly tabernacles are disordered and desolate, shaken and out of repair, the spirit delights to dwell within them ; as houses are said to be haunted when they are forsaken and gone to decay." The countenances acquired by the mistaken endeavours of these men to insure themselves against the fires of the next world, remind one of the brazen Gorgons and chimæras nailed upon our houses, as insurance plates against fire in this world. Some, like the Phœnix, tell us that they are seeking regeneration amid flames and agony ; some, like the Pelican, are emblems of the tortures they inflict upon their own breast.

> Fanaticism's flame arises,
> Like a volcano's, by surprises,
> Foretells its coming by a grumbling
> Or inward motion, stir and rumbling,
> Breaks out at length, and roars hubbubish,
> Throwing up endless loads of rubbish,
> With gleams that only show the gloom,
> And heat that serves but to consume ;
> And when its baleful sulphurous light
> Has shed around a withering blight,
> The fierce, but evanescent flashes,
> Subside again in smoke and ashes.

FANATICISM — the daughter of ignorance, and the mother of infidelity. Like every other excess, fanaticism provokes a reaction ; the cold fit of spiritual sickness succeeds the hot one ; and the patients forgetting that the reverse of wrong is not always right, swing to the contrary extreme of profligacy and irreligion. Our English puritans, with their ascetical bigotry, generated the profane licentiousness of Charles the Second's reign, just as the intolerant spirit, and invidious splendours of the French Hierarchy, provoked that anti-religious fanaticism which swept away both the throne and the altar. These are examples from which our Irvingites and our bench of bishops might equally draw instruction, if the voice of the past were not as an unknown tongue to both parties.

FASHION—a power as invisible and as despotic as the grand Lama of Thibet. It is said she is a goddess, but no one has ever seen her face, though all aspire to be acquainted with her Proteus forms. Her mandates, of which the origin is utterly unknown, are nevertheless understood and communicated by some inscrutable instinct, and obeyed with a still more inexplicable and unenquiring submission. The rich and the independent are the most eager to become her abject slaves; and as spaniels are the most fawning, when worst treated, so do her votaries delight in their idol, in proportion as her reign is tyrannical, her fancies capricious, and her tastes preposterous. In the service of this fickle and ungrateful despot, who casts off her most faithful followers, unless they will blindly conform to her ever-changing vagaries, the timid and delicate willingly encounter pain, the indolent inconvenience and labour, the parsimonious expense. Many leave the tradesman and the tax-gatherer unpaid, that they may voluntarily tax themselves to supply offerings to this mysterious goddess, who finds her strongest supporters among the weak, her most faithful adherents among the inconstant, her warmest admirers among those who admire nothing but themselves. One would not object to the prevalent notion that whatever is fashionable is right, if our rulers of the mode would contrive that whatever is right should be fashionable.

FAVOURITES—persons undervalued by the many because they are over-valued by one.—Hatred, however, of favourites is only the love of favour. We dislike them, not because they are unworthy of their elevation, but because we ourselves cannot attain it. Even where their demerits may justify our censure, it proceeds from envy rather than an abstract sense of rectitude. In like manner the justice which we refuse to great men when living, and willingly concede to them after death, does not emanate from our love of their virtues, but from our hatred of those who have succeeded to their high offices. We are not less liberal of our praise when it can do no good, than of our abuse when it can annoy and injure. For an exemplification of this double injustice, we may refer to some of our critics. In proportion as they lowered an author beneath his fair standard while living, they will raise him above it after death, in order to make his survivors look little. Their generosity is all posthumous : they tear the laurels from your head to hang them on your tomb ; they pick your pocket to pay you in post obits ; your winding-sheet is the only one with which they find no fault; they accelerate your death, and then do their best to make you live.

" *La faveur*," says La Bruyere, " *met l'homme au dessus de ses égaux, et sa chute au dessous.*"

FEAR—a real evil often created by the anticipation of an imaginary one. As we can but be frightened when the danger arrives, our previous terrors are but so much unnecessary addition to the annoyance. They who are most afraid of a cold, or the cholera, are the most likely to catch them : so it is with many other evils, mental as well as bodily. Like the nettle, they only sting the timid ; grasp them firmly and they are innocuous. Fly from them and they pursue you ; face them and they are gone. " The fear of ill exceeds the ill we fear," and there are circumstances in which men have been known to rush headlong into danger, in order to get rid of the intolerable apprehension of it. This is to be terrified out of terror.—Fear is a prodigious magnifier, especially where it has been excited by any unusual object. No traveller ever saw a small wolf; no landsman ever experienced a gale at sea that did not appear to be a tornado : every thing is comparative. Fear, in short, makes us imitate the silly wheatear, who flies into the fowler's snare, in order to avoid the shadow of a passing cloud. There are occasions, however, upon which no man should fear Fear, for it is the most potent of moralists.

What anchorites—as my punning friend T. H. justly observes—we all became in England, when our stomachs were literally turned by the fear of the cholera. Esculent vegetables were pronounced uneatable—even the tailors forswore cabbage : people looked black upon green-peas, and eschewed with horror the salads they once chewed with pleasure. As to fruits, it was fruitless to put them on the table : the dessert was deserted; every apple was a forbidden one; currants were no longer current; it was dangerous to pare a pear, and still more so to pine for pine. Some forsook their French wines, and took to port, as the only safe harbour; others gave up their spirits at the very moment when they most wanted to keep them up; and a few paid more than usual attention to their temper, because they had been cautioned against every thing liable to turn sour.

An inveterate dram-drinker being told that the cholera with which he was attacked was incurable, and that he would speedily be removed to a world of pure spirits, replied, "Well, that's a comfort at all events, for it's very difficult to get any in this world."

FEE, Doctor's—often the purchase-money for that which the vendor cannot sell. See Fee Simple. A certain Esculapian, never known to refuse his golden honorarium, not having received it one morning from a patient whom he had been long attending, affected to be searching about very earnestly upon the floor. "What are you looking for, Doctor?" inquired the sick man. "For my fee," was the reply; "not finding it in my hand, I suspect I must have dropped it." "No, Doctor, no; you have made a small mistake; it is I who have dropped it!"

FEUDALISM—holding lands by tenure of military service, and thus perpetuating war and usurpation. The spirit and principle of the feudal system being that of the many for the few, its main pillars are the supremacy of the sword—primogeniture—hereditary nobility—and despotic monarchy. Such are the distinguishing features of the dark ages. The spirit of the present era is federalism, commerce, peace, the principle of the few for the many, and the attainment of the greatest possible happiness for the greatest possible number, which is silently but surely leading to the modification of primogeniture, the probable suppression, at no distant period, of hereditary legislators, and the encompassment of limited monarchy with republican institutions. England, France, Spain, and Portugal, are assuming the federal form, while the northern states of Europe retain the feudalism, which they were the first to inflict upon the south.

FICTION, Works of.—Among other objections to these fascinating productions, it has been urged that they create a habit of feeling pity or indignation, without affording us an opportunity to relieve distress, or resist oppression, and by thus awakening our sympathies to imaginary claims, dispose them to slumber when called upon by real ones. The heart, it is argued, may be softened till it is hardened, as there are metals which acquire a greater induration the oftener they are melted. This ingenious theory is more plausible than true. All our benevolent sympathies will be corroborated by exercise, even when not called forth by any real object, as the archer will strengthen his arm by the practice of shooting into the air, and the soldier by engaging in sham-fights learns how to conduct himself in real ones. To suppose that figments weaken our susceptibility to facts, is to imagine that dreams will unfit us for waking realities, and that smoke is more tangible than solids. If the maintainer of this theory will request some kind friend to throw at his head the most pathetic volume ever written, it may safely be predicted that the shadow, if it misses him, will make a less sensible impression upon his feelings, than the substance, if it hits him.

FLATTERY, see Flummery.—The hocus-pocus non-sense with which our ears are sometimes cajoled, in order that we may be more effectually bamboozled and deceived. Unbounded is the respect and politeness with which the practised adulator throws dust in your eyes, when he wants to pick your pocket, or to make a fool of you. A man's flattery, to be really good, ought not only to be as keen as his sword, but as polished. By no means is it so easy a weapon to wield as many people imagine: it is like a flail, which if not adroitly used, will box your own ears, instead of tickling those of the corn. Let it be taken for granted, that while many women will accept a compliment to their beauty at the expense of their understanding, very few will relish a compliment to their talents if it derogate from their personal charms. Lady G——, whose ten lustres have somewhat dimmed the lustre of her attractions, consented in a Parisian party to assist in getting up an extemporaneous *Proverbe*, and to appear as Calypso. In answer to the compliments she received at the conclusion, she declared that she had done her best, but added, that to represent Calypso properly, one should be young and handsome. "Not at all," said an old General, wishing to be very polite, "your ladyship is a proof to the contrary; nothing could look better from the further end of the Saloon, and nothing could be better acted: as to youth and beauty, the distance supplies all that." "In that case, General! I wonder that you do not always keep at a distance," was the retort.

FLOWERS—the terrestrial stars that bring down heaven to earth, and carry up our thoughts from earth to heaven:—the poetry of the Creator, written in beauty and fragrance.

"He who does not love flowers," says Ludwig Tieg, a German writer, "has lost all fear and love of God." Another German author defines woman as something between a flower and an angel.

FOOL.—The Dandy reader may please to see——Looking-glass. Folly, nevertheless, has found other defenders than the author of the *Encomium Moriæ*, for it has been seriously maintained by a modern writer, that none but a fool will attempt to live without folly, and that the greatest of all follies is to be wiser than others. Let the fool then be comforted; he was never guilty of *this* absurdity.

FORGIVENESS—is not always the noblest revenge for an injury, since it may proceed from spite, rather than from a generous forbearance. "I never used revenge," says Lord Herbert, of Cherbury,—"as leaving it alway to God, who, the less I punish mine enemies, will inflict so much the more punishment on them." Perhaps his lordship had been reading the 25th chapter of Proverbs, where it is said, "If thine enemy be hungry, give him bread to eat, and if he be thirsty, give him water to drink, for then shalt thou heap coals of fire upon his head, and the Lord shall reward thee." This may be questionable morality, but it is at all events better to do good with a bad motive, than evil with a good one; for a virtuous action may benefit many, whereas a wrong feeling can only implicate the single individual from whom it emanates. In the former case, too, the example may be imitated without the unworthy impulse; as in the latter it may be followed without the redeeming incitement.

FORTUNE—a blind goddess, who sometimes bestows her smiles upon fools, in order to reconcile men of sense to her frowns; and often runs from the proud, to revisit the wretched.—A man of fortune is one who is so unfortunate as to be released from the necessity of employment for the mind, and exercise for the body, the two great constituents of health and happiness; who has every thing to fear and nothing to hope; and who consequently pays in anxiety and ennui more than the value of his money. Fortune is painted blind, in order to show her impartiality; but when she cheers the needy with hope, and depresses the wealthy with distrust, methinks she confers the richest boon on the poorest man, and injures those upon whom she bestows her favours.

Te colimus, Fortuna, Deam, is, nevertheless, the motto to almost every man's conduct, however he may disclaim the confession with his lips; and few have a more ready excuse for their homage than the Grecian sage, who being asked why philosophers always ran after rich men, while rich men never courted philosophers, replied, " Because the latter know that they want money, while the former do not know that they want wisdom." Who so independent of the blind goddess as the ruined gamester, when he exclaimed, after a run of ill luck, " O spiteful Fortune! you may make me lose as much as you please, but I defy you to make me pay!"

Dryden evinces no great respect for this deity, when he exclaims—

> " Fortune a goddess is to fools alone,
> The wise are always masters of their own."

FORTUNE-TELLER—a pickpocket, discerning enough to limit his or her depredations to gulls and simpletons. The girl who told the gipsy by whom she had been promised a large fortune, that she might deduct another sixpence, provided she would realize her prediction, and pay over the remainder of the money at once, little dreamt that she **was** translating a thought of old Eunius, the Roman poet, who says, speaking of fortune tellers—

" Quibus divitias pollicentur, ab iis drachmam petunt,
De divitiis deducant drachmam, reddant cætera."

It is remarkable that in our aspirations after wealth, we never betake ourselves to the wealthy, who might be the most likely to communicate the secret of its acquisition; but rather lend ourselves to the delusions of the ragged and the starving, whose poverty is the surest proof that they are totally ignorant of the *magnum arcanum.* One must have the ears of Midas to listen to those who pretend to possess his touch.

FOX-HUNTING—tossing up for lives with a fox, and running the risk of being in at your own death, instead of that of the animal you are pursuing. A fox-hunter lays a very fair wager when he pits his own head against an animal's tail. Bull, bear, and badger-baiting are prohibited by the magistrates, if not by law: there is a society for the prevention of cruelty to animals, the secretary of which evinces a laudable activity in punishing drovers, coachmen, and carmen, who are unmerciful towards their cattle ; but gentlemen may kill and mangle game, and put stags, hares, and foxes, to a lingering and cruel death, without molestation or impeachment. This may appear an unjust and invidious distinction ; but it must be recollected, that the plebeians are naturally ignorant, and torment their animals to urge them forward, or with some other appearance of excuse ; whereas the gentry are, or ought to be, well-informed, and perpetrate their various cruelties solely for their own pastime and amusement !

If a fox-hunter possess the accompaniments of being a toper and a gambler, he may be said to pass his mornings in running through other people's estates, and his nights in running through his own.

FREETHINKER.—This word, by a strange abuse of terms, has come to be synonymous with a libertine and a contemner of religion, whereas the best security, both for morality and piety, is a perfect freedom of thought. If it be a reproach to be a freethinker, it must be a merit to think like a slave; and mental bondage, always more degrading than that of the body, must be more honourable than the liberty of both ! The right of examining what we ought to believe, is the foundation of Protestantism, and to deny it, is to revert to the Popish claim of infallibility. We may as well suppose a man can reason without thinking at all, as reason without thinking freely ; and it has been maintained, even by dignitaries of the Church, that a verbal, uninquiring assent even to a truth, is less meritorious than the con- scientious error which is the result of patient investigation. If thought is to be restricted, or excluded altogether from the consideration of the most important of all subjects, it necessarily follows, that idiots, and irrational beings, are as competent to decide upon them as the most enlightened philosophers ; a *reductio ad absurdum*, which we commend to the attention of the mind-chainers. Those are the real free- thinkers, using the word in its most invidious sense, who imagine that the unshackled exercise of man's noblest and most distinguishing attribute, can ever lead to any other results than a still more deep, and more soul-felt conviction of the greatness, goodness, and glory of its divine Giver. For myself, I desire no better epitaph, in this respect, than the words of Juvenal—

> " Civis erat qui libera posset
> Verba animi proferre, et vitam inpendere vero."

FRIEND, Real—one who will tell you of your faults and follies in prosperity, and assist you with his hand and heart in adversity.—See Phœnix, and Unicorn.

Strange as it may sound, we are sometimes rather disposed to choose our friends from the unworthy than the worthy; for though it is difficult to love those whom we do not esteem, it is a greater difficulty to love those whom we esteem much more than ourselves. A perfect friendship requires equality, even in virtue. He who has merited friends, will seldom be without them; for attachment is not so rare as the desert that attracts and secures it.

Some there are, who, with an apparent zeal, vindicate their friends from all their little peccadilloes, whitewash them as carefully as they can, and then knock them on the head by lamenting their addiction to some gross impropriety. This resembles the conduct of the Roman priests, who, when an ox was not completely white, chalked over the dark spots, and leading him up to the altar, made him an immediate sacrifice.

Favours, and especially pecuniary ones, are generally fatal to friendship; for our pride will ever prompt us to lower the value of the gift by diminishing that of the donor. Ingratitude is an effort to recover our own esteem, by getting rid of our esteem for our benefactor, whom we look upon as a sort of toothdrawer, that has cured us of one pain by inflicting another.

As friendship must be founded on mutual esteem, it cannot long exist among the vicious; for we soon find ill company to be like a dog, which dirts those the most whom it loves the best. After Lady E. L., and her female companion, had defied public opinion for some time, her ladyship was obliged to say—" Well, now, my dear friend, we must part for ever; for you have no character left, and I have not enough for two."

FRIENDS.—There may be the same vitiated taste in the choice of friends, as of food. Many who like their game to be high and rank, seem to choose their associates for the same recommendation; not objecting to those whose reputations are in the worst odour. Others lay the foundation of future quarrels by forming inconsiderate and incongruous attachments,—a union, as Cowper wittily observes—

> " Like Hand-in-Hand insurance plates,
>   Which unavoidably creates
>   The thoughts of conflagration."

A fashionable friend is one who will dine with you, game with you, walk or ride out with you, borrow money of you, escort your wife to public places—if she be handsome, stand by and see you fairly shot, if you happen to be engaged in a duel, and slink away and see you fairly clapped in a prison, if you experience a reverse of fortune.—Such a man is like the shadow of the sun-dial, which appears in fine weather, and vanishes when there comes a rainy day.

People are always pleased with those who partake pleasure with them; and hence there is a maudlin sympathy among brother topers,—but this is fellowship, not friendship. Never was the term more thoroughly desecrated than by the heartless Horace Walpole, who, in one of his letters, says, " If one of my friends happens to die, I drive down to St. James's Coffee House, and bring home a new one."

FURNITURE—inanimate society. I like appropriate emblems in furniture, though I would not adopt the pedantry of Mr. Hope in its full extent, and make every joint stool, by its classical and hieroglyphical mysteries, puzzle the head instead of supporting the body. Where pleasant associations can be awakened,—and I would admit none of a contrary tendency,—why should not our chairs, tables, and sideboards be made to enhance the attractions and the resources of home, by ministering to a refined taste, and stimulating the imagination? To study how every decoration may express an emblem, and even to pun in marble, by sculpturing horses' heads beside a bust of Philip, because that word signifies, in Greek, a lover of horses, is a pitiful conceit; but it is pleasant, nevertheless, to impart to mahogany some of the properties of mind, to lift upholstery out of its materiality, and make it the medium for conveying the fancy through the whole range of time and space.

FUTURITY—what we are to be, determined by what we have been.—An inscrutable mystery, of which we can only guess at a solution, by referring to the present and the past. These assure us, by millions of incontestable proofs, that the benevolent Creator sympathises with our happiness; then he must sympathise still more tenderly with our sufferings. To suppose that He would scatter all sorts of delights around us in this evanescent world, and yet doom the great mass of mankind to everlasting anguish in the next, is an irreconcileable contradiction. The earth, upon which we are merely flitting passengers, is everywhere enamelled with flowers, equally exquisite for varied beauty and perfume, but useless, except for the purpose of diffusing pleasure; and yet our eternal abode is to be horrent with fire and agony! The best way of combating the terrors with which superstition has darkened futurity, is to appeal from the unknown to the known, from the unseen to the visible, from imaginary torment to real enjoyment, from the frightfulness and the stench of Tophet to the beauty of a tulip, and the fragrance of a rose.

ALLOWS—a cure without being a prevention of crime. It is calculated, that since the suspension of bank payments, 800 human beings have been executed for forgery alone ! In the year 1832, an important improvement was effected in our penal code, by the entire repeal of the punishment of death, as it regarded five classes of criminals.

It is curious to observe how, in all cases, the good sense and humanity of the public outstrip those of judges and legislators, who, being generally both hardened and blinded by habit, neither feel for the criminal, nor see the iniquity of the law. Singular inconsistency ! that many of the same clear-sighted and kind-hearted people, who rail against the severity of our code, as utterly inconsistent with the special injunctions and mild spirit of Christianity, will still subject those who differ from them in matters of faith to all the damnatory clauses of their vindictive creed. They are religiously bent upon mitigating every code but the religious, and would alleviate the punishment of all offenders, except those who have committed the irremissible crime of differing from them in opinion. And yet, what are the comparatively painless three or four minutes of hanging, to an eternity of exquisite anguish ? Oh ! why will not men adopt the healing, the consolatory, the blessed and blessing spirit of Christianity, instead of the occasional bitterness of its letter ? why will they not read the universe, instead of the perversions and anathemas of gloomy fanatics, and believe, that in a future state the doom, even of the guilty, will be measured by the wisdom, the justice, the mercy of the Creator, rather than by the misdeeds of the creature ?

GAME LAWS—acts passed for the careful protection

of birds and beasts, and the ruthless proscription of human beings. If these barbarous enactments, instead of proceeding from the mere caprices of tyranny, were governed by anything like principle and common sense, we might venture to ask, why one sort of wild beast or bird should be pronounced game in preference to another?—why pigeons, and plovers, and weazles, should not receive that appellation, as well as pheasants, partridges, and hares?—why, in short, the Squirearchy should not, in imitation of King John, lay a total interdict upon all the winged, as well as four-footed creatures; while such of them as are fond of angling, claimed all the fishes as their exclusive privilege and property. There are no natural distinctions. If they have a right in one instance, they have a right in all, and the *feræ naturæ* must have been meant by heaven for the sole enjoyment and amusement of sportsmen and country gentlemen, who have the least need of them, and, therefore, the least claim to them. It was once made felony to steal a hawk; and he who took its eggs, even in his own grounds, was liable to imprisonment for a year and a day, besides a fine at the King's pleasure. Hawking is no longer an amusement of the gentry, and therefore, this barbarous law has been repealed; but how horrible, that the lives and liberty of the commonalty should thus depend upon the fashion of a day, and the occasional pastimes of that narrow class, who dub themselves the gentry. What remains of our game laws is conceived in the same atrocious spirit, and is too monstrous to endure much longer against the growing knowledge of the people, and a reformed Parliament.

In the dark ages, when rude warriors could find no other employment in peace than to make field sports serve as a sort of apprenticeship to the arts of war, there might be some excuse for an eager addiction to them; but in these days, when even the Squirearchy can read and write, when, besides the whole unlimited range of intellectual pursuit, they may command exercises and amusements of all sorts, when some have magisterial functions to discharge, and all may occupy themselves in works of local charity, and parochial or county utility, to affirm that they have no resources and no inducement to reside upon their estates, if they may not worry poor hares to death, and mangle and destroy partridges, is to stultify themselves, to confess that they are at once weak, and cruel, and utterly worthless members of society.

Then comes the pithy question, why our rural districts should be disturbed, demoralised, and stained with blood ; why the fields of the industrious husbandman should be overrun and damaged, and his fences broken down ; why the crops of the farmer should be wasted by the depredations of game, against whose ravages it is punishable to defend himself? why our prisons and transport-ships should be crowded with victims, in order to afford occasional pastime to a sporting Squirearchy, who stand self-convicted as the idlest, the most unfeeling, the least meritorious class of the whole community ?

The good sense and humanity of the lower orders have induced them to forego bear and badger-baiting altogether ; bull-baiting and cock-throwing are falling fast into desuetude, and most of their other cruel pastimes are discontinued ; an improvement which, it is to be hoped, will not be altogether thrown away upon those patrician sportsmen, who ought to have set the example which they are now called upon to follow.

GAMING, see Beggar and Suicide.— The gamester begins by being a dupe, speedily becomes a knave, and generally ends his career as a pauper. A dice-box, like that of Pandora, is full of all evils, with a deceitful Hope at the

bottom, which generally turns into Despair. There is but
one good throw upon the dice, which is, to throw them away.

GENIUS—a natural aptitude to perform well and easily
that which others can do but indifferently, and with pains.
Locke has exploded the theory of innate ideas. The mind
of a newly-born infant is as a new mirror, which, with a
capacity to reflect all objects, is, in itself, objectless. There
is nothing innate or original in either case, except the
capacity to reflect, which will vary according to the peculiar
construction of the mind or the mirror; some presenting
objects with a true or a false, with a beautifying or a discoloured and unbecoming hue; while others will enlarge,
diminish, distort, or absolutely reverse the forms presented
to them. These different tendencies of minds, originally
idealess, constitute the diversities of human character, or
form what is commonly called genius.

GHOSTS.—There is more meaning and philosophy than
at first sight appears in Coleridge's answer to Lady Beau-
mont, when she asked him whether he believed in ghosts—
" O no, Madam, I have seen too many to believe in them."
He had sense enough to see that his senses had been
deceived.

GLORY, Military—sharing with plague, pestilence, and
famine, the honour of destroying your species; and partici-
pating with Alexander's horse the distinction of transmitting
your name to posterity.

GLUTTONY.—Pope's line—

" Is there no help then, Helluo, bring the jowl,"

was suggested by what Athenæus records of Philoxenus, the

Dithyrambic poet, who, having nearly completed, at one meal, an enormous polypus, was seized with convulsive spasms, and being told his last hour was at hand, exclaimed —" Since Charon and Atropos are come to call me away from my delicacies, it is best to leave nothing behind, so bring the remainder of the polypus." According to the same veracious author, Cambles, being given to gastromargism, *ate up his wife*, and in the morning, found her hands in his throat! Many a poor man now-a-days, when he finds the hands of his shrewish wife in his throat, would be glad to dispose of the rest of her body after the fashion of Cambles.

GNATS.—" To what base uses may we not return !" exclaims Hamlet,—" Imperial Cæsar dead and turned to clay," &c. It is a humiliating fact, which cannot be denied ; but, on the other hand, there are many forms of matter, which, in their decomposition, are as much elevated, as the ingredients of Cæsar's body were temporarily degraded. Gnats, for instance, and other annoying insects devoured by birds, are ultimately converted into music; their importunate buzzing being but an inharmonious prelude, or tuning of instruments for the warbling of the nightingale, the cheerful song of the thrush, and the full concert of the winged choristers, who turn the summer air into melody. Our own daily food, ministering to the spirit of which the body is only the shrine, may be sublimised into wit, wisdom, and poetry. In the economy of nature, there is a perpetual interchange of life and death, of mind and matter. We draw existence and intellect from the earth ; we return to it, and contribute, by resolving into our first elements, to supply life and intellect to our successors.

GOETHE—said that he considered no work complete, unless it involved some mystery which the author left unexplained, for the express purpose of stimulating the curiosity and the faculties of the reader. In this confession we have a key to his *Faust*, to much of the Kantian philosophy, and to a large portion of the German literature in general. The mystical—the obscure—the enigmatical, where there is no real riddle to be solved, as in the case of Faust, Coleridge's Christabel, and similar productions, are so much sheer impertinence, and one feels a contemptuous pity for those laborious Œdipi, who puzzle their brains in endeavouring to solve the imaginary enigma of a sham Sphinx. German writers and readers seem to find a delight in thus stultifying each other, but it is foreign to the plain, straightforward, intelligible, useful, matter-of-fact character of England,—and therefore is it, that German literature will never become popular among us. Goethe—the Shakspeare and Voltaire of Germany—is little known in this country, except by his Werther and his Faust.

GOOD, in things evil.—

> " ' There is a soul of goodness in things evil,
> Would men observingly distil it out.'

" So with equal wisdom and good-nature, does Shakspeare make one of his characters exclaim.—Suffering gives strength to sympathy. Hate of the particular may have a foundation in love for the general. The lowest and most wilful vice may plunge deeper out of a regret of virtue. Even in envy may be discerned something of an instinct of justice, something of a wish to see universal fair-play, and things on a level." Leigh Hunt, from one of whose delightful papers in the Indicator this passage is extracted, might easily have expanded his idea, and illustrated it by further examples ; for while body and soul retain their alliance, their joint offspring will ever bear a likeness to either parent. " The web of our life is of a mingled yarn, good and ill together; our virtues would be proud if our faults whipped them not; and our crimes would despair if they were not cherished by our virtues." To begin with the latter;—what we call patriotism, is often a blind and mischievous prejudice against other nations, rather than an enlightened preference of our own. Love is as often sensual as sentimental. Parental affection, where it is not instinctive, is only reflected self-love. Charity not seldom proceeds from pride, from our desire to get rid of an uneasy sensation, or from the hope of being repaid with usurious interest what we "lend to the Lord." Dispensing justice may spring from the thirst of domination over our fellow creatures; and religion itself, even when sincere, may be instigated by that selfish regard to future reward, which has been termed—other-worldliness.

As our virtues are tainted occasionally by degrading associations, so may our vices be mingled with redeeming ones. Conjugal jealousy and the hatred of a rival, spring from the intensity of our love. Revenge, which, like envy, is an instinct of justice, does but take into its own hands the execution of that natural law which preceded the social. Avarice is only prudence and economy pushed to excess; intemperance has its source in fellowship and hospitality; and wasteful extravagance springs from an unregulated generosity. These considerations are not urged to encourage moral Pyrrhonism and doubt; still less to confound the barriers of right and wrong; but to inculcate humility as well as forbearance, to teach us that we should neither be too overweening in estimating our own virtues, nor too severe in condemning the failings of others.

GOODNESS—a synonyme for Deity. "When all the good of a system," says G. L. Le Sage, of Geneva, "can easily be traced to general principles, and when all the evils appear to be exceptions, closely connected with some good, the excess being evidently, though, perhaps, but in a small degree, on the side of good, the contriver must be regarded as beneficent." If the existence of pain and evil render it difficult for a reflecting man to be an optimist, there is no reason why he should not, at all events, be an *agathist.* It is an observation of Dr. Johnson, that as the greatest lie tells more truth than falsehood, so may it be said of the worst man, that he does more good than evil.

"When a common soldier," observes Adam Smith, "is ordered upon a forlorn hope, his courage, and his sense of duty, make him march to his doom with alacrity; but how few are philosophers enough to imitate this brave devotion, when they are ordered out upon the forlorn hope of the universe." The moral courage that will face obloquy in a good cause, is a much rarer gift than the bodily valour that will confront death in a bad one.

With a double vigilance should we watch our actions, when we reflect, that good and bad ones are never childless; and that, in both cases, the offspring goes beyond the parent, —every good begetting a better, every bad a worse.

GOOSE—a bird, and word of reproach, but I know not why. M. de Cottu, the French jurist, who came to this country to digest our laws and our dinners, and who pronounced our *cuisine* to be *fade et bornée*, records, with an affectation of delicate disgust, that even at decent tables he had often seen a goose!—Gadso! I can easily believe it, if he sat opposite the mirror. Why this calumniated fowl should be a byword for ridicule in our discourse, or an object of abomination at polite tables, is an enigma, which it might puzzle Œdipus to solve. Every one knows that the Roman State was saved by the cackling of geese; a hint which has by no means been thrown away upon some of our own short-witted and long-winded senators. Among the Romans, the gander and his spouse were a favourite and a fashionable dish ; but learned commentators maintain, that the particular brood to which the commonwealth was so much indebted was preserved, as well as all its immediate descendants, with the utmost care ; a circumstance which must have been much deplored by the epicures of that day, since it became impossible to have a Capitol goose for dinner. Then, as now, the little giblets were thought great delicacies, and good livers deemed the livers good, as appears by the following extract from Francis's Horace, b. ii. sat. 8 :—

> " And a white gander's liver,
> Stuffed fat with figs, bespoke the curious giver."

Whence, also, we may see that their epicurism extended even to the colour. A modern white gander is a *rara avis*. Queen Elizabeth was cutting up a goose, when she learnt that the Spanish armada had been cut up by a Drake. Why, then, should a bird, ennobled by so many historical, and endeared by so many culinary recommendations, be treated with scorn and contumely? If the reader sympathise with the writer in wishing to see some zealous, though tardy reparation, made by a featherless biped to the biped who supplies us with feathers, he will peruse with a kindred com- placency and indulgence the following

ODE TO A GOOSE,

Written after dinner on the Feast of St. Michael,

STROPHE I.

O BIRD most rare ! although thou art
Uncommon common on a common,
What man or woman
Can in one single term impart

A proper name for thee ?—An ancient Roman
Would answer—" *Anser*."   Sure I am that no man,
Knowing thy various attributes, would choose
        To call thee Goose !

ANTISTROPHE I.
No, Goose ! thou art no Goose.   Well stuffed with sage
   And titillating things both dead and living,
        For ever art thou giving
Solace to man in life's brief pilgrimage.

EPODE I.
Jove's eagle wielding the avenging thunder,
Is but a folio hawk, a bird of plunder.
        Minerva's owl,
        (Both are foul fowl !)
Shunning the light, should ne'er have been preferr'd
To rank as Wisdom's bird.—
As for the young and stately swan,
A Scottish lawyer is the man
        To sing its praises.
I am no writer to the cygnet—so,
        Avoiding further periphrases,
For thee alone, O Goose ! my verse shall flow.

STROPHE II.
O bird of Morpheus ! half our lives are sped,
(Ay, and the happiest too) upon a bed
Stuffed with thy feathers.   On thy breast
        Thou hushest us to rest,
        As if we were thy goslings,
        Till we forget life's hubble-bubble,
            Its toil and trouble,
Its crossings and its jostlings,
And borne in dreams to empyrean latitudes,
Revel in ecstasies and bright beatitudes.

ANTISTROPHE II.
 Churls that we are ! what snoozing hum
   Ascends to thee ?—what pæans, what adorings?
Our mouths, perchance, are open, but they're dumb :
        Our sole harangues
        Are nasal twangs,
And all our gratitude consists of snorings.

EPODE II.

Bird of Apollo ! worthy to pluck grass
  On the Parnassian mountain,
  Beside the classic fountain
Of Hippocrene, what Muse with thee can class,
To whose inspiring wing we owe
 All that the poets past have writ ;
From whose ungathered wings shall flow
 All our whole store of future wit ?
   Well may'st thou strut,
   Proud of thy pens uncut,
   Which shall cut jokes,
   In after times, for unborn folks ;—
Well may'st thou plume thyself upon thy plumage—all
  Is erudite and intellectual,
  Each wing a cyclopædia, fraught
  With genius multiform, a world of thought !
  Ah! when thou putt'st thy head
  Beneath that wing to bed,
In future libraries thou tak'st a nap,
And dream'st of Paternoster Row, mayhap !
What are *they* dreaming of, that they forget
  (The publishing and scribbling set)
  To apotheosise thee, Goose !
  As the tenth Muse?

ANTISTROPHE III.

  And then the darling driblets,
  That constitute thy giblets,
  Whether in soup or stew'd,
O ! what delectable and dainty food !
Full of my subject ('twas my dinner dish,)
  No wonder that I feel all over goosy,
  Fired with what Braham calls *entusimusy*
So much so, I could almost wish,
  If fate were nothing loth,
  To be a Goose instead of man.
" Be doubly happy on thy present plan,"
  (Methinks the reader cries,)
  " And thank the favouring destinies,
  For now thou'rt *both !*"

GOUT—sometimes the father's sin visited upon the child, but more often the child of our own sins visiting its father. A man of the latter stamp once asked Abernethy what he should do to avoid the infliction.—" Live upon a shilling a day—and earn it," was the reply, at once pertinent and impertinent.

GOVERNMENT.—According to Milton, it should be the first object in a representative commonwealth, " to make the people fittest to choose, and those chosen fittest to govern." According to the Conservatives, the people should be defrauded, as much as possible, of the elective franchise, in order that an oligarchy may the more easily defraud them of everything else. A despotic government is an inverted cone, resting upon a point, and liable to be toppled down by the smallest movement. A popular government is a pyramid, the firmest and most enduring of all forms.

Government, as a science, has by no means kept pace with the advancement of other arts. It might be expected, that legislatures, like individuals, although headstrong, violent, and passionate, in the outset of their career, would become mild, moderate, and wise in their old age; but experience does not justify this inference. In human nature, there are two leading principles, or motives of conduct,—the hope of reward, and the fear of punishment; but most governments either address themselves exclusively to the latter, or if they bring the former into operation, they begin at the wrong end, showering titles, ribands, emoluments, honours, and distinctions upon the upper classes, who should be taught to consider virtue as its own reward, while the lower orders are only attempted to be influenced by pains, penalties, and terror.

Were the art of government left to its official functionaries, it would probably be stationary, even in England; but it is fortunately pushed forward on the road of improvement by public opinion, the power of which, developing itself through a free press, is becoming every day more manifest and irresistible. If there be truth in the *vox populi vox Dei*, this must be the best, the most legitimate, the most hallowed of all authority. Every man has a voice in the formation of that public opinion, which confers the privileges, without incurring the dangers, of universal suffrage. Some, it is true, have more weight than others, but it is the superior influence of talent and information, a much better element of representation than property, upon which the elective franchise is usually based. Government will have attained its perfection when the people, being universally educated and competent to judge, and the press being untaxed and unfettered, so as to give power and certainty to their voice, the rulers of the State, obeying while they govern, and following while they seem to lead, shall be merely the official mouthpieces of the national will.

These, however, will be deemed the notions of a visionary; a *beau ideal*, for the realization of which good men may sigh, while practical ones will smile compassionately, and refer the experiment to the millennium.

GRATITUDE.—If this be justly defined as "a lively sense of benefits to come," ingratitude is so far preferable, that it is free from hypocrisy and sordid motives, and releases the benefactor as well as the benefited. If the one be a calculating virtue, the other is at least a frank vice. Great ingratitude cannot be common, because great beneficence is rare, and its alleged frequency, therefore, is often a pretext trumped up by the parsimonious to save their pockets. To be deterred by such a plea from practising charity, when we have the means, is to commit towards heaven the very offence which we are imputing to our fellow-creatures. Besides, one man's ingratitude is not another man's ingratitude. Beneficent people are rarely grateful; they look upon common favours like common politeness, as a matter of course. An apparent gratitude may sometimes be the sharpest revenge. Sir Charles Sedley, when he joined the Prince of Orange, said of King James the Second—" He has made my daughter a Countess, and I will show my gratitude by endeavouring to make his a Queen." It will be recollected, that Sedley's daughter, created Countess of Dorchester, was James's mistress, and that the Prince of Orange's wife, afterwards Queen Mary, was James's daughter.

GRAVE—the gate through which we pass from the visible to the invisible world.

" GRAVITY"—says Rochefoucauld, " is a mystery of the body, invented to conceal the defects of the understanding."

GRIEFS—are like the beings that endure them,—the little ones are the most clamorous and noisy; those of older growth, and greater magnitude, are generally tranquil, and sometimes silent. Our minds are like ill-hung vehicles; when they have little to carry, they raise a prodigious clatter, —when heavily laden, they neither creak nor rumble.

GRUMBLERS—who are perpetually publishing the mal-treatment they have experienced, excite but little sympathy; for, without going the length of Rochefoucauld's maxim, it may safely be maintained, that there is nothing which people in general bear with more equanimity than the misfortunes of their neighbours. It is natural that those who feel themselves aggrieved, should give vent to complaint; but it is equally so, that their hearers should at length listen to the catalogue of their wrongs with indifference.

> " If you are treated ill and put on,
>   'Tis natural to make a fuss ;
> To see it and not care a button,
>   Is just as natural for us.
> Like people viewing, at a distance,
>   Two persons thrown out of a casement,
> All we can do for your assistance,
>   Is to afford you our amazement :—
> For an impartial looker-on
> In such disasters never chooses ;
> 'Tis neither Tom, nor Will, nor John,—
>   'Tis the phenomenon amuses." *

Not to enjoy all the innocent happiness we can, is so far impious, that it is defrauding the Creator of that purpose in our creation, which we may consider to be the most congenial to the divine nature.

ABIT—a second nature, which often supersedes the first. The habit which enables one man to dispense with necessaries, may render superfluities indispensable to another. Extremes touch ; he who wants no favours from Fortune, may be said to have obtained the very greatest that she can bestow, in realizing an independence which no changes or reverses can diminish. What king or conqueror can say as much ?

The late Sir W——r S——g, as he hurried along the streets of London, had contracted a habit, whenever he met

* Hall Stevenson's Works, vol. i. p. 120 ; a writer already forgotten, although he died so lately as 1785. His fables, a poor imitation of Fontaine, deriving their sole interest from the politics of the day, and the indelicacy of his " Crazy Tales," in imitation of Chaucer and Prior, have hurried his productions into a quick oblivion, spite of the marvellous ease of his versification, which has rarely been equalled.

any of his numerous acquaintance, of saluting them with a passing bow, a touch of the hat, and the words—" Sir, I wish you a very good morning." As High Sheriff of a county, it once became his duty to attend the execution of a criminal, when, having seen that all the preliminary arrangements were complete, and that his services were no longer needed, he bowed, and touched his hat to the culprit, whose cap was already over his face, and took leave of him with his habitual —" Sir, I wish you a very good morning !"

A friend of the author's, who had purchased a *post-obit*, dependent on the life of an elderly female, being asked, some years afterwards, whether he had yet come into possession, replied—" Oh no !—and I have quite given it up ; for the old cat has now acquired such a habit of living, that I do not suppose she could die if she would." It must be confessed, that this obstinate habit is the very last that we resign.

HAPPINESS—a blessing often missed by those who run after pleasure, and generally found by those who suffer pleasure to run after them. Like a Will-o'-the-wisp, it is sometimes farthest off when we imagine we can grasp it, and nearest to us when it appears to be at a distance. The most effectual way to secure it to ourselves, is to confer it upon others.

None are either so miserable or so happy as they are thought, for the mind soon habituates itself to its moral atmosphere, whether rough or gentle. If there be no difference between possessing a thing, and not wishing for it, happiness may be best attained by indifference ; at all events there is a greater approximation than is generally supposed, between those who have lost, and those who retain their happiness ; since the former are always hoping to recover, what the latter are always fearing to be deprived of.

Pyrrhus, denying the reality of any beatitude, maintained

that life and death were equal, and when asked why he did not seek the grave, since existence was so little attractive, replied, " Because both are indifferent to me."

In the progress of time and general improvement, the aggregate of human enjoyment may be incalculably increased, without diminishing the stock of comparative discontent; for as we measure our portion in life not by our superiority to our predecessors, but by our inferiority to our contemporaries, we forget abstract benefits in relative disadvantages. Notwithstanding this drawback, human happiness must be constantly augmenting. As civilization advances, every peasant enjoys luxuries and securities from which nobles and monarchs were formerly debarred. That there is much less misery and suffering in the world than formerly, is incontestably proved by the remarkable increase in the mean duration of life, while the years thus added to our span, derive a double value from the almost universal diffusion of the means of enjoying them.

As important disappointments do but rarely occur, and yet many men are unhappy during the greater part of their lives, it is evident that they must fret their spirit about trifles. The great secret of cheerfulness and content is not to be annoyed by petty thwartings, and not to aspire to unattainable objects. Children are always happy, because they are always pursuing trifles of easy acquisition.

Exaggerating the misery of mankind is a species of impiety, because it is an oblique reflection on the benevolence of the Deity. If man had been made involuntarily happy, he would have been without motives to exertion, and would have lost that noblest species of felicity which arises from the virtuous and successful development of his faculties. If virtue, moreover, always ensured happiness, while vice entailed inevitable misery, we should lose one of the strongest arguments for a future state of retribution.

HARDSHIPS—pleasures when they are self-imposed, intolerable grievances when they are required by our duty. What sportsman ever complains of fatigue, what card-player of sedentariness, what angler of solitude and dulness, what bookworm of confinement, what miser of poverty, what lover of slavery?—Ay, but these annoyances may be endured with patience, because they are voluntary. Well, and what prevents us from performing with an equal good-will the tasks enjoined by our station in life, and which all our ill-will cannot enable us to avoid? We conquer our fate when we submit to it cheerfully. Vain repinings only serve to aggravate it.

So prone, however, are we to discontent and complaint, that even when men bear their real hardships with tolerable composure, they are apt to invent imaginary ones, to which they cannot submit with any degree of patience.

HARMONY, Musical—a sensual pleasure, which, in well regulated minds, seldom fails to produce moral results.

> Hark! to the voice of yonder sour
>   And gloomy monitor, who cries—
> " Why do ye waste life's fleeting hour
>   In idle songs and melodies?
> The tongue that sings—the hands that play,
>   Shall soon be mute and cold in death,
> And ye who listen to the lay
>   As soon shall yield your parting breath."
>
> But hark! I hear an angel's voice—
>   " Mortals!" exclaims the dulcet chant,
> " Sing! and with instruments rejoice,
>   For music is a heavenly grant.
> 'Twas meant to charm your cares away,
>   The thoughts to raise—the heart to mend,
> And hallow'd thus, its lightest lay
>   Attains a high and moral end."

He who has a spirit of harmony in his nature will exhibit

it in every other direction, as well as in that of music. There will be a pleasing concord and consentaneousness in all his thoughts, words, and actions. As the sound of music enables him to walk in a sustained and regular step over uneven ground, so will the moral harmony of his nature, responding to the unheard music of the spheres, or in other words, to the voice of God, speaking by his revelations, empower him to pursue the right way with a steady and orderly step, amid all the quicksands and inequalities of his life's pilgrimage.

HEAD—a bulbous excrescence, of special use to many as a peg for hanging a hat on—as a barber's block for supporting wigs—as a target for shooting at when rendered conspicuous by a shining helmet—as a snuffbox or a chatterbox— as a machine for fitting into a halter or guillotine—as a receptacle for freaks, fancies, follies, passions, prejudices, predilections—for anything, in short, but brains.

HEALTH.—See Temperance, Exercise, and Virtue as often as you can, and the doctor as seldom as you can. The mind's health is the best security for that of the body—*Qui medicè vivit miserè vivit.*

HEART.—According to a French author, those men pass the most comfortably through the world, who have a good digestion and a hard heart; the former preserving them from all the annoyances of dyspepsia, and the latter from those painful feelings to which the compassionate and the sympathising are perpetually subject. Such a man, indeed, may have fewer pains, but can he enjoy any pleasure, except the vulgar ones of sense? He that possesses a susceptible heart, has an inexhaustible mine of sweet emotions. Let him cherish its tenderness, and guard, above all things, against those outpourings of envy or uncharitableness, which inevitably harden the heart, as the foam exuded by testaceous animals encrusts into shell.

HEREDITARY DISTINCTIONS—bestowing personal rewards and honours without the smallest regard to personal qualifications, or even to flagrant *dis*-qualifications. The winner of a title generally deserves it ; he who succeeds to it, even though he may deserve nothing but to lose it, is allowed to signalize his demerit by retaining all the pride, pomp, and circumstance of rank. Frederick of Prussia knew better. In the hopeful project of propagating procerity, he compelled his grenadiers to marry giantesses, intending to recruit his body-guards with their offspring ; but when he found that the children fell short of the parents' standard, he refused to enrol them, and either placed them in the regiments of the line, or made them drummers and fifers. If we ejected, in like manner, from our House of Lords, the sons who fell short of the mental stature by which the winners of their title had achieved distinction, there would be a certainty of our possessing a more enlightened upper house ; but, alas ! there might also be a chance of our having none at all !

Fame, titles, and wealth, the great incentives to patriotism, virtue, and exertion, have a signal moral effect on the whole nation when they are bestowed upon those who have merited them. Their example, thus rendered conspicuous to all, excites in all a noble emulation, the surest source of generous and lofty deeds. But when the distinctions thus honourably achieved are rendered hereditary, the whole process is reversed, and the result is often positively demoralising, both upon the inheritor and the spectators. Already possessing all the public rewards of merit, and feeling not the smallest motive for exertion, the hereditary nobleman naturally sinks into indolence, even if he do not abandon himself to dissolute courses ; while the inferior classes of society, seeing all the recompences of excellence heaped upon the slothful and the depraved, feel the distinctions of right and wrong confounded in their minds, and conclude that vice has as good a chance for attaining eminence as virtue. We must recollect, too, that the beneficial example of the original achiever of the title, supposing it to have been honourably earned, operates but for one life, or rather for a portion of it, while this demoralising influence can only cease with the extinction of the family. Doubtless there are many noblemen, and more probably in England than in any other country, who instead of making their titles their honour, are an honour to their titles, and who have each a much higher merit than that of being "the tenth transmitter of a foolish face ; " but though we are glad to see such a man in possession of honours, we should respect him more, had he earned his distinctions instead of inheriting them.

As to making a man, whether knave, dotard, or idiot, for there are no disqualifications, a hereditary legislator, the very term involves an absurdity, at which nothing but its familiarity prevents our laughing.—What should we say to an hereditary poet, or philosopher, or member of the House of Commons? Our history scarcely affords a single instance of a name continuing illustrious beyond two generations at the most, after which the glory of the an-cestor often serves but to signalize the degeneracy of the descendant.

" But," says a grave reader in spectacles, " if men could not transmit their titles and honours, they would be much less solicitous to earn them, and thus we should lose the noblest incentive to noble deeds." My dear Sir, as Dr. Johnson once said to Boswell,—clear your mind of cant. Many heroes, besides Lord Nelson, having no sons to care about, knew when they were seeking distinctions, that they would bequeath them to relatives whom they positively disliked. If a man be so indifferent to fame and reward, as not to exert himself for his own sake, depend upon it he will never do it for the sake of his son. Our love of offspring, is only self-love at second-hand : and it is never powerful enough to supersede the first. That men would be quite satisfied with titles and honours for life, is incontestably proved by the eagerness with which the proudest of our aristocracy struggle for ribands, and orders, and appointments about the Court, which are not transmissible to descendants. We do not find that the Scotch and Irish peers of parliament set the less value on that distinction, because it expires with the life of the individual, or the dissolution of parliament.

In former times, an order of nobility was a barrier against the encroachments of the Crown ; in the present, it is more frequently an impediment to the progress, improvement, and just rights of the commonalty ; coming between the king and the people, as has been remarked by Champfort, much in the same manner as the hound comes between the hunter and the hare.

When Locke exploded the theory of innate ideas, there should have been an end to the system of innate distinctions. Many wise, and good, and liberal-minded men are nevertheless strenuous advocates for the maintenance of an hereditary nobility, asserting it to be consonant to the order and intentions of nature. Upon this intricate question, I agree with Rumbold, the Roundhead maltster of Charles the Second's time, who said that he should firmly believe in the divine origin of hereditary distinctions, when he saw one class of men born with saddles on their backs, and another class with whips and spurs, all ready to ride them.

HETERODOXY — is another man's doxy :— whereas Orthodoxy is a man's own doxy. The definition is an old one, but it might be difficult to give a new one which should be more accurate. Hales defines heresy and schism as religious scarecrows :—they might be efficient ones formerly, but now-a-days they will scare few birds except gulls and dotterels.

HINT — a jog of the mental elbow. Lord M., a Scottish judge, well known for his penurious habits, being compelled to give a dinner to the barristers upon circuit, and having neglected to order any claret, with which they had been accustomed to be regaled on such occasions, Harry Erskine endeavoured by several oblique hints to make him sensible of the omission. His lordship, however, who had an acute misapprehension where his pocket was in danger, affected to receive all these innuendoes in a different sense, and at length, seeking to turn the conversation to the war in which we were then engaged, abruptly exclaimed, "I wonder what has become of the French fleet?"—"Just at present, my lord," replied his waggish persecutor, "I believe it is, like ourselves, *confined to port!*"

A sportsman, who during the shooting season had gone to pass a week with his friend in the country, on the strength of a general invitation, soon found, by a gentle hint, that he would have done better to wait for a special one. "I saw some beautiful scenery," was the visitor's first remark,—"as I came to-day by the upper road." "You will see some still finer," was the reply, "as you go back to-morrow by the lower one."

HISTORY—the Newgate calendar of kings and rulers, which finds no materials in the happiness or virtue of states, and is therefore little better than a record of human crime and misery. It may be doubted whether we should tempt children to become misanthropes, by perusing it too early. At a more mature age they may beneficially distinguish the momentary triumph of crime, from the eternal lot of virtue. To form an opinion of human nature from a perusal of history, is like judging of a fine city by its sewers and cess-pools.

HOLIDAYS—the Elysium of our boyhood : perhaps the only one of our life. Of this truth Anaxagoras seems to have been aware. Being asked by the people of Lampsacus, before his death, whether he wished any thing to be done in commemoration of him,—" Yes," he replied ; " let the boys be allowed to play on the anniversary of my death." " Men are but children of a larger growth," and, in this working-day country, where we have neither half holidays enough, nor even enough half-holidays, it might be well if some patriot would bequeath to the whole labouring community a legacy similar to that of Anaxagoras.

HOPE—though sometimes little better than the deferring of disappointment, is, nevertheless, a compensation for many of life's painful realities. Its fruition terminates its enjoyment ; but why should we complain that expectation renders us more happy than possession, since the former is a long-enduring pleasure, and the latter only a brief regret ?—A presentiment of coming gladness is the summit of terrestrial felicity. Hope, however, is a better dependance, at the outset, than at the close, of our career. To use the language of Lord Bacon, it is a good breakfast, but an idle supper.

All wings—like a cherub, Hope builds upon nothing, floats, self-supported, like the clouds, catching every flitting ray of the sun, and can raise itself to heaven, even by clinging to a film or gossamer.   If there be any truth in the poet's averment, that

> " Hope springs eternal in the human breast,"

who shall say that man is unhappy?

HORSE—an article in the sale of which you may cheat your own father without any imputation upon your honesty, or your sense of filial duty.   Dr. Burnet, having good reason for disposing of his nag, got upon its back, and rode it up and down, without succeeding, however, in concealing its defects.   "My good doctor," said the expected purchaser, "when you want to take me in, you should mount a pulpit, not a horse."

HOUR-GLASS.—Every thing, we are told, has its hour, and an hour-glass offers no exception to the rule ; its period of utility is but a short one.   The sands gradually wear and file away the aperture through which they pass, at the same time that they themselves are constantly diminishing their particles by friction and collision, so that they flow faster and faster through the enlarged opening, and the machine, turn it which way you will, becomes deranged and useless. So it is with the state machine : by struggling against the restraints of the monarchical or oligarchical principle, the people do but too often enlarge and extend its capacity, while they weaken and wear out themselves, until the proper and useful balance between the two is entirely destroyed. All governments, therefore, however well poised at first, have as constant a tendency towards derangement as the hour-glass.   The balance may be restored in either case, by diminishing the power that has been enlarged, and extending that which has been lessened in the wear and tear of years— this is Reform.   Or you may wait till the machine is obliged to be turned topsy-turvy and thrown into total disorder, or dashed to pieces—this is Revolution.

HOUSEKEEPING, Regular.—When Sheridan, by the assistance of his friends, was installed in a house in Savile Row, he boasted to one of his relations how comfortably and regularly he was living, so much so, that everything went on like clock-work.—"That I can easily believe," was the reply, "it goes on by tick! tick! tick!"

HUMANITY—is much more shown in our conduct towards animals, where we are irresponsible, except to heaven, than towards our fellow-creatures, where we are restrained by the laws, by public opinion, and by the fear of retaliation. The more defenceless and humble the creature, the greater is the merit of treating it kindly, since our tenderness must spring from a high principle or a feeling heart. Show me the man that is a lover of animals, and I will answer for his philanthropy.

How refined and considerate was the humanity of the master butcher, who, in defending his drover for inflicting a tremendous blow upon the eye of an ox, exclaimed, " What harm could he do by striking the beast over the head, where it does not injure the meat?"

HUMILITY—the best evidence of real religion, as arrogance, self-conceit, and pretension, are the infallible criteria of a Pharisaical devotion.

> As the best laden branches bend
>   To Earth with an augmented press,
> So do the fruits of virtue tend
>   To bow our hearts in humbleness ;
> While the vain Pharisee, inflate
> With all the puff'd and windy state,

> That owes to emptiness its birth,
> Like a balloon, a void inside,
> Without—all varnish, pomp and pride,
> Only seeks Heaven to be descried,
>   Admired and gaz'd at from the earth.—
> What though the sound and sane Divine
>   Neglected lives, forgotten dies,
> While sects and devotees combine
>   To puff some bigot to the skies ;
> A diamond's still a precious stone
>   Although upon a dunghill cast,
> And worthless dust, though upwards blown,
>   Retains its vileness to the last.

That false humility, which only stoops to conquer, and prostrates itself that it may rise with the more certainty, may be compared to bottled beer, which is laid flat in order that it may get up. As the soil which is richest in precious ores, generally presents the most barren surface, so genuine humility, proud of nothing but the consciousness of virtue, " Disdains to wear the prize she loves to win."

HUNGER—that which gives the poor man his health and his appetite, and the want of which often afflicts the rich with satiety and disease.

HUNTINGDON.—The author of " The Bank of Faith," however strange and unauthorized may have been his doctrine, seems to have entertained most orthodox notions as to the proper purposes of a flock, and the great objects of the Spiritual Shepherd, if we may judge by the following passage. " Who, but a fool, when God has used a shepherd to call a flock together, would lead that flock from post to pillar on purpose to shear them, and give the wool to men whom I know not whence they be? Bless my God ! these board-men have taught me better things. I keep my flock at home, and shear them for my own profit."

HYPOCHONDRIA—the imaginary malady with which those are taxed who have no real one.

HYPOCRISY—may assume the mask of vice as well as of virtue. Such is the vanity of some men, that they would rather be notorious, and even infamous, than unnoticed. Lord Byron sometimes pretended to be more profligate than he really was, in order, as he affirmed, that he might ingratiate himself with the women ! Satirizing the sex is, generally, spitting against the wind, which blows back in our own face, what we vainly spurt forth against it. It has been said of hypocrites, that they go to the Devil's abode by the road of Paradise ; but this, at all events, evinces a better taste than to journey towards the same destination by the most revolting road that can be selected. If it gives us a more favourable opinion of the Devil, to believe that he is not so black as he is painted by others, it should deepen our contempt for certain pseudo-human devils, when we learn that they are not so black as they paint themselves.

There is much hypocrisy in affecting to give up the pleasures of the world, from religious motives, when we only withdraw from it because we find a greater gratification in the pleasures of retirement.

"My dear children," said an old rat to his young ones, " the infirmities of age are pressing so heavily upon me, that I have determined to dedicate the short remainder of my days to mortification and penance, in a narrow and lonely hole which I have lately discovered : but let me not interfere with your enjoyments ; youth is the season for pleasure ; be happy, therefore, and only obey my last injunction—never to come near me in my retreat. God bless you all !"

Deeply affected, snivelling audibly, and wiping his paternal eyes with his tail, the old rat withdrew, and was seen no more for several days, when his youngest daughter, moved rather by filial affection, than by that curiosity which has been attributed to the sex, stole to his cell of mortification, which turned out to be a hole, made by his own teeth, in—an enormous Cheshire cheese!

.

I DLENESS—hard work for those who are not used to it, and dull work for those who are. Idleness is a moral leprosy, which soon eats its way into the heart and corrodes our happiness, while it undermines our health. Nothing is so hard to do, as to do nothing. The hypochondriacal Countess, who "envies every cinder-wench she sees," is much more to be pitied than the toiling drudge, who "sighs for luxury and ease."

Idleness is costly without being a luxury. Montaigne always wound up the year's account of his expenses with the following entry: "Item—for my abominable habit of idleness—a thousand livres."

Idlers may deserve our compassion, but few things are more misplaced than the contempt lavished upon them as useless members of society; sometimes such scorn is only masked envy; where it is real, it is wrong. All rich idlers may be termed the representatives of former industry and talent; they must either have achieved independence by their own exertions or by those of their ancestors, for almost all wealth can be traced back to labour, or genius, or merit, of some sort. And why do the revilers of the idle, labour and toil with such perseverance?—that they may imitate those whom they abuse, by acquiring an independence and becoming themselves idle. The sight of luxurious ease is the best stimulus to exertion. To suppose that the pleasure of overtaking is greater than that of pursuing the game, may be a mistake, but it is a beneficial one, and keeps society from stagnating. Rich idlers are the advancers of civilization, the best encouragers of industry—the surest patrons of literature and the arts. Nor is there any thing invidious in their good fortune, for every one may aspire to rival or surpass it, which is not the case with hereditary distinctions.

We toil for leisure only to discover, when we have succeeded in our object, that leisure is a great toil. How quickly would the working classes be reconciled to what they term the curse of compulsory occupation, if they were doomed, only for a short time, to the greater curse of compulsory idleness! Quickly would they find, that it is much better to wear out than to rust out.

IDOL—what many worship in their own shape, who would be ashamed to do so in any other.

IMAGINATION, Dreams of—an atonement for the miseries of reality. Philosophers in all ages have delighted in appealing from this incorrigible world to a creation of their own, where all the evils to which mankind are subjected, should be rectified or mitigated. It was with this feeling that Plato, after the death of Socrates, wrote his Atlantis. Tacitus, shocked at the profligacy and subjection of his countrymen, endeavoured to shame them by holding up to their imitation the wisdom, virtue and liberty of the German forests. Sir Thomas More transported himself from the tyranny of Henry VIII. into Utopia. Harrington established the republican government, for which he panted, in his Oceana; and Montesquieu developed his own benevolent views in his fabulous history of the Troglodytes.

IMPRESSIONS, First—are sometimes involuntarily betrayed. Much of the spectator's mind may be gathered by his almost unconscious exclamation when he encounters any novel and striking sight, or is thrown into strange and unexpected situations, which have as sure an effect as wine, in eliciting the truth. Running against a surprise, is like running against a post,—it forces the breath out of your mouth, before you have time to consider how you shall modulate it. Pope, the actor, who was a great epicure, ejaculated in a transport, on his first catching the prospect from Richmond Hill—" a perfect haunch, by heaven !" One of the French Savans, after risking his life in penetrating into the square chamber of the great Egyptian pyramid, had no sooner ascertained its dimensions, by holding up his torch, than he cried to his companion.—" *Quel emplacement pour un Billard !* "

IMMORTALITY of modern authors—drawing in imagination upon the future, for that homage which the present refuses to pay :—at best a protracted oblivion. A poet, however illustrious in his day, is like the statue set up by Nebuchadnezzar, the feet of which were of clay. A living language is a painting, perpetually changing colour, and then perishing ; a dead one is a marble statue—always the same. Even this distant reversion of fame is denied to a modern, for there is little chance that the English tongue of the nineteenth century should live as a dead language after it is dead as a living one. Some vainglorious author boasted that his poems would be read when those of Pope and Dryden were forgotten. " But not till then," added a bystander.

INCONSISTENCY—the only thing in which men are consistent. We are certainly compounded of two contrary natures, impelling us, under different circumstances and influences to actions apparently irreconcileable. To this must it be attributed that the gravest and most saturnine, will sometimes indulge in fits of jocularity, a fact which T. H. would otherwise explain, but in my opinion with too strict a leaning towards anatomy, by referring it to man's possessing a funny bone and an *os humerus*. The stupidest person I ever knew, a mere sensualist, a *gourmand*, and a *gourmet*, composed one of the prettiest little poems I ever read. Scaliger said that he would rather have written Horace's Ode—"*Quem tu, Melpomene*," than be made King of Arragon ; and for my own part, I would rather have indited the following stanzas, than be promoted to the Laureatship !

That my friend, a dull, plodding fellow, whose great business it had hitherto been to eat, drink, and sleep, should spread his fancy's wings, and indulge in a poetical flight, is perhaps less marvellous, than that the first and only essay of his muse, should exhibit a tenderness so touching, combined with aspirations so delicate and ethereal. But we must not tantalise the reader by withholding from him any longer our author's

LOVE SONG.

What mistress half so dear as mine,
    Half so well dress'd, so pungent, fragrant,
Who can such attributes combine,
    To charm the constant, fix the vagrant?
Who can display such varied arts,
    To suit the taste of saint and sinner,
Who go so near to touch their hearts,
    As thou, my darling, dainty dinner?

Still my breast holds a rival queen,
    A bright-eyed nymph, of sloping shoulders,
Whose ruddy cheeks and graceful mien,
    Entrance the sense of all beholders.

> Oh! when thy lips to mine are press'd,
> What transports titillate my throttle !
> My love can find new life and zest,
> In thee, and thee alone, my bottle !

INDEPENDENCE, The boast of—is a trait of vulgarity, and sometimes of insincerity, since professors are not always performers. In reality we are all more independent than is generally imagined, for the whole world can neither take from us what nature has given, nor give us what nature has denied.

INDIGESTION—INDUSTRY—two things which were never before found united.

INFALLIBILITY.—To adopt the doctrines of a pretended infallible church, in order that you may be free from doubt and error, is like putting out your eyes because you cannot find your way, or have been misled by a Jack-o'-Lantern.

INFERIORS—a term which we are ever ready to apply to those beneath us in station, without considering whether it be applicable in any other sense. Many men may be our superiors without being our equals; and many may be our nominal inferiors to whom we are by no means equal.

Inferiority, in others, whether of rank, fortune or talent, never offends, because it conveys a silent homage to our self-love. This is the secret of condescension in the great.

INNOVATION — the unanswerable objection urged against all improvement. We have already quoted the dictum of Bacon—that a froward retention of custom is as turbulent a thing as an innovation. This was not the opinion of Ignatius Loyola, who in order to avoid any innovation in the shape of his boot, after having fractured his leg, ordered a considerable part of the bone to be sawed off, thus proving himself to be a conservative of the true discriminating stamp. To say that all new things are bad, is to say that all old things were bad in their commencement, for the most ancient were once new; and whatever is now most firmly established was once innovation, not even excepting Christianity itself. Even Moses sometimes altered his own laws, and others were introduced into the religious ordinances of the Jews long after his death. " The last chapters of Ezekiel contain a representation of a more pure and holy service imparted to the prophet in a vision ; and we cannot suppose that they would account anything sinful among the improvements of divine worship." * The forms of our Christian Church are of human institution, and therefore liable to original error, while they must necessarily require a new adaptation to the changes in the times, unless we follow Loyola's plan, and cut the world so as to fit the Church, instead of fitting the Church to the world. Who would like to live under our political government, such as it was when our " venerable Church establishment" was founded? And if the former has required a constant series of improvements in the course of centuries, are we to believe that experience and greater enlightenment can add nothing to the perfect excellence of the latter?—" I would only ask," said Lord Bacon, two hundred years ago, " *why* the civil state should be purged and restored by good and wholesome laws, made every third or fourth year in parliament assembled, devising remedies as fast as time breedeth mischief; and *contrariwise*, the ecclesiastical state should still continue upon the dregs of time, and receive no alteration?" Are no additional alterations required since Lord Bacon's time? Unquestionably they are, and such have been the sentiments

* Commentaries on the Laws of Moses, by Michaelis, vol. i. n. 30.

of the most eminent and pious men who have considered the subject. Hooker, in his "Ecclesiastical Polity," maintains broadly that—" Neither God being the author of laws, nor his committing them to scripture, nor the continuance of the end for which they are instituted, is reason sufficient to prove they are unchangeable."* Was not the Reformation an innovation, and have not the clergy, ever since, been virtually though not literally changing our Calvinistical articles, by giving them an Armenian interpretation? How well does this illustrate the remark of a church dignitary : " Creeds and confessions," says Dr. Paley, " however they may express the persuasion or be accommodated to the controversies or to the fears of the age in which they are composed, in process of time, and by reason of the changes which are wont to take place in the judgment of mankind upon religious subjects, they come at length to *contradict the actual opinions* of the church whose doctrines they profess to contain." †

Let us advance from an archdeacon, for authority sometimes carries more weight than an argument, and hear what ?. Bishop says, " The innovations introduced into our religious establishment at the Reformation were great and glorious for those times ; but *some further innovations are yet wanting*, (would to God they may be quietly made !) to bring it to perfection." ‡

Another Bishop confesses that, " it pleased God in his unsearchable wisdom to suffer the progress of this great work, the Reformation, to be stopped in *the midway*, and the effects of it to be greatly weakened by many unhappy divisions among the Reformed." §

* Third Book, section 10.
† Moral and Political Philosophy, b. vi. c. 10.
‡ Dr. Watson's, Bishop of Llandaff, Misc. Tracts, vol. ii. p. 17.
§ Dr. Louth's, afterwards Bishop of London, Visitation Sermon, 1758.

Many other of the brightest ornaments of our Church have maintained the necessity of a further reformation. Tillotson, Patrick, Tenison, Kidder, Stillingfleet, Burnet, all endeavoured to effect it, but in vain. The best friends of the Church will be most anxious that the living successors of these pious men may inherit their sentiments, and be more successful in carrying them into execution ; especially when they recollect that the cry of innovation is totally inapplicable. That word signifies change by the introduction of novelty, whereas the proposed alterations are mostly a return, or an approach to the primitive forms and discipline of the Christian Church.

INQUISITIVENESS—an itch for prying into other people's affairs, to the neglect of our own ;—an ignorant hankering after all such knowledge as is not worth knowing ; —a curiosity to learn things that are not at all curious. People of this stamp would rather be put to the question, than not ask questions ; silence is torture to them. A genuine quidnunc prefers false news to none ; he piques himself upon having the very first information of things that never happened. It is supposed that the Americans have attained the greatest art in parrying inquisitiveness, because they are more exposed to it ; but a well-known civic wag, at a late period of political excitement, maintained a defensive colloquy with a rustic inquisitive, which could hardly have been excelled by any Transatlantic performer. In travelling post, he was obliged to stop at a village to replace a horse's shoe, when the Paul Pry of the place bustled up to the carriage window, and, without waiting for the ceremony of introduction, exclaimed—" Good morning, Sir !—horse cast a shoe, I see—I suppose, Sir, you be going to—" Here he paused, expecting the name of the place to be supplied ; but the citizen answered—" You are quite right, Sir ; I generally go there at this season."—"Ay—hum—do ye?—and no doubt you be come now from—"—"Right again, Sir; I live there." —"Oh, ay, do ye? But I see it be a London shay; pray, Sir, is there anything stirring in London?"—"Yes; plenty of other chaises, and carriages of all sorts."—"Ay, ay, of course; but what do folks say?"—"Their prayers every Sunday."— "That is not what I mean; I wish to know whether there is anything new and fresh?"—"Yes, bread and herrings." —"Anan! you be a queer chap. Pray, Muster, may I ask your name?"—"Fools and clowns call me 'muster,' but I am, in reality, one of the frogs of Aristophanes, and my genuine name is Brekekekex Koax. Drive on, postillion."

INSCRIPTIONS, Monumental.—What a strange people are the Americans! Instead of setting up splendid cenotaphs for kings and heroes, the oppressors or the destroyers of their species, they erect monuments to the benefactors of mankind, containing no other inscription than the name of the deceased, and the improvement or discovery for which he was celebrated. At Charleston, in South Carolina, there is a monument, made after the model of that of Scipio at Rome, with the following inscription—

" Eli Whitney,
The *Inventor of the Cotton Gin.*"

The superficial reader who may never have heard of this useful machine, and who cannot clear his mind from the ludicrous or ignoble associations connected with the word, will smile, perhaps, as he peruses it; but let us hear the opinions of an American judge upon the subject.

" How few of the inscriptions in Westminster Abbey could be compared with that! Who is there, that, like him, has given his country a machine, the product of his own skill, which has furnished a large part of its population, from childhood to old age, with a lucrative employment; by which their debts have been paid off; their capitals increased; *their lands trebled in value.* It may be said, indeed, that this belongs to the physical and material nature of man, and ought not to be compared with what has been done by the intellectual benefactors of mankind,—the Miltons, the Shakspeares, and the Newtons. But is it quite certain that any thing short of the highest intellectual vigour—the brightest genius—is sufficient to invent one of these extraordinary machines? Place a common mind before an oration of Cicero and a steam engine, and it will despair of rivalling the latter as much as the former; and we can by no means be persuaded that the peculiar aptitude for combining and applying the simple powers of mechanics, so as to produce these marvellous operations, does not imply a vivacity of imagination, not inferior to that of the poet and orator. And then, as to the effect on society, the machine, it is true, operates, in the first instance, on mere physical elements, to produce an accumulation and distribution of property. But do not all the arts of civilization follow in the train? and has not he who has trebled the value of the land, created capital, rescued the population from the necessity of drudgery, covered a waste with plenty; has he not done a service to the country of the highest moral and intellectual character? Prosperity is the parent of civilization and all its refinements; and every family of prosperous citizens, added to the community, is an addition of so many thinking, inventing, moral and immortal natures."

These are the words of Mr. Justice Johnson, of South Carolina, and I will not injure their effect by a single comment beyond the expression of a hope, that as we have begun a similar course in this country, by setting up a statue to WATT, the inventor or perfecter of the steam engine, we may continue in this career, and only erect public monuments to those who have really deserved well of their country.

INSTINCT, Animal — the exertion of mental power, without the exercise of reason or deliberation :—the implanted principle that determines the will of brutes, and is generally limited to the great objects of nature—self-preservation, the procurement of food, and the continuance of the species.   An intelligent being, having a motive in view for the performance of any particular operation, will set about it either similarly to others, or in a different mode, according to circumstances, his views and powers of action being almost infinitely varied ; but irrational beings never deviate from the instincts with which they are born, and which are adapted to their particular economy.   Hence, animals are stationary, while man is progressive.   Beavers construct their habitations, birds their nests, bees their hive, and the spider its web, with an admirable ingenuity; but the most sagacious of them cannot apply their skill to purposes beyond the sphere of their particular wants, nor do any of them improve, in the smallest degree, on their predecessors.   Exactly as they respectively built at the time of creation, so will they continue to build until the end of the world.   To illustrate the contrary tendency, and the progressiveness of man in his habitations, we should compare a Hottentot's kraal with St. Peter's, or St. Paul's.

INSTINCTS, Human—natural prejudices, to reject the influence of which, in the education of youth, is, itself, one of the most unreasonable of prejudices. "Why should we scruple," asks Mrs. Barbauld, "to lead a child to right opinions, in the same way by which nature leads him to right practices? He may be left to find out that mustard will bite his tongue, but he must be prejudiced against ratsbane."

INSTITUTIONS—must be fitted to the different ages of the world's mind, just as his clothes are altered and adjusted to the different ages of an individual's body. When we have outgrown either, they should be cast aside; unless we wish our movements to be cramped, or that which restrains them to be violently rent asunder.

Institutions may be compared to certain fruits: when unripe, no storm disturbs them; when ripe, a puff will blow them down. What have they to expect when they are rotten? The answer will be found in Schedule A of the Reform Bill.

INTOLERANCE—being irreligious for the sake of religion, and hating our fellow-creatures, out of a pretended love of their Creator. Intolerance has more lives than a cat; you cannot even starve it to death. Deprive its right hand of its cunning, by taking away the sword wherewith it smote infidels; its nostrils of the soul-rejoicing odour of a roasting heretic; its ears of the delightful groans of imprisoned or tormented non-conformists; its heart of what it best loved, in Corporation and Test Acts, and Catholic disabilities, it will still pick up its crumbs of comfort, and contrive to subsist upon the remaining modicum of religious pains and penalties, or of legal punishments for the freedom of opinion. And while thus employed, the fiend Intolerance boasts of her godlike qualities, and especially of her marvellous liberality. Supported by jails and judges, she employs the sword of law (not justice) to clip the wings of thought, and then complacently exclaims to her mutilated victim —" Behold! you are free as the air—you may fly whithersoever you please: who so liberal, so generous, so tolerant, as I ?"

IVY—a vegetable corruptionist, which, for the purpose of its own support, attaches itself, with the greatest tenacity, to that which is the most antiquated and untenable, and the fullest of holes, flaws, and imperfections.

EALOUSY — tormenting yourself, for fear you should be tormented by another. "Why," asks Rochefoucauld, "does not jealousy, which is born with love, always die with it?" He would have found an answer to this question, had he reflected that self-love never dies. Jealousy is the greatest of misfortunes, and excites the least pity.

JEWS, The modern—are proofs, we are told, of the truth of Christianity. Are they not, at the same time, proofs of the want of Christianity in those who profess, without feeling, its charitable doctrine? As the Scriptures, when they enjoin love of our neighbour, carefully warn us to put the most enlarged construction upon the word, it is difficult to reconcile the virulent denunciations, and the incentives to scorn and hatred of the Jews, which so many of the clergy infuse into their sermons, either with Christianity, good taste, or right feeling. Our Saviour was a Jew; the greater portion of the Bible is Jewish; the ten commandments, which constitute the basis of our morality, are Jewish. Why, then, should we dislike our fellow-subjects, and spiritual half-brethren, because they happen to be Jews, more even than we hate Turks and Pagans, who are utter aliens and infidels?

All persecution is demoralizing, and the Jews have been long exposed to its worst species,—that of public prejudice, aggravated by civil and other disabilities. Abolish all religious pains, penalties, and distinctions, and this oppressed race will quickly become elevated in the moral, as well as in the political scale.

What a picturesqueness do these descendants of Abraham impart to the otherwise monotonous surface of society! Far and wide do we travel, to behold the inanimate mouldering remains of Greece and Rome; while in the Israelites, our neighbours and fellow-townsmen, we may contemplate the living ruins of a nation still more ancient and illustrious. Who can survey their adust complexions, oriental physiognomies, and dark-flowing beards, converting them into unfaded portraits of the old Scripture characters, without being carried back, in imagination, to the crowded streets of Solyma, and the glories of King David?

There are moral points of view, also, in which they cannot be contemplated without exciting respect and admiration in every candid mind. For eighteen hundred years, under persecutions more relentless and unremitting than the world ever witnessed, have they clung to their ancient faith with an indomitable and unparalleled heroism. Martyrdom is comparatively nothing;—death, the affair of a moment, is easily confronted;—but the life-long death of continual oppression, scorn, and hatred, all which might be avoided by the utterance of a single word, none but a high-principled soul can endure. Their inflexible tenacity, in this respect, presents a grand, I had almost said a sublime spectacle. " But they are so sordid," objects blind Prejudice. You have made them so, may be replied, by leaving no other career open to them but that of money getting. Besides, they are *not* sordid, where any principle or duty prompts them to be otherwise. While we ourselves are forming societies to compel a due observance of the Sabbath, on the part of Christian tradesmen, the Jews, a whole people of traders and dealers, already debarred from the seventh day of the week, spontaneously deprive themselves of another, from a sense of religious duty. The poorest, the most starving of their tribe, shuts up his miserable shop on the Saturday, and willingly sacrifices a sixth part of his income upon the altar of his religion. Are such men to be taunted by the sanctified dealers and traders, who cannot refrain from transacting business, even on an annual Fast-day?

By the necessity under which they labour, of submitting to test oaths and declarations, opposed to their conscience, the Jews are excluded from the common privileges of citizenship, from the learned professions, and other channels of honourable distinction ; all in manifest contravention of that principle of our reformed constitution, which declares, that religious difference shall not form any ground of civil disability. And yet we are not persecutors ! What odious cant !

JOKES—the cayenne of conversation, and the salt of life. "A joke's prosperity," says Shakspeare, "lies in the ear of the hearer;" and indeed it is sometimes exceedingly difficult to pronounce whether it be a good one or a bad one, risibly speaking, for a *bon mot* may be too witty to be pleasant, or at least to elicit laughter; while a poor pleasantry, by the help of some ludicrous turn, or expression, or association of ideas, may provoke cachinnation, *à gorge déployée*. Nay, there are cases, in which a joke becomes positively good from its being so intolerably bad, and is applauded, in the inverse ratio of its merit, as the greatest honours are sometimes showered upon men who have the least honour. The admiration excited by the highest order of wit is generally serious, because it sets us thinking. It was said of a crafty Israelite, who deserted the Hebrew faith, without embracing that of the Christians, and yet endeavoured to make both parties subservient to his selfish views, that he resembled the blank leaf between the Old and New Testament, belonging to neither, and making a cover of both. No one would laugh at this; it is exactly that description of wit which has been defined "an unexpected association of apparently dissimilar ideas, exciting pleasure and surprise." Lord Byron was once asked by a friend, in the green room of Drury Lane Theatre, whether he did not think Miss Kelly's acting in the "Maid and the Magpie" exceedingly natural?—"I really cannot say," replied his lordship; "I was never innocent of stealing a silver spoon." This is drollery rather than wit, and excites our laughter, without claiming any portion of our admiration.

One of our poets, a remarkably cadaverous-looking man, recited a poem, descriptive of a country walk, in which the following couplet occurred :—

> "The redbreast, with his furtive glance,
> Comes and looks at me askance ;"—

upon which a wag exclaimed—"Gad ! if it had been a carrion-crow, he would have stared you full in the face ;" a remark so humorous and unexpected, that it was received with an unanimous shout of laughter. Here the absurdity of the idea, if it did not amount to wit, was something better, or, at all events, more stimulative of the risible faculties.

JUDGMENT—a faculty of which very few people have enough to discover that they want more. In forming a judgment of each other, the sexes usually proceed upon the falsest and most deceitful grounds. If a woman be struck by a man's exterior, she invariably thinks well of his morals and his talents : gain her love, and you secure her esteem ; she judges of everything by the impression made upon herself, and in the credulity that prompts her to believe what she wishes, is easily led away by her confiding and affectionate nature. Men, sexually speaking, are still more blind and rash in their judgment, or, rather, in their total want of it. If they are smitten by a pretty face, they inquire no further, and ask but one question—Will you have me ?

They marry the face, of which the beauty is to last, perhaps, for one year only,—at most for ten,—and they know little or nothing of the mind with which they are to be associated until death. In balancing the respective motives of the sexes, the advantage is, as usual, all on the side of the females. Both are precipitate, and both wrong; but women are misled by their trust and their affections, while men fall into the same error from the influence of their passions and their senses. If any of my male readers doubt this judgment, let them doubt their own.

ING—according to the doctrine of despots and their worshippers, the hereditary proprietor of a nation;—according to reason, its accountable first magistrate. Monarchs are the spoilt children of fortune; and, like the juvenile members of the class, are often wayward, peevish, and ill at ease. We talk of being "as happy as a king;" but which of us is not happier,—at least, in love and friendship, the great sweeteners of life? There is no courtship in Courts. A king goes a wooing in the person of his privy councillors; marries one whom he never saw, in order to please the nation, of which he is the ruler, only to be its slave; and is generally cut off from those domestic enjoyments that constitute the highest charm of existence. Friendship cannot offer him a substitute, for equality is its basis; and he who wears a crown is at once prevented by station, and prohibited by etiquette, from indulging in any communion of hearts. Truly he ought to be exempted from all other taxes, since he pays quite enough for his painful preeminence.

A wise man, however well qualified to shine in Courts, will seldom desire to share their dangerous splendour.

Diogenes, while he was washing cabbages, seeing Aristippus
approach, cried out to him—" If you knew how to live upon
cabbages, you would not be paying court to a tyrant."—" If
you knew how to live with kings," replied Aristippus, " you
would not be washing cabbages."

" Of all kinds of men," says a French writer, " God is
least beholden to kings ; for he does the most for them,
and they the least for him." And yet the patriot king,
who confers happiness upon a whole nation, must render
a more acceptable service to the Deity than any other
mortal can proffer.

KISSES—admit of a greater variety of character than
perhaps even my female readers are aware, or than Joannes
Secundus has recorded. Eight basial diversities are mentioned in Scripture ; viz.—The kiss of

Salutation . . .	Sam. xx. 41. 1 Thess. v. 26.
Valediction . . .	Ruth ii. 9.
Reconciliation . .	2 Sam. xiv. 33.
Subjection . . .	Psalms ii. 12.
Approbation . .	Proverbs ii. 4.
Adoration . . .	1 Kings xix. 18.
Treachery . . .	Matt. xxvi. 49.
Affection	Gen. xlv. 15.

But the most honourable kiss, both to the giver and receiver,
was that which Queen Margaret of France, in the presence
of the whole Court, impressed upon the lips of the ugliest
man in the kingdom, Alain Chartier, whom she one day
found asleep, exclaiming to her astonished attendants—" I
do not kiss the man, but the mouth that has uttered so
many charming things." Ah ! it was worth while to be a
poet in those days.

KITCHEN—the burial-place of the epicure's health and fortune.—"What a small kitchen!" exclaimed Queen Elizabeth, after going over a handsome mansion.—"It is by having so small a kitchen, that I am enabled to keep so large a house," replied its owner.

KNOWLEDGE—a molehill removed from the mountain of our ignorance. Where shall we discover a finer illustration of disinterestedness than the outcry raised against the taxes on knowledge by Alderman ——, who can never be affected by the impost. To call the newspaper stamp, however, a tax upon knowledge, is to term the duty upon gin a tax upon provisions. Away with the former, nevertheless, in order that men of respectability and talent may enter into the arena, and compete with the authors of the illegal penny and twopenny publications. If danger be apprehended from the darkness or perversion of the popular mind, what security so effectual as that of enlightening and guiding it? How preposterous to clamour against the poison, and interdict the antidote! If the people *will* endanger their own constitution, and that of the country, by plucking sour apples from the forbidden tree of knowledge, the only way to cure them of their propensity, is to allow them free access to a sweeter and better fruit.

" What will be the best method of saving this small beer from depredation?" said a lady to her butler.—"By placing a cask of strong beer at the side of it," was the reply.

A knowledge of useful things, of which others are ignorant, is never considered an excuse for an ignorance of trifles that are generally known.

After a scholar has attained a certain age, no knowledge that you can let in upon his mind will do him any harm.

Cattle may be admitted into an orchard, to graze it after the trees are grown up, but not when they are young.

Partial instruction may be a partial evil, but universality of knowledge, however high the standard, will never take the poor out of their sphere. Elevating the lower, without depressing the upper classes, it will be an unmixed good to both. But if knowledge be power, will not its universality give a dangerous ascendancy to the multitude? No—for the few will be still wiser than the many. The most ignorant will then run the greatest risk. In a general illlumination, it is only the unlighted windows that are pelted and broken by the mob.

KNOWLEDGE of the world—the fancied wisdom of those whose reflections are created by a mirror. There is a class of persons who think they evince prodigious penetration into the human heart, when they ascribe every action to the worst possible motives, taking it for granted that all men are sordid, profligate, or designing, all women dissipated, thoughtless, and inconstant. This misanthropical ignorance they presume to term knowledge of the world. So it may be, but it is of that world only which is comprised in their own persons.

AMPS.—When these were brought in at night, the ancient Greeks used to salute them with the words, Χαιρε, φιλον φως—*Salve amica lux!*—The human owls of modern times, when the intellectual light is spreading around them, are so far from hailing it with a blessing, that they retire to their cells and lurking places, and hoot at it as a pestilent innovation. While stabbing at the liberies and happiness of mankind, they would rather cry out, with Macbeth,—

> " Come, thick night,
> And pall thee in the dunnest smoke of hell,
> That my keen knife see not the wound it makes,
> Nor Heaven peep through the blanket of the dark,
> To cry hold ! hold ! "

LANDSCAPE GARDENING—artificial nature : the finest of the fine arts. He who lays out grounds and gardens, calling new beauties into existence, not only for his own gratification, but for that of his contemporaries and successors, is exercising a benevolent power which makes him a species of creator. Like all the pure and simple pleasures, this is an enjoyment which rewards itself, and retains its attraction under all circumstances, and at every period of life. The word Paradise is synonymous with garden, and the Elysium of the ancients consisted of sylvan fields. Happy the man who can secure a living apotheosis, amid the beatitudes of a terrestrial garden !

LANGUAGES—in several instances have derived their names from a single word. Sismondi, writing on the literature of the Trouveres, says, " The Provençal was called the *Langue d'Oc*, and the Wallon the *Langue d'Oil*, or *d'Oui*, from the affirmative word of each language, as the Italian was then called the *Langue de Si*, and the German the *Langue de Ya*." Not only to a whole language, but to a whole life may the word *yes* give its colour and character, as many an unhappy wife has found to her cost.

Language, which is the uniting bond and the very medium of communion between men, is at the same time, by the great variety of tongues, the means of severing and estranging nations more than anything else. In this respect it may be compared to the Ourang-outang, which, according to the travelling showman, "forms the connecting link which separates mankind from the human race."

LAUGH, A horse—the sorry hack upon which buffoons and jesters are fain to ride home, when they want to make a retreat, and are at a loss for any other conveyance. Such Merry Andrews save their credit as the Romans did their Capitol, by the cackling of geese. To succeed in this object all expedients are considered fair ; to win the laugh, is to win the battle ; if you cannot, therefore, check-mate your adversary by reasoning, dumb-found him by your superior learning, or surpass him in the brilliancy of your wit, knock him down by a poor pun, the worse the better ; set the example of a hearty laugh, for this is catching, though wit is not, and make your escape while the company are exercising their risible muscles ; they will generally be with you, for they like to see a conqueror capsized. The late Jack Taylor, of pleasant memory, who was no mean proficient in thus turning the tables upon his opponent, when he found himself losing, has recorded one of his exploits. He was rapidly losing ground in a literary discussion, when the opposite party exclaimed, " My good friend, you are not such a rare scholar as you imagine ; you are an every-day man." " Well, and you are a *weak* one," replied Taylor, who instantly jumped upon the back of a horse laugh, and rode victoriously over his prostrate conqueror.

LAUGHTER—a faculty bestowed exclusively upon man, and one which there is, therefore, a sort of impiety in not exercising as frequently as we can. We may say with Titus, that we have lost a day if it have passed without laughing. The pilgrims at Mecca consider it so essential a part of their devotion, that they call upon their prophet to preserve them from sad faces. "Ah!" cried Rabelais, with an honest pride, as his friends were weeping around his death-bed, "if I were to die ten times over, I should never make you cry half so much as I have made you laugh." "*Risu inepto res ineptior nulla est*," says an anti-risible reader; but if laughter be genuine, and consequently a means of innocent enjoyment, can it be inept?"

LAW, English—see Hocus Pocus, and Chicanery. The following character, or rather sentence of condemnation, was pronounced upon it, by one well acquainted with his subject —the lecturer over the remains of the late Jeremy Bentham. In answer to the question, what is this boasted English law, which, as we have been told for ages, renders us the envy and admiration of surrounding nations, he replies, "The *substantive* part of it, whether as written in books or expounded by judges, a chaos, fathomless and boundless; the huge and monstrous mass being made up of fiction, tautology, technicality, circuity, irregularity, and inconsistency; the *administrative* part of it, a system of exquisitely contrived chicanery; a system made up of abuses; a system which constantly places the interest of the judicial minister in opposition to his duty; so places his interest in opposition to his duty, that in the very proportion in which it serves his ends, it defeats the ends of justice; a system of self-authorised and unpunishable depredation; a system which encourages mendacity, both by reward and punishment; a system which puts fresh arms into the hands of the injurer, to annoy and distress the injured; in a word, a system which maximises delay, sale, and denial of justice." And yet, what an outcry was raised by the disinterested reverers of our time-hallowed institutions, when Lord Brougham attempted to sweep some of the filth from the mere margin of this sink of iniquity. His reforms were too rough, forsooth. They would have him cleanse the Augean stable with a white cambric handkerchief.

Most lawsuits are a juggle, whose sole object seems to be the plunder of both plaintiff and defendant by the prolongation of their quarrel. "Strange," says Old Fuller in his "Worthies," "that reason continuing always the same, law, grounded thereon, should be capable of so great alteration." It is not grounded upon reason, but upon the artifices of pettifoggers, and therefore its perversions and metamorphoses are infinite. *In Republicâ corruptissimâ plurimæ leges.* When Justinian compiled his Institutes, the writings on the civil law alone amounted to many camel loads. *Ours* may be reckoned by ship loads, and the money annually expended upon law and lawyers (not upon justice), may be counted by millions. Such is the magnitude and vitality of this hundred headed Hydra, that we may well doubt the power of Lord Brougham to crush it, even though he dip his arrows in the monster's gall. Hercules as he is, he will find it difficult to outlaw the lawyers.

LAWYERS—generally know too much of law to have a very clear perception of justice, just as divines are often too deeply read in theology, to appreciate the full grandeur and the proper tendencies of religion. Losing the abstract in the concrete, the comprehensive in the technical, the principal in its accessories, both are in the predicament of the rustic, who could not see London for the houses.

It has been invidiously said, that lawyers pass their time in taking advantage of their contemporaries; but if we may credit the authority of Foote, they sometimes outwit the undertaker even after their death. That facetious person being once summoned into the country, by the relatives of a respectable practitioner, to whom he had been appointed executor, was asked what directions should be given respecting the funeral? "What may be your practice in the country," said the wag, "I do not exactly know ; but in London, when a lawyer dies, his body is disposed of in a very cheap and simple manner. We lock it up in a room over night, and by the next morning it has always totally disappeared. Whither it has been conveyed we cannot tell to a certainty ; but there is invariably such a strong smell of brimstone in the chamber, that we can form a shrewd guess at the character of the conveyancer."

LEARNING—very often a knowledge of words, and an ignorance of things ; a common act of memory, which may be exercised without common sense. A mere scholar is generally known by his unacquaintance with everything but languages, which have so filled his head, that they have left room for nothing else. He mistakes the steps for the temple of Minerva ; the shrine for the goddess herself; and is as proud of his mind's empty purse, as if there were money in it ! Pedantry's jargon will no more improve our under-standings, than the importunate clink of a smoke-jack will fill our bellies. The elaborate triflings of scholiasts and commentators, the jingling sophistries of logic, and what has been technically termed the learning of the schools, all of which were so many antidotes to sound sense and reflection, may well be thrown overboard, when many a member of our Mechanics' Institutes, possesses useful knowledge that might puzzle a whole convent of college monks.

Of all learning the most difficult department is to un-learn. Drawing a mistake or prejudice out of the head, is as painful as drawing a tooth, and the patient never thanks the operator for the "*demptus per vim mentis gratissimus error.*" No man likes to admit·that his favourite opinion (perhaps the only child of his mind, and cherished accordingly) is an illegitimate one. Sluggish intellects are ever the most obstinate, for that which it has cost us much to acquire, it costs us much to give up; and the older we get, the more tenaciously we cling to our errors, as those weeds are most difficult to eradicate that have had the longest time to root themselves. Harvey could find no physician, turned of forty, who would admit the circulation of the blood. Numbers of these quadragenarian owls are now to be found in every profession, while we have Jesuits enough of all ages, who sigh for the suppressed Inquisition, whenever a political or religious Galileo promulgates any truth that threatens to interfere with established falsehoods. These buzzards have yet to acquire the most useful of all learning—that of unlearning.

LIARS—verbal forgers, stiflers of truth, and murderers of fact. They will sometimes attempt to conceal their failing by affecting a scrupulous adherence to veracity. B—, who rarely shamed the Devil, once said of his friend, " Jack is a good fellow, but, it must be confessed, he has his failings. I am sorry to say so, but I will not tell a lie for any man. Amicus Jack—*sed magis amica veritas,*—I love my friend, but I love truth still more."—" My dear B—," said a bystander, laying his hand upon his shoulder—" I never expected that you would have preferred a perfect stranger to an old acquaintance."

The *ci-devant* civic dandy, who, from his rising in the east and setting in the west, or, perhaps, from his want of personal beauty, *quasi lucus à non lucendo*, had acquired the nickname of Apollo, once received a visit from a peer, whose propensity to fibbing is well known.—" I find," said his lordship, who is apt to mistake impertinence for jocularity, " that you are going to the fancy-ball to-night, and I presume you will appear in the character of Apollo."—" I had some such idea." replied ——, " and I am glad your lordship has called, because you can now accompany me as my *lyre.*"

LIBEL, Law of—a libel upon the law. Even under the tyranny of some of the Roman emperors, there seems to have been a greater latitude of speech and writing than is permitted by the laws of modern England. Adverting to the reigns of Trajan and Aurelius, Tacitus says—"*Rara temporum felicitate, ubi sentire quæ velis, et quæ sentias dicere licet.*"—"By the rare happiness of those days you might think what you wished, and speak as you thought."

LIBELLERS—literary bravos, supported by illiterate cowards. If the receiver of stolen goods be worse than the thief, so must the purchaser of libels be more culpable than their author. As the peruser of a slanderous journal would write what he reads, had he the talent, so the actual maligner would become a malefactor, had he the opportunity and the courage.—"*Maledicus à malefico, nisi occasione, non differt,*" says Quinctilian.—"He who stabs you in the dark, with a pen, would do the same with a pen-knife, were he equally safe from detection and the law."

A libeller's mouth has been compared to that of a volcano —the lighter portions of what it vomits forth are dissipated by the winds; the heavier ones fall back into the throat whence they were disgorged. The aspersions of libellers may, perhaps, be better compared to fullers' earth, which, though it may seem to dirt you at first, only leaves you more pure and spotless, when it is rubbed off.

LIBRARY—a precious catacomb, wherein are embalmed and preserved imperishably, the great minds of the dead who will never die.

"In the library of the world," says Champfort, "men

have hitherto been ranged according to the form, the size, and the binding. The time is coming when they will take rank and order according to their contents and intrinsic merits."

LIFE—a momentary convulsion between two tranquil eternities;—an avenue to death, as death is the gate that opens to a new and more enduring life. Our tables and bills of mortality, within the last hundred years, show a remarkable and unprecedented increase in the average duration of human life; while our capacities for taking advantage of this prolonged term have, at least, been doubled within the term mentioned. The existence of a rational and improvable creature, is not to be measured by years and months, but by ideas and sensations—by what we can see, enjoy, learn, and accomplish during our pilgrimage upon earth, in which point of view every educated individual is as a Methuselah when compared to his remote ancestors. Look how we have conquered space and time, and all the elements that surround us, making an impalpable vapour, in England alone, perform the work of many millions of men, and thus leading us to the cheering hope that iron and steam may eventually supersede, to a considerable degree, the employment of human and animal bones and muscles, so that the meanest artizan may have leisure for recreation and the culture of his mind. Consider how the pangs of separation are diminished and the affections solaced, by those facilities of rapid travelling which may be said to have almost brought the uttermost ends of the earth together, and to have made each nation participate in the advantages of all. Easy is it now for any man or woman to be a literal cosmopolitan. A week takes us to St. Petersburg—four weeks to Grand Cairo—a few months to the East Indies, or to any part of the world.

It is the activity of the mind, not the functional vitality of the body, that constitutes life. By the enlargement of our ideas, and the general diffusion of knowledge, consequent upon our increased powers of locomotion and comparison, we may condense a whole existence into a narrow compass of time, and enjoy a dozen such lives as were passed by the most enlightened of our ancestors. And yet, doubly precious as this state of being has become, how many are compelled to throw away life for a livelihood, *et propter vitam vivendi perdere causas.* Nevertheless, their mere vitality, even in spite of their discontents, is an inexhaustible source of gratification, and might be rendered much more so, would they but contemplate it in the proper light. "Enjoy thy existence," says Jean Paul Richter, "more than thy manner of existence, and let the dearest object of thy consciousness be the consciousness of life."

Though nothing is so closely allied as life to death, no two things are so utterly different from each other.

The ancient Egyptians considered every part of the universe to be endowed with an inherent life, energy and intelligence; worshipping the active phenomena of nature, without discriminating cause from effect. They believed the elements themselves to be animated; and why should they not be?—All of them have motion and a voice—the great constituents of vitality: and, if not themselves alive, they are all instinct with life.

Life has been compared to tragedy, comedy, and farce. It was reserved for Talleyrand to consider it as a one-act piece. "I know not why the world calls me a wicked man," said Rulhière, "for I never, in the whole course of my life, committed more than one act of wickedness."—"But when will this act be at an end?" asked Talleyrand.

LIGHT, The new.—It was said of Burns, that the light

which led him astray, was light from heaven; a false and unguarded assertion, for no light from heaven can ever lead man astray. The spiritual new light is a Jack-o'-lantern, which sometimes lures its followers into quagmires and pit-falls; or it may be the glitter of gold, and the dazzling lustre of worldly greatness, by which they are lighted to dignities and high places. Of this latter we will cite an instance from the Life of Andrew Melville, by Dr. M'Crie:—"When Cowper was made Bishop of Galloway, an old woman, who had been one of his parishioners, and a favourite, could not be persuaded that her minister had deserted the Presbyterian cause. Resolved to satisfy herself, she paid him a visit at the Canongate, where he had his residence, as Dean of the Chapel Royal. The retinue of servants, through which she had to pass, staggered the good woman's confidence, and being ushered into a room, where the bishop sat, she exclaimed—'Oh, Sir! what's this?—and ye ha' really left the guid cause, and turned prelate!'—'Janet!' said the bishop, 'I have got a new light on this subject.'—'So I see,' replied Janet; 'for when ye was at Perth, ye had but ae candle, and now ye ha' got twa before ye.—That's your *new* light.'"

LIGHT—like the circulating blood, which returns to the heart, is supposed to return to the sun, after having performed the functions for which it was emitted from that body. Even so will the soul, our intellectual light, return to its divine source, when released from the body, to whose earthly purposes it has ministered.

LITERATI—may be divided into two classes: those who live to study, and those who study to live; the former, tending to elevate literature, and the latter, to degrade it. The first generally survive their own death; the last often die and are forgotten in their lifetime, for that which is written for the day must expire with it.

LOVER—see Lunatic. A man, who, in his anxiety to obtain possession of another, has lost possession of himself. Lovers are seldom tired of one another's society, because they are always speaking of themselves. Let us not, however, disparage this fond infatuation, for all its tendencies are elevating. He who has passed through life without ever being in love, has had no spring-time—no summer in his existence; his heart is as a flowering plant which hath never blown—never developed itself—never put forth its beauty and its perfume—never given nor received pleasure.

The love of our youth, like Kennel coal, is so inflammable, that it may be kindled by almost any match; but if its transient blaze do not pass away in smoke, its flame, too bright and ardent to last long, soon exhausts and consumes itself. The love of our maturer age is like coke, which, when once ignited, burns with a steady and enduring heat, emitting neither smoke nor flame.

No wonder that we hear so much of the sorrows of love, for there is a pleasure even in dwelling upon its pains.—Revelling in tears, its fire, like that of naphtha, likes to swim upon water.

Lovers must not trust too implicitly to their visual organs. A tender swain once reproached his inamorata with suffering a rival to kiss her hand, a fact which she indignantly denied. —" But I *saw it.*"—" Nay, then," cried the offended fair, " I am now convinced you do not love me, since you believe your eyes in preference to my word."

LUCK, Good and bad—is but a synonyme, in the great majority of instances, for good and bad judgment. The prudent, the considerate, and the circumspect, seldom com-

lain of their ill luck; but I should shrewdly suspect the
iscretion of the grumbler who protested that fortune always
ıade clubs or spades trumps, when he had not a single
lack card in his hand; and that even when he fell back-
·ards he was sure to break his nose.

LUXURY—the conqueror of conquerors—the consump-
on of states—the dry-rot of the constitution—the avenger
f the defeated and the oppressed. Poverty, conquest, wealth,
ıxury, decay; such is the Round-Robin history of the
·orld—

<blockquote>

"Sævior armis
Luxuria incubuit, victumque ulciscitur orbem."

</blockquote>

Mandeville's position, that private vices are public benefits,
nd that individual luxury, even when pushed to a faulty
ҡcess, is a public advantage, cannot be maintained; for
othing that is injurious to one, can be good for many.

AGNANIMITY—is as often littleness as
greatness of mind. There is a cheap species,
which prompts us to feel complacently towards
our enemy when he has enabled us to make a
happy repartee.
We forgive him all his previous attempts to lower us,
ecause he has unintentionally furnished us with a momen-
ıry triumph; so completely does our love of self predomi-
ate, even over our dislike of others. The more cruelly we
ave mauled our poor vanquished opponent, the more ten-
erly do we regard him; and if we have well nigh blown
im to atoms, we feel as if we could never again injure a hair
f his head. As there is no magnanimity so cheap, there is
one so gratifying as this, for we like to purchase our virtues

on good terms. One of Sheridan's creditors, after having long and vainly dunned him, at length suggested, that if he could not discharge the principal of the debt, he might, at least, pay the interest. "No," said the wag; "it is not my interest to pay the principal, nor my principle to pay the interest." Though he had previously hated the man for his vulgar importunity, it is recorded that he took him into favour from that moment, and actually defrayed the amount of his bill, a rare instance of preference, considering that he seldom discharged any debt till he paid that of nature.

Pleasant enough was the magnanimity of the person who, being reproached with not having revenged himself of a caning he had received, exclaimed, " Sir, I never meddle with what passes behind my back ! "

MAN—an image of the Deity, which occasionally acts as if it were anxious to fill up a niche in the temple of the Devil. The only creature which, knowing its mortality and immortality, lives as if it were never to die, and too often dies as if it were never to live :—the sole being gifted with reason, the only one that acts irrationally :—the nothing of yesterday— the dust of to-morrow. Man is a fleeting paradox, which the fulness of time alone can explain ; a living enigma, of which the solution will be found in death.

MARRIAGE—a state of which it is unnecessary to describe the great happiness, for two reasons ;—first, because it would be superfluous to those who are in the enjoyment of its blessings : and secondly, because it would be impossible to those who are not.

Habituated as we are to the association of doves with loves, it seems startling to learn, on the authority of Pliny, that the Romans considered the hawk a bird of particularly good omen in marriage, because it never eats the hearts of other birds ; thus intimating that no differences, or quarrels, in the marriage state, ought ever to reach the heart.

The difficulty of effecting marriages, in these times of expensive establishments, is one of the great evils of our social system, and the principal source of corrupt manners. Malthus's prudential restraint is actively operative among the middling, and utterly neglected by the lower classes ; hence the predominance of celibacy in the one, and of a redundant population and consequent pauperism, in the other.

" Marriage," says Dr. Johnson, " is the best state for a man in general ; and every man is a worse man, in proportion as he is unfit for the married state." It may be doubted, however, whether another of his positions could be maintained—"that marriages in general would be as happy, and often more so, if they were all made by the Lord Chancellor, upon a due consideration of character and circumstances, without the parties having any choice in the matter."

In the pressure that now weighs upon all persons of limited fortune, sisters, nieces, and daughters, are the only commodities that our friends are willing to bestow upon us for nothing, and which we cannot afford to accept, even gratuitously. It seems to have been the same, at a former period, in France. Maitre Jean Picard tells us that, when he was returning from the funeral of his wife, doing his best to look disconsolate, such of the neighbours as had grown-up daughters and cousins came to him, and kindly implored him not to be inconsolable, as they could give him a second wife.—" Six weeks after," says Maitre Jean, " I lost my cow, and, though I really grieved upon this occasion, not one of them offered to give me another."

It has been recorded by some anti-connubial wag, that when two widowers were once condoling together, on the recent bereavement of their wives, one of them exclaimed, with a sigh, " Well may I bewail my loss, for I had so few differences with the dear deceased, that the last day of my marriage was as happy as the first."—" There I surpass you," said his friend, " for the last day of *mine was happier !* "

MARTYR—that which all religions have furnished in about equal proportions, so much easier is it to die for religion than to live for it. Our high church conservatives cry out, with a lusty voice, " Touch not that which has been cemented by the blood of the holy martyrs ! " Why, these very martyrs, whose devotedness proves nothing but their sincerity, died in the cause of reform ; and yet their example is cited as a warning against it ! If their blood appeal to us at all, it may rather be supposed to cry out against the monstrous abuses of that Christianity, for whose cause they became martyrs.

MASQUERADE—a synonyme for life and civilised society. There are two sorts of masquerade, simulation, or pretending to be what you are not: and dissimulation, or concealing what you are ; and we are all mummers under one or the other of these categories, excepting a few performers at the two extremes of life—those who are above, and those who are beneath all regard for appearances. As a secret consciousness of their defects is always prompting hypocrites to disguise themselves in some assumed virtue, the only way to discover their real character, is to read them backwards, like a Hebrew book.

Many masqueraders on the stage of real life betray themselves by overacting their part. With religious pretenders this is more especially the case, and for an obvious reason: they increase the outward and visible sign, in proportion as they feel themselves deficient in the inward and spiritual grace. Can we wonder at their sanctimonious looks, and puritanical severity? Even when they flounder and fail in their hypocrisy, they would persuade us that their very blunders proceed from a heavenly impulse. They remind one of the fat friar, who being about to mount his mule, called upon his patron saint to assist him, and gave such a vigorous spring at the same time, that he fell over on the other side, when he exclaimed with an air of complacency, "Hallo! the good saint has helped me too much!"

So difficult is it to avoid overacting our part, that we cannot always escape this error, when we are agents and accessaries, instead of principals, in imposing upon the world. The Regent of France, intending to go to a masquerade in the character of a lackey, and expressing an anxious wish to remain undetected the Abbé Dubois, suggested that this object might easily be attained, if he would allow him to go as his master, and to give him two or three kicks before the whole company. This was arranged accordingly, but the pretended master applied his foot so rudely and so often, that the Regent was fain to exclaim, "Gently, gently, Monsieur l'Abbé! you are disguising me too much!"

MASTER.—Being our own master, means that we are at liberty to be the slave of our own follies, caprices and passions. Generally speaking, a man cannot have a worse or more tyrannical master than himself. As our habits and luxuries domineer over us, the moment we are in a situation to indulge them, few people are in reality so dependent as the independent. Poverty and subjection debar us from many vices by the impossibility of giving way to them: when we are rich, and free from the domination of others, we are corrupted and oppressed by ourselves. There was some philosophy, therefore, in the hen-pecked husband, who being asked why he had placed himself so completely under the government of his wife, answered, "To avoid the worse slavery of being under my own."

MEDICAL PRACTICE—guessing at Nature's intentions and wishes, and then endeavouring to substitute man's.

MELANCHOLY—ingratitude to Heaven.—

> O impious ingrates ! cast your eyes
> On the fair earth—the seas—the skies,
> And if the vision fail to prove
> A Maker of unbounded love ;—
> If in the treasures scattered wide,
> To guests of earth, and air, and tide ;
> If in the charms, with various zest,
> To every sense of man addressed,
> Ye will not see the wish to bless
> With universal happiness,
> Nor judge that mortals best fulfil
> A bountiful Creator's will,
> When, with a cheerful gratitude,
> They taste the pleasures He has strew'd,
> What can avail the wit, the sage,
> The love of man, the sacred page,
> When, by such evidence assailed,
> Your God and all His works have failed !

As a good antidote to gloomy anticipations, we should all of us do well to recollect the saying of Sir Thomas More,—

> " If evils come not—then our fears are vain,
> And if they do—fear but augments the pain."

MEMORY.—Rochefoucauld says, " Every one complains of his memory, no one of his judgment." And why ? Because we consider the former as depending upon nature; and the latter upon ourselves. Alleged want of memory is a most convenient refuge for our self-love, since we can always throw it as a cloak over our ignorance. It is astonishing how much people are in the habit of forgetting what they never knew.

"Strange," says the same writer, "that we can always remember the smallest thing that has happened to ourselves, and yet not recollect how often we have repeated it to the same person."

It is a benevolent provision of nature, that in old age the memory enjoys a second spring—a second childhood, and that while we forget all passing occurrences, many of which are but painful concomitants of old age, we have a vivid and delightful recollection of all the pleasures of youth. Many a greybeard, who seems to be lost in vacancy, as he sits silently twiddling his thumbs, is in fact chewing the mental cud of past happiness, and enjoying a tranquil gratification, which youngsters might well envy.

Objects become shadowy to the bodily eye, as they are more remote, but to the mental eye of age, the most distant are the most distinct. A man of eighty may forget that he was seventy, but he never forgets that he was once a boy. Who can doubt the immortality of the soul, when we see that the mind can thus pass out of bodily decrepitude into a state of rejuvenescence? for this process amounts to a Palingenesia—a partial new birth out of a partial decease, preparatory to a total resurrection out of total dissolution.

MINDS.—Large ones, like pictures, are seen best at a distance. Their beauties are thus enhanced, and their blemishes concealed,—a process which is reversed by a close inspection. This is the reason, to say nothing of envious motives, why we generally undervalue our contemporaries, and overrate the ancients.

MIRROR.—John Taylor relates in his Records, that having restored sight to a boy who had been born blind, the lad was perpetually amusing himself with a hand-glass, calling his own reflection his little man, and enquiring why he could make it do everything that he did *except shut its eyes.* A French lover, making a present of a mirror to his mistress, sent with it a poetical quatrain, which may be thus paraphrased :—

> " This mirror *my* object of love will unfold,
>   Whensoe'er your regard it allures :—
> Oh ! would, when I'm gazing, that I might behold
>   On its surface the object of *yours /* "

But the following old epigram, on the same subject, is in a much finer strain :—

> " When I revolve this evanescent state,
>   How fleeting is its form, how short its date !
> My being and my stay dependant still,
> Not on my own, but on another's will ;
> I ask myself, as I my image view,
> Which is the real shadow of the two ?"

MISADVENTURE, Mischance, and Misfortune—are all the daughters of Misconduct, and sometimes the mothers of Goodluck, Prosperity, and Advancement. To be thrown upon one's own resources, is to be cast into the very lap of Fortune ; for our faculties then undergo a development, and display an energy, of which they were previously unsusceptible. Our minds are like certain drugs and perfumes, which must be crushed before they evince their vigour, and put forth their virtues. Lundy Foot, the celebrated snuff manufacturer, originally kept a small tobacconist's shop at Limerick. One night, his house, which was uninsured, was burnt to the ground. As he contemplated the smoking ruins on the following morning, in a state bordering on despair, some of the poor neighbours, groping among the embers for what they could find, stumbled upon several canisters of unconsumed, but half-baked snuff, which they tried, and found it so grateful to their noses, that they loaded their waistcoat pockets with the spoil. Lundy Foot, roused from his stupor, at length imitated their example, and took a pinch of his own property, when he was instantly struck by the superior pungency and flavour it had acquired from the great heat to which it had been exposed. Treasuring up this valuable hint, he took another house in a place called Black Yard, and preparing a large oven for the purpose, set diligently about the manufacture of that high-dried commodity, which soon became widely known as Black Yard snuff; a term subsequently corrupted into the more familiar word—Blackguard. Lundy Foot, making his customers pay literally through the nose, raised the price of his production, took a larger house in Dublin, and ultimately made a handsome fortune by having been ruined.

MISANTHROPE.—Quite unworthy of Goethe's genial and penetrative mind is his misanthropical remark, that " each of us, the best as well as the worst, hides within him something, some feeling, some remembrance, which, if it were known, would make you hate him." More consonant would it have been to truth, as well as to an enlightened spirit of humanism, had he reversed the proposition, and exclaimed, in the words of Shakspeare—

> " There is some soul of goodness in things evil,
> Would men observingly distil it out ! "

Law's observation, " that every man knows something worse of himself than he is sure of in others," savours not of misanthropy, but of that doubly beneficial feeling which inculcates individual humility, and universal charity.

Rochefoucauld, and misanthropical writers of the same class, cannot succeed in giving any man, of a generous and clear intellect, an unfavourable opinion of human nature. Like the workers of tapestry, who always behold the wrong side, they themselves may see nothing but unfinished outlines, coarse materials, crooked ends, and glaring defects, and yet produce a portrait which, to those who contemplate it in front, and from a proper point of view, shall be full of grace, beauty, harmony, and proportion.

MISER—one who, though he loves himself better than all the world, uses himself worse ; for he lives like a pauper, in order that he may enrich his heirs, whom he naturally hates, because he knows that they hate him, and sigh for his death. In this respect, misers have been compared to leeches, which, when they get sick and die, disgorge, in a minute, the blood they have been so long sucking up. La Bruyere tersely says—"*Jeune on conserve pour la vieillesse : vieux on épargne pour la mort.*"

Pithy enough was the reply of the avaricious old man, who, being asked by a nobleman of doubtful courage what pleasure he found in amassing riches which he never used, answered—"Much the same that your lordship has in wearing a sword."

Perhaps the severest reproach ever made to a miser, was uttered by Voltaire. At a subscription of the French Academy for some charitable object, each contributor putting in a *louis d'or*, the collector, by mistake, made a second application to a member noted for his penuriousness. —"I have already paid," exclaimed the latter, with some asperity.—"I beg your pardon," said the applicant : "I have no doubt you paid ; I believe it, though I did not see it."— "And I saw it, and do not believe it," whispered Voltaire.

MISFORTUNE—is but another word for the follies, blunders, and vices, which, with a greater blindness, we attribute to the blind goddess, to the fates, to the stars, to any one, in short, but ourselves. Our own head and heart are the heaven and earth which we accuse, and make responsible for all our calamities.

The prudent make the reverses by which they have been overthrown supply a basis for the restoration of their fallen fortunes, as the lava which has destroyed a house often furnishes the materials for rebuilding it. Fools and profligates, on the contrary, seek solace for their troubles, by plunging into sensual and gross pleasures, as the wounded buffalo rolls himself in the mud.

The misfortune of the mischievous and evil-minded, is the good fortune of the virtuous ; the failure of the guilty, is the success of the innocent : to pity, therefore, the former, is, in some sort, to injure the latter, and to destroy the effect of the great moral lesson afforded by both. Let us keep our sympathies for the sufferings of the good.

All men might be better reconciled to their fate, if they would recollect that there are two species of misfortune, at which we ought never to repine ;—viz., that which we can, and that which we cannot, remedy ; regret being, in the former case, unnecessary, in the latter, unavailing.

The same vanity which leads us to assign our misfortunes or misconduct to others, prompts us to attribute all our lucky chances to our own talent, prudence, and forethought. Not a word of the fates or stars when we are getting rich, and everything goes on prosperously. So deeply-rooted in our nature is the tendency to make others responsible for our own misdeeds, that we lapse into the process almost unconsciously. When the clergyman has committed a peccadillo, he is doubly severe towards his congregation, and does vicarious penance in the persons of his flock. Men scold their children, servants, and dependants, for their own errors ; coachmen invariably punish their horses after they themselves have made any stupid blunder in driving them ; and even children, when they have tumbled over a chair, revenge themselves for their awkwardness, by beating and kicking the impassive furniture. Wine, the discoverer of truth, sometimes brings out this universal failing in a manner equally signal and ludicrous. An infant being brought to christen to a country curate, at a time when he was somewhat overcome by early potations, he was unable to find the service of Baptism in the book ; and, after fumbling for some time, peevishly exclaimed—"Confound the brat ! what is the matter with it ? I never, in all my life, knew such a troublesome child to christen ! "

MISSIONS, Religious—an attempt to produce, in distant and unenlightened nations, a uniformity of opinion on subjects upon which the missionaries themselves are at fierce and utter variance; thus submitting a European controversy of 1800 years to the decision of a synod of savages. Where the missionary begins with civilising and reclaiming the people among whom he is cast, he cannot fail to improve their temporal condition, and he is likely to contribute to their spiritual welfare; neither of which objects can be attained by the hasty zealot, who commences by attempting to teach the five points of Calvinism to barbarians unable to count their five fingers.

There is no reason to suppose, that the rapid conversion of the whole world to Christianity forms any part of the scheme of Providence, since, in eighteen centuries, so little comparative progress has been made towards its accomplishment. Still less shall we be warranted in concluding, that all those who remain in spiritual darkness will be eternally shut out from the mercy of their Creator, if we duly perpend the spirit of the Scriptures—" The Gentiles, which have not the law, do by nature the things contained in the law." Rom. ii. 14.—" God is no respecter of persons; but in every nation he that feareth him, and worketh righteousness, is accepted with him." Acts x. 34, 35.—" If there be a willing mind, it is accepted according to that a man hath, and not according to that he hath not." 2 Cor. viii. 12. And St. Paul seems to intimate that the Lord will accomplish his own work of conversion in his own time—" I will put my laws into their mind, and write them in their hearts. And they shall not teach every man his neighbour, and every man his brother, saying, Know the Lord; for all shall know me, from the least to the greatest." Heb. viii. 10, 11.

It is to be feared, that the conduct of the Europeans among savage nations, especially if we recollect the horrors of the slave trade, will plead much more powerfully than the Gospel precepts of our missionaries. Even where our example has not nullified our doctrine, it is difficult to adapt the latter to the capacities of barbarians. We learn from " Earle's Residence in New Zealand," that when some of the missionaries were expounding the horrors of Tophet and eternal fire, their auditors exclaimed—" We will have nothing to say to your religion. Such horrid punishments can only be meant for white men. We have none bad enough among us to deserve them ; but, as we have listened to you patiently, perhaps you will give us a blanket !"

MODERATION, Religious—an unattainable medium, since the world seems to be divided between the enthusiastic and the indifferent, or those who have too much and those who have too little devotion. One party make religion their business; the other make business their religion. Two commercial travellers meeting at an inn near Bristol, and conversing upon spiritual subjects, one asked the other whether he belonged to the Wesleyan Methodists. " No," replied the

man of business—"what little I do in the religious way is in
the Unitarian line."

MONASTERY — a house of ill-fame, where men are
seduced from their public duties, and fall naturally into
guilt, from attempting to preserve an unnatural innocence.
"It is as unreasonable for a man to go into a Carthusian
Convent for fear of being immoral, as for a man to cut off his
hands for fear he should steal. When that is done, he has
no longer any merit, for though it is out of his power to
steal, he may all his life be a thief in his heart. All
severity that does not tend to increase good or prevent evil,
is idle."

MONEY—a very good servant, but a bad master. It
may be accused of injustice towards mankind, inasmuch as
there are only a few who make false money, whereas money
makes many men false. We hate to be cheated, not so much
for the value of the commodity, as, because it makes others
appear superior to ourselves. Being defrauded would be
nothing, were it not so galling to be outwitted. Crates, the
Greek philosopher, left his money in the hands of a friend,
with orders to pay it to his children in case they should be
fools; for, said he, if they are philosophers, they will not
want it. Money is more indispensable now than it was then,
but, still, a wise man will have it in his head rather than his
heart.

MORALITY—keeping up appearances in this world, or
becoming suddenly devout when we imagine that we may
be shortly summoned to appear in the next.

MORAL CHOLERA.—"It is easier," says St. Gregory
Nazianzen, "to contract the vices of others than to impart to

them our own virtue; just as it is easier to catch their diseases than to communicate to them our own good health."*
Our anxiety to avoid bodily infection can only be exceeded by our total indifference to that which is mental. There is a moral, as well as a physical cholera, and yet, while we are frightened to death at the approach of the one, we voluntarily expose ourselves, during our whole life, to the attacks of the other. One of our jails was lately emptied because it contained a single case of Asiatic cholera; all the rest are kept crowded, until the patients, labouring under moral cholera, shall have corrupted the whole mass of their fellow prisoners. It seems to be the object of these institutions to propagate and disseminate the miasmata of vice, instead of preventing their circulation. Such of our malefactors as have the disease, in the natural way, are employed to inoculate the others, and then we wonder that there is a plague in the land. If an offender have broken one of the commandments, we guard against a repetition of the crime by sending him to a place where he not only learns to break the other nine, but to break prison also, when he presently begins to exercise his newly-acquired knowledge upon the community. We hang and transport rogues on a large scale, but we produce them on a still more extensive one.

MOTHERS. — Four good mothers have given birth to four bad daughters:—Truth has produced hatred; Success, pride; Security, danger; and Familiarity, contempt. And, on the contrary, four bad mothers have produced as many good daughters, for Astronomy is the offspring of astrology; Chymistry of alchemy; Freedom, of oppression; Patience, of long-suffering.

* Facilius est vitium contrahere quam virtutem impertire; quemadmodum facilius est morbo alieno infici, quam sanitatem largiri.

MOUNTAINEERS—are rarely conquered, not so much on account of the facility for defence afforded by their craggy heights, as from their hardier habits and greater patriotism. In the rich lowlands, art becomes the principal pursuit ; art leads to riches and luxury, and these to enervation and subjection.   On the high and barren places, man's occupations render him more conversant with nature, an intercourse which inseparably attaches him to "the mountain nymph—sweet liberty."—When in danger of being worsted, Highlanders are renovated, like Antæus, by a touch of their native earth ; and so might we, when attacked by the cares and sickliness of money-getting and money-spending, if we would only quit our crowded cities, take a walk in the fields, and touch the earth.   When the leafless and embittering metropolis turns our moral honey into gall, we may always reverse the process by straying amid the flowers of the country.

MOUTH—a useless instrument to some people, in its capacity, by the organs of speech, of rendering ideas audible ; but of special service to them in its other capacity of rendering victuals invisible.

MUSES, The—nine blue-stocking old maids, who seem to have understood all arts except that of getting husbands, unless their celibacy may be attributed to their want of marriage portions.   These venerable young ladies are loudly and frequently invoked by poetasters, writers in albums and annuals, and other scribblers; but, like Mungo in the farce, each of them replies, "Massa, massa !—the more you call, the more me won't come."   One of our tourists, at Paris, observing that there were only statues of eight muses on the Opera House, which was then incomplete, inquired of a labouring mason what had become of the ninth. *"Monsieur, je ne vous dirois pas,"* replied the man;—*" mais probablement elle s'amuse avec Apollon!"*—An English operative would hardly have given such an answer. A gentleman once expressed his surprise that, in so rich a literary country as England, the Muses should not attain their due honours.—"Impossible!" cried a whist-playing old lady—"They are nine, and of course cannot reckon honours."

MUSIC.—"Music, like man himself, derives all its dignity from its subordination to a loftier and more spiritual power. When, divorcing itself from poetry, it first sought to be a principal instead of an accessory, to attach more importance to a sound than to a thought, to supersede sentiment by skill, to become, in short, man's play-fellow, rather than his assistant teacher, a sensual instead of an intellectual gratification, its corruption, or at least its application to less ennobling purposes, had already commenced. As the art of music, strictly so called, was more assiduously cultivated, as it became more and more perplexed with complicated intricacies, only understood by a few, and less and less an exponent of the simple feelings and sentiments that are intelligible to all, it may be said to have lost in general utility and value, what it gained in science, and to have been gradually dissolving that union between sound and sense, which imparted to it its chief interest and influence."

So entirely do I agree with the writer from whom the above extract is taken, that I have often rode back after a morning concert, to my residence in the country, that I might enjoy the superior pleasures of natural music. It was upon such an occasion, while strolling in the fields, that my thoughts involuntarily arranged themselves, as the novelists say, into the following stanzas:—

THE TIN TRUMPET;

I.

There's a charm and zest when the singer thrills
The throbbing breast with his dulcet trills,
And a joy more rare than the sweetest air
    Art ever combined,
When the poet enhances,
By beautiful fancies,
The strain, and entrances
    Both ear and mind.
Thy triumph, O music ! is ne'er complete,
Till the pleasures of sense and of intellect meet.

II.

Delights like these, to the poor unknown,
Are reserved for the rich and great alone,
In diamonds and plumes, who fill the rooms
    Of some grand abode,
And think that a guinea,
To hear Paganini
Or warbling Rubini,
    Is well bestow'd ;
Since then, only then, they the pleasures share
Of science, voice, instrument—equally rare.

III.

But the peasant at home, in gratuitous boon,
Has an opera dome and orchestral saloon,
With melody gay from the peep of day
    Until evening dim :
Whenever frequented,
With flowers it is scented,
Its scenes all invented
    And painted by Him,
Who suspended its blazing lamps on high,
And its ceiling formed of the azure sky.

IV.

Oh ! what can compare with the concert sublime,
When waters, earth, air, all in symphony chime ?

> The wind, herds, and bees, with the rustle of trees,
>   Varied music prolong ;
> On the spray as it swingeth,
> Each bird sweetly singeth,
> The sky-lark down flingeth
>   A torrent of song,—
> Till the transports of music, devotion, and love,
> Waft the rapturous soul to the regions above.

MUSICIANS—machines for producing sounds ; human instruments, generally so completely absorbed by their own art, that they are either ignorant of all others, or undervalue them. In a company at Vienna, where the conversation was nearly engrossed by the praises of Goethe, Catalani exclaimed, with great *naïveté*, " Who is this Goethe?—I have never heard any of his music!" A poor German composer being introduced to Mozart, whom he considered the greatest man in the world, was so overcome with awe, that he dared not lift his eyes from the ground, but remained, for some time, stammering—" Ah, Imperial Majesty! Ah, Imperial Majesty!" In the same spirit Cafarielli, when told that Farinelli had been made a sort of Prime Minister in Spain, replied—" No man deserves it better, for his voice is absolutely unrivalled."

MYSTERY. — To him who has been sated and disappointed by the actual and the intelligible, there is a profound charm in the unattainable and the inscrutable. Infants stretch out their hands for the moon ; children delight in puzzles and riddles, even when they cannot discover their solution ; and the children of a larger growth desire no better employment than to follow their example, however it may lead them astray. The mystery of the Egyptian hieroglyphics was a frequent source of idolatry ; the type being taken for the prototype, until leeks and onions received the homage originally meant for their divine Giver. The attractive mystery of Irving's unknown tongues has engendered a fanaticism, at which we need the less wonder, if we remember the confession of the pious Baxter, that, in order to awaken an interest in his congregation, he made it a rule, in every sermon, to say something that was above their capacity.

There is a glorious epoch of our existence, wherein the comprehensible appears common and insipid, and in abandoning ourselves to the enthusiasm of imagination, we attain a middle state between despair and deification ;—a beatific ecstacy, when the spirit longs to fly upward—when the finite yearns for the infinite, the limited in intellect for the omniscient, the helpless for the omnipotent, the real for the impossible. Thus to flutter above the world, on the extended wings of fancy, is to be half a deity. And yet the forward-springing and ardent mind, which, running a-head of its contemporaries, stands upon the forehead of the age to come, only renders itself the more conspicuous mark for obloquy and assault. Like a Shrovetide cock, tethered to the earth, it can but partially raise itself, when it again sinks down, amid the sticks and stones of its cruel persecutors.

AMES.—The character of different eras may, to a certain extent, be discovered by the various ways in which our ambitious nobility, and others, have endeavoured to achieve an enduring celebrity. When chivalry was the rage, they gave their names to new inventions in arms and armour: —now-a-days, they court notoriety by standing godfathers to some new fashion in clothes and cookery, and eclipsing all competitors in their coats, cabs, and castors. A ducal Campbell, whose ancestors were always spilling hot blood, endeavours to win celebrity in another way, by inventing an Argyle for preserving hot gravy; a Sandwich embalms his name between two slices of bread and ham; a Pembroke immortalises himself in a table;—a Skelmersdale goes down to future ages, like an Egyptian divinity, in a chair;—a Standish, surpassing the bottle conjuror, creeps into an ink-stand, by which means "he still keeps his memory BLACK in our souls;"—a Stanhope expects to be wheeled down to posterity, by harnessing his name to a gig of a peculiar con-struction;—a Petersham, hitting upon the easiest device by which he could prove to after ages that he wore a head, gives his title to a hat. Another nobleman, *clarum et venerabile nomen*, one who was said to have driven all the tailors into the suburbs, by compelling them to live on the skirts of the town, wraps up his name in the mummy-cloth of a Spencer, and secures a long-enduring fame by inventing a short coat.

It is not generally known, that names may be affected, and even completely changed, by the state of the weather. Such, however, is, unquestionably, the case. The late Mr. Suet, the actor, going once to dine about twenty miles from London, and being only able to get an outside place on the coach, arrived in such a bedraggled state, from an incessant rain, and so muffled up in great coats and pocket handker-chiefs, that his friend inquired, doubtingly—"Are you *Suet?*" —"No!" replied the wag—"I'm *dripping!*"

Contracting a name sometimes lengthens the idea. Kean mentions an actor of the name of Lancaster, whom his com-rades called Lanky, for shortness.

NEGRO—a human being treated as a brute, because he is black, by inhuman beings, and greater brutes, who hap-pen to be white. The Ethiopians paint the devil white; and they have much better reason for making him look like a European, than we have for giving him an African complexion.

NOBLEMAN—one who is indebted to his ancestors for a name and an estate, and sometimes to himself, for being unworthy of both. It was said of an accomplished and amiable Earl, who was weak enough to be always boasting his title and his birth—"What a pity he is a nobleman; he really deserves to have been born a commoner."

NON-RESIDENCE and PLURALITIES — the best securities for an effectual Church Reform. "These scandalous practices," says Bishop Burnet, "are sheltered among us by many colours of law; whereas the Church of Rome, from whence we had these and many other abuses, has freed herself from this under which we labour, to our great and just reproach. This is so shameful a profanation of holy things, that it ought to be treated with detestation and horror. Do such men think on the vows they made at their ordination, on the rules in the Scriptures, or on the nature of their functions, or that it is a cure of souls? How long, how long shall this be the peculiar disgrace of our Church, which, for aught I know, is the only Church in the world that tolerates it?"—*Hist. of his own Times*, p. 646.

When, by an official return to Parliament, the great extent of these scandalous abuses was first made known to Lord Harrowby, "it struck me," says he, "with surprise—I could almost say with horror." Alas! when temporal peers are horror-struck by the scandals that are tolerated and practised by their spiritual teachers!

Many ecclesiastics, particularly from Ireland, whose influence or command of money has procured them a handsome tithe income, and who are leading idle and luxurious lives, at places of fashionable resort, either in England or upon the

Continent, without ever dreaming of their flock, except as to the best mode of fleecing them, boast, nevertheless, of being staunch supporters of the Church. Verily, it must be as its buttresses, rather than its pillars, since they are never seen inside the sacred building. The Rev. Dr. ENGLAND, of H——, as one of his parishioners very logically remarked, is the only divine who has a valid excuse for non-residence, and always employing curates, since we have the authority of Lord Nelson for asserting, that "ENGLAND expects every man to do his duty."

It is related of Philip of Narni, that he once preached a sermon upon non-residence, before Pope Gregory XV., which had the effect of driving thirty Bishops to their respective dioceses the day after. Alas! we have few preachers and no bishops of this stamp in Protestant England.

NONSENSE—sense that happens to differ from our own, supposing that we have any. If matter and mind, blending together in two incoherent substances, form the connecting link that separates physics from metaphysics, the real from the imaginary, and the visible from the unapparent, it follows as a precursive corollary, that the learned comments of the scholiasts, the dogmas of theologians, and the elaborate treatises of the Byzantine historians, can never be recognized as evidences of a foregone conclusion. Statistics and algebra, as well as logic and analogy, equally rebut the inference that in a case of so complicated a nature, the deposition of a mere functionary can be received as the spontaneous evidence of a compulsory principal. Cases may doubtless arise, where legal deductions, drawn from federal rather than from feudal institutes, will vary the superstructure upon which the whole theory was based; but in the present instance, such objections must be deemed rather captious than analytical. On the whole it is presumed that the reader, who has carefully

perused and reconsidered our arguments, will be at little loss
to understand the nature of the word, of which we have
written this clear and explanatory definition.   Should he,
however, not be satisfied, he is referred to Voltaire's Galima-
thias, beginning " *Un jour qu'il faisoit nuit,*" &c.

NON SEQUITUR — a grammatical Adam, being a
relative without an ante-cedent :—something that is *apropos*
to nothing, and comes after without following from.   Of this
figure there are various sorts ; but the most common form is
putting the cart before the horse, or taking the effect for the
cause.   The industrious, prudent, and enlightened people of
this country have thriven and grown great and rich, not
always in consequence of good, but in spite of bad government.   Their native shrewdness and energy have enabled
them to triumph over impediments, political, fiscal, and commercial, which would have completely crushed a less active
and enterprising nation.   When, therefore, they are desired
to reverence the mis-governed and the unreformed institu·
tions, to which alone they are told to consider themselves
indebted for all the advantages they enjoy, one cannot help
recalling the *non sequitur* of the Carmelite Friar, who in-
stanced as a striking proof of the superintendence and goodness of Providence, that it almost invariably made a river
run completely through the middle of every large city.
Somewhat akin to this instance of *naïveté* was the reply of
the Birmingham boy, who being asked whether some shillings,
which he tendered at a shop, were good, answered with
great simplicity, " Ay, that they be, for I seed father make
'em all this morning."

NOVELTY—what we recover from oblivion.   We can
fish little out of the river Lethe that has not first been thrown
into it.   The world of discovery goes round without advancing,

like a squirrel in its cage, and the revolution of one century differs but little from that of its predecessor. New performers mount the stage, but the pieces and its accompaniments remain pretty much the same. Trumpets and taxes are the characteristics of the present era. No security without immense standing armies, no armies without pay, no pay without taxes. It is a grievance which we cannot avoid, and of which, therefore, it were as well to say nothing ; but if Tacitus is not silent on the subject, who *can* be ? "*Neque quies gentium*," says that historian, "*sine armis, neque arma sine stipendiis, neque stipendia sine tributis haberi queunt.*"

In the two extremes of life we have the most acute sense of novelty. To the boy all is new : to the old man, when this world no longer offers variety or change, is presented the most stimulating of all novelties—the contemplation of a new existence.

Shakspeare " exhausted worlds, and then imagined new ;" but this is a privilege conceded to none but the chosen sons of genius. Common writers can only become original, when they have exhausted nature, by becoming unnatural. Like a mountebank at a fair, they surprise our attention by their extravagance, but they cannot keep it. We shrug our shoulders, and forget them. Many are the writers, nevertheless, who prefer a momentary fool's cap to a distant laurel.

NOVEMBER—the period at which most Englishmen take leave of the sun for nine months, and not a few of them for ever. A demure Scottish lady having been introduced to the Persian ambassador when in London, exclaimed with an incredulous air, " Is it possible that ye are such idolators in Persia as to worship the sun ? " " Yes, madam," was the reply, " and so you would in England, if you ever saw him."

ATH, Legal — making the awful and infinite Deity a party to all the trivial and vulgar impertinences of human life : an act of profanation equally required from a churchwarden and an archbishop, from a petty constable and the chief justice of England. "Let the law," says Paley, "continue its own functions, if they be thought requisite ; but let it spare the solemnity of an oath, and, where it is necessary, from the want of something better to depend upon, to accept a man's word or own account, let it annex to prevarication penalties proportionable to the public consequence of the offence."

Where they are made a test of religious belief, for the purpose of excluding any class of our fellow-subjects from their civil rights, oaths, being equally opposed to Christianity, policy, and justice, ought to be totally and finally abolished. He who first devised the oath of abjuration, profligately boasted that he had framed a test which should "damn one half of the nation, and starve the other ;"— a vaunt well worth the consideration of those who have placed themselves within the first clause of his prophecy.

To the utterance of oaths, as execrations, a practice equally hateful for its blasphemy and vulgarity, there seems to be little other inducement than its gratuitous sinfulness, since it communicates no pleasure, and removes no uneasiness, neither elevates the speaker, nor depresses the hearer. "Go," said Prince Henry, the son of James I., when one of his courtiers swore bitterly at being disappointed of a tennis match—"Go ! all the pleasures of earth are not worth a single oath."

OBEDIENCE, Military—must be implicit and unreasoning. "Sir," said the Duke of Wellington to an officer of engineers, who urged the impossibility of executing the directions he had received, "I did not ask your opinion, I gave you my orders, and I expect them to be obeyed." It might have been difficult, however, to yield a literal obedience to the adjutant of a volunteer corps, who, being doubtful whether he had distributed muskets to all the men, cried out—"All you that are without arms will please to hold up your hands."

ODOURS, Bad—the silent voice of nature, made audible by the nose. The worst may, in some degree, be sweetened to our sense, by a recollection of the important part they perform in the economy of the world. Those emitted by dead animals attract birds and beasts of prey from an almost incredible distance, who not only soon remove the nuisance, but convert it into new life, beauty, and enjoyment. Should no such resource be at hand, as is often the case in inhabited countries, the pernicious effluvia disengaged from these decaying substances, occasion them to be quickly buried in the ground, where their organised forms are resolved into chemical constituents, and they are fitted to become the food of vegetables. The noxious gas is converted into the aroma of the flower, and that which threatened to poison the air, affords nourishment and delight to man and beast. Animals are thus converted into plants, and plants again become animals ;—change of form and not extinction—or, rather, destruction for the sake of reproduction, being the system of nature. Pulverised human bones are now largely imported into England for manure, and the corn thus raised will again be eventually reconverted into human bones.

OLD AGE—need not necessarily be felt in the mind, as

in the body; time's current may wear wrinkles in the face
that shall not reach the heart: there is no inevitable decrepitude or senility of the spirit, when its tegument feels
the touches of decay. We sometimes talk of men falling
into their second childhood, when we should rather say that
they have never emerged from their first, but have always
been in an intellectual nonage. Vigorous minds very rarely
sink into imbecility, even in extreme age. Time seems
rather to drag them backwards, to their youth, than forwards
towards senility. Like the Glastonbury thorn, they flower in
the Christmas of their days. Hear how beautifully the venerable Goethe, in the Dedication to the first part of *Faust*,
abandons himself to this Palingenesia.

" Ye approach again, ye shadowy shapes, which once, in
the morning of life, presented yourselves to my troubled
view! Shall I try, this time, to hold you fast? Do I feel
my heart still inclined towards that delusion? Ye press
forward! well then, ye may hold dominion•over me as ye
arise around out of vapour and mist. My bosom feels
youthfully agitated by the magic breath which atmospheres
your train.

" Ye bring with you the images of happy days, and many
loved shades arise; like to an old, half-expired tradition,
rises First-love with Friendship in their company. The pang
is renewed; the plaint repeats the labyrinthine, mazy course
of life, and names the dear ones who, cheated of fair hours
by fortune, have vanished away before me.

" They hear not the following lays—the souls to whom
I sang the first. Dispersed is the friendly throng—the first
echo, alas, has died away! My sorrow voices itself to the
stranger many: their very applause makes my heart sick;
and all that in other days rejoiced in my song—if still living,
strays scattered through the world.

" And a yearning, long unfelt, for that quiet, pensive,

Spirit-realm seizes me. 'Tis hovering even now, in half-formed tones, my lisping lay, like the Æolian harp. A tremor seizes me : tear follows tear ; the austere heart feels itself growing mild and soft. What I have, I see as in the distance ; and what is gone, becomes a reality to me."

What a cordial is this apocalypse of youth to all "grave and reverend seniors !"—Why should any of us doubt that the mind may be progressive, even when the body loses ground? If we are wiser to-day than yesterday, what is to prevent our being wiser to-morrow than to-day?—Women rarely die during pregnancy ; and while the mind can be made to conceive and bear children, we may be assured that nature means to preserve its full vitality and power.

Privation of friends by death, is the greatest trial of old age ; for, though new ones may succeed to their places, they cannot replace them. For this, however, as for all other sorrows, there is a consolation. When we are left behind, and feel as exiles upon earth, we are reconciled to the idea of quitting it, and yearn for that future home, where we shall be united to our predecessors, and whither our survivors will follow us.

Old age is still comparative, and one man may be younger at eighty, than another at forty. "Ah ! madam !" exclaimed the patriarch Fontenelle, when talking to a young and beautiful woman—" if I were but fourscore again !"

How powerful is sympathy ! The mere mention of this anecdote has sent me courting to the muse, and ha. thrown into verse what I had intended further to say on the subject of

OLD AGE.

Yes, I am old ;—my strength declines,
And wrinkles tell the touch of time,

Yet might I fancy these the signs
  Not of decay, but manhood's prime ;
For all within is young and glowing,
Spite of old age's outward showing.

Yes, I am old ;—the ball, the song,
  The turf, the gun, no more allure ;
I shun the gay and gilded throng ;
  Yet, ah ! how far more sweet and pure
Home's tranquil joys, and mental treasures,
Than dissipation's proudest pleasures !

Yes, I am old ;—Ambition's call,—
  Fame, wealth, distinction's keen pursuit,
That once could charm and cheat me—all
  Are now detected, passive, mute.
Thank God ! the passions and their riot
Are barter'd for content and quiet.

Yes, I am old ;—but as I press
  The vale of years with willing feet,
Still do I find life's sorrows less,
  And all its hallow'd joys more sweet ;
Since Time, for every rose he snatches,
Takes fifty thorns, with all their scratches.

My wife—God bless her ! is as dear
  As when I plighted first my truth ;
I feel, in every child's career,
  The joys of renovated youth :
And as to Nature—I behold her
With fresh delight as I grow older.

Yes, I am old ;—and death hath ta'en
  Full many a friend, to memory dear ;
Yet, when I die, 'twill soothe the pain
  Of quitting my survivors here,
To think how all will be delighted,
When in the skies again united !

Yes, I am old ;—experience now,
  That best of guides, hath made me sage,

And thus instructed, I avow
My firm conviction, that old age,
Of all our various terms of living,
Deserves the warmest, best thanksgiving !

"OLD MEN"—says Rochefoucauld, "like to give good advice, as a consolation for being no longer in a condition to give a bad example." May we not turn the dictum of the writer against himself, and infer that he gave us all his bad advice from a contrary feeling?—Well may the portrait be dark, when the misanthrope draws from himself !

OMEN—the imaginary language of heaven speaking by signs. An oracle is the same, speaking by human tongues, but both have now become dumb. If we wish to know who believes in this Latin word, we must get our Latin answer by reading it backwards.

OPINION—a capricious tyrant, to which many a free-born Briton willingly binds himself a slave. Deeming it of much more importance to be valued than valuable;—holding opinion to be worthier than worth, we had rather stand well in the estimation of others, even of those whom we do not esteem, than of ourselves. This is, indeed, the

" Meanness that soars, and pride that licks the dust."

The greater the importance we attach to our opinions, the greater our intolerance, which is wrong, even when we are right, and doubly so when we are in error; so that persecution for opinion's sake, can *never* be justifiable. Our own experience might teach us better, for every man has differed, at various times, from himself, as much as he ever has differed at any one time from others.

Suffering others to think for us, when Heaven has supplied us with reason and a conscience for the express purpose of enabling us to think for ourselves, is the great fountain of all human error. "There cannot," says Locke, "be a more dangerous thing to rely on than the opinion of others, nor more likely to mislead one; since there is much more falsehood and error among men than truth and knowledge; and if the opinions and persuasions of others, whom we know and think well of, be a ground of assent, men have reason to be heathens in Japan, Mahometans in Turkey, Papists in Spain, Protestants in England, and Lutherans in Sweden." *

Were a whole nation to start upon a new career of education, with mature faculties, and minds free from prepossessions or prejudices, how much would be quickly abandoned that is now most stubbornly cherished! If we have many opinions, in our present state, that have once been proscribed, it is presumable that we cling to many more which future generations will discard. The world is yet in its boyhood—perhaps in its infancy; and our fancied wisdom is but the babble of the nursery. However quickly we may take up an error, we abandon it slowly. As a man often feels a pain in the leg that has been long amputated, so does he frequently yearn towards an opinion after it has been cut off from his mind,—so true is it that

> " He that's convinced against his will,
> Is of the same opinion still."

So wedded are some people to their own notions, that they will not have any persons for friends, or even for servants, who do not entertain similar views. Lord L—— makes a point of strictly cross-questioning his domestics, as to their religious and political faith, before he engages them. While

* On the Human Understanding, l. iv. c. xv.

residing on his Irish estates, a groom presented himself to be hired, resolving, beforehand, not to compromise himself by any inconsiderate replies.—" What are your opinions ?" was the peer's first demand.—" Indeed, then, your lordship's honour ! I have just none at all at all."—" Not any ! nonsense !—you must have some, and I insist upon knowing them."—" Why, then, your honour's glory, they are for all the world just the same as your lordship's."—" Then you can have no objection to state them, and to confess frankly what is your way of thinking."—" Och ! and is it my way of thinking you mane by my opinions ?—Why, then, I am exactly the same way of thinking as Pat Sullivan, your honour's gamekeeper, for, says he to me, as I was coming up stairs, Murphy, says he, I'm thinking you'll never be paying me the two-and-twenty shillings I lent you, last Christmas was a twelvemonth.—Faith ! says I, Pat Sullivan ! I'm quite of your way of thinking."

OPTIMISM—a devout conviction that, under the government of a benevolent and all-powerful God, everything conduces ultimately to the best in the world he has created, and that mankind, the constant objects of his paternal care, are in a perpetual state of improvement, and increased happiness. This is a great and consoling principle, the summary of all religion and all philosophy, the reconciler of all misgivings, the source of all comfort and consolation. To believe in it, is to realize its truth, so far as we are individually concerned; and indeed it will mainly depend upon ourselves, whether or not everything shall be for the best. Let us cling to the moral of Parnell's hermit, rather than suffer our confidence in the divine goodness to be staggered by the farcical exaggerations of Voltaire's Candide. If the theory of the former be a delusion, it is, at least, a delightful one; and, for my own part—" *malim cum Platone errare,*

quam cum aliis rectè sentire"—where the error is of so consolatory and elevating a description.

An optimist may be wrong, but presumption and religion
are in his favour; nor can we positively pronounce anything
to be for final evil, until the end of all things has arrived,
and the whole scheme of creation is revealed to us. "Does
not every architect complain of the injustice of criticising a
building before it is half finished?—Yet, who can tell what
volume of the creation we are in at present, or what point
the structure of our moral fabric has attained?—Whilst we
are all in a vessel that is sailing under sealed orders, we
shall do well to confide implicitly in our government and
Captain."*

ORIGINALITY—unconscious or undetected imitation.
Even Seneca complains, that the ancients had compelled
him to borrow from them what they would have taken from
him, had he been lucky enough to have preceded them.
" Every one of my writings," says Goethe, in the same candid spirit, " has been furnished to me by a thousand different
persons, a thousand different things: the learned and the
ignorant, the wise and the foolish, infancy and age, have
come in turn, generally without having the least suspicion of
it, to bring me the offering of their thoughts, their faculties,
their experience: often have they sowed the harvest I have
reaped. My work is that of an aggregation of human beings,
taken from the whole of nature; it bears the name of
Goethe."

It is in the power of any writer to be original, by deserting
nature, and seeking the quaint and the fantastical; but
literary monsters, like all others, are generally short-lived.
"When I was a young man," says Goldsmith, "being anxious

* Ed. Review, I. 309.

to distinguish myself, I was perpetually starting new propositions; but I soon gave this over, for I found that generally what was new was false." Strictly speaking, we may be original without being new: our thoughts may be our own, and yet common-place.

ORTHODOXY—says a reverend writer, will cover a multitude of sins, but a cloud of virtues cannot cover the want of the minutest particle of orthodoxy:—whatever you do, be orthodox. Nevertheless, it might be easily shown, that all Christian Churches have suffered more by their zeal for orthodoxy, and by the violent methods taken to promote it, than from the utmost efforts of their greatest enemies.

S and Qs.—The origin of the phrase "Mind your Ps and Qs," is not generally known. In alehouses, where chalk scores were formerly marked upon the wall, or behind the door of the tap-room, it was customary to put these initial letters at the head of every man's account, to show the number of pints and quarts for which he was in arrears; and we may presume many a friendly rustic to have tapped his neighbour on the shoulder, when he was indulging too freely in his potations, and to have exclaimed, as he pointed to the score—"Giles! Giles! mind your Ps and Qs."

When Toby, the learned pig, was in the zenith of his popularity, a theatrical wag, who attended the performance, maliciously set before him some peas; a temptation which the animal could not resist, and which immediately occasioned him to lose his *cue*. The pig exhibiter remonstrated with the author of the mischief on the unfairness of what he had done, when he replied, that his only wish was, to see whether Toby knew his Ps from his Qs.

PANACEA, Advertised—see Poison.　There would be little comfort for the sick, either in body or mind, were there any truth in the averment, that philosophy, like medicine, has plenty of drugs and quack medicines, but few remedies, and hardly any specifics.　So far from admitting this discouraging statement, a panacea may be prescribed, which, under ordinary circumstances, will generally prevent, and rarely fail to alleviate, most of the evils that flesh is heir to. The following are the simple ingredients:—occupation for the mind, exercise for the body, temperance and virtue for the sake of both.　This is the *magnum arcanum* of health and happiness.　Half of our illness and misery arises from the perversion of that reason which was given to us as a protection against both.　We are led astray by our guide, and poisoned by our physician.

PARENT.—It may be doubted, whether a man can fully appreciate the mysterious properties, and the thought-elevating dignity of his nature, until, by becoming a parent, he feels himself to be a creator as well as a creature.　The childless man passes through life like an arrow through the air, leaving nothing behind that may mark his flight.　A tombstone, stating that they were born and died, is the sole brief evidence of existence which the mass of bachelors can transmit to the succeeding generation.　But the father feels that he belongs to the future, as well as the present; he has, perhaps, become a permanent part and parcel of this majestical world "till the great globe dissolve;" for his descendants may not impossibly make discoveries, or effect reforms, that shall influence the destiny of the whole human race, and thus immortalise their name.　These may be baseless dreams, fond and doting reveries, but, like all the aspirations connected with our offspring, they serve to soothe and meliorate the heart, while they send the delighted spirit into the future, wreathed with laurels, and mounted upon a triumphal car of glorious hopes.

PARTRIDGE—a bird to which the Squirearchy are so strangely attached, that they will shoot, trap, and transport their fellow-creatures for the pleasure of destroying it themselves.

PARTY-SPIRIT—a species of mental vitriol, which we bottle up in our bosoms, that we may squirt it against others; but which, in the meantime, irritates, corrodes, and poisons our own hearts. Personality and invective are not only proofs of a bad argument, but of a bad arguer; for politeness is perfectly compatible with wit and logic, while it enhances the triumph of both. By a union of courtesy and talent, an adversary may be made to grace his own defeat, as the sandal tree perfumes the hatchet that cuts it down. Cæsar's soldiers fought none the worse for being scented with unguents, nor will any combatant be weakened by moral suavity. The bitterness of political pamphlets, and newspaper writing, so far from acting as a tonic, debilitates and dishonours them. A furious pamphleteer, on being reproached with his unsparing acrimony, exclaimed, " Burke, and Curran, and Grattan, have written thus, as well as I."— " Ay," said his friend, "but have you written thus *as well* as they?" Political writers and orators must not mistake the rage, the mouthing, and the contortions of the Sybil for her inspiration.

PASSIONS.—Were it not for the salutary agitation of the passions, the waters of life would become dull, stagnant, and as unfit for all vital purposes as those of the Dead Sea. It should be equally our object to guard against those tempests and overflowings which may entail mischief, either upon ourselves or others; and to avoid that drowsy calm, of which the sluggishness and *inertia* are inevitably hostile to the health and spirits. In the voyage of life, we should imitate the ancient mariners, who, without losing sight of the earth, trusted to the heavenly signs for their guidance. Happy the man, the tide of whose passions, like that of the great ocean, is regulated by a light from above !

St. Evremond compares the passions to runaway horses, which you must tame by letting them have their run; a perilous experiment, in which the rider may break his neck. Much better to restrain and conquer them before they get head; for if they do not obey, they will be sure to command, you.

PASSIVE RESISTANCE—succeeding to that doctrine of passive obedience, which was once so strenuously inculcated, promises to be not less efficient as a public weapon, than the helplessness of woman is often found to be in private life. This formidable, though negative power, may be compared to a snowball,—the more you push against it, the greater it becomes; it continues giving way before you, until it finally comes to a stand still, conquers your strength, and defies your utmost efforts to move it. The Quakers were the first to discover this important secret;—the Catholic tithe-payers of Ireland are now acting upon it;—the English dissenters are betaking themselves to it in the question of Church-rates;—and it threatens to be the common resort of the whole people, wherever there is a grievance to be redressed, for which they are compelled to take the remedy into their own hands.

PATRIOTISM—too often the hatred of other countries disguised as the love of our own; a fanaticism injurious to the character, and fatal to the repose of mankind. In the subjects of small states, it is more especially odious, for they must hate nearly the whole of their fellow-creatures. Were the world under the domination of one monarch, patriotism would be a virtue. Let us view it as under the government of one celestial king; let us consider the children of our common Father, whatever be their creed or country, as our brethren, and the narrow feeling of patriotism will soon expand into the nobler and more exalted principle of an all-embracing humanism. Most delightful is it to contemplate the friendly intercourse now in active operation between the people of different countries, and more especially between those of France and England. There is rapidly springing up a holy alliance of nations, not of kings, and a European public opinion, from which the philanthropist may confidently anticipate the controlling of governments, the diminished frequency of wars, the improvement of the human race, and the completion of what a benevolent Providence has designed for the destiny of man.

Public opinion, when it has once ascertained its own power, will direct, while it seems to obey; as a vessel, while it appears to be governed by the elements, is, in fact, compelling them to conduct her into the desired port.

PEN—the silent mouthpiece of the mind, which gives ubiquity and permanence to the evanescent thought of a moment.

PERSECUTION—disobeying the most solemn injunctions of Christianity, under the sham plea of upholding it. How admirable the humility of the spiritual persecutor, when he kindly condescends to patronise the Deity, to assist Omniscience with his counsels, and lend a helping hand to Omnipotence! In such an attempt, the failure is generally as signal as the folly, the cruelty, and the impiety; for martyrs, like certain plants, spring up more stubbornly, the more you endeavour to crush and trample them down. The rebound is always proportioned to the percussion, the recoil to the discharge. To conquer fanaticism, you must tolerate it: the shuttlecock of religious difference soon falls to the ground, when there are no battledores to beat it backwards and forwards.

Power should never be given to any class, as religionists; for morality, and even humanity, are but sorry securities against the promptings of that heartless monster, bigotry. Hence the danger of what is called an established religion, or, in other words, of a religion wielding the sword of the civil magistrate—the source of persecution in all creeds, and all ages. "It was the State religion of Rome that persecuted the first Christians."—"Who was it that crucified the Saviour of the world for attempting to reform the religion of his country? The Jewish priesthood.—Who was it that drowned the altars of their idols with the blood of Christians, for attempting to abolish Paganism? The Pagan priesthood.— Who was it that persecuted to flames and death those who, in the time of Wickliffe and his followers, laboured to reform the errors of Popery? The Popish priesthood.—Who was it, and who is it, that both in England and in Ireland, since the Reformation—but I check my hand, being unwilling to reflect upon the dead, or to exasperate the living."*

"It was the State religion in this country that persecuted the Protestants; and since Protestantism has been established, it is the State religion which has persecuted Protestant dissenters. Is this the fault principally of the faith of these Churches, or of their alliance with the State? No man can be in doubt for an answer."†

The clergy, indeed, are apt to tell us, that they require no

* Miscellaneous Tracts, by the Bishop of Llandaff, vol. ii.
† Dymond's "Church and the Clergy."

further favour for their doctrines and discipline, than a fair
and impartial inquiry; and this is perfectly true, so long as
they are satisfied with the results of the inquiry; but should
the contrary be the case, the luckless investigator is liable to
be refuted by the Canon Law, and the irresistible arguments
of fine, pillory, and imprisonment. This is freedom of inquiry
with a vengeance !

PESSIMISTS—moral squinters, who, being incapable of
a straightforward view, " imagine that penetration is evinced
by universal suspicion and mistrust; who hope, perhaps, to
exalt themselves by degrading others; who discredit every
thing that is noble, believe all that is base; who would persuade their hearers, that the pure wholesome temple of moral
beauty and virtue, is a lazar-house of noisome corruption and
festering abomination. A more false and pestilent treason
against human nature, a more impious profanation of the
divinity of goodness that is within us, a more self-condemn-
ing calumny upon the world, it is not easy to conceive; and
yet, upon this paltry, mischievous basis, have weak-headed
and bad-hearted men, in all ages, not only contrived to
obtain a reputation for shrewdness and sagacity, but sometimes have been enabled to distress, with painful misgivings,
those nobler spirits, who would wish to sympathise with
fellow-creatures, in the fulness of love and charity, and to
believe themselves surrounded with congenial hearts and
kindred souls."

PHILANTHROPY—was not ill-defined by Cicero, when
he says, alluding to the purposes of man's creation—" *Ad
tuendos conservandosque homines, hominem natum esse.
Homines hominum causâ sunt generati, ut ipsi inter se alii
aliis prodesse possint. Hominem, naturæ obedientem,
homini nocere non posse.*"

Why was man made with wide-spreading arms, except, as Dryden beautifully supposes—

" To satisfy a wide embrace ?"

The only way we can evince our gratitude to our great Creator and Benefactor, for all that he has given us, is to be as useful as we can to his creatures, and "to love our neighbour as ourselves."

" I fear," said a country curate to his flock—" when I explained to you in my last charity sermon, that Philanthropy was the love of our species, you must have understood me to say *specie*, which may account for the smallness of the collection. You will prove, I hope, by your present contributions, that you are no longer labouring under the same mistake."

PHYSICIANS—always cherish a sneaking kindness for cooks, as more certain and regular purveyors of patients than plague and pestilence; and there is this advantage in their advice, that no two of them agree, so that the taste of an invalid may always be accommodated. "Are you out of sorts," says Montaigne, "that your physician has denied you the enjoyment of wine, and of your favourite dishes?—Be not uneasy; apply to me, and I engage to find you one of equal credit, who shall put you under a regimen perfectly opposite to that settled by your own adviser."

Blunt, and even rude, as he sometimes was, our countryman, Abernethy, would not have hazarded so unfeeling a speech as is recorded of Andrea Baccio, the celebrated Florentine physician. Being called on to attend a woman of quality, he felt her pulse, and asked her how old she was.—She told him, "about four score."—"And how long *would* you live?" demanded the surly practitioner, quitting her hand, and making the best of his way out of the house.

Physicians may well smile at the many jokes and malicious pleasantries of which they are the butt, for they must share the consciousness of their patients, that there is no greater benefactor to his species than the successful practitioner. No wonder that such men received divine honours in the olden times, since they seem to approximate to the attributes of the gods—"*Neque enim ullâ aliâ re homines propius ad Deos accedunt, quam salutem hominibus dando.*"

PHYSIOGNOMY—reading the hand-writing of nature upon the human countenance. If a man's face, as it is pretended, be like that of a watch, which reveals without, what it conceals within, silence itself is no security for our thoughts, for a dial tells the hour as well as a clock. If, in addition to this self-betrayal, the suggestion of Momus could be realized, and a window be placed in our bosoms, so that "he who runs may read," the best of us might well change colour, for many a heart would look black when it was *read*.

PIC-NIC—the most unpleasant of all parties of pleasure.

If sick of home and luxuries,
  You want a new sensation,
And sigh for the unwonted ease
  Of *un*accommodation,—
If you would taste, as amateur,
  And vagabond beginner,
The painful pleasures of the poor,
  Get up a Pic-nic dinner.

Presto ! 'tis done—away you start,
  All frolic, fun, and laughter,
The servants and provision cart
  As gaily trotting after.

THE 'TIN TRUMPET;

The spot is reach'd, when all exclaim
  With many a joyous antic,
" How sweet a scene !— I'm glad we came !
  How rural—how romantic ! "

Pity the night was wet !—but what
  Care gipsies and carousers ?
So down upon the swamp you squat
  In porous Nankeen trowsers.—
Stick to what sticks to you—your seat,
  For thistles round you huddle,
While nettles threaten legs and feet,
  If shifted from a puddle.

Half starved with hunger—parch'd with thirst,
  All haste to spread the dishes,
When lo ! 'tis found, the ale has burst,
  Amid the loaves and fishes.
Over the pie, a sodden sop,
  The grasshoppers are skipping,
Each roll's a sponge, each loaf a mop,
  And all the meat is dripping.—

Bristling with broken glass, you find
  Some cakes among the bottles,
Which those may eat who do not mind
  Excoriated throttles.
The biscuits now are wiped and dried,
  When squalling voices utter,
" Look ! look ! a toad has got astride
  Our only pat of butter ! "

Your solids in a liquid state,
  Your cooling liquids heated,
And every promised joy by fate
  Most fatally defeated ;
All, save the serving men are sour'd,
  They smirk, the cunning sinners !
Having, before they came, devoured
  Most comfortable dinners.

Still you assume, in very spite,
  A grim and gloomy gladness,
Pretend to laugh—affect delight—
  And scorn all show of sadness.—
While thus you smile, but storm within,
  A storm without comes faster,
And down descends in deaf'ning din
  A deluge of disaster.

'Tis *sauve qui peut;*—the fruit dessert
  Is fruitlessly deserted,
And homeward now you all revert,
  Dull, desolate, and dirtied,
Each gruffly grumbling, as he eyes
  His soaked and sullen brother,
" If these are Pic-nic pleasantries,
  Preserve me from another ! "

" PILGRIM'S PROGRESS."—The hero of this popular and pious allegory, as has been justly observed by Mr. Dunlop, in his " History of Fiction,"—" is a mere negative character, without one good quality to recommend him. There is little or no display of charity, beneficence, or even benevolence, during the whole course of his pilgrimage. The sentiments of Christian are narrow and illiberal, and his struggles and exertions wholly selfish."

In proof of the latter part of this imputation, mark with what a heartless indifference to everything but himself, he abandons his wife and family.—" Now he had not run far from his own home, but his wife and children, perceiving it, began to cry after him to return, but the man put two fingers into his ears, and ran on, crying Life ! Life ! Eternal Life ! So he looked not behind him, but fled towards the middle of the plain."

So uniform are the results of fanaticism, even when engendered by different views of religion, that a precisely similar trait is related of the Catholic, St. Francis Xavier.

" It is well," says Sir Walter Scott, speaking of his general character, as given by Dryden, " that our admiration is qualified by narrations so shocking to humanity, as the account of the Saint passing by the house of his ancestors, the abode of his aged mother, on his road to leave Europe for ever, and conceiving he did God good service in denying himself the melancholy consolation of a last fare-well."—*Life of Dryden*, p. 338.

PLAGIARISTS—purloiners, who filch the fruit that others have gathered, and then throw away the basket.

PLEASING ALL PARTIES.—This hopeless attempt usually ends by pleasing none, for timeservers neither serve themselves nor any one else. As the endeavour involves a contemptible compromise of principle, it is generally despised by the very parties whom we seek to conciliate. What opinion can we have of a man who has no opinion of his own ?—A neutral, we can understand and respect ; but a Janus-faced double-dealer, who affects to belong to both sides, will not be tolerated by either. His fear of giving offence is the greatest of all offences. Of this, a ludicrous instance was afforded at the time of the riots, in 1780, when every one was obliged to chalk " No Popery " upon the wall of his house, in order to protect it from violence.—Delpini, the clown, particularly anxious to win " golden opinions from all sorts of men," since his benefit was close at hand, scrawled upon his house, in large letters —" No Religion."

PLEASURES — see Will-o'-the-wisp. Some, like the horizon, recede perpetually as we advance towards them ; others, like butterflies, are crushed by being caught. Plea-sure unattained, is the hare which we hold in chase, cheered

on by the ardour of competition, the exhilarating cry of
the dogs—the shouts of the hunters—the echo of the horn—
the ambition of being in at the death. Pleasure attained, is
the same hare hanging up in the sportman's larder, worthless, disregarded, despised, dead.

The keenest pleasures of an unlawful nature are poisoned
by a lurking self-reproach, ever rising up to hiss at us, like a
snake amid the flowers—

> " —— medio de fonte leporum,
> Surgit aliquid amari ;"

while there is a secret consolation, even in the heaviest
calamity, if we feel that it has not been incurred by our
own misconduct. Upon this subject the great and golden
rule is, so to enjoy present, as that they may not interfere
with future pleasures. Burns has happily compared sensual
pleasure to

> " Snow that falls upon a river,
> A moment white, then gone for ever."

POETRY—the music of thought conveyed to us in the
music of language :—the art of embalming intellectual
beauty, a process which threatens to be speedily enrolled,
together with the Egyptian method of immortalising the body,
among the sciences which are lost.

The harmony of the works of nature is the visible poetry
of the Almighty, emblazoned on the three-leaved book of
earth, sea, and sky.

If Hayley could talk, even in *his* days, of—" the cold
blank bookseller's rhyme-freezing face," what would he say
in ours, when we have seen Crabbe, Wordsworth, and
Coleridge, condemned to an involuntary silence ; Moore,
the first lyrical writer of the age, " *vir nullâ non donandus
lauru*," one whose very soul is poetry, driven to the ungenial

toil of Biography; and Southey, not only necessitated to waste his fine poetical talents and kindly feelings in the fierce arena of criticism and politics, but absolutely obliged to consult the public taste, or rather the total want of it, by discontinuing the Laureate odes?

Absurd as it was to expect a rational answer from T. H., I ventured to ask him how it came that all our best poets were obliged to write prose?—" Because poetry is *prose-scribed*," was his reply.

POINT, One good.—So various are the estimates formed of us by our fellow-creatures, that there never, perhaps, existed an individual, however unpraiseworthy, who was not acknowledged to have *one* good point in his character, though it by no means follows, that this admission is always to be taken as a compliment. A gentleman, travelling on a Sunday, was obliged to stop, in order to replace one of his horse's shoes. The farrier was at church; but a villager suggested, that if he went on to Jem Harrison's forge, he would probably be found at home. This proved to be true, when the rustic who had led the horse to the spot exclaimed —" Well, I must say that for Jem—for it is the only good point about him—he do never go to Church!"

POLITENESS—of the person exhibits itself in elegance of manners, and a strict adherence to the conventional forms and courtesies of polished life. Politeness of the heart consists in an habitual benevolence, and an absence of selfishness in our intercourse with society of all classes. Each of these may exist without the other.

POOR LAWS*—premiums upon idleness and improvi-

* How far the author might have modified this article, had he lived

dence—reversing the moralising effect of the prudential restraints, and of the domestic affections, as devised for the welfare of society by the wisdom of God, through the instrumentality of a demoralising system, invented by the folly of man. Our poor laws, making the industrious support the indolent, the moral the profligate, and the prudent the improvident, are not only dissuasions from good, but stimulants to evil, by encouraging selfishness, recklessness, and inconsiderate marriages, and thus perpetuating pauperism, misery, and vice. This mischievous system tends inevitably to impoverish the rich, without enriching the poor; but in the harm thus done to both classes, the latter are by far the greatest sufferers,—their industry being paralysed, their affections seared, their minds demoralised, and their poverty confirmed.

What cruelty! exclaims some sanctimonious anti-Malthusian, to discourage the marriages of the lower orders, and what scandalous immorality would be the consequence of success in this object! Why, the prudential restraint which prevents improvident matches, is in full operation throughout the whole of the middling and upper classes, without being felt as an oppression, and without any increase of immorality. Even if their temporary celibacy were to increase *one* vice of the lower orders, it would diminish fifty others, by improving their circumstances, and removing the temptations of want and destitution. Pauperism is the hot-bed of crime, and good circumstances are the best security for good conduct.

POPULARITY—the brightness of a falling star,—the fleeting splendour of a rainbow,—the bubble that is sure

to witness the recent modification of the Poor Laws, it is impossible to say.—ED.

to burst by its very inflation. The politician who, in these lunatic times, hopes to adapt himself to all the changes of public opinion, should qualify for the task by attempting to make a pair of stays for the moon, which assumes a new form and figure every night.

POPULATION. — The proportion between the sexes seems to be governed by a general and permanent law, which, doubtless, keeps them at the standard best adapted for human happiness. Wherever accurate registers are kept, we know that the number of males born exceeds the females; the ratio being between fifteen to fourteen, and twenty-five to twenty-four. In England and Wales, from 1810 to 1820, they were as sixteen to fifteen, very nearly the same as in France. And yet, partly owing to the greater longevity of females,—to the loss of male life in the military and naval service, or in unwholesome manufactures,—to emigration, and other circumstances, it is found, throughout Europe, that the females exceed the males. In this uniformity of the laws of population, we behold a new and gratifying proof of a superintending Providence—of a common Father, who, making no distinctions of clime or religion, of rank or station, subjects the whole family of mankind to the same paternal control.

POSSIBLE.—In order to effect the utmost possible, we must be careful not to throw away our strength in straining after the impossible, and the unattainable, least we exemplify the fable of the dog and the shadow. " Search not into the things above thy strength."

" Sors tua mortalis ; non est mortale quod optas."

POSTHUMOUS GLORY--a revenue payable to our

ghosts; an *ignis fatuus;* an exhalation arising from the ashes and corruption of the body; the glow-worm of the grave; a Jack-o'-lantern, of which a skeleton is the Jack, and the lantern a dark one; protracted oblivion; the short twilight that survives the setting of the vital sun, and is presently quenched in the darkness of night. "Ashes to ashes, and dust to dust," may be said of our fame, as well as of our frame: one is buried very soon after the other. When the rattling earth is cast upon our coffin, it sends up a hollow sound, which, after a few faint echoes, dies and is buried in oblivious silence. That fleeting noise is our posthumous renown. Living glory is the advantage of being known to those whom you don't know;—posthumous glory is enjoying a celebrity from which you can derive no enjoyment, and enabling every puppy in existence to feel his superiority over you by repeating the old dictum, that a living dog is better than a dead lion, or by quoting from Shakspeare—" I like not such grinning honour as Sir Walter hath !"

POSTS and PLACES.—It was a complaint of D'Alembert, that men so completely exhausted their industry in canvassing for places, as to have none left for the performance of their duties. Query—Have public men improved in this respect since the days of D'Alembert?

POVERTY.—To the generous-minded, it is the greatest evil of a narrow fortune that they must sometimes taste the humiliation of receiving, and can rarely enjoy the luxury of conferring benefits. None can feel for the poor so well as the poor, and none, therefore, can so well appreciate the painfulness of being unable to relieve the distress with which they so keenly sympathise.

Riches, it was once observed, only keep out the single evil

of poverty. True! was the reply—but how much good do they let in! Whatever may be the talents of a poor man, they will not have their fair share of influence; for few will respect the understanding that is of so little advantage to its owner, and still fewer is the number of those who will doubt the abilities that have made a fool rich. Nevertheless, there are many chances in favour of the sufferers under impecuniosity; for, if Necessity be the mother of Invention, Poverty is the father of Industry; and the child of such parents has a much better prospect of achieving honours and distinction than the rich man's son. Chief Justice Kenyon once said to a wealthy friend, who asked his opinion as to the probable success of his son at the Bar—"Let him spend his own fortune forthwith; marry, and spend his wife's, and then he may be expected to apply with energy to his profession."

PRACTICE — does not always make perfect. Curran, when told by his physician, that he seemed to cough with more difficulty, replied—"That is odd enough, for I have been practising all night."

PRAISE—that which costs us nothing, and which we are, nevertheless, the most unwilling to bestow upon others, even where it is most due, though we sometimes claim it the more for ourselves, the less we deserve it; not reflecting that the breath of self-eulogy soils the face of the speaker, even as the censer is dimmed by the smoke of its own perfume.

Which of us would desiderate the expressive silence recommended by Scaliger as the most appropriate compliment to Virgil?—"*De Virgilio nunquam loquendum; nam omnes omnium laudes superat.*" Few people thank you for praising the qualities they really possess; to win their hearts, you must eulogise those in which they are deficient. As this is the most subtle of all flattery, so is it the most acceptable. In general, we have little reason to be grateful to those who speak the strict truth of us, and we are the more bound to acknowledge the kindness of those who flatter us by agreeable falsehoods. Stratonice, the bald wife of Seleucus, gave six hundred crowns to a poet, who extolled the beauty and profusion of her hair. One thing I would counsel to authors —never to make any allusion to themselves. If from sheer modesty, they speak disparagingly of their own works, their averments are set down for gospel; if they assume the smallest modicum of merit, their claim is cited as an instance of inordinate vanity. Silence is sapience.

The best praise which you can bestow on an author, or an artist, is to show that you have studied and understand his works. When Augustin Caracci pronounced a long discourse in honour of the Laocoon, all were astonished that his brother Annibal said nothing of that celebrated *chef-d'œuvre*. Divining their thoughts, the latter took a piece of chalk, and drew the group against the wall as accurately as if he had it before his eyes; a silent panegyric, which no rhetoric could have surpassed.

"Our praise of beginners," says Rochefoucauld, "often proceeds from our envy of those who have already succeeded." This is a secret well known to critics; but they do not seem to be aware that sincerely to praise merit is, in some degree, to share it.

PRAYER-BOOKS—answer many useful purposes, besides that of being carefully laid on the drawing-room table every Sunday morning. Were it not for these little manuals, people would have nothing to hold before their faces at church, when they are gaping, or ogling their neighbours, or quizzing a new bonnet in the next pew. But the most appropriate, praiseworthy, and important object to which a prayer-book can be applied, is its enabling you to afford incontestable proof that you keep a man-servant, when you enter the house of God to forswear the pomps and vanities of this wicked world. I have known ladies of all ages who could carry, for any distance, a pet poodle, weighing twenty-nine pounds and twelve ounces; but I have seldom known a female of any age who, having a man-servant, could carry a prayer-book, weighing four ounces and four pennyweights, from the church-door to the door of her pew. As there is a great inconvenience in crowding the aisles with lacqueys, going and returning, both at the commencement and the end of service, I would propose that all ladies should either carry their own prayer-books, or lock them up in their pews; and that those who are entitled to that pious distinction, should have a large label upon their backs, inscribed, " I keep a footman." By this measure we should avoid the inconvenience of which I have complained, while the fair label-bearers, carrying their footman at their back, instead of having him always in their head, would still obtain due credit for that Christian humility and devout sense of the proper objects of church-going, which are so clearly evidenced by the display of a handsome man, in a handsome blue livery, with crested buttons, crimson collar and facings, tufted shoulder knots, long worsted tags, and silken tassels !

PRECEDENT, Authority of—substituting a decision or an opinion for a principle, or a truth, and thus running the risk of perpetuating error, by making another man's folly the guide of your wisdom. Had the precedent of one age always been a rule for the next, the world would have been stationary, and we should never have emerged from barbarism. If this slavish adherence to former decisions gave us a fixed and immutable system, there would be some compensation for its being a wrong one; but the glorious uncertainty of the

law, based as it is upon precedent, has passed into a by-word.
A weathercock, even when it has become so rusty that it will
not traverse, may occasionally point in the right direction;
but one that hangs so loosely as to be perpetually shuffling
and veering, without reference to the quarter whence the
wind blows, can only serve to puzzle and mislead.

PRECEPT—without example, is like a waterman, who
looks one way and rows another. What avails the knowledge of good and evil, if we do what we ought to avoid, and
avoid what we ought to do? A direction post may point out
the right road, without being obliged to follow it; but human
finger posts, especially teachers and preachers, have not the
same privilege. When a man's life gives the lie to his tongue,
we naturally believe the former, rather than the latter. Pharisaical professions are but as a tinkling cymbal; we cannot
listen patiently to the voice of the hypocrite, charm he never
so wisely; but there is a silent eloquence in the morality of a
whole life, that is irresistible. Precept and example, like the
blades of a pair of scissors, are admirably adapted to their
end, when conjoined: separated they lose the greater portion
of their utility. Tertullian says, that even our writings blush
when our actions do not correspond with them. Ought not
this inconsistency rather to produce a contrary effect, and to
prevent our writings from being *read?*

He who teaches what he does not perform, may be compared to a sun-dial on the front of a house, which instructs
the passenger, but not the tenant. "*Equidem beatos puto,*"
says Pliny, "*quibus Deorum munere datum est, aut facere
scribenda, aut legenda scribere; beatissimos verè quibus
utrinque.*" "Happy are they to whom the gods have given
the power, either to perform actions worthy to be recorded,
or to write things worthy to be read: happier still are they
in whom both powers are united."

PRECOCIOUS CHILDREN—whose early intellectual development is often the harbinger of a premature decay, may be compared to Pliny's Amygdala, or almond tree, of which the early buds and immature fruits were cut off by the frosts of spring.

PRESS—the steam engine of moral power, which, directed by the spirit of the age, will eventually crush imposture, superstition, and tyranny. The liberty of the press is the true measure of all other liberty, for all freedom without this must be merely nominal. To stifle the nascent thought, is a moral infanticide, a treason against human nature. What can a man call his own, if his thought does not belong to him? King Hezekias is the first recorded enemy to the liberty of the press: he suppressed a book which treated of the virtues of plants, for fear it should be abused, and engender maladies; a shrewd and notable reason, well worthy of a modern Attorney-general.

PRIDE.—"My brethren," said Swift in a sermon, "there are three sorts of pride—of birth, of riches, and of talents. I shall not now speak of the latter, none of you being liable to that abominable vice."

If we add to our pride, what we cut off from less favourite faults, we are merely taking our errors out of one pocket to put them into another.

PRIESTHOOD.—When the word of God, chained up in the Latin tongue, was a sealed book to the public; when the mere ability to read entitled a man to the *privilegium clericale;* when the nation, steeped in ignorance, and consequently in superstition, looked up to the clergy as the means of salvation, and the sole depository of that learning and knowledge which are always worldly power; we can understand why their authority should be almost unlimited, and little marvel, that, like all despotism, it should be grossly abused. The laws, of which the clergy then had the chief enactment, having exempted them from almost every personal duty, they attempted a total exemption from almost every secular tie. " But, as the overflowing of waters," says Sir Edward Coke, "doth many times make the river to lose its proper channel, so, in times past, ecclesiastical persons, seeking to extend their liberties beyond their due bounds, lost those which of right belonged to them."

Of these perversions and usurpations the most grievous were abolished by the Reformation; which, however, effectually provided for the corruption, and final unpopularity of the Church, when it bequeathed to it a spiritual nobility, tithes, pluralities, wealthy sinecures, and non-residence. In morals, piety, and learning, the clergy, as a body, are not only unexceptionable, but most exemplary; and yet, in the most religious country in the world, they are confessedly not so popular as they ought to be. Why? Because, instead of being a-head of the people, as has always hitherto been the case, they are only on a par with them in general information, and occasionally behind them in the desire of improvement, in liberality, and in the spirit of the age, the only articles whereof some of their body do not seem anxious to take tithe. This censure must not be passed without excepting many distinguished individuals, to whose enlightened views the writer is proud to do justice. A substitution for the obnoxious tithes, and a reform of the Church abuses, may restore to the clergy all their lost influence and popularity, nor yet encroach upon that decent and sufficing provision, beneath which, or above which, no minister can long preserve the respect of his flock. Upon the aggregate property of the Church none seek to make inroad, but all must feel that it would be much better secured by a more equal distribution, and by a timely reform, which, in order to ensure its friendly spirit, ought to emanate from the Church itself.

PRIMOGENITURE—disinheriting a whole unoffending family, in order that the accident of an accident, viz., the eldest son of an eldest son, very possibly the last in merit, though the first in birth, may be endowed with the patrimony of his brothers and sisters, each of whom may exclaim—

> " Sum pauper, non culpa mea, sed cu'pa parentum,
> Qui me fratre meo non genuere priùs."

Equally opposed to nature, reason, morality, and sound policy, this barbarous remnant of the doctrine which main-tains the many to be made for the few, not the few for the many, has been a pregnant source of private as well as public corruption. The father whose estate is entailed has lost much of his moral influence over his children, being equally unable to reward the duty and affection of the juniors, or to control and punish the excesses of his heir, whose independence too often occasions him to be prema-turely extravagant, profligate, and unfilial. Numerous and notorious are the family feuds thus engendered, for Primo-geniture destroys all the ties of consanguinity. An observant foreigner has noticed, that the English aristocracy, generally alienated from their eldest son, doat, nevertheless, on their eldest grandson, because they see in him an avenger of their wrongs, and the future tormenter of him by whom they themselves have been tormented. What a revolting picture of perverted affection !

Nor are the social and fraternal feelings less distorted. With what a calm heartlessness will an elder son, rolling in wealth and luxury, see his brothers struggling with poverty, nor feel himself bound to offer them the least assistance ! " I must live," sorrowfully exclaimed a poor *cadet*, when soliciting a small loan from the heir of a rich family. " *Je n'en vois pas la nécessité*," was the brother's reply ; and his unfeeling rejection of the suit was abundantly justified by that law of Primogeniture, which has completely superseded the law of nature. So much for its corrupting effects upon private life.

That it is not less demoralising in a public point of view, is established by the fact, that our aristocracy, for ages past, have had no other means of providing for their younger sons, than by making them state-paupers, and procuring them pensions, sinecures, civil or military appointments, and places in the colonies or the Church; so that they have a deep interest in upholding abuses of every description, and in monopolising for their own order, and by an undue influence, those employments which ought to be open to merit, and to candidates of every class. What can we then expect from an unreformed House of Lords ? Primogeniture, as a constituent element of nobility, begins in injustice, continues by acquiescence, and is perpetuated by habit, until at last, the hoary abuse shakes the grey hairs of antiquity at us, and gives itself out for the wisdom of ages.

" It is a fact highly honourable to the character of the French nation, that when De Villele attempted to revive the ' *droit d' aînesse*,' there were amongst the numerous petitioners against the measure, the names of many who would have benefited by the change, but who paid less regard to their own interest than to the suggestions of natural affection. They were too noble-minded to barter the rights and honour of their brothers for wealth or worldly distinction. The same feelings of justice and generosity have distinguished the citizens of Virginia, where, when the paternal estate has been bequeathed entire to the eldest son, he has frequently been known to divide it equally among his brothers and sisters. In both these cases an opposite conduct would have been censured by public opinion, and would have incurred a degree of odium which is to be found in those countries only where the natural instinct of justice is not perverted by luxury, and the sympathies and charities of life are pure and unsullied. How different is the picture which the mother country would present to the eye of the indignant North American! The portions of our younger nobility, like the wages of our peasantry, are made out of a poor-rate; pride and poverty are encouraged by the same policy, and the gentleman and the labourer are equally paupers."—*English-man's Magazine.*

It has been urged, that the abolition of primogeniture and entail would rapidly pauperise the land, by its continual sub-division into small allotments. But it is already pauperised, where it is not fattened into disease; for the few are as much too rich, as the many are too poor; and if that be the best system which confers the greatest happiness upon the greatest number, a more equal distribution of the general wealth would surely be an improvement for all. The fine arts might suffer, for want of wealthy patrons; but the useful arts would receive an impulse from the greater diffusion of competency; and what would be gained in the latter direction might well atone for the loss in the former. A nation may pay too dear for the arts. It is, doubtless, fine to talk of an Augustan era, and Augustus himself was said to boast that he had found Rome of brick, and left it of marble; but if he had added, as in truth he might, that he had found Rome free, and had left it enslaved, what patriot would not have felt the city dishonoured by its architectural honours?

The constant reports, in our papers, of law-suits between relations, mostly originating in the unjust system of Primogeniture, reminds one of Malherbe, when he was reproached for being always at law with his family.—" With whom, then," he asked, " would you have me be at variance? The Turks and Muscovites will not quarrel with me."

It was well said by one whose elder brother, a dissolute and unhappy man, had been vaunting the extent of the family estate—" I should envy you for what you have, did I not pity you for what you are." The same, when once walking with his senior, suddenly seized his arms, hurried him on, and exclaimed, with a look of pretended alarm— "Away! away! your life is in danger—save me from the entailed estate!"—at the same time pointing to a board set up in an old gravel-pit, with the following inscription— " Any one may shoot rubbish here."—T. H. is made responsible for the truth of this anecdote, though it may possibly be as old as the venerable Josephus Molitor.

PROMULGATION—the most essential part of a law, and one, nevertheless, which is the most completely neglected, hundreds and thousands of poor wretches having been punished under enactments of whose existence they were utterly ignorant.—" You are rather hard upon the canine race, unless they can read," said a foreigner, " for I see written up in various places, ' All dogs found in these grounds will be shot.' " Our laws are still harder upon the human race, for, though the quadrupeds cannot read, we presume them to have owners who can, and who will keep them out of danger; whereas the biped, even if he be able to spell, has no warning set up to put him on his guard,— and if he cannot, has no pastor or master who will apprise him of his danger. We have declared it illegal to set steel traps and spring-guns in unenclosed grounds; and yet we thickly plant those murderous weapons, under the name of Acts of Parliament, in the highways and thoroughfares, keeping the people in the dark, as if on purpose to entrap the greater number of them. It has been objected, that they would not understand the Acts if they were placed before their eyes. Then they are not bound to obey them. Reason, justice, and humanity proclaim, that no enactment, especially a penal one, can be obligatory it it be utterly unintelligible. The barbarous jargon in which they are now written, should make way for brevity and plain English. It might be well if a summary or digest of every law affecting the people were printed for circulation, and affixed to every church door. It might be better still, if every clergyman were obliged to recapitulate and comment upon it from the pulpit. We are not always sure that, by expounding the laws of God, the preacher can show us the way to heaven; but by explaining the laws of man, there is little doubt that he might prove a very valuable guide to the poor in their earthly pilgrimage.

PROPHECIES, The—were never meant as a Moore's Almanac, or as riddles for every blind Œdipus to guess at; and yet a year rarely passes without some new version of the Book of Revelation, ingeniously adapted to the gazettes and current events of the period, by the half-crazy enthusiasts who seem to have succeeded to the old dabblers in judicial astrology. Vanity and self-love persuade these modern seers, not only that the era to which they belong —that insignificant and fleeting point of time called the present—must be the all-important one shadowed forth by the inspired writers, but that they must be the chosen instruments to establish the connection between the Apocalypse and last Saturday's newspaper. This year's expounder regularly falsifies the last, but, as

> " Fools rush in where angels fear to tread,"

new ones constantly arise, who being, if possible, still more peremptory and still more wrong than their predecessors, entangle themselves with the first little horn, and the second little horn, and are generally left in a dilemma between the two.

This gipsy-like irreverence should be discountenanced by all sober Christians. The Apostle tells us that—" the things of God knoweth no man but the Spirit of God : "—and it cannot be for edification to see the interpreters warring with each other, as well as with the sacred volume, and thus encouraging the scoffer, while they bewilder the devout inquirer.

PROSELYTISM—self-love, seeking to make converts to our own opinion, disguised as the love of God, seeking to win votaries to the true faith. If all religions were to be engaged in this pursuit, and all have an equal right, the crusades would be renewed, and the whole world would soon become an arena for theological strife.

A Frenchwoman, who had married a Lutheran, made an offering to her patron Saint, for the purpose of procuring her husband's conversion to Catholicism. While she was waiting the effect of her prayers and donations, the good man fell sick and died, upon which the grateful wife exclaimed—" Ah ! there is no Saint like the holy St. Catherine. She has graciously given me even more than I asked ! "

A traveller, who had resided some time in Southern Africa, being asked whether the missionaries had been successful in civilising the natives, replied—" So much so, that I have known hundreds of negroes, who thought no more of lying, drinking, or swearing, than any European whatever."

PROSPERITY—indurates; adversity intenerates. The human heart is like a feather-bed—it must be roughly

handled, well shaken, and exposed to a variety of turns, to
prevent its becoming hard and knotty. Not without good
reason does our liturgy instruct us to pray for divine protection " in the hour of our wealth," for Satan,

> " —— wiser than before,
> Now tempts by making rich, not making poor :"

and our dangers and trials invariably increase with our
prosperity. Then comes the withering discovery that opulence is not happiness, for the shadows that surround us
are invariably the darkest when the sun of our fortune shines
the most brightly. Very often, too, we are only the more
ridiculous, as well as unhappy, for being tossed in Fortune's
blanket, and elevated above the heads of our fellows, a process which often turns our own. It matters little to be worth
money, if we are worth nothing else.

PROVINCIALISM.—There is a provincialism of mind
as well as of accent—a nationality of counties. Manners
make the man, and localities tend to make the manners.
The character of a whole people may be homogeneous,
though compounded of many opposite ingredients; as spirit
and water, sugar and acid, are necessary to the integrity of
punch.

PRUDENCE—is of relative merit, according to its degree and the necessity for its exercise. It should no more
be prominently noticeable in the conduct of a prosperous
man, than prudery in the demeanour of a virtuous woman.
When the rainy day comes, for which over-cautious niggards
have been long providing, Fortune often delights to take
them by the head and shoulders, and thrust them into the
middle of the shower.
When thus limited to self-interest, prudence is inferior

to the instinct of animals, which is sometimes generous and disinterested. Calculation, the first attribute of Reason, should never render us incapable of the first of the virtues— a sacrifice of self. The head must not be allowed to predominate over the heart. An expansive humanism, which is only a more enlarged calculation, would confirm the Scripture injunction, and teach us to love our neighbour as ourself.

Over-caution and over-preparation not seldom defeat their own object. Washington Irving tells us of a Dutchman, who, having to leap a ditch, went back three miles, that he might have a good run at it, and found himself so completely winded, when he arrived at it again, that he was obliged to sit down on the wrong side to recover his breath. —*Reculer pour mieux sauter* is only advisable when the preparation bears a due proportion to the thing to be performed.

All, however, must admire the prudence and caution of the banker's clerk in America, in giving evidence on a trial for forgery. "When I do hold the check this way, it do look slick like the handwriting of Malachi Hudson;— when I do hold it that way, it is not at all like Malachi's signature, so that upon the whole I should say it's about middling."

PUBLIC OPINION—is a river which digs its own bed. We may occasionally moderate or quicken its course, but it is very difficult to alter it.

PUFFING—a species of cozenage and trickery much resorted to by the vendors of quack medicines, blacking, novels, and other trash, for the purpose of gulling the public and cajoling them into a purchase of their wares. The abettors of this derogatory practice maintain that, so far as literature is concerned, it is an act of self-defence against the abuse of Reviews.—"What!" they exclaim, "is a bane to exist without its antidote? are malevolence, scurrility, perversion, and all the captious chicaneries of corrupt hyper-criticism, to have undisputed possession of the literary field? are authors, *ex necessitate*, such nefarious felons as not to be allowed benefit of clergy? Nature, where she plants a vegetable poison, generally provides an antidote, so in the moral world she causes sympathies to spring up by the side of antipathies. Extremes, moreover, have an inherent tendency towards each other; the pessimist makes the optimist: and thus it is that the unfairness, the bitterness, the rancour of reviewers have generated those much more excusable failings, if such they may be termed, of superlative, fulsome, high-flown panegyrics."

Be it observed, that in all these mutual malpractices, acting and re-acting with aggravated effect upon each other, the author has no share; he has parted with his copyright, has no interest in the conflict, and can find no more pleasure in being made the shuttlecock between the black and white battledore, than would a well-dressed gentleman in being alternately jostled by a miller and a chimney-sweeper. Philautical hyperboles are not less ridiculous and offensive than vain, for we may be assured that the more we speak of ourselves in superlatives, the more will others speak of us in diminutives; and the less we put ourselves forward, the more will the public be disposed to advance us.—"*Præfulgebant Cassius et Brutus eo ipso quod eorum effigies non visebantur,*" says Tacitus.

It must be confessed that the publisher, when, by constant puffing, he spreads and diffuses the leaves of his favourite book, and purifies the peccant humours of the critical world, has before him the example of nature, who, by a similar process, unfolds the vegetable leaves, and disperses the foul-ness and ill-humours of the atmosphere. Even should the amiable encomiast undesignedly bring grist to his own mill, surely he is not more culpable than the miller, who confessedly lives by puffs, and yet pursues his avocation without impeachment: so true is it that one man may steal a horse, while another must not look over the hedge! Both evils will work out their own cure, and puffing the most speedily, if there be any truth in the dictum, that

> " Praise undeserved is censure in disguise ;"

or, that

> " A vile encomium doubly ridicules,
> Since nothing blackens like the ink of fools."

Sheridan, in " The Critic," has described the puff-collusive, which is not yet by any means extinct :—

" If booksellers, now-a-days, do not venture to recommend their publications upon the ground of their indelicacy, they scruple not to attract readers by openly setting forth the personality and scandalous nature of the work they are puffing, thus pandering to a vice which is the stigma and opprobrium of the day, adducing as a merit that which ought to condemn the book with every right-thinking and right-feeling reader, and perverting public morals by an unblushing substitution of wrong for right. ' That 's villanous, and shows a most pitiful ambition in him that uses it. Oh, reform it altogether !' "

PUN—a verbal equivocation. If the highest legitimate wit be only a play upon ideas, why may we not tolerate a play upon words, which are the signs of ideas? Such a recreation is at least dabbling in the elements of wit, whereas a starch and formal gravity is an evidence of nothing but dullness. It is much easier to condemn a good pun than to make one, and Dr. Johnson evinced his envy rather

than his contempt, when he associated punsters and pick-
pockets.—We are seldom angry with that which we really
despise.

PUNISHMENTS—being meant for prevention, not revenge, should be so regulated—"*ut pœna ad paucos, metus
ad omnes perveniat.*"—Wise is that maxim which says, "*Non
minus turpe principimulta supplicia, quam medico multa
funera;*" and yet we have only lately made the discovery in
England, that hanging is the very worst use that a man can
be put to.

Some writers have thought that the state should be not
less solicitous to recompense good deeds, than to punish
evil ones ; but, perhaps, it is better not to disturb the
moralising impression, that virtue is its own best reward.
The noblest actions, too, would instantly become liable to a
tainting suspicion of motives, if the virtues were to be
scheduled, and remunerated according to a fixed tariff.
Experience has shown us to what infamous purposes the
rewards for the apprehension of malefactors have been
perverted by trading informers, and other dealers in *blood
money.*

Disproportionate punishments are attended with five
evils :—they deter prosecutors from coming forward—they
draw attention to the crime—awaken pity for the criminal
—excite hatred of the law—and occasion the magnitude of
the temptation to offence to be measured by the magnitude
of the punishment.

PURGATORY—one of the few inventions of priestcraft
that almost deserves to be true ; for a medium was wanting
between the two extremes of perdition and salvation. Infinite and eternal torment for offences committed in a few
brief years of existence, appeared so irreconcileable with the

divine attributes, that purgatory, as an intermediate and terminable state of punishment, was invented at a very early period of the Church. Harmless and reconciling in theory, it soon became practically perverted by the clergy into a device for the extortion of mass-money, under the pretext of shortening its duration. Had this abuse been corrected, and the supposed benefits of purgatory extended equally to the poor and the rich, our Church Reformers would, perhaps, have done well to leave this consolatory doctrine as they found it. It may not have the clear warranty of Scripture, but how much did they leave untouched, which was equally unsanctioned by divine authority ! Quevedo, in his Visions, tells us, that an old Spanish nobleman once met his coach-man in purgatory, when the latter exclaimed—" O master, master ! what can ever have brought so good a catholic as you into this miserable place?"—" Ah, my worthy Pedro ! I am justly punished for spoiling that reprobate son of mine. But you, who were ever such a sober, steady, well-conducted man, what can have brought you hither ?"—" Ah, master, master !" snivelled Pedro, " I am brought here for being the father of that reprobate son of yours !"

PURITANISM—the innocence of the vicious—external sanctimony, assumed as a cover for internal laxity. When-ever we smell musk or other pungent perfumes, we may fairly suspect that the wearer must have some strong effluvium to conquer ; and where we observe a Pharisaical display of prudery and piety, we shall seldom err in pro-nouncing that it is the disguise of some wolf in sheep's clothing. A nice man, according to Swift, is a man of nasty ideas; and a pretender to superior purity will often be found much dirtier than his neighbours. Some of these Pharisees will occasionally betray themselves by over-acting their part. " I never saw such an indelicate gentleman as that at the opposite house!" exclaimed a young female saint, " he must have seen that I did not choose to pull down the blind, and yet he has been watching me the whole time I have been changing my dress." Two damsels, of the same puritanical stamp, encountering Dr. Johnson, shortly after the publication of his Dictionary, complimented him on his having omitted all the gross and objectionable words. "What, my dears!" said the doctor, "have you been looking out for them already?"

UAKER.—"If external rites," Archbishop Tillotson affirms, "have ate out the heart of religion in the Church of Rome, religion should seem to have made the deepest impression on the Quakers, who are the most averse from external ceremonies and observances, and are therefore hated by the formalists of all churches." That no honours might be wanting to this truly Christian sect, they have been dignified by the abuse of Cobbett, who, in allusion to their dress, and their rejection of the ceremony of baptism, terms them, in choice Billingsgate, "a set of unbaptized, buttonless blackguards!"

Many have admired and eulogised the mild creed, the universal charity, the fraternal love, the well-directed industry, the moral rectitude, the commercial probity, the strict veracity, the general amiability, of these religionists, among whom are to be found no malefactors, no beggars, no infamous members of any sort, and who imagine that they best prove themselves to be good Christians, by being good subjects, good neighbours, good men. But how indiscreet, how dangerous, nay, how immoral, is such eulogy! What! can we forget that they arrogantly presume to be pious and virtuous, without paying tithes;—that they dare to have a church, not only without sacraments, but even without a priesthood;—and that they constitute the best organised and most harmonious religious society in the world, not only without a spiritual aristocracy, but even without a head? What profanation, too, that they should consider marriage a simple civil contract, should solemnize it as such, and yet never offer to the public a single instance of adultery or divorce! What a pestilential example is all this, and how injurious to true, primitive, unadulterated Christianity, as it is maintained and illustrated in our venerable Established Church!! Let us hear no more of the Quakers, unless it be for the purpose of proscribing and persecuting them!

"QUARRELS—would never last long," says Rochefoucauld, "if the fault were only on one side." The Spanish proverb, which tells us to beware of a reconciled friend, inculcates an ungenerous suspicion. In the case of lovers, we have the authority of Terence for affirming that—*Amantium ira amoris redintegratio est;*—and many are the instances among friends, where a momentary rupture has only served to consolidate the subsequent attachment, as the broken bone, that is well set, usually becomes stronger than it was before.

QUIBBLE—QUIRK—QUIDDET—see Law Proceedings. "True!" cried a lady, when reproached with the inconsistent marriage she had made, " I have often said I never would marry a parson, or a Scotchman, or a Presbyterian; but I never said I would not marry a Scotch Presbyterian parson."

Roger Kemble's wife had been forbidden to marry an actor, and her father was inexorable at her disobedience; but, after having seen her husband on the stage, he relented, and forgave her, with the observation of—" Well, well, I see you have not disobeyed me after all ; for the man is not an actor, and never will be an actor."

QUID PRO QUO.—Every one has heard the reply of Montague Matthew, when he was spoken to for Matthew Montague,—that there is a great difference between a chestnut horse and a horse chestnut ; but this seems to have been forgotten, nevertheless, by an unlucky wight, who, being engaged to dine at the Green Man at Dulwich, desired to be driven to the Dull Man, at Greenwich, and lost his dinner by a *quid pro quo*.

T. H. observed of the mate of a Whitby merchant ship, who could do nothing without his quid, that he had classical authority for "*Nil actum reputans dum* quid *superesset agendum*."

AILLERY—has been compared to a light which dazzles, but does not burn : this, however, depends on the skill with which it is managed; for many a man, without extracting its brilliance, may burn his fingers in playing with this dangerous pyrotechnic. Pleasant enough to make game of your friends, by shooting your wit at them, but if your merry bantering degenerates into coarse and offensive personality, nobody will pity you, should you chance to be knocked down by the recoil of your own weapon. He who gives pain, however little, must not complain should it be retorted with a disproportionate severity; for retaliation always adds interest in paying off old scores, and sometimes a very usurious one. Wags should recollect, that the amusement of fencing with one's friends is very different from the anatomical process of cutting them up.

A coxcomb, not very remarkable for the acuteness of his feelings or his wit, wishing to banter a testy old gentleman, who had lately garnished his mouth with a complete set of false teeth, flippantly inquired,—" Well, my good Sir ! I have often heard you complain of your masticators—pray, when do you expect to be again troubled with the tooth-ache ?"—" When you have an affection of the heart, or a brain fever," was the reply. Not less ready and biting was the retort of the long-eared Irishman, who, being banteringly asked—" Paddy, my jewel ! why don't you get your ears cropped ? They are too large for a man !" replied—" And yours are too small for an ass."

A well-known scapegrace, wishing to rally a friend who had a morbid horror of death, asked him, as they were passing a country church during the performance of a funeral, whether the tolling bell did not put him in mind of his latter end.—" No ; but the rope does of yours," was the caustic reply.

REASON—the proud prerogative which confers on man the exclusive privilege of acting and conversing irrationally. No man is opposed to reason, unless reason is opposed to him ; to protest against it, is to confess that you fear it, and they who interdict its use, on account of the danger of its abuse, may as well build a house without windows, for fear the lightning should enter it, or put out their eyes, lest they should go astray. To give reasons against the employment of reason, is to refute yourself, and to close up your mind till it resembles the bower described by Shakspeare,—

> " Where honeysuckles, ripened by the sun,
> Forbid the sun to enter."

And yet we have theologians, who, proscribing the exercise of man's distinguishing and most noble attribute, in the most exalted object to which it can be directed—the contemplation of the Deity, and the study of his revealed will,—would confine human nature, in its highest aspirations, to mere animal instincts.   Surely this is a triple treason;—first, against the majesty of God; secondly, against the dignity of his human image; thirdly, against the writings he inspired.   In various places do the Scriptures themselves repudiate this degrading doctrine.   St. Paul desires us to "prove all things;" and St. Peter, in his first epistle, expressly says, "Be ready always to give an answer to every man that asketh you *a reason* of the hope that is in you."—iii. 15.   And as we are elsewhere told that the letter killeth, how are we to discover the saving spirit, except by the exercise of our intellectual faculties?   To imagine that the Bible is opposed to reason, is to impugn its veracity.   Mark the opinion of the pious Locke upon the subject: "No mission can be looked on to be divine, that delivers anything derogating from the honour of the one, only, true, invisible God; or inconsistent with natural religion, and the rules of morality; because God, having discovered to men the unity and Majesty of his eternal Godhead, and the truths of natural religion and morality by the light of reason, he cannot be supposed to back the contrary by revelation; for that would be to destroy the evidence and use of reason, without which, men cannot be able to distinguish divine revelation from diabolical imposture."*

And to the same purport, Bishop Burnet, in his "Exposition of the 19th Article," tells us, "that if we observe the style and method of the Scriptures, we shall find in them all over a constant appeal to men's reason, and to their intellectual faculties.   If the mere dictates of the Church, or of *infallible men* had been the resolution and foundation of

* Posthumous Works, p. 226.

faith, there had been no need of such a long thread of reasoning and discourse, as both our Saviour used when on
earth, and the Apostles used in their writings. We see the
way of authority is not taken, but explanations are offered,
proofs and illustrations are brought, to convince the mind;
which shows that God, in the clearest manifestation of his
will, would deal with us as with rational creatures, who are
not to believe, but on persuasion; and to use our reason, in
order to the attaining that persuasion."

Well would it have been for sound and rational theology,
had controversial writers always attended to the dictum of
another learned and pious divine, who affirms — "That
which has not reason in it, or for it, is man's superstition,
and not religion of God's making."—*Dr. Whichcote's Sermons*, p. 117.

Prohibiting the exercise of this faculty, in matters of
opinion, is but an imitation of the Papists, who will not allow
the senses to be judges in the case of transubstantiation.
Strange! that instinct, which is the reason of animals, is to
be allowed to the feathered, and not to the featherless biped.
These irrationalists seem to think, that the intellectual faculties of man are like hemlock and henbane, poisonous to the
human, but not to the feathered race—*Hyosciamus et cicula
homines perimunt, avibus alimentum præbent.* Reason,
however, does us all yeoman's service in the defence of anything unreasonable. When Paley was asked why he always
kept his horse three miles off, he replied—" For exercise."—
" But you never ride."—" That is the reason why I keep
him at such a distance, for I get all the exercise of the
walk."

Still more ingenious was the logic of the schoolboy, whose
companion thought it absurd that Homer should describe
Vulcan as being a whole day in falling from the clouds to
the earth.—" Nay," argued the acute youth, " this shows his

close adherence to nature; for you can hardly expect Vulcan to fall as fast as another man, when you recollect that he was lame." His lameness being the consequence of his fall, it must be confessed, that there was unreasonableness enough in this reason to satisfy the most zealous irrationalist.

REFORM—an adaptation of institutions to circumstances and knowledge, or a restoration to the original purposes, from which they have been perverted, demanded as a right by those who are suffering wrongs, and only denied and abused by those who have been fattening upon abuse. The real Conservatives are the Reformers, the real revolutionists are the corruptionists, who, by opposing quiet, will compel violent change. When the ultras, and men of this class, whose long misrule, and denial of justice, have inflamed the public mind, charge the Reformers with having thrown the whole country into a blaze, thus accusing the extinguisher of being the firebrand, one is reminded of the incendiary, who, in order to avoid detection, turned round and collared the foreman of the engines, exclaiming—"Ha, fellow! have I caught you?—This is the rascal who is first and foremost at every fire—seize him! seize him!" There is no Reform Bill in Turkey,—no factious opposition,—no free press,—no twopenny trash,—yet, in no country are revolutions so frequent.

Reform, however, to be useful and durable, must be gradual and cautious. To those radical gentry of the movement party, who would be always at work, without calculating the mischief or the cost of their vaunted improvements, I recommend the consideration of the following anecdote:—The celebrated orator Henley advertised, that, in a single lecture, he would teach any artisan, of ordinary skill, how to make six pair of good shoes in one day;—nay, six-and-twenty pair, provided there was a sufficiency of materials. The sons of

Crispin flocked in crowds, willingly paying a shilling at the door, to be initiated in such a lucrative art, when they beheld the orator seated at a table, on which were placed six pair of new boots.—"Gentlemen!" he exclaimed, "nothing is so simple and easy as the art which I have undertaken to teach you. Here are a new pair of boots,—here are a large pair of scissors;—behold! I cut off the legs of the boots, and you have a new pair of shoes, without the smallest trouble; and thus may they be multiplied, *ad infinitum*, supposing always that you have a sufficiency of materials."

REFORMATION.—"The freedom for which our first Reformers contended, did not include any freedom of dissent from the Athanasian Creed. Grotius and Lardner, and Locke and Newton, those great and pious men, who were an honour to human nature, and the most illustrious advocates of Christianity, would have been adjudged by the first Reformers, as well as by the Catholics, by Cranmer and Knox, as well as by Bonner and Beaton, to be worthy of death in the present world, and of everlasting misery in the world to come. The martyrdoms of Servetus in Geneva, and of Joan Bocher in England, are notable instances of the religious freedom which prevailed in the pure and primitive state of the Protestant churches."—*Ed. Review*, vol. xxvii. p. 165.

The Reformation was not a struggle for religious freedom, but for Protestant intolerance, instead of Catholic intolerance; and the struggle of modern Christians should be for emancipation from *all* intolerance. To every man thus engaged, may we not piously ejaculate—"*Dii tibi dent quæ velis!*"

RELIGION, Fashionable—going to Church; making devotion a matter of public form and observance between man and man, instead of a governing principle, or silent communion between the heart and its Creator;—converting the accessory into the principal, and mistaking the symbol and stimulant of pious inspiration for the inspirer;—worshipping the type, instead of the archetype;—being visibly devout, that is to say, when anybody sees you.

RELIGION, General—an accidental inheritance, for which, whether it be good or bad, we deserve neither praise nor censure, provided that we are sincere and virtuous.

Let us not, however, be mistaken. Far be it from us to assert, that men should be indifferent to the choice of religion, still less that all are alike. We maintain only, that in the great majority of instances, little or no choice is allowed; and it is our object to inculcate that humility as to our own opinions, and that toleration for others, in which the most devout are very apt to be the most deficient.

> " Religion is the mind's complexion,
> Governed by birth, not self-election,
> And the great mass of us adore
> Just as our fathers did before.
> Why should we, then, ourselves exalt
> For what we casually inherit,
> Or view, in others, as a fault,
> What, in ourselves, we deem a merit?"

The religion that renders good men gloomy and unhappy, can scarcely be a true one. Dr. Blair says, in his Sermon on Devotion—" He who does not feel joy in religion, is far from the kingdom of heaven." Never can a slavish and cowering fear afford a proper basis for the religion of so dignified a creature as man, who, in paying honour, must feel that he keeps his honour, and is not disunited from himself, even in his communion with God. Reverence of ourselves is, in fact, the highest of all reverences; for, in the image of the

Deity, we recognise the prototype; and thus elevated in soul, we may humbly strive to imitate the divine virtues, without pride or presumption. Religion has been designated as the love of the good and the fair, wherever it exists, but chiefly when absolute and boundless excellence is contemplated in "the first good, first perfect, and first fair." With this feeling in their hearts, the virtues could never wander from the right faith; and yet, how many good men seek it amid the dry spinosities and tortuous labyrinths of theology! It was a homely saying of Selden, "that men look after religion, as the butcher did after his knife, when he had it in his mouth."

Even a sincere religion may be unconsciously mixed up with carnal impulses; for when we cannot bring heaven down to earth, we are very apt to take earth up to heaven. That ardent adoration of the Virgin Mary, which has procured for Catholicism the not inappropriate designation of the Marian Religion, was derived probably from the days of chivalry, when a sexual feeling impassioned the worship paid to the celestial idol, and a devout enthusiasm sanctified the homage offered to the earthly one. These spiritual lovers would have done well to perpend the fine saying of the philosopher, Marcus Antoninus—"Thou wilt never do anything purely human in a right manner, unless thou knowest the relation it bears to things divine; nor anything divine, unless thou knowest all the relations it has to things human."

RELIGION, "Pure and undefiled before God and the Father."—We have placed this last, because it is the last that enters into the contemplation of the numerous classes of Christians, most of whom are too busy in fashioning some fantastical religion of their own, to seek for it in the Scriptures. The devout and rational reader is referred to

the twenty-seventh verse of the first chapter of James. And
if he still harbour a doubt which be the works of the flesh,
and which of the Spirit, let him peruse St. Paul's Epistle to
the Galatians, chap. v. ver. 19—26.

REPARTEE—a smart rejoinder, which, when given *impromptu*, even though it should be so hard a hit as to merit
the name of a knock down blow, will still stand excused,
partly from the ready wit it implies, and partly from its
always bearing the semblance of self-defence. When time,
however, has been taken to concoct a retort, and an opportunity sought for launching it, not only does it lose all the
praise of extemporaneous quickness, but it assumes a character of revenge rather than of repartee.

Those repartees are the best which turn your adversary's
weapons against himself, as David killed Goliah with his
own sword. Abernethy, the celebrated surgeon, finding a
large pile of paving stones opposite to his door, on his returning home one afternoon in his carriage, swore hastily at
the paviour, and desired him to remove them. "Where will
I take them to?" asked the Hibernian. "To hell!" cried
the choleric surgeon. Paddy leant upon his rammer, and
then looking up in his face, said with an arch smile, "Hadn't
I better take them to heaven?—sure they'd be more out of
your honour's way."

REPLY, A ready.—"Carnivorous animals," said a collegian to the Rev. S. S——, "are always provided with claws
and talons to seize their prey; hoofed animals are invariably
graminivorous. Is it, therefore, consistent with the analogies
of nature to describe the devil when he goes about seeking
whom he may devour, as having a cloven foot?" "Yes,"
replied the divine; "for we are assured, on scriptural authority, that all flesh is grass." Few better replies are upon

record than that of young De Chateaunœuf, to whom a
bishop once said, " If you will tell me where God is, I will
give you an orange? " " If you will tell me where He if
not, I will give you two," was the child's answer.

REQUEST, A modest.—When the Duke of Ormonde was
made Lord Lieutenant of Ireland, in Queen Anne's reign,
one of his friends applied to him for some preferment,
adding, that he was by no means particular, and was willing
to accept either a Bishopric, or a Regiment of Horse—or to
be made Lord Chief Justice of the King's Bench.   This,
however, is surpassed by Horace Walpole's anecdote of a
humane jailor in Oxfordshire, who made the following application to one of his condemned prisoners. " My good friend!
I have a little favour to ask of you, which from your obliging
disposition, I doubt not you will readily grant. You are
ordered for execution on Friday week. I have a particular
engagement on that day: if it makes no difference to you,
would you say *next* Friday instead? "

RESOLUTION.—He who sets out by considering all
obstacles well — *non obstantibus quibuscunque*, has half-
accomplished his purpose, for the difficulty in human affairs
is more often in the mind of the undertaker, than in the
nature of the undertaking. With this feeling, and the *nil
actum reputans dum quid superesset agendum,*—nothing is
impossible.

RESPECTABILITY—keeping up appearances, paying
your bills regularly, walking out now and then with your
wife, and going occasionally to church.   On the trial of
a murderer, a neighbour deposed that he had always considered him a person of the highest respectability, as he had
kept a gig for several years. This could only have occurred

in England, where it is held that a man who is worth money, must be a man of worth.

RETIREMENT from business—a mistake in those wh. have not an occupation to retire *to*, as well as *from*. Such men are never so well or so happily employed, as when they are following the avocation which use has made a second nature to them. The retired butcher in the neighbourhood of Whitby, must have found idleness hard work, when he gave notice to his friends, that he should kill a lamb every Thursday, just by way of amusement.

RETORT-COURTEOUS.—" I said his beard was not cut well; he was in the mind it was; this is called the retort-courteous," says one of the characters in Shakspeare; but this *lucus à non lucendo,* does not come up to our modern idea of the term, which should involve some portion of the sharpness or smartness of a repartee. Lord G——, who is vehemently suspected of being descended from Ferdinand Mendez Pinto, since he never opens his mouth without fibbing, made some disparaging statement at White's concerning one of the members. The party implicated, who happened to overhear him, came up to his accuser, and said emphatically, " My Lord, you have made an assertion," inferring as a matter of course, that he had uttered a falsehood. It is impossible to imagine a more polite, and yet more cutting way of giving the lie.

Two of the guests at a public dinner having got into an altercation, one of them, a blustering vulgarian, vociferated, " Sir, you are no gentleman !" " Sir," said his opponent in a calm voice, and with a derisive smile,—" you are no judge." Both these *bon mots* are complete and literal instances of the retort-courteous.

There are retorts uncourteous which can only be justified

by the occasion. Talleyrand being pestered with importunate questions by a squinting man, concerning his broken
leg, replied, " It is quite crooked,—as you see."

H. C——, a keen sportsman, provoked by a cockney
horseman who had ridden over two of his hounds, could not
forbear swearing at him for his awkwardness. " Sir !" said
the offender, drawing up both himself and his horse, and
assuming a very consequential look, " I beg to inform you,
that I did not come out here to be damned."—" Why then,
Sir, you may go home, and be damned."

" Ah ! Dr. Johnson," exclaimed a Scotchman, " what
would you have said of Buchanan, had he been an English-
man ?" " Why, Sir," replied Johnson, " I should not have
said of Buchanan, had he been an Englishman, what I will
now say of him as a Scotchman, that he was the only man
of genius his country ever produced."

REVENGE—a momentary triumph, of which the satisfaction dies at once, and is succeeded by remorse; whereas forgiveness, which is the noblest of all revenges, entails a
perpetual pleasure. It was well said by a Roman Emperor,
that he wished to put an end to all his enemies, by converting them into friends.

REVIEW—a work that overlooks the productions it professes to look over, and judges of books by their authors, not
of authors by their books.

REVIEW, Retrospective. — When we cast a Parthian
glance backwards, and embrace in one far darting retrospect
our whole existence, divided as it has been into infancy, boyhood, manhood, and old age, each a sort of separate life,
from the variety of thoughts, feelings, and events that it
comprises, what a long, long, course of time seems to be con-

densed into the mental operation of a single moment. The period from our own birth to the present hour, appears more extensive and eventful than all that has preceded it, even from the birth of the world ; so different is the impression made by time experienced, and time imagined. In the former case, the view is broken by a succession of land-marks, each throwing back the distance, and giving to the whole the semblance of covering a much larger space than it really occupies. In the latter, we are gazing over an object-less sea, where the horizon is brought nearer to us for want of any standard by which to measure its remoteness. History is the shadow of time; life its substance, and they bear the same relation to one another, that the dim twilight does to the up-risen and visible sun. It is in vain to talk to men of throwing their minds into the past, or into the future, you may as well bid them leap out of themselves, or beyond their shadow. The present is all in all to us. As to the past ages, and those which are to come, " *De non apparentibus et non existentibus eadem est ratio.*"

REVIEWER.— With certain honourable exceptions, a reviewer is one who, either having written nothing himself, or having failed in his own literary attempts, kindly under-takes to decide upon the writing of others. " Let those teach others, who themselves excel," was the maxim of former times, but in the march of no-intellect, we have reversed all this: the dunce wields the magisterial rod, the ass sits in the professor's chair, and both are severe, because they have found it much more easy and pleasant not to like, than to do the like. *Hi præ cæteris alios liberiùs carpere solent, qui nil proprium ediderunt :*—those men are most disposed to depreciate others, who have done nothing them-selves. Such a critic contemplates a book, as a carpenter views a tree, not to weigh the time and contrivance that have been required for its production, not to admire its just proportions, or the beauty of its leaves, not to consider what pleasure or advantage it may bestow upon others, if left to flourish and expand, but merely to calculate how he himself may best turn it to account, by undermining, overthrowing, and cutting it up. As to the poor author, he is merely used as a stalking-horse, behind which the critic levels at the surrounding game, giving his steed a lash or two as he ends his diversion.

Messieurs the Reviewers ! you are like Othello, not for your black looks, nor because of your smothering the innocent in their own sheets, but because, " your occupation's gone." Having found out the motives both of puffers and abusers, the public are no more to be deterred from purchasing a clever book by the latter, than cajoled into buying a stupid one by the former. Parodying the words of a well known epigram, we may therefore exclaim :—

> Peace, idiots,—peace ! and both have done,—
>   Each kiss his empty brother,
> For Genius scorns a foe like one,
>   And dreads a friend like 't'other.

Should any of the fraternity, nevertheless, feel disposed to notice this little work, they will please to consider themselves among the honourable exceptions alluded to in the commencement of this article. We scorn to truckle to any man for the poor honours of " full blown Bufo," but candour, is candour !

RHETORIC—appealing to the passions instead of the reason of your auditors, and claiming that value for the workmanship, which ought to be measured by the ore alone. An orator is one who can stamp such a value upon counterfeit coin as shall make it pass for genuine. Pitt was a rhetorician, or rather declaimer, of this sort, and unfortunately, we are now paying in sterling coin for his Birmingham flash money.

RICHES—are seldom really despised, though they may be vilipended upon the principle of the fox, who imputed sourness to the unattainable grapes. We cannot well attach too much value to a competency, or too little to a superfluity, but we may and do err in generally defining the former as a little more than we already possess. Riches provide an antidote to their bane, for though they encourage idleness, they will purchase occupation, by change of scene, variety of company, pastimes of all sorts, and by that noblest employment of any, the exercise of beneficence. Robinson Crusoe might despise riches—so may a savage; but no sane and civilised man will hold them in contempt.

" If you live," says Seneca, "according to the dictates of nature, you will never be poor; if according to the notions of the world, you will never be rich."

RIGHTS—and constitutional improvements, are generally the results of a struggle, for no wrong makes a voluntary surrender; it must be met, fought, and conquered. Liberty has seldom been brought into the world without a convulsion. Treason and rebellion are terrible afflictions, but they gave us Magna Charta in one age, and in another the Constitution of 1688. Tyranny and abuse never imitate the well-bred dog, who walks quietly down stairs, just as he sees preparations are making for kicking him down. They wait for the application of the foot, and are kicked twice as far as was first intended. Had the boroughmongers conceded representation to three or four of the large towns, they would not have been all consigned to Schedule A, and smothered in their own rottenness.

ROMAN CATHOLIC RELIGION.—Horace Walpole in his Letters mentions a sceptical *bon-vivant*, who, upon being urged to turn Roman Catholic, objected that it was a religion enjoining so many fasts, and requiring such implicit faith:—"You give us," he observed, "too little to eat, and too much to swallow."

ABBATH, Observance of.—The Americans are before us in sound opinions on this subject. In the report of the House of Representatives upon petitions for the prohibition of the conveyance of the mail on the Sabbath, the proposition is broadly laid down, that questions of religious obligation lie out of the province of legislation. It says, "The principles of our government do not recognise in the majority any authority over the minority, except in matters which regard the conduct of man to his fellow-men." And it defines the duty of the representative "to guard the rights of man—not to restrict the rights of conscience." We here quote the passage.

"Religious zeal enlists the strongest prejudices of the human mind, and, when misdirected, excites the worst passions of our nature under the delusive pretext of doing God service. Nothing so infuriates the heart to deeds of rapine and blood. Nothing is so incessant in its toils, so persevering in its determinations, so appalling in its course, or so dangerous in its consequences. The equality of rights secured by the constitution may bid defiance to mere political tyrants, but the robe of sanctity too often glitters to deceive. The constitution regards the conscience of the Jew as sacred as that of the Christian, and gives no more authority to adopt a measure affecting the conscience of a solitary individual than that of a whole community. That representative who would violate this principle, would lose his delegated

character, and forfeit the confidence of his constituents.
If Congress shall declare the first day of the week holy, it
will not convince the Jew nor the Sabbatarian. It will dis-
satisfy both, and, consequently, convert neither. Human
power may extort vain sacrifices, but Deity alone can command the affections of the heart. If Congress shall, by the
authority of the law, sanction the measure recommended, it
would constitute a legislative decision of a religious controversy, on which even Christians themselves are at issue.
However suited such a decision may be to an ecclesiastical
council, it is incompatible with a republican legislature, which
is purely for political, and not religious purposes."

Josephus records, that when God was determined to
punish his chosen people, the inhabitants of Jerusalem, who,
while they were breaking all his other laws, were scrupulous
observers of that *one* which required them to keep holy the
Sabbath-day, he suffered this hypocritical fastidiousness to
become their ruin; for Pompey, knowing that they obstinately refused even to defend themselves on that day, selected
it for a general assault upon the city, which he took by storm,
and butchered the inhabitants with as little mercy as he
found resistance.

" Pleasant but wrong," was the *naïveté* of the little urchin,
who, on being brought before a magistrate for playing
marbles on a Sunday, and sternly asked,—" Do you know,
sirrah, where those little boys go to, who are wicked enough
to play marbles on a Sunday?" replied very innocently,—
" Yes, your vorship, some on 'em goes to the Common, and
some on 'em goes down by the river side."

SACRIFICES—killing and burning the harmless to save
the hurtful, so that the less innocent men become, the more
they destroy innocent animals. What must have been
Solomon's opinion of his own sins, and those of his people,

when, at the consecration of the temple, he offered a sacrifice of 22,000 oxen, and 120,000 sheep !—Ovid was clear-sighted enough to see the folly of the heathen system of sacrifice, and there is a remarkable conformity between his—

" Non bove mactato cœlestia numina gaudent,
    Sed quæ præstanda est, et sine teste, fide"—

and sundry passages in the New Testament. The priesthood made no very heavy sacrifice when they gave up their share of slaughtered animals for tithes, offerings, and other pecuniary oblations.

SANCTUARY—the abuse of impunity, arising originally from the abuse of legal severity;—two evils aggravating, in the endeavour to correct, each other. All local privileges, the remnants of this ancient compromise, should be abolished. We need no other sanctuary than mild laws impartially administered. The king being the first magistrate of the State, and, as head of the Church, the guardian of the public morals, why should the verge of his court enable debtors to defy their just creditors, and to defraud honest tradesmen with impunity? Why should Peers, or Members of the House of Commons, perverting their honour into a source of dishonour, violate the laws which themselves have made, and set themselves above pecuniary responsibility by their freedom from arrest? How these privileges have been abused, is well known:—why they should be still retained, is by no means so manifest.

SATIRE—a glass in which the beholder sees everybody's face but his own.

SAW—a sort of dumb alderman which gets through a great deal by the activity of its teeth.—N.B. A bona-fide alderman is not one of the " wise saws " mentioned by Shakspeare, at least in "modern instances."

SCANDAL—what one half the world takes a pleasure in inventing, and the other half in believing.

SCANDALOUS REPORTS — says Boerhaave, are sparks, which, if you do not blow them, will go out of themselves. They have, perhaps, been better compared to volcanic explosions, of which the lighter portions are dispersed by the winds, while the heavier fall back into the mouth whence they were ejected. Our scandalous journals, professedly dealing in personality and abuse, have been justly termed the opprobrium of the age ; but it is some consolation to know, that few or none of them have disgraced the liberal cause. The Conservatives have all the discredit of their support; the Reformers, all the honour of their enmity. Nuisances as they are, it is, perhaps, wise not to molest them, but to let them die of their own stench. Prosecutions for libel avail little against men of straw, and as to personal chastisement, the rogues—

> " Have all been beaten till they know,
> What wood the cudgel's of by the blow ;
> Or kick'd, until they can tell whether
> A shoe be Spanish or neat leather."

SCEPTICISM.—" The dogmatist," says Watts, " is sure of everything, and the sceptic believes nothing." Both are likely to be wrong, but we need not impute wrong motives to either. Scepticism *may* be assumed as an excuse for immorality : but Faith also *may* be assumed as a substitute for good works. To say that the doubters are all profligates, and the orthodox all hypocrites, would be equally removed from truth and liberality. As the worldly temptations all lean towards an acquiescence in received opinions, those who profess them should be the last to suspect the motives of those who differ from them. Both may be good Christians, if they will but think each other to be such.

SCHISM.—" The restraining of the Word of God, and the understanding of men, from that liberty wherein Christ and the Apostles left them, is, and hath been, the only fountain of all the schisms of the Church, and that which makes them immortal;—the common incendiary of Christendom, and that which tears in pieces, not the coat, but the bowels and members of Christ, *Ridente Turca nec dolente Judæo.*"—(Chillingworth's *Religion of Protestants,* pt. i. p. 152.)

SCHOOLS.—It may be questioned whether the separation of brothers and sisters from each other, and of both from their parents, by sending them to school, be not injurious to domestic morals, and therefore hurtful to all parties. That scholars may derive many advantages from attending public or private institutions cannot be denied; but their residence should be at home, for such would seem to be the intention of nature; and the constant intercourse of parents and children cannot be otherwise than mutually beneficial. Men should be fathers of their sons' minds as well as bodies. Whatever a youth may lose in the classics, by being educated *altogether* at home, he will gain in morality, and the family affections; while he will pick up, by what may be termed insensible education, more general knowledge than will be generally possessed by an Etonian or Harrow boy of twice his age. Latin and Greek are worth having, but not if they cost more than their value. The licentious intrigues of heathen gods, and the loose morality of Pagan writers, are not the safest reading at that period of life, when evil impressions are the most easily made, and the most difficult to eradicate. What is the value of mere scholarship? There ought to be a satisfactory answer to this question, for a whole life is often given for its acquirement. And after all, it is not the knowledge locked up in the learned languages; it is not the treasure, but the casket; not the nut, but the shell, upon which our classical students crack their critical teeth. Bowing down to the shrine, not to the divinity, what wonder that we so rarely hear of a learned Theban or senior wrangler after he quits his monkish Alma Mater. He knows nothing, does nothing, thinks of nothing, by which the world may be benefited or enlightened. Modern History—the British Constitution—Political Economy—General Science, have formed but a small part of his education, for they are not noticed by the commentators, either upon Lycophron's Cassandra, or the Prometheus Vinctus. If only one half of the time lavished upon the dead languages had been devoted to philosophical researches, many a scholar, who is now forgotten, might have left behind him an imperishable name. Since the days of the illustrious Robert Boyle, few of our patricians have distinguished themselves in the higher sciences, or as experimental philosophers. Boyle, it must be confessed, had an advantage—he was never at college; no more were Newton, Maclaurin, Wallis, Simson, Napier; nor, in our own more immediate times, Sir Humphry Davy, and some of our most eminent philosophers.

SCHOOLMASTER—a dealer in boys and birch;—often an academical tyrant, who in his utter ignorance of proper management, renders his victims intractable by maltreatment, and then treats them worse for being intractable. Cudgel a little jackass as often as you will, and if he survives your cruelty, he will only end with being a great jackass.

Many of our pedagogues, ever ready to apply the birch and the ferula, make no allowance for natural deficiency of talent, while they will often terrify a lad of good abilities, but weak nerves, into an asinine stupidity. The boys from whom they gather their harvest, they seem to consider as so much corn, which must be threshed and knocked about the ears before any grains of sense can be extracted; or perhaps they liken them to walnut trees, which shower down their fruit in return for being well beaten. " The schoolmaster's joy is to flog," says Swift; since when a hundred years have elapsed, and it still remains the favourite pastime of our pedagogues, who seem to think that boys, as well as sylla-bubs, are to be raised by flogging. Ships and fishes may make their way when steered by the tail; but when we attempt to guide or impel youngsters by a similar process, we only retard or turn them out of their right line. Flagel-lation, whether of pupils or of soldiers, invariably hardens and depraves those whom it seeks to reclaim. In nothing is a thorough reform so much wanted as in some of our old-fashioned seminaries and teachers.

An empty-headed youth once boasted that he had been to two of the most celebrated schools in England. "Sir," said a bystander, "you remind me of the calf that sucked two cows." "And what was the consequence?" "Why, sir, he was a very great calf."

SCIENCE—presents this advantage to its cultivator, that he may always hope for progression, whereas the arts, at least the ornamental ones, move in a perpetual Round Robin, the demand for novelty constantly requiring that even the most faultless perfection should be superseded by something new, which, of necessity, must be something inferior. Were Phidias, Vitruvius, and Raphael to revive, they would find that the world has retrograded in statuary, architecture, and painting;—but could Leibnitz or Newton revisit us, they would be amazed at our advances in mathematics and general science.

SCOTCHMEN—the inhabitants of every country except their own. " No wonder," says Dean Lockier, " that we meet with so many clever Scotchmen, for every man of that country, who has any sense, leaves it as fast as he can."

SCOTT, Sir Walter.—Twenty-two bad poets have already written epitaphs upon this celebrated author. What a gain would it be to the world if Sir Walter were now writing theirs !

SCULPTURE—the noble art of making an imperishable portrait in marble or bronze. There are various ways of contemplating these exquisite productions of genius. We may be delighted by the beauty of a statue, amazed by the triumph of manual dexterity which it exhibits, or we may be interested in its associations with the past or the future. Or there is a Utilitarian and economical way of considering the matter, which was well illustrated by two artisans, when Chantry's bronze statue of George the Fourth was first exhibited, " What a lot o' penny pieces all this here copper would have made," observed one.—" Ay, never mind, Jack !" said his companion, pointing at the figure—" it will cost a deal less to keep he, than it does to keep the live un ! "

A contemporary writer has asked, why we attach so little value to the wax figures in the perfumers' shops, which approach much nearer to nature than the most elaborate marble bust; but he must have forgotten that all works of art are estimated in the mingled ratio of their difficulty, utility, and permanence, not by their mere similitude to the object imitated.—" You would not value the finest head cut out upon a carrot," said Dr. Johnson. Here he was right, but he was wrong when he added that the value of statuary was *solely* owing to its difficulty; for its durability, we might almost say its perpetuity, gives it an immeasurable advantage over a perishable painting.

SEA, The—three-fourths of what we might call the earth; the dwelling-place of whales, walruses, porpoises, seals, sailors, and other monsters.

Strange that we often lose our way in travelling by land, where we have only to follow our nose, pursue the high roads chalked out for us, and read the sign posts set up for our guidance; while in traversing the pathless deep, with none to ask, and no sea-marks to direct, with nothing to peruse but the blank main and the illegible sky, a vessel seldom fails, however long and remote may be her voyage, to steer direct into her destined harbour. This is the proudest victory of science; the greatest triumph of man over the elements. The little round compass is the ring that marries the most distant nations to each other. Commerce is the parent of civilisation; the coasts and ports of a country will be always found more polished than the inland parts. The sea, therefore, shall ever receive the homage of my profound respect, but I cannot admire it. Hunt has justly defined it as a great monotonous idea. So little do I like it, that I care not to dwell upon it, even with my pen.

SECRETS.—A secret is like silence—you cannot talk about it, and keep it; it is like money—when once you know there is any concealed, it is half discovered.—"My dear Murphy!" said an Irishman to his friend, "why did you betray the secret I told you?"—"Is it betraying you call it? Sure, when I found I wasn't able to keep it myself, didn't I do well to tell it to somebody that could?"

SECTS — different clans of religionists, the very variety and number of which should inculcate mutual respect and toleration, instead of hatred, and that odious self-worship, which many people imagine to be worship of the Creator.—

Embracing those whom Europe holds,
The Christian catalogue unfolds
    About a hundred different sects,
And due indulgence it should teach
To every follower of each ;
    If for a moment he reflects,
The chances are against his own,
Just as one hundred are to one.

SELF-LOVE—thinking the most highly of the individual that least deserves our regard. The self-love of most men consists in pleasing themselves, but there are some cases where it displays itself in pleasing others. In neither is it altogether to be condemned, for our sensibilities may be too weak, as well as too strong, and they who feel little for themselves, will feel little or not at all for others. Nothing can be more different than fortitude and insensibility; the one being a noble principle, the other a mere negation; and yet they are often confounded.

SERMONS—sometimes theological opiates—sometimes religious discourses, attended by many who do not attend to them, and when published, purchased by many who do not read them. It is in vain to expect much eloquence or originality in these productions ;—first, because most clergy-men have a horror of novelty, lest it should be deemed unorthodox: and, secondly, because they want all motive for the bold and full development of their talents. To rise above the regular routine of the pulpit, will neither improve their present position, nor add to their chances of future preferment; for the ruling church powers, jealous of all enthusiasts, and still more so of original thinkers, had much rather promote a weak respectable man, who will submit to be led, than a strong-minded zealous divine who might aspire to lead—and, perhaps, to innovate !

" How comes it," demanded a clergyman of Garrick—"that I, in expounding divine doctrines, produce so little effect upon my congregation, while you can so easily arouse the passions of your auditors by the representation of fiction?" The answer was short and pithy.—"Because I recite falsehoods as if they were true, while you deliver truths as if they were false."

SERVANTS—liveried deputies, upon whose tag-rag-and-bobtail shoulders we wear our own pride and ostentation; household sinecurists, who invariably do the less, the less they have to do; domestic drones, who are often the plagues, and not seldom the masters of their masters. Many who have now become too grand for grand liveries, and will not shoulder the shoulder-knot, are only to be distinguished from those whom they serve by their better looks and figures, and more magisterial air. Let no man expect to be well attended in a large establishment; where there are many waiters, the master is generally the longest waiter. A Grand Prior of France, once abusing Palapret for beating his lackey, he replied in a rage—" Zooks, Sir, he deserves it; I have but this one, and yet I am every bit as badly served as you who have twenty."

SET-DOWN.—That species of rebuke familiarly termed a set-down, when it has been merited by the offending party, and is inflicted without an undue severity, is generally very acceptable to every one but its object. An empty coxcomb, after having engrossed the attention of the company for some time with himself and his petty ailments, observed to Dr. Parr, that he could never go out without catching cold in his head. " No wonder," cried the doctor, pettishly, " you always go out without anything in it." Another of the same stamp, who imagined himself to be a poet, once said to Nat. Lee, "Is it not easy to write like a madman, as you do?" "No; but it is very easy to write like a fool, as you do."

SETTLER.—Tom Hood, in one of his delightful Comic Annuals, has an .engraving of a colonist meeting a settler in the form of an infuriated lion, who with bristling mane seems prepared to give the stranger a passport down his throat. We may encounter a less formidable, but equally conclusive settler, without stirring from our own fire-sides, and afford a proof at the same time, that a bad thing put into the mouth will sometimes bring a good thing out of it.—An epicure, while eating oysters, swallowed one that was not fresh. "Zounds, waiter!" he ejaculated, making a wry face, "what sort of an oyster do you call this?" "A native, Sir," replied the wielder of the knife. "A native! —*I* call it a *settler*, so you need not open any more.— What's to pay?"

SHOOTING THE LONG-BOW—stretching a fact till you have made it as long as you want it. Lord Herbert of Cherbury s tastes have descended to some of our modern nobility, for he tells us in his Autobiography, "The exercises I chiefly used, and most recommended to my posterity, were, riding the great horse and fencing. I do much approve likewise of *shooting in the long-bow*." So does our ingenious contemporary, Lord G——, who never suffers himself to be outstripped in the marvellous. The Marquis of H—— had engaged the attention of a dinner party, by stating that he had caught a pike, the day before, which weighed nineteen pounds. "Pooh!" cried Lord G——, "that is nothing to the salmon I hooked last week, which weighed fifty-six pounds." "Hang it," whispered the Marquis to his neighbour, "I wish I could catch my pike again; I would add ten pounds to him directly."

SICKNESS—without reference to the religious impressions it is calculated to awaken, is well worth enduring, now and then, not only for the pleasure of convalescence, but that we may learn a due and grateful sense of the blessing of health. "Every recovery," says Jean Paul Richter, "is a *palingenesia*, and bringing back of our youth, making us love the earth, and those that are on it, with a new love."

SIDE WIND ATTACK—the not uncommon custom of pelting a friend, after he has left the company, seems to have been derived from the practice of the ancient tribes, who erected a monument to a departed hero, by throwing stones upon him.

SILENCE—a thing which it is often difficult to keep, in exact proportion as it is dangerous not to keep it. So frail that we cannot even speak of it without breaking it, and yet as easily and as completely to be restored as it was destroyed, few people understand the use, or appreciate the value of this mysterious quality. All men when they talk, think that they are conferring pleasure upon others, because they feel it themselves; but none suspect that the same object may sometimes be more effectually obtained by their silence. A good listener is much more rare than a good talker, because the conversation of general society seldom fixes the attention, and thus in the hopelessness of curing

the evil, we aggravate it. "When I go into company," said
L——, "I am compelled to become as great a chatterbox as
the rest, because I had rather hear my own nonsense than
that of other people." "After all," observed his niece one
day, when he was twitting her with her loquacity,—"I know
many men who talk more than women : "—"Ay," was the
reply, "more to the point."

L—— was once overturned in a carriage with his niece,
who, finding after all her screams, that she had received no
hurt, asked her uncle how, in such an imminent danger, he
could have preserved so perfect a silence. "Because I was
tolerably sure that death would not be frightened away by
my making a noise."

Socrates, when a chatterbox applied to him to be taught
rhetoric, said that he must pay double the usual price,
because it would first be necessary to teach him to hold his
tongue. We may be sometimes gainers by practising this
difficult art, even at a festive meeting. "Silence," exclaimed
an epicure to some noisy guests, "you make so much noise
that we don't know what we are eating."

SILK—the refuse of a reptile, employed to give distinction
and dignity to the lord of the creation. Compare the caterpillar in its cocoon, with the king's counsel in his silk gown,
and in adjusting the claims of the rival worms, the palm of
ingenuity must be conceded to the former, because it spins
and fashions its own covering, whereas the latter can only
spin out the thread of empty elocution, and weave a web of
sophistry. The Abbé Raynal calls silk, "*l'ouvrage de ce ver
rampant, qui habille l'homme de feuilles d'arbres élaborées
dans son sein.*" Hear how the pompous Gibbon gives the same
information. "I need not explain that silk is originally spun
from the bowels of a caterpillar, and that it composes the
golden tomb, whence a worm emerges in the form of a

butterfly." There is an Arabian proverb which conveys the same fact in a much more moral and poetical form. "With patience and perseverance, the leaf of the mulberry tree becomes satin."

SLANDERER—a person of whom the Greeks showed a due appreciation, when they made the word synonymous with devil. Slanderers are at all events economical, for they make a little scandal go a great way, and rarely open their mouths, except at the expense of other people. We must allow that they have good excuse for being defamatory, if it be their object to bring down others to their own level. It may be further urged in their extenuation, that they are driven to their trade by necessity; they filch the fair character of others, because they have none of their own; and with this advantage, that the stolen property can never be found upon them. There is a defence also for their covert and cowardly mode of attacking you, for how can you expect that backbiters should meet you face to face? Nay, they have even a valid plea for being so foul-mouthed, considering how often they have been compelled to eat their own words. Hang them ! let us do the fellows justice !

SLAVE-DRIVER—a white brute employed to coerce and torture black men. Old Fuller calls Negroes, " images of God carved in ebony." May we not say of their white taskmasters, that they are images of the devil carved in ivory.

SNUFF—dirt thrust up the nostrils with a pig-like snort, as a sternutatory, which is not to be sneezed at. The moment he has thus defeated his own object, the snuffing snuff-taker becomes the slave of a habit, which literally brings his nose to the grindstone; his Ormskirk has seized him as St. Dunstan did the devil, and if the red hot pincers could occasionally start up from the midst of the rappee, few persons would regret their embracing the proboscis of the offender. Lord Stanhope has very exactly calculated that in forty years, two entire years of the snuff-taker's life will be devoted to tickling his nose, and two more to the agreeable processes of blowing and wiping it, with other incidental circumstances. Well would it be if we bestowed half the time in making ourselves agreeable, that we waste in rendering ourselves offensive to our friends. Society takes its revenge by deciding, that no man would thrust dirt into his head, if he had got any thing else in it.

SOCIETY.—If persons would never meet except when they have something to say, and if they would always separate when they have exhausted their pleasant or profitable topics, how delightful, but alas! how evanescent would be our social assemblages.

SOLDIER—a man machine, so thoroughly deprived of its human portion, that at the breath of another man machine, it will blindly inflict or suffer destruction. Divested of his tinsel trappings, his gold lace, feathers, music, and the glitter of the false glory with which it has been attempted to dazzle the world as to his real state, it is difficult to imagine any thing more humiliating, than the condition of a soldier.

Nothing so much shows the triumph of opinion and usage over fact, of the conventional over the abstract, as that a profession, apparently so much at variance with all their feelings, should be chosen by gentlemen of independence, humanity, and reflection. Nothing is more redeeming to our common nature than that such men, placed in a sphere so expressly calculated to make them both slavish and tyrannical, should generally preserve their good qualities from contamination. Few characters so honourable, few gentlemen so courteous, few companions so agreeable as a British officer; but this is not in consequence, but in spite of his being in the army. Why he ever entered it, we presume not to inquire, but we are bound to believe that his motive was not less rational and amiable than that of the affectionate Irishman, who enlisted in the seventy-fifth regiment, in order to be near his brother, who was a corporal in the seventy-sixth.—(*Vide* Josephus Molitor.)

SPECULATION—a word that sometimes begins with its second letter.

SPINSTER—an unprotected female, and of course a fine subject for exercising the courage of cowards, and the wit of the witless.

STEAM.—Strange that there should slumber in yonder tranquil pond, a power so tremendous, that could we condense and direct its energies, it might cleave the solid earth in twain, and yet so gentle that it may be governed, and applied, and set to perform its stupendous miracles by a child! The discovery that water would resist being boiled above 212 degrees, has conferred upon England its manufacturing supremacy, and will eventually produce changes, both moral and physical, of which it is difficult to limit the extent. One bushel of coals, properly consumed, will raise seventy millions of pounds weight a foot high. The Menai Bridge, weighing four millions of pounds, suspended at a medium height of 120 feet, might have been raised where it is, by seven bushels of coals. M. Dupin estimates the steam engines of England to possess a moving power equivalent to that of 6,400,000 men at the windlass. And this stupendous agent is at present only in its infancy!

STOMACH—the epicure's deity. Buffon gave it as his deliberate conviction, that this portion of our economy was the seat of thought, an opinion which he seems to have adopted from Persius, who dubs it a master of arts, and the dispenser of genius. So satisfied are we of its reflecting disposition, that we call a cow, or other beast with two stomachs, a ruminating animal *par excellence*. To judge by the quantity they eat, we might infer some of our own species to have two stomachs; but when we listen to their discourse, we find it difficult to include them in the class of ruminating animals.

STONE, The Philosopher's—the folly of those who have inherited Midas's ears without his touch. A will-o'-the-wisp, however, does not always lead us into quagmires; in running after shadows we sometimes catch substances, and in following illusions overtake the most valuable realities. The pursuit of the philosopher's stone has by no means been a vain one. Alchymy has given us chymistry, and we are indebted to the astrologers for the elucidations of the most difficult problems in astronomy. The clown, who in running to catch a fallen star, stumbled, and kicked up a hidden treasure, has found many an unintentional imitator among scientific visionaries and stargazers. Perhaps more has been gained by long and vainly seeking the quadrature of the circle, the longitude, and perpetual motion, than would have arisen from immediate success. Morals, too, have their philosopher's stone, in other shapes than those of Plato's Atlantis, or More's Utopia; and it is healthy to chase such chimeras, if it were only for the sake of air and exercise, in an atmosphere of purity. Many real virtues may be acquired by straining after an imaginary and unattainable perfection. *Crede quod habes, et habes.* When a thing is once believed possible, it is half realized.

STONE to pelt with.—Dr. Magee affirms, that the Roman Catholics have a Church without a religion;—the Dissenters, a religion without a Church;—the Establishment, both a Church and a religion. "This is false," observes Robert Hall of Leicester; "but it is an excellent stone for a clergyman to pelt with."

STUPIDITY—is often more apparent than real; it may be indisposition rather than incapacity. The human mind is not like logic—the major does not always contain the minor; and men who feel themselves fit for great things, cannot always accomplish little ones. Claude Lorraine was dismissed by the pastry-cook to whom he had been apprenticed, for sheer stupidity. The difficulty did not consist in bringing his mind up, but in bringing it down to the manufacture of buns and tartlets.

STYLE.—To have a good style in writing, you should have none; as perfect beauty of face consists in the absence of any predominant feature. Mannerism, whether in writing or painting, can never be a merit. Swift is right when he decides, that "Proper words in proper places, make the true definition of a good style."

"He who would write well," says Roger Ascham, "must follow the advice of Aristotle,—to speak as the common people speak, and to think as the wise think." Style, however, is but the colouring of the picture, which should always be held subordinate to the design. "We may well forgive Tertullian his iron style," says Balzac, "when we recollect what excellent weapons he has forged out of this iron, for the defence of Christianity, and the defeat of the Marcionites and Valentinians."

SUBSCRIPTIONS, Private—paying your creditors by

taxing your friends; an approved method for getting rid of
both. Many years ago a worthy and well-known Baronet,
having become embarrassed in his circumstances, a Subscription was set on foot by his friends, and a letter,
soliciting contributions, was addressed to the late Lord
Erskine, who immediately dispatched the following answer :—

"My dear Sir John,
"I am in general an enemy to Subscriptions of this nature;
first, because my own finances are by no means in a flourish-
ing plight; and secondly, because pecuniary assistance, thus
conferred, must be equally painful to the donor and the
receiver. As I feel, however, the sincerest gratitude for your
public services, and regard for your private worth, I have
great pleasure in *subscribing*—(Here the worthy Baronet,
big with expectation, turned over the leaf, and finished the
perusal of the note, which terminated as follows):—in *subscribing* myself,

"My dear Sir John,
"Yours very faithfully,
"ERSKINE."

SUGGESTION, A friendly.—A man who had had his
ears cuffed in a squabble, without resenting the affront,
being shortly afterwards in a party, and in want of a pinch
of snuff, exclaimed, "I cannot think what I have done with
my box; it is not in either of my pockets."—"Try your ears,"
said a bystander.

SUPERSTITION,—as Plutarch has well observed, is
much worse than atheism, since it must be less offensive to
deny the existence of such a deity as Saturn, than to admit
his existence, and affirm, that he was such an unnatural monster, as even to devour his own children.

Archbishop Tillotson says, " According as men's notions of God are, such will their religions be; if they have gross and false conceptions of God, their religion will be absurd and superstitious. If men fancy God to be an ill-natured Being, armed with infinite power, who takes delight in the misery and ruin of his creatures, and is ready to take all advantages against them, they may fear him, but they will hate him, and they will be apt to be such towards one another, as they fancy God to be toward them; for all religion doth naturally incline men to imitate him whom they worship."—*Sermons*, vol. i. p. 181.

" Atheism," observes a Christian philosopher, " leaves a man to sense, to philosophy, to natural piety, to laws, to reputation; all which may be guides to an outward moral virtue, though religion were not; but superstition dismounts all these, and erecteth an absolute monarchy in the minds of men."—(*Bacon's Essays*, p. 96.) In point of fact, the misrepresentation of a deity, leads immediately to the denial of his existence; a result which has not escaped the acuteness of Plutarch. " The atheist," says that writer, " contributes not in the least to superstition; but superstition, having given out so hideous an idea of the Deity, has frightened many into the utter disbelief of any such being; because, they think it much better, nay, more reasonable, that there should be no deity, than one whom they see more reason to hate and abominate, than to love, honour, and reverence. Thus inconsiderate men, shocked at the deformity of Superstition, run directly into the opposite extreme of atheism, heedlessly skipping over true piety, which is the golden mean between both."

How certainly should we avoid the degrading superstition of demonism, did we but act upon the following position of Archbishop Tillotson:—" Every good man is, in some degree, partaker of the divine nature, and feels that in himself, which he conceives to be in God; so that this man does experience what others do but talk of;—he sees the image of God in himself, and is able to discourse of him from an inward sense and feeling of his excellency."—(*Sermons*, vol. iii. p. 42.) If we thus behold the Deity reflected in our own hearts, no wonder that the religion of the good man should be rational and cheerful, and that of the bad man superstitious and gloomy. How forcibly does the latter recall the passage in Bacon's noble essay—" Of Unity in Religion," where he says—" It was a great blasphemy when the devil said, 'I will ascend, and be like the Highest;' but it is greater blasphemy to personate God, and bring him in, saying—'I will descend, and be like the Prince of Darkness.' Surely this is to bring down the Holy Ghost, instead of the likeness of a dove, in the shape of a vulture, or raven; and to set out of the bark of the Christian Church a flag of a bark of pirates and assassins."

SUPPER — a receipt for indigestion, and a sleepless night. A Spanish proverb says—A little in the morning is enough; enough at dinner is but little; a little at night is too much. This agrees pretty nearly with the Latin dictum—

> Pone gulæ metas, ut sit tibi longior ætas,
> Esse cupis sanus?—Sit tibi parca manus.

SYMPATHY —a sensibility, of which its objects are sometimes insensible. It may be perilous to discourage a feeling, whereof there is no great superabundance in this selfish and hard-hearted world; but even of the little that exists, a portion is frequently thrown away. Such is the power of adaptation in the human mind, that those who seem to be in the most pitiable plight, have often the least occasion for our pity. A city damsel, whose ideas had been

Arcadianised by the perusal of pastorals, having once made an excursion to a distance of twenty miles from London, wandered into the fields in the hope of discovering a *bonâ fide* live shepherd. To her infinite delight, she at length encountered one, under a hawthorn hedge in full blossom, with his dog by his side, his crook in his hand, and his sheep round about him, just as if he were sitting to be modelled in china for a chimney ornament. To be sure, he did not exhibit the azure jacket, jessamine vest, pink tiffany inexpressibles, peach-coloured stockings, and golden buckles of those faithful portraitures. This was mortifying; still more so, that he was neither particularly young nor cleanly; but, most of all, that he wanted the indispensable accompaniment of a pastoral reed, in order that he might beguile his solitude with the charms of music. Touched with pity at this privation, and lapsing, unconsciously, into poetical language, the civic damsel exclaimed—" Ah! gentle shepherd, tell me where's your pipe?"—" I left it at home, Miss," replied the clown, scratching his head, "cause I ha'nt got no baccy."

A benevolent committee-man of the Society for superseding the necessity of climbing boys, seeing a sooty urchin weeping bitterly, at the corner of a street, asked him the cause of his distress;—" Master has been using me shamefully," sobbed the sable sufferer;—" he has been letting Jem Hudson go up the chimney at No. 9, when it was my turn! He said it was too high, and too dangerous for me, but I'll go up a chimney with Jem Hudson any day in the year; that's what I will!"

There is a local sympathy, however, in which we cannot well be mistaken, and which it is lamentable not to possess; for that man—to use the words of Dr. Johnson—"is little to be envied, whose patriotism would not gain force upon the plain of Marathon, or whose piety would not grow warmer among the ruins of Iona."

Even the most obdurate and perverse natures cannot always resist the power of sympathy. Indecorous as it is, we must quote Lord Peterborough's observation on the celebrated Fénélon;—"He is a delicious creature; I was forced to get away from him as fast as I possibly could, else he would have made me pious." As a profane man may be pleased with piety, so may a wise one be occasionally pleased with folly, through sympathy with the pleasures of others.

Most misplaced and mischievous of all, is that spurious sympathy, by which some of our journalists and novel writers seek to enlist our feelings in the cause of the basest malefactors.—"To make criminals the object of a sentimental admiration, and of a sort of familiar attachment; to hold up as a hero the treacherous murderer, whose life has been passed in reckless profligacy, merely because, at his death, he displays a firmness which scarcely ever deserts the vilest, is a task as unworthy of literary talents, as it is unfit for cultivated and liberal minds."—*Ed. Review*, vol. xl. p. 202.

ALENT.—What we want in natural abilities may generally and easily be made up in industry; as a dwarf may keep pace with a giant, if he will but move his legs a little faster. "Mother!" said the Spartan boy, going to battle, "my sword is too short."—"Add a step to it," was the reply.

TALKERS, Great—not only do the least, but generally say the least, if their words be weighed, instead of reckoned. He who labours under an incontinence of speech, seldom gets the better of his complaint; for he must prescribe for

himself, and is sure of having a fool for his physician. How
many a chatterbox might pass for a wiseacre, if he could
keep his own secret, and put a drag chain, now and then,
upon his tongue. The largest minds have the smallest
opinion of themselves; for their knowledge impresses them
with humility, by showing the extent of their ignorance, and
this discovery makes them taciturn. Deep waters are still;
wise men generally talk little, because they think much:
feeling the annoyance of idle loquacity in others, they
are cautious of falling into the same error, and keep
their mouths shut, when they cannot open them to the
purpose.

Small wits, on the contrary, are usually great talkers.
Uttering whatever comes uppermost, and everything being
superficial, their shallowness makes them noisy, and their
confidence offensive. If we might perpetrate, at the same time,
a pun and paradox, we should affirm, that the smaller the
calibre of the mind, the greater the *bore* of a perpetually open
mouth. Human heads are like hogsheads—the emptier they
are, the louder report they give of themselves. The chatterbox,
according to the Italians, "*parla prima e pensa poi;*" but
we have specimens in this country, who never think, either
before or after. The clack of their word-mill is heard even
when there is no wind to set it going, and no grist to come
from it.

M. de Bautré, being in the antechamber of Cardinal Riche-
lieu, at the time that a great talker was loudly and incessantly
babbling, begged him to be silent, lest he should annoy the
Cardinal.—"Why do you wish me not to speak?" asked the
chatterbox;—"I talk a good deal, but I talk well."—"*Half*
of that is true," said M. de Bautré.

TASTE—a quick and just perception of beauty and deformity in the works of nature and art.

TAVERN—a house kept for those who are not house-keepers.

TEST ACTS—devices for letting in the unscrupulous and irreligious, and for excluding the conscientious and the pious. All churches have had them, and all have found them equally inefficacious. Requiring a man to receive the Sacrament, and thus profane a sacred ordinance, as a qualification for the proper discharge of a civil office, is about as germane to the matter, as if you were to stipulate that your dairymaid should go through the process of being vaccinated, as a security for her making good butter, and never attempting to injure your cow.

They who imagine that a particular form of test, because it succeeds perfectly well in one instance, must be equally efficacious in all, without reference to the circumstances of the case, or the materials upon which the experiment is to be made, fall into the same mistake as the simple country girl, who, having seen a laundress spit upon a flat iron, to ascertain whether it were too hot, spat in her smoking porridge, to see whether it would burn her mouth.

TEXT, Scriptural—a fertile source of delusion and bigotry to those particularly clear-sighted people, who prefer the letter which killeth, to the spirit which giveth life.

> From drugs intended to impart
>   Relief to sickness, care, and pain,
> The chymist, with transmutive art,
>   Extracts a poison and a bane.
> So does the bigot's art abuse
>   The sacred page of love and life,
> And turn its sweet and hallowed use
>   To deadly bitterness and strife.

As purblind or short-sighted elves
Measure their glasses by themselves,
And deem those spectacles most true
Which suit their own distorted view,
So every weak, fanatic creature
Makes of himself a Bible-meter ;
Chooses those portions of the word
Which with his blindness best accord,
And closes up his darkened soul
Against the spirit of the whole.

Learn this, ye flounderers in the traps
Of insulated lines and scraps,—
Though all the texts of Scripture shoot,
   Like hairs within a horse's tail,
From one consolidated root,
   Where beauty, strength, and use prevail,
Singly, they're fit, like single hairs,
Only for springes, nets, and snares.*

Tertullian gives the best advice upon this subject when he says—"We ought to interpret Scripture, not by the sound of words, but by the nature of things."—*Malo te ad sensum rei, quam ad sonum vocabuli exerceas.*

THEOLOGY, Controversial—is to religion what law is to justice, a science which darkens by its illustrations, and misses its object in its over anxiety to attain it. If truth may be called the sun of religion, controversial theology is assuredly its Will-o'-the-wisp.

Theology, says Le Clerc, is subject to revolutions as well as empires, but though it has undergone considerable changes, yet the humour of divines is much the same.

TIME—the vehicle that carries everything into nothing. We talk of *spending* our time, as if it were so much interest

---

* Versified from Dr. Donne.

of a perpetual annuity; whereas we are all living upon our capital, and he who wastes a single day, throws away that which can never be recalled or recovered.

TINDER—a thin rag, such for instance as the dresses of modern females, intended to catch the sparks, raise a flame, and light up a match.

TITHES—being a remuneration for a particular service, ought not only to be fairly proportioned to the talent and industry of the performer, but to be subject to regulation like any other salary, where the duty is improperly discharged, or altogether omitted. To pretend that tithes are absolute property, is a mere fiction. If they were like an estate, why do men complain of the scandal of pluralities or of simony? Who ever hears of the scandal of possessing three or four estates, or of simoniacal contracts for lands and houses? Except by consent of another, the Tithe-owner has no property whatever, for the landholder, if he please, may refuse to cultivate the soil, and then the former has no interest in it, and the assumed *property* of tithe is *pro tempore* annihilated.

That tithes are sacred, and inalienable, is another fiction. If the assertion were true, they would still belong, of right, to the Roman Catholic clergy, from whom Henry VIII. wrested them, with very little form of law. In point of fact, they have repeatedly been made the subject of legislative interference, and from a very early period, as will be seen by the following extract :—

" *William the Conqueror and his Clergy.*—With such enormous riches at their disposal, they became unduly powerful; and William, jealous of that power, and suspicious of their fidelity, reduced all their lands to the common tenure of knights' service and barony—(equivalent to reducing a freehold to a lease for fourteen years, subject to be renewed at the pleasure of the real owner). The prelates were required to take an oath of fealty, and to do homage to the king, before they could be admitted to their temporalities, and they were also subject to an attendance before the king in his Court Baron, to follow him in all his wars with their knights and quota of soldiers, and to perform all other services incident to feudal tenures. The clergy remonstrated most bitterly against this new revolution, equalled only by the revolution which took place in church property five centuries afterwards; but William, like Henry VIII., was inexorable, and consigned to prison or banishment all who opposed his will."—From *Baines' History of the County Palatine of Lancaster.*

It is, we believe, upon this tenure, and as feudal barons, that the bishops claim the right of sitting in the House of Peers.

But tithes have been legally alienated or abolished, though not quite so unceremoniously, since the time of Henry VIII. Waste lands for the purpose of removing the obstacle to their improvement, were exempted by a statute of Edward VI. from all tithe for seven years. Madder, on account of the expense of its cultivation, has been relieved altogether from this payment. In Scotland, as it is well known, tithes were entirely abolished by a very pious monarch, Charles I., who sets forth in the preamble to his famous *Decret Arbitral*, that it is " expedient for the well-being of the realm, the better providing of kirks and stipends, and the establishment of schools and other pious uses, that each proprietor shall have and enjoy his own *teind* (tithe); and therefore decrees that all *teinds* shall be valued and sold, according to certain rules for making the estimate; which was ratified in Parliament by the act 1633, cap. 17." However sacred, therefore, may be the Church's claims and rights, they have been repeatedly abrogated or

encroached upon when the common weal required the in-
fringement.

The most eminent and pious men in all ages have been
opposed to this mode of supporting the clergy. Wicliff repeatedly asserts that the spirit of Christianity was wounded
by clerical endowments; and that venom was poured into
the Church, on the very day which first invested her ministers, as such, with the rights of property. Archdeacon Paley,
who can hardly be considered unfriendly to the real interests
of the Church, says, "Of all institutions adverse to cultivation and improvement, none is so noxious as that of tithes.
They are a tax not only upon industry, but upon that industry
which feeds mankind, upon that species of exertion which it
is the aim of all wise laws to cherish and promote."

When any attempt is made to correct the evils of this
impolitic and vexatious impost, without injury to existing
rights, a cry of robbery and sacrilege is incontinently raised
by the very pastors who value their flocks, as if they were
Merino sheep, solely for the sake of the fleece. And after
all, who have been such unblushing alienators, not to say
usurpers of tithe, as the clergy themselves? Originally, as
Southey admits in his Book of the Church, c. vi., "the
whole was received into a common fund, for the fourfold
purpose of supporting the clergy, repairing the church, re-
lieving the poor, and entertaining the pilgrim and stranger."
Who are the parties that have perverted this fund from its
original pious uses, and turned it all into their own pockets?
If the clergy were not the first instigators of this abuse, they
are at all events the greatest gainers by it, not seeming ever
to have thought of their Master's injunction—"Freely ye
have received, freely give." (Matthew, ch. x. v. 8.)

The opinion that every man should be allowed, not only
to choose his own religion, but to contribute as he thinks
proper towards the support of the pastor, whose duties he

exacts, has been maintained by Dr. Adam Smith, as well as other enlightened and devout philosophers, and has been successfully carried into practice by a vast empire—the United States of America. To plead that the voluntary system in England would not adequately support the Church, is to give up the Church, by admitting that it has no hold upon the affections of the people; and that the Catholics and Dissenters have so much more zeal in the cause of religion, as to contribute both to the established system and their own, while the Episcopalians would not even maintain one priesthood, except upon compulsion. A spiritual institution, which, after so many centuries of power and wealth, would immediately fall to the ground, unless propped up by force of law, is surely self-condemned.

To render tithes at all consistent with policy and justice, they should only be imposed to support the religion of the great majority of the people. Where the contrary is the case, as is signally exemplified in Ireland, such an impost is an oppression so unwarrantable and irritating, that we can little wonder at the national misery and disturbance of which it has been the fruitful source. In no way, however, are the existing Clergy answerable for the present mischievous system of tithe, either in England or Ireland. They have found, not made it, and are entitled to a just and liberal compensation for any rights that they may surrender. But for Heaven's sake—or if this plea have lost its efficacy—for the sake of earth, and its peace and prosperity, let us have some quick composition for these blood-stained tithes, at least in Ireland. When assailed by the legislature, it is to be hoped that they will not receive the same supernatural support once experienced in France, the annals of which country assure us that in the year 793, the ears of corn were all void of substance, and demons were heard in the air, proclaiming that they had ravaged

the harvests, in order to avenge the clergy, for the reluctance
of the people to the payment of tithes !— St. Foix, who
relates this story, asks, "how did the devils come to interest
themselves so warmly in behalf of the priesthood?"

It is maintained by some, that in England the tithes are
no hardship, or that they solely affect the landlord : nay, it
is affirmed by one writer, that the agricultural interest in
general desire their conservation. My friend T. H., who
will have his joke, however serious may be the subject, or
pitiful the pun it elicits,—asserts, that the burthen of this
impost falls upon the farmer, and that if he be really in
favour of the tithe, it must be for the same reason that the
Mahometan respects Mecca—because it is the burial-place
of his *prophet*.

TITLES of BOOKS — decoys to catch purchasers.
There can be no doubt that a happy name to a book is
like an agreeable appearance to a man; but if in either
case the final do not answer to the first impression, will
not our disappointment add to the severity of our judgment? "Let me succeed with my first impression," the
bibliopolist will cry, " and I ask no more. The public
are welcome to end with condemning, if they will only
begin with buying. Most readers, like the Tuft-hunters
at college, are caught by titles." How inconsistent are
our notions of morality ! No man of honour would open
a letter that was not addressed to him, though he will
not scruple to open a book under the same circumstances.
Colton's " Lacon," has gone through thirteen editions, and
yet it is addressed " TO THOSE WHO THINK." Had the
author substituted for these words "those who think they
are thinking," it might not have had so extensive a sale,
although it would have been directed to a much larger class.
He has shown address in his address.

TOLERATION—being wise enough to have no difference with those who differ from us. The mutual rancour of conflicting sects is inversely as their distance from each other; no one hating a Jew or a Pagan half so much as a fellow-Christian, who agrees with him in all but one unimportant point.

If a Hindoo or Mahometan philosopher were to contemplate five hundred different sects of Christians, spitting fire and eternal perdition at each other, in flagrant defiance of the very Scriptures which they profess to teach and obey, would he not be tempted to exclaim—" Unhappy men ! ye are all likely to be equally right in your denunciations, for when ye condemn each other, ye condemn yourselves !"

> Fain would the bard on all impress
>   The hatred of intolerance,
> Teach them their fellow men to bless,
>   Whatever doctrines they advance,
> Bid every fierce contending sect
> Humble its passions, and reflect,
> That real Christians love the souls
>   Of those by whom their own are doom'd,
> As frankincense perfumes the coals
>   By which it is itself consumed.

TOMB—a house built for a skeleton :—a dwelling of sculptured marble, provided for dust and corruption :—a monument set up to perpetuate the memory of—the forgotten.

TONGUE—the mysterious membrane that turns thought into sound. Drink is its oil—eating its drag-chain.

TRAGEDY—is preferred to comedy—(unless it be the *comédie larmoyante;*)—and novels with a distressing conclusion, to those which end happily, because they occasion

a greater excitement. By nature, we are all more acutely
sensible of pain than pleasure, and can therefore sympathize
more intensely with the former than the latter. All persons
like strong sensations, and the novel-reading world in particular, consisting mostly of male or female idlers of the
better class, little conversant with real miseries, fly for a
relief from the monotony and mental stagnation of tranquil
life, to the stimulus of fictitious distress. Their sympathy
with imaginary happiness is too tame to deserve the name
of an emotion.

TRIALS—moral ballast, that often prevents our capsizing.
Where we have much to carry, God rarely fails to fit the
back to the burthen; where we have nothing to bear, we
can seldom bear ourselves. The burthened vessel may be
slow in reaching the destined port; but the vessel without
ballast becomes so completely the sport of the winds and
waves, that there is danger of her not reaching it at all.

TRIFLES—may be not only tolerated but admired, when
we respect the trifler. Little things, it has been said, are
only valued when coming from him who can do great things.
It has been affirmed that trifles are often more absorbing
than matters of importance ; but this can only be true when
said of a trifler—of a mean mind pursuing mean objects.
Mirabeau maintains that morality in trifles, is always the
enemy of morality in things of importance; a position not
less untrue than dangerous; for it is precisely in trivial
affairs that a delicate sense of honour and rectitude is most
certainly exhibited, as we throw up a feather and not a stone
to ascertain the direction of the wind.

TRUTHS.—Many a truth is like a wolf which we hold by
the ears—afraid to let it escape, and yet scarcely able to

retain it. And why should we let it go, if it be likely to worry or annoy our neighbour? To promulgate truth with a malicious intention, is worse than to infringe it with a benevolent one, inasmuch as a pleasant deception is often better than a painful reality. It was a saying of the selfish Fontenelle, that if he held the most important truth, like a bird in his hand, he would rather crush it than let it go. Lessing, the German, on the contrary, found such a delight in the investigation of truth, that he professed his readiness to make over all claim as its discoverer, provided he might still be allowed to pursue it. Nor can we wonder at his holy ardour, for to follow truth to its source, is to stand at the footstool of God.

GLINESS — an advantageous stimulus to the mind, that it may make up for the deficiencies of the body. Medusa's head was carried by Minerva; and it will generally be found, that as beauty remains satisfied with exterior attractions, plainness strives to recommend itself by interior beauty. Talent and amiability, which are more loveable than mere loveliness, will always impart a charm to their possessor, as the want of them will render even a Venus unattractive. Countenance, or moral beauty, the reflection of the soul, is as superior to superficial comeliness, as mind is to matter. It is a halo, which indicates the *mens divinior*, and will win worshippers, however unadorned may be the shrine whence it emanates, for she who looks good cannot fail to be good-looking.

UMBRELLA—an article which, by the morality of society, you may steal from friend or foe, and which, for the same reason, you should not lend to either.

UNIFORMITY, Religious—a chimera, not less unattainable than identity of taste, or consimilarity of face, form, and stature.   And why should we believe that God, being recognised as he is, by all nations, should delight in consentaneousness as to the mode of worship, when the whole genius of the world, both moral and physical, evinces a design to introduce the greatest possible diversity into every department of creation?   Varieties of doctrine are but modifications of the moral creation, under the influence of the religious principle.

> The gems of soul that God hath set
> In frames of silver, gold, and jet,
> Tinged by their tegument of clay,
> May shed a varicolour'd ray ;
> Yet, like the rainbow's motley dyes,
> Unite, and mingle in the skies.
>   Man, like the other plants of earth,
> Takes form and pressure from his birth ;
> And since, in various countries, each
> Prays in a different form of speech,
> Why may not God delight to view
> Variety of worship too ;—
> All to one glorious source address'd,
> Although in different forms express'd ?
> The vast orchestra of the earth
>   Millions of instruments displays ;
> But when its countless sounds go forth,
>   To hymn the same Creator's praise,
> The mighty chorus swells on high,
> In one accepted harmony.

USURY, Law of—punishing a man for making as much as he can of his money, although he is freely allowed to make as much money as he can.   Usury (*ab usu æris*) is rent for money, as rent is usury for land.

ANITY—like laudanum, and other poisonous medicines, is beneficial in small, though injurious in large quantities. No man, who is not pleased with himself, even in a personal sense, can please others; for it is the belief of his own grace that makes him graceful and gracious. If it be a recommendation to dress our minds to the best advantage, and to render ourselves as agreeable as possible, why should it be an objection to bestow the same pains upon personal appearance? Dress often influences character; for the man whose well-regulated mind has a due sense of propriety and fitness, will train himself from the outside inwards, and act up to his externals. Our present uniformity, and plainness of attire, have given a monotony to character, and lowered the general standard of manners. Who can look upon a cloth sleeve and drab trowsers with the elevating feelings inspired by embroidered silk and the dangling sword, which, in determining the rank, conferred, to a certain degree, the sentiments and the demeanour of a gentleman? When men, too, wore different dresses according to their age, they naturally adapted their deportment and conversation to their attire, which tended still further to produce individual consistency, and general variety. As old and young now wear the same habiliments, there is as little difference in their manners as in their coats; a sameness which cannot be right in one direction, and may be wrong in both.

VERSE.—There seems to be no peculiar adaptation of the rhythm or verse to the subject, whether grave or gay, which custom and association may not conquer. The French Alexandrine, in which Racine composed his tragedies, and Voltaire his Henriade, is the burlesque verse of the English. Compare the following, or any line of the *Phèdre*—

"D'un mensonge—aussi noir—justement—irrité,"

and its rhythm will be found nearly identical with this, from Anstey's Bath Guide—

"For his wig—had the luck—a cathartic—to meet."

On the contrary, the French burlesque verse is nearly the same as the heroic ten syllable verse of the English.

VICE—miscalculation; obliquity of moral vision; temporary madness. A single vice, thrown aside only because it was worn out, is often considered a valid set off against all those that we still retain. Heaven, it is said, rejoices over one penitent sinner, more than over ninety and nine that have never erred; but it is not written that one sin, by which we have been abandoned, is to give us acquittance for the ninety and nine that we continue to practise. And yet there are many who seem to imagine, that squeamishness upon a single point will give them warrant for a want of scruple upon all others. Brissot, to whose writings and conduct the horrid massacres of the Tuileries, on the 10th of August, 1792, have been principally ascribed, exclaimed, in defending himself to Dumont,—"Look at the extreme simplicity of my dwelling, and see whether you can justly reproach me with dissipation or frivolity. For two years I have not been near a theatre!" The man whose starch morality will not allow him to witness tragedies at a playhouse, may surely be allowed to perpetrate them on the stage of real life !

It may be doubted, whether vice be so effectually repressed by the fear of future, as of immediate punishment. Jack Ketch exercises a more potent influence than the devil;

for none can doubt the existence of the former, while evil
men have a strong motive to be sceptical as to the existence
and avenging power of the latter. The hope of future reward is the best consolation to the good under affliction ;
but the belief that virtue and vice are their own reward and
punishment, even in this world, will moralise many from
a sense of interest, who might not have been so certainly
reclaimed by a sense of duty.

VULGARITY—is not found in uncivilized life, because,
in that state, there is little difference of rank, and less
of manners; nor is it, in a civilized country, a deficiency
of politeness or refinement, as compared with the most
polished classes; for a peasant may be a gentleman, and
a peer a vulgarian.

Vulgarity of manners may co-exist with a polished mind,
and urbanity with a vulgar one : the union of both constitutes the gentleman, whatever may be the grade in which it
is found.

ITCHCRAFT, Belief in—a reproach to reason, and a monument of folly and atrocity,
composing part and parcel of the wisdom and
humanity of our ancestors. The most magical
circumstance, attending imputed magic, is the
apparent impossibility of its being believed, even by the
parties implicated, whether witches or witchfinders. Sorcery
was a convenient crime to fix upon those who had no other ;
but how could it be credited that helpless, lonely, infirm,
and suffering old women,—for such were generally reputed
to be witches,—if they had obtained command over the
powers of light or darkness, would not exercise it for their
own benefit and relief, before they thought of directing it to

the good or evil of others? A wretched creature, from mere malignity, is supposed to inflict injuries upon her neighbours; and yet these identical parties scruple not to provoke her terrible malice to the utmost, by bringing her to a painful and ignominious death, from which her puissant ally, Satan, can do nothing to save her. Was ever such a tissue of glaring impossibilities! Apuleius, who was accused of magic, availed himself of this argument—"*Sin verò, more vulgari, cùm isti propriè magum existimant, qui communione loquendi cum Diis immortalibus, ad omina quæ velit, incredibili quadam vi, contingere polleat; oppidò miror cur accusare non timuerint quem posse tantum fatentur.*"

James the First, as it is well known, wrote a treatise on Demonology; the large-minded Bacon countenanced witchcraft; Sir Matthew Hale thanked God, upon his knees, that he had lived to condemn sorcerers to death; the lawyers, quoting from the Malleus Maleficarum, stickled as stoutly as usual for the maintenance of the old law, and the wisdom of our ancestors; while the clergy, citing the Bible, and the witch of Endor, stigmatised, as infidels and atheists, those who objected to the burning of all old women known to be partial to black cats, or suspected of taking nocturnal rides through the air, upon an enchanted broomstick. If it had not been for the efforts of unprofessional teachers, the common people would still remain plunged in a Serbonian bog, of the darkest ignorance and superstition. Truly they are much indebted to their pastors and masters!

WAGS AND WITS—lamps that exhaust themselves in giving light to others. Their gibes, their gambols, their songs, their flashes of merriment, their puns and bon-mots, and bright, and sharp, and pointed sayings, are but as so many swords, which, the oftener they are drawn forth, do but the sooner wear out the scabbard. It is much easier to make others forget time, than to prevail on old Chronos to forget us. The *fêtes* to which a man of wit is invited, only afford an excuse to the fates for shortening his thread. He finds it is no joke to be always joking; his stomach and his convivial reputation fail him at once; his jests die because he cannot digest; so many good things have gone into his mouth, that none can come out of it; and the fellow of mark and likelihood, without whom no party was deemed complete, no laughter-loving guests assured of constant coruscations and cachinnations, becomes used **up,** worn out, stultified, superannuated, and is left to his obscure lodging, to digest, if he can, his own indigestions, to be taken by the hand by no one but the gout, and to try solitary conclusions with the grim sergeant — death. An old joke, especially if it be very little of its age, is a bad thing, as the readers of this work must often have exclaimed; but an old joker is a sad thing, as many a facetious ancient has found to his cost.

WANTS — Suicides and self-destroyers. Man's bodily wants have been the great stimulus to all the arts, sciences, and discoveries, which have elevated him to his present civilization. The nakedness, helplessness, and necessities of the " bare forked animal," combined with the amazing powers and lofty aspirations of his reason, have enabled him to become the true lord of the creation, to conquer the elements by which he is surrounded, and to make them minister not only to the removal of his minutest wants, but to the supply of his most superfluous luxuries. Had he been born with the fur coat, or the stomach of a bear, he would have remained a brute, or at best a savage.

WAR—National madness. An irrational act confined to rational beings; the pastime of kings and statesmen, the

curse of subjects. Admitting the social instinct of man,
Montesquieu was not afraid to confess, that the state of war
begins with that of society; but this desolating truth, which
Hobbes has abused to praise the tranquillity of despotism,
and Rousseau, to celebrate the superior independence of
savage life, is with the philosopher the sacred and salutary plea for government and laws, which are an armistice
between states, and a treaty of perpetual peace between
citizens.

WHIGS—in power, are often Tories, as Tories, out of
power, are Whigs. The public may well say with Mercutio,
"A plague on both your houses," having found, to their
cost, that whichever party comes in, *they* are sure to be
losers, and that—

> " C'st pour le peuple une chose moins aigre,
>   D'entretenir un gras, que d'engraisser un maigre."

When, in the history of this country, we see one party
driven out for incapacity, and their opponents claiming
the reins of government as a matter of course, although
they had not long before been expelled for a similar in-
competency, we are reminded of the argumentative answer
of the Irish peasant,—" Paddy, do you know how to drive?"
—" Sure I do; never a better coachman in all Connaught.
Wasn't it I who upset your honour into a ditch two years
ago?" As the present Whigs, however, who have given
us Reform, have made abundant atonement for the errors
of their predecessors, they should be free from any reproach
that may attach to the name. It has now merged into the
more noble one of Reformers, and so long as they continue
to direct their power to the same patriotic and beneficial
ends, no lover of his country will wish to see them dis-
possessed of it. As to the Tories, they have confessed

everything laid to their charge, by acknowledging the very
name to be so odious, that they have been fain to betake
themselves to an *alias.*

WHISKERS.—"I cannot imagine," said Alderman H—,
" why my whiskers should turn grey, so much sooner than
the hair of my head."   " Because you have worked so much
more with your jaws than your brains;" observed a wag.

WINDMILLS—machines which are only kept going by
being perpetually puffed, in which respect they bear a
*p*ointed resemblance to certain authors.   The latter raise
the wind by increasing their sale, whereas the former
diminish their sail as the wind increases.

WISDOM OF OUR ANCESTORS—the experience of
the inexperienced, and the superior knowledge of the ignorant.   Old women in pantaloons, who object to the smallest
reform in our antiquated establishments, because they suited
our forefathers, recall to memory the debate in the assembly
of the Sorbonne upon the propriety of ordering new table-
cloths. —" What !" exclaimed a grey-bearded doctor, the
conservative of the college, " are we wiser than our grand-
fathers ?   Are not these the identical cloths of which they so
long made use ? "—" Yes," said another, " and that is the
reason why they are completely worn out."

WIT—consists in discovering likenesses—judgment in
detecting differences.   Wit is like a ghost, much more often
talked of than seen.   To be genuine, it should have a basis
of truth and applicability, otherwise it degenerates into mere
flippancy; as, for instance, when Swift says,—"A very little
wit is valued in a woman, as we are pleased with a few
words spoken plain by a parrot ;" or when Voltaire remarks,

that "Ideas are like beards; women and young men have none." This is a random facetiousness, if it deserves that term, which is equally despicable for its falsehood and its facility.

Where shall we discover that rarer species of wit, which, like the vine, bears the more clusters of sweet grapes the oftener it is pruned; or like the seven-mouthed Nile, springs the faster from the head, the more copiously it flows from the mouth?

The sensations excited by wit are destroyed, or at least impaired, if it excites the stronger emotions, or even if it be connected with purposes of utility and improvement. We may laugh where it is bitter, as the Sardinians did when they had tasted of their venomous herb; but this is the risibility of the muscles, allied to convulsion, rather than to intellectual pleasure.

You may sometimes show that you have not got your own wits about you, by thinking that other people *have*. When Mrs. M'Gibbon was preparing to act Jane Shore, at Liverpool, her dresser, an ignorant country girl, informed her that a woman had called to request two box orders, because she and her daughter had walked four miles on purpose to see the play. "Does she know me?" inquired the mistress. "Not at all," was the reply, "What a very odd request!" exclaimed Mrs. M'G.—"Has the good woman got her faculties about her?"—"I think she have, Ma'am, for I see she ha' got summut tied up in a red silk handkercher."

WOMAN—an exquisite production of nature, between a rose and an angel, according to a German poet; the female of the human species, according to the zoologists; the redeeming portion of humanity, according to politer fact and experience. Woman is a treasure of which the profligate and the unmarried, can never appreciate the full value, for he who possesses many does not possess one. Malherbe, says in his Letters, that the Creator may have repented the creation of man, but that He had no reason to repent having made woman? Who will deny this: and which of us does not feel, though in due subjection to a holier religion, the devotion of Anacreon, who, when he was asked, why he addressed so many of his hymns to women, and so few to the deities? answered, "Because women are my deities."

In England the upper classes are generally so much occupied with public affairs, or with local and magisterial duties, to say nothing of the uncongenial sports of the field, that women are obliged to associate with frivolous danglers and idlers, to whose standard they necessarily lower their minds and their conversation. To appear a *blue-stocking*, subjects a female to certain ridicule with those coxcombs who adopt the silly notion of *Lessing*, "that a young lady who thinks, is like a man who rouges," and who maintain that she should address herself, not to the sense, but to the senses of her male companions. Politics have thus tended to effect a mental dissociation of the sexes, the jealousy of dunces to trivialise the conversational inter-course that still subsists, and women whose unchecked intellectual energies would be " Dolphin-like, and show themselves above the element they move in," are compelled to bow to this subjection, unless they have the courage to set up for blue-stockings — and old maids. Were their supremacy to effect no change in the present general cha-racter of the sex, I believe the world would be an in-calculable gainer by making them lords of their lords, and committing to them the sole direction of all affairs, both national and domestic. As some of our most distinguished sovereigns have been females, is it unreasonable to conclude that we should insure permanent good government for the whole human race, by acknowledging the sovereignty of the sex?

To the French must be assigned the honour of the following just encomium, "*Sans les femmes les deux extrémités de la vie seraient sans secours, et le milieu sans plaisirs.*"

WORDS—sometimes signs of ideas, and sometimes of the want of them. When so many are coining new words, it is a security against a superfluous supply to know that old ones are occasionally lost. An Eton scholar, whose faculties had been bemuddled with the spondees and dactyls of prosody, having got out of nominal into real nonsense verses, carried up a *soi-disant* Latin epigram to his master. After reading it over two or three times very carefully, the pedagogue exclaimed, " I cannot find any verb here."—" That is the reason that I brought it to you," said the boy with great *naïveté*, " I thought you might perhaps tell me where it was."

WORDSWORTH.—The cheerful piety of this writer, his penetrative wisdom, most profound when it appears the most simple, and his ennobling aspirations, all modulated into the most exquisite music of which our language is susceptible, touch a chord, as we are reading him, with which every heart may be proud to beat in unison. Not in cities, not in colleges, nor even in the solitary cell, can his writings be properly appreciated. We should wander forth with them to the fields and groves, where we may imbibe the kindred influences of nature, and hold communion with the Creator through the medium of the beauty and magnificence He hath everywhere created; until the hallowed and invigorated soul, throwing off all its petty cares and misgivings, effuses itself in a serene delight. To feel the poems of Wordsworth, we should peruse them with the fresh air of heaven blowing round about us, amid the scenes that he pictures, where we may compare the face of nature with its reflection in the printed mirror before us; where we may acknowledge the presence and the influence of that exhilarating Spirit which he loves to evoke, and yielding ourselves to the devout reveries he has so described, may gradually sink into—

<blockquote>
————" that serene and blessed mood,
In which the affections gently lead us on,
Until, the breath of this corporeal frame,
And even the motion of our human blood,
Almost suspended, we are laid asleep
In body, and become a living soul;
While with a heart made quiet by the power
Of harmony, and the deep sense of joy,
We see into the life of things."
</blockquote>

WORLD, The—a great inn, kept in a perpetual bustle by arrivals and departures: by the going away of those who have just paid their bills (the debt of nature), and the coming of those who will soon have a similar account to settle:— *Decessio pereuntium, et successio periturorum.*

WRITING—painting invisible words—giving substance and colour to immaterial thought, enabling the dumb to talk to the deaf.

WRONG—may be aggravated without any increase of evil doing, as good may be diminished without any abatement of actual beneficence. "Joyful remembrances of wrong actions," says Jean Paul, "are their half repetitions, as repentant remembrances of good ones are their half abolishment. In law, the intention, not the act, constitutes the crime; and in the moral law, virtue should be measured by the same standard.

AWNING—opening the mouth when you are sleepy, and want to shut your eyes; an infectious sensation very prevalent during the delivery of a tedious sermon, or the perusal of a dull novel, but never experienced when reading a work like the present!

YEARS—of discretion. The young and giddy reader is requested to see—Greek Calends.

YOUTH—a magic lantern, that surrounds us with illusions which excite pleasure, surprise, and admiration, whatever be their nature. The old age of the sensual and the vicious is the same lantern without its magic—the glasses broken, and the illusions gone, while the exhausted lamp, threatening every moment to expire, sheds a ghastly glare, not upon a fair tablecloth, full of jocund associations, but upon what appears to be a dismal shroud, prepared to receive our remains.

And now, gentle reader, or rather may I call you simple, if you have waded through this strange farrago, here will I bring it to a close, hoping by its example the better to impress upon you the pithy precept, that all our follies and frivolities, all our crude and undigested notions, all our "bald and disjointed talk," should, like this little volume, terminate with—YOUTH.

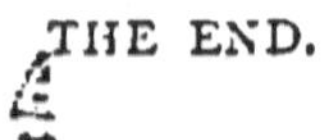

THE END.

BRADBURY, AGNEW, & CO. LIMD., PRINTERS, WHITEFRIARS.

www.ingramcontent.com/pod-product-compliance
Lightning Source LLC
Chambersburg PA
CBHW021537110726
47902CB00004B/921